WITHDRAWN

SAND AND FIRE

ALSO BY TOM YOUNG

FICTION

The Mullah's Storm

Silent Enemy

The Renegades

The Warriors

NONFICTION

The Speed of Heat:
An Airlift Wing at War in Iraq and Afghanistan

SAND AND FIRE

TOM YOUNG

G. P. PUTNAM'S SONS • NEW YORK

G. P. PUTNAM'S SONS
Publishers Since 1838
Published by the Penguin Group
Penguin Group (USA) LLC
375 Hudson Street
New York, New York 10014

USA · Canada · UK · Ireland · Australia
New Zealand · India · South Africa · China

penguin.com
A Penguin Random House Company

Library of Congress Cataloging-in-Publication Data

Young, Thomas W., date.
Sand and fire / Tom Young.
p.   cm.—(A Parson and Gold Novel; 5)
ISBN 978-0-399-16688-4
1. Parson, Michael (Fictitious character)—Fiction.   2. Gold, Sophia (Fictitious
character)—Fiction.   3. Terrorism—Prevention—Fiction.   4. Soldiers—Fiction.
5. Africa, North—Fiction.   6. Suspense fiction.   I. Title.
PS3625.O97335S26   2014   2014012102
813'.6—dc23

Printed in the United States of America
1 3 5 7 9 10 8 6 4 2

Book design by Gretchen Achilles

For my parents, Bob and Harriett Young

SAND AND FIRE

CHAPTER 1

The fine sands of the Sahara Desert lifted into the sky and crossed the Mediterranean. Scirocco winds whipped the dust over miles of water, and the particles in the air added a golden tinge to the twilight's glow. At Sigonella Naval Air Station in Sicily, Gunnery Sergeant A. E. Blount took a deep puff of his Cohiba, looked up at a blood-red moon.

Blount sat at a table outside the base coffee shop. From across the street, just outside the air station, he could hear the thump and pulse of music. Some of his Marines, along with sailors and Air Force fliers, were starting the evening early at the Route One nightclub. Blount cared little for the crowds, the dancing, the hookups of the nightclub. And, anytime he entered a club or restaurant anywhere in the world, his size invited stares. Blount stood six feet, eight inches. Two hundred and forty-five pounds, close to the USMC's max weight for his height, but with the body mass index of a creekbed stone.

The big Marine did not begrudge the loud partying. Those boys needed to have fun while they could, because they might go into action any day now. The hopes of the Arab Spring were curdling into despair as terrorists took town after town in Egypt, Libya, Algeria, and Tunisia. Where unsteady administrations lacked control, Islamic militancy rushed into the vacuum. Revolutions had led to coups, and coups had led to chaos.

Blount, however, was going home. He had just wrapped up an exercise at Sig as a team chief with his unit, Fox Company, Second Marine Special Operations Battalion. His uniform bore the golden wings and canopy of a parachutist, and he held a hard-earned military occupational specialty: MOS 0372, Critical Skills Operator. Blount had put in for retirement with an effective date in three weeks. His twenty years of service had taken him through firefights in Fallujah, sniper duty in the Korengal Valley, even hand-to-hand combat in an Afghan cave. He still carried scars on both hands and under his right arm from the cave fight.

Those battles had earned him the Navy Cross, the Bronze Star with a combat V, the Purple Heart, and every right in the world to spend the rest of his days in peace. Tomorrow, the freedom bird would take him to Marine Corps Air Station Beaufort in South Carolina. From there, he'd make his way to that big country house he'd bought on ten acres outside Beaufort for his wife and two baby girls. The girls didn't like it when he called them babies. They were eight and twelve.

They'd like it when he got them that pony, though. He had a plan for those ten acres, and most of it involved a pasture. The rest he'd plow into a great big vegetable garden. As he'd sweated in the Sunni Triangle or shivered in the Hindu Kush, Blount had planned every square foot of that garden: two rows of sweet corn, a row of Irish potatoes, a row of yams, two rows of tomatoes, two of okra, along with rows for black-eyed peas, butter beans, string beans, bell peppers, and hot peppers. Squash and cucumbers, too. Of course, his family could eat only a fraction of that. Bernadette would freeze and can some of it. The rest he'd place in baskets, load into the back of his Dodge Ram, and donate to the local A.M.E. Zion Church. The church held suppers for the homeless every Wednesday night.

The sound of a door squeaking open behind him interrupted his thoughts of home. A young corporal, Tony Fender, came out of the coffee shop with a steaming paper cup.

"May I join you, Gunny?" Fender asked.

Blount blew out a long plume of cigar smoke. "You may," he said.

With the tip of his boot, Blount shoved a chair out from under the table. He sat up straighter in his own chair and adjusted the blouse of his MARPAT camo. The tip of an aged and cracked leather knife sheath showed from under the blouse. The knife hung on a black web belt earned in the Marine Corps Martial Arts Program. A vertical red stripe on the belt indicated Blount's status as an instructor trainer.

"Still got that old KA-BAR, Gunny?" Fender said as he took his seat. "They could have issued you a new knife, you know."

"I'll keep this one."

His grandfather had carried that knife in the Pacific. Grandpa had served as a Montford Point Marine, one of the first black men to wear the Eagle, Globe, and Anchor. The knife had a more recent history, too. Not a lot of people knew about that. Just the Marines who were there at the time and a couple of folks from other services—an Air Force flier named Michael Parson and a real sharp Army interpreter named Sophia Gold. But Blount didn't like to tell war stories.

"We're gonna miss you, Gunny. You sure you can't stay with us a while longer?"

None of your business, Blount thought. This boy Fender wasn't a bad Marine; he just talked too much. Hair cut in a proper high-and-tight. Small tattoo on the inside of his left wrist—nothing badass, just a girl's name. *Anne*.

Blount took another pull at his cigar. The tip reddened like the moon above, and he held the smoke long enough to make it clear that was the only answer Fender would get. In the distance, twilight blurred the outline of Mount Etna's summit. Blount had heard the story of some ancient philosopher who threw himself into the mouth of Etna, an active volcano. Maybe the dude just got tired of dumb questions.

"Didn't mean to pry," Fender said. "Sorry about that."

Blount exhaled, tapped away a round of ash the size of a shot glass. "It's all good," he said.

"If you don't mind my asking, Gunny, I've always wondered what your initials, A. E., stood for."

"You can keep wondering, Corporal."

Before either man could say anything else, a loud crump sounded from across the street. The thud came almost in time with the thumping of music. But it stopped the music. A power failure, maybe? Then Blount heard screams.

The two Marines looked at each other. Blount dropped his cigar and crushed it out with his heel.

"Let's get over there," he said.

With a clatter of overturned chairs, Blount and Fender sprinted for the front gate. The German shepherds in the K-9 compound just inside the perimeter fence began barking; even they knew something was wrong.

Blount ran up to two Navy MPs manning the gate, flashed his ID. Both MPs held rifles and stood guard behind concrete barriers. One spoke into his radio, called for backup. Blount understood why they held their position instead of rushing to help at the nightclub. Whatever had just happened at Route One could serve as a diversion for terrorists trying to get inside the base.

"What's going on?" Blount asked.

"Don't know," one of the MPs said. "Some kind of blast, but it sounded weird."

More screams came from inside the club. Blount could see people stumbling out into the parking lot.

Blount charged across the road. Fender caught up behind him. Some of the victims pouring out of Route One had bloodied faces and arms. Blount saw no serious injuries like limbs torn off; perhaps it was worse inside. He forced his way through the door as nightclub patrons staggered past him.

Inside, at least twenty people lay on the floor amid shattered furniture and spilled beer. Some wailed and writhed while others lay silent. Some moaned and cursed in English and Italian. The air smelled of explosives, sweat, perfume, and . . . feces. Somebody had lost control of his bowels. Blount looked around, still saw no one with severe trauma. But some of the people on the floor weren't moving at all. A couple others were twitching uncontrollably. Blount kneeled beside a man suffering from convulsions, placed a hand on the man's shoulder.

The man rolled over and tried to look at Blount. He wore black jeans and an Under Armour polo shirt. Anchor tattoo on his bicep. Young guy, maybe twenty. A sailor out on a Saturday night.

"Where are you hurt?" Blount asked.

The sailor shivered and arched his back. Mucus ran from both nostrils. The man's eyes looked strange; his pupils had shrunk to pinpoints. He tried to speak.

"Can't . . . can't."

"You can't what, bud?"

"B-b-b . . . breathe."

Just a few feet away, Fender tried to help an Italian girl. Her black dress clung to her thighs, the fabric wet with something. Blount caught a whiff of urine. On her knees, she pitched forward until she went down on all fours.

Fender put his hand on her back. "What's wrong?" he asked.

The girl muttered something in Italian, and then vomited onto the floor.

Blount put it all together.

"Nerve gas!" he shouted. "Fender, get out of here!"

The corporal looked over at Blount, glanced around the room.

"I ain't leaving without you, Gunny."

Blount thought for a second. If they'd gotten exposed to nerve gas, it was already too late. He felt all right, though. If he'd inhaled sarin, he'd know it. But he could still touch a droplet of it and get exposed through his skin. Didn't matter. These people needed help. And he did not have the only thing that could help them.

"Go to the fleet warehouse and tell 'em you need all the auto-injectors they can give you," Blount ordered. "I'll check the clinic. These folks all gon' die if they don't get some antidote."

"Aye, aye, Gunny."

Outside, flashing blue lights of military police cars and ambulances pierced the deepening twilight. Sirens split through shouts and screams. Blount and Fender pulled out their ID cards, held them aloft as they pushed their way to the base gate. No sense getting shot by an excited cop. MPs now swarmed the guard post. Some headed into the nightclub.

"Looks like a nerve gas attack in there," Blount told an MP. "They show all the symptoms. I'm coming back with some antidote kits if I can find 'em."

One of the cops started to ask a question, but Blount ignored him. Blount ran past a sign that read NAS SIGONELLA. THE HUB OF THE MED.

At the clinic, Blount gripped a door handle, pressed his thumb on the latch release, pulled. Locked tight. He shook the door in frustration. But he saw a light on in an interior room. Someone moved around inside. The gunnery sergeant banged on the door and began yelling.

"Open up!" he shouted. "Open up!"

A woman in Navy fatigues came to the door and unlocked it. She wore the insignia of a lieutenant commander in the Nurse Corps. Black hair tied in a bun. Rimless glasses.

"Ma'am," Blount said, breathing hard. "We got a mass casualty event right outside the gate, and I'm pretty sure it's nerve gas."

"I thought I heard something," the nurse said. "How do you know it's nerve gas?"

"Symptoms," Blount said. "Drooling and twitching. Ma'am, we gotta get out there with some antidote. You got any?"

The nurse frowned. "Wait a minute, Gunnery Sergeant," she said. "Atropine is a controlled drug."

Blount felt a surge of impatience. People were dying out there.

"Sweet Jesus, ma'am," he said. "You folks gave it to me to carry in Iraq. I didn't need it there but I need it here." He used to keep doses right in his pocket. Why couldn't he have it now?

The nurse picked up a phone and dialed a number, maybe the main hospital on the other side of the base. When someone answered, she said, "I have a Marine here who says that incident off base involves chemical weapons. You might want to get your chem response ready in case he's right."

In case I'm right, Blount thought. The Marine Corps taught me those symptoms. She thinks I'm just some dumb bruiser.

Blount followed the nurse down the hall and into a storage room. She unlocked a cabinet and began searching, but not nearly fast enough for Blount.

"Where is it, ma'am? Can I help you look?"

The woman unlocked another cabinet, motioned across its shelves. Blount rummaged, knocked over bottles and boxes. He found a case of the old Mark 1 kits, pairs of injectors stored together in vinyl pouches.

"Wait, Gunnery Sergeant," the nurse said. "I have to . . ."

Blount didn't hear the rest of the sentence. He grabbed the Mark 1 kits and a box of medical gloves, took off at a run.

A memory of childhood came to him. Back on the farm, in the summer of his tenth year, his beagle puppy was bounding around the trash barrel. The pup carried something white in its mouth. Young Blount called to his dog and took away the object, a screw-on cap from a plastic jug. Around the trash barrel lay several empty jugs, each bearing the label of an insecticide used in the tobacco fields.

"Stop it, Digger," Blount said. "You ain't supposed to play with that."

Young Blount walked back to the weathered frame house where he lived with his mother—and his father, whenever the man wasn't off on a drunk. The puppy followed him home, playful as ever.

Blount went inside and turned on the television. After the old set warmed up, Blount tried all three channels but couldn't find any cartoons. So he went back outside to play with Digger.

He found the pup lying in the weeds, trembling. Vomit covered its front paws. Green diarrhea issued from the other end. Digger looked up with misty eyes. He didn't have the strength to wag his tail.

Blount wrapped the puppy in a burlap sack and ran down the dirt road to the most reliable source of help he knew—his grandfather. He found Grandpa on the porch, smoking a Camel and reading the newspaper.

"Grandpa," Blount called. "Digger's real sick and needs to go to the vet."

The old man folded his paper, crushed out his cigarette in a bean-bag ashtray.

"What's wrong with him, boy?"

"He's throwing up and going to the bathroom. He's shaking all over." Blount thought for a moment. "He poisoned hisself."

"What did he get into?" Grandpa asked. "Show me."

Blount handed the puppy to his grandfather and ran back to the trash barrel. He returned with the empty jug. By then, Grandpa was getting into his pickup; Blount jumped into the truck's passenger side. Grandpa looked at the jug's label, started the engine. He'd placed the dog in the middle of the bench seat, right where duct tape covered a rip.

On the ride into Beaufort, the pup kept shaking and throwing up.

"Son," Grandpa said, "we'll see what Doc Albright can do, but I don't believe Digger's gon' make it."

Tears slid down Blount's cheeks. He wished the old Chevy could go faster. Please, Lord, just let Digger have some medicine.

At the animal hospital, Blount ran inside with the dog in his arms. His grandfather brought the pesticide jug and showed it to the veterinarian.

"I'll be right back," Doc Albright said.

The veterinarian returned with a syringe. He didn't even take Digger into the examination room. Right there in the waiting room, with the puppy in Blount's lap, the vet pinched fur from the scruff of the animal's neck, inserted the needle. Doc Albright depressed the plunger, and Blount watched the clear liquid disappear into his best friend's veins. As soon as the needle came out, the beagle stopped shaking. The pup relaxed immediately. His eyes changed color. He wagged his tail, licked Blount's thumb.

"That was quick," Grandpa said.

"It usually is, if it works," Doc Albright said. "Bring him back if he don't look right tomorrow, but I think he'll be fine."

"What do you say?" Grandpa asked.

"Thank you," Blount said. "Sir."

On the ride home, Grandpa said, "I'm proud of you, boy. You found a problem, but you didn't go squalling like a child. You figured out the situation and took action. That's thinking like a man."

Digger lived long enough to greet Private Blount on his return from boot camp.

Back at Route One, Gunnery Sergeant Blount found men in full MOPP chem-protection gear: gas masks, charcoal-impregnated suits, butyl gloves. Blount snapped on a set of medical gloves and went to work.

In the parking lot, he found the Italian girl in the black dress. Somehow she'd crawled or staggered outside. Lying on the pavement, she looked even worse. Sweat beaded on her cheeks as if she'd just run a desert marathon. Wrinkles radiated out from her eyes, her face contorted. She continued to heave, though nothing came up from her stomach. The girl made a primal groaning sound and spat out a mouthful of mucus and saliva. Blount took a knee beside her, pulled out a pair of injectors.

"I gotcha, miss," he said. "I got what you need."

He took the first injector, a plastic cylinder the size and shape of a felt-tip marker. Blount removed the yellow safety cap at one end, arming the spring-loaded needle at the other end. The girl moaned again and rolled onto her side. That position was good; it exposed the fleshy backs of her thighs, and Blount didn't want to punch a needle into her bone. With his left hand, the Marine held her knees to keep her from moving again. With his right, he pressed the atropine injector to the girl's upper leg.

A click from inside the injector told Blount the two-inch needle had rammed home. If the Italian felt pain, she did not show it. She only continued to twitch and drool. Poor girl's nervous system is so jacked up, Blount thought, she probably can't tell one hurt from another. He counted ten seconds and pulled out the needle. Then he uncapped the other injector, the one labeled PRALIDOXIME CHLORIDE.

He pressed the injector against her other thigh, felt the snap of the spring. After another ten-count, he removed the needle. Blount rolled the girl over on her back.

The wrinkles around her eyes faded as the muscles in her face relaxed. She coughed, glanced around, focused on Blount. Now she looked at him with the eyes of a human instead of a dying wild animal.

"*Grazie,*" she breathed. A barely audible whisper, but Blount understood.

He stretched out her sleeve and poked both needles through the fabric. Using his thumb and forefinger, he bent the needles into fish-hook shapes so they'd hang from the dress. That way, other rescuers would know the girl had received one dose.

One was apparently enough. The girl probably didn't weigh a hundred pounds. She'd have been gorgeous, Blount thought, if she hadn't just been poisoned nearly to death. Her chest rose and fell evenly now. Blount left her and surveyed the mess around him.

The nurse from the clinic ran up, looked around, and bent over a patient. She held an injector to his leg. A few feet away, Fender worked on another victim. Blount threw the box of gloves to the corporal.

"Put these on," Blount ordered.

"Aye, Gunny."

Sarin tended to disperse quickly. Blount figured that was the only reason he and Fender hadn't dropped dead like tobacco worms sprayed with malathion.

Yards away, between two parked cars, a man lay shaking on the ground. Maybe he'd stumbled that far before collapsing. Blount stepped over both moving and motionless bodies to reach him. Blount felt a shock of recognition when he saw the face, twisted and smeared with vomit: his old platoon commander, Lieutenant Kelley. At least a major by now. Kelley wore a white civilian dress shirt streaked with dirt, blood, and spit.

"Sir, it's me, Blount. Sir, can you talk?"

Kelley showed no sign that he even heard the question. He let out a long keening sound through chattering teeth. Blount uncapped a set of injectors, pressed both of them against the officer's leg. The needles snapped simultaneously, and Blount felt the antidotes coursing through the plastic housing of the injectors.

Please let this fix him, Blount thought. Please don't let me be too late. Blount counted to ten, pulled out the needles.

Kelley entered some deeper form of spasms. The officer's fists clasped so tightly that his fingernails cut into his palms. His head slammed against the front tire of the car beside him. His knees knocked together, and his skin took on a gray cast. In the course of two wars, Blount had witnessed all manner of dying. But he had never seen anything like this. Nerve gas turned its victims into ghouls right before it killed them.

From his training he knew that, in severe cases, you administered three doses, one right after the other. If this wasn't severe, then the word had no meaning. He armed another pair of injectors, jammed them against Kelley's thigh. Once again he heard the twin snaps. Kelley continued to twitch and shake. After ten seconds, Blount pulled out the needles and uncapped a third pair of injectors.

Once more, he jammed the injectors against Kelley's leg, watched the spring-loaded needles strike through fabric and into flesh. He tried to hold the needles in place. In deep convulsions, Kelley wrenched and thrashed. As Kelley twisted to his left, he jerked his leg away from Blount's hand. Both needles came out of the officer's thigh. Blount found himself holding two injectors, each needle spewing liquid uselessly into the air.

"Damn it," Blount hissed.

Blount stabbed the needles back into Kelley's leg and held them there as the injectors emptied.

Kelley stopped trembling. Blount thought the triple dose had finally worked. But Kelley did not move at all. Blount yanked out the spent injectors and tried to roll the officer onto his back. The man's eyes appeared dull and fixed, pupils constricted to dots. Kelley had quit breathing. No pulse, either. If those shrunken pupils saw anything, it was not in this world.

Blount stared for a moment, a fistful of Kelley's shirt still in his hand. The antidote was supposed to work; he'd just seen it work fine on that girl.

He had shared long deployments and deadly firefights with this officer. But after all that, Kelley had to die like this? Without even getting a chance to fight back?

CHAPTER 2

The Omni Air International DC-10 rotated off the runway at Sigonella and climbed into the dusty Mediterranean sky. Blount had stayed up all night helping treat victims of the gas attack and load them into ambulances. At last count, the sarin had killed twelve American service members and four Italians. Twice that many people remained in hospitals.

Blount had wanted his final homecoming to be a joyous event, bringing him a sense of satisfaction and completion. Like the old song said, a time to lay down his sword and shield, down by the riverside, and study war no more. Enter a life of community and tranquility, family, and friends. Summer evenings with the girls on the porch, making ice cream the good kind of way, turning the crank by hand. Bass fishing and rabbit hunting.

But now he could feel only anger and guilt. Somebody had poisoned his friends and comrades-in-arms, along with defenseless civilians. Made them die in one of the worst ways you could think of. And for what? Even if the bad guys had any kind of legitimate grievance—and Blount didn't believe they did—nothing justified their tactics. His own people had suffered worse than anything most jihadists had ever experienced, and his elders had overcome through dignity and nonviolence. Nothing excused terrorism. Ever.

So Blount was mad, for sure. But what kept him awake now, even in his sleep-deprived state, were the questions. Could he have saved Kelley? Blount had let the needles come loose when administering the third dose, and some of the drugs had squirted onto the pavement.

Would that wasted antidote have been just enough, just in time, to help his friend? Maybe not. But guilt was the enemy that stalked Blount in his dreams, and now that enemy carried even more ammunition.

As the island of Sardinia slid under the wings, a flight attendant came by.

"Is there anything you need, sir?" she asked.

Blount liked the civilian crews of these Defense Department charters. Always respectful and appreciative. They saw the faces of the warriors every day, so they had some idea of war's cost. For too many folks back stateside, combat amounted to nothing but a reality-TV show. A channel to flip through between *Wheel of Fortune* and the Home Shopping Network.

"No, ma'am," Blount said. "I'm good."

What he needed waited a few thousand miles across that water. Bernadette and his daughters, Ruthie and Priscilla.

The DC-10 made a refueling stop at Naval Station Rota in Spain. Blount waited in the passenger terminal and saw a group of Marines who had just flown in from Camp Lejeune, North Carolina. Their battalion was attached to the 24th Marine Expeditionary Unit. Blount's battalion was attached to another Lejeune-based MEU, the 22nd. A young sergeant dropped his seabag on the floor and sat next to Blount.

"Where you headed?" Blount asked.

"Getting on the boat from here, Gunny. Sailing out on the *Iwo Jima*."

The USS *Iwo Jima* was an amphibious assault ship, built specifically for taking Marines to a fight. With all the recent trouble in North Africa, maybe a strong force floating in the Med would make terrorists think twice.

Blount knew well the mix of excitement and apprehension the Marines of the 24th MEU would be feeling about this deployment. Another challenge, another chance to back up your buddies and prove your worth to the organization you loved. But along with the anticipation came the fear of what might happen to some of those buddies.

In the snack bar next to the passenger terminal, Blount bought an egg sandwich and a half pint of orange juice. He didn't really feel hungry, just tired, but he still couldn't sleep. He sat in a booth, pulled off the sandwich's top slice of bread, and shook black pepper onto the fried egg. Put the bread back into place. As he ate, he gazed idly at the snack bar's display of a matador's sword, cape, and felt hat. Then he ordered the only thing the snack bar made really well, a cup of *café con leche*. He stirred the Spanish-style coffee, sat down at another booth under a television tuned to CNN. The anchor handed off the broadcast to a reporter speaking live from Sigonella:

> *"The death toll has risen to twenty in the nerve gas attack on a nightclub outside the American naval air station here. Some officials have compared this strike to the 1995 Tokyo subway incident, when the Aum Shinrikyo cult killed thirteen people with sarin gas.*
>
> *"However, the Japanese attack involved liquid sarin carried in plastic bags. Last night's incident used weaponized sarin delivered by some sort of munition. Investigators say it appears an explosive device was planted inside the nightclub. The attack targeted only the club; the air station's security was never breached.*
>
> *"The base here remains on its highest level of alert, which the military calls Force Protection Condition Delta. So far, no terrorist group has claimed responsibility."*

A voice on the PA system called Blount's flight. Blount swallowed the last of his coffee, then joined the passengers filing up the air stairs into the DC-10. Minutes later, the jet thundered away from the ground and banked to the west. Blount watched the wide beaches of Rota pass beneath him; across the bay, he saw the ancient port of

Cádiz. Years ago he'd taken a walking tour of Cádiz's Old Town and learned how this region had once come under the rule of Moors campaigning north from the Sahara. For centuries, swords had crossed at this meeting place of continents. He thought of the Marines about to board the *Iwo Jima*, and he wished them Godspeed.

Blount finally fell asleep after the DC-10 leveled off above the Atlantic. About two hours later, he woke from his nap with a blank mind. For just a second, he had to ask himself why he felt anxiety. What was wrong? Then all the events of the night before came back to him, with the image of Kelley as he trembled, drooled, then stared blankly out of dead eyes.

Kelley and Blount had fought together a decade ago across the rooftops and back alleys of Fallujah. The town hosted a hornet's nest of insurgents, many of them not even Iraqi. Intel thought one of them might be Abu Musab al-Zarqawi, the Jordanian terrorist infamous for the on-camera beheading of American contractor Nicholas Berg. When the networks ran the Berg story, they cut away from the video after al-Zarqawi drew his knife. But at an intel briefing, Blount saw the entire thing. The sight sickened him and filled him with determination. Apparently, it had the same effect on his commanders. They decided Fallujah had to be cleared.

So the Marines, along with some real bad Scottish dudes called the Black Watch, sealed off the place after encouraging civilians to leave. Then Blount's platoon helped sweep through the town, house by house, bullet by bullet. They called it Operation Phantom Fury.

From Blount's point of view, the op went pretty well until Corporal Lane got hit. As the platoon advanced by ones and twos across a street, a boom scattered pigeons from the power lines drooping overhead. Warm blood spattered Blount's face like spray from a hot shower. Just in front of Blount, Lane collapsed.

Blount grabbed Lane by his tactical vest and dragged him to a house that the platoon had already cleared. The rest of the platoon took cover among riddled buildings lining the street. Kelley and a medical corpsman followed Blount into the house. Just to make sure they were safe, Kelley swept the room with his rifle and checked a stairway at the back. No shots, no bad guys inside. Blount wiped his eyes and face. His glove came away bloody, with some kind of sticky matter mixed in.

The corpsman dropped his medical ruck beside Lane, who had taken a round in the mouth. Or maybe the cheek or chin. The high-velocity slug had torn up his face so badly it was hard to tell. Lane gurgled and coughed once. The cough sprayed blood. Then he seemed to struggle to inhale. Lane stared up at the ceiling, scraped the floor with his heels as if he needed to push himself up out of water to breathe.

"Damn it," the corpsman said. "I gotta open his trachea."

"How can I help, Doc?" Blount asked.

"Hold his head steady. Extend his neck just a little bit."

Blount placed his knees on either side of Lane's helmet. He put one hand under the wounded man's neck and lifted as gently as he could.

"That's good," the corpsman said. "Keep him in that position."

Kelley looked on as he spoke on his radio. "Anybody got eyes on that shooter?"

An answer came back amid electronic blips and pops: "Negative, sir."

The corpsman dug a gauze pad and a curved plastic tube from his medical kit. He opened the blade of a folding knife. Tapped two fingers on Lane's Adam's apple. Lane clawed at the floor and tried to sit up. Blount held him down.

"Hold still, bud," Blount said. "I know it feels like you're suffocating. Doc's gon' fix you right up." Funny thing, Blount thought, to cut a man's throat to save him.

The corpsman placed the tip of his blade on Lane's throat and made a vertical incision about an inch and a half long. A little line of blood appeared. He stroked with the knife again to deepen the cut, and then pulled the edges of the incision farther apart. Dabbed away the blood with the gauze, then cut again.

The depth of the cut surprised Blount. He'd always thought a man's windpipe lay right under the skin. The corpsman sliced through yet another layer of tissue, and the light-colored rings of Lane's trachea became visible. Doc twisted his wrist and made a horizontal cut, this one much smaller. Air hissed through the opening. The corpsman shoved the tube into the hole, and the edges of the cut closed around the tube.

Lane's breath sounded strangely hollow as it flowed through the tube. He stopped struggling.

"You the man," Blount told Doc.

The corpsman ignored the compliment. "We gotta get him out of here," he said.

Automatic-weapons fire sputtered from somewhere outside. The rip of an AK. Two pops on semiauto answered. That's what Fallujah usually sounded like: hajjis spraying and Marines aiming. The single shot that got Lane was an exception.

Outside, from behind doorways and courtyard walls where they'd taken cover, other members of the platoon sized up the situation and checked in with Kelley. Blount heard the calls over the officer's MBITR radio.

"We got multiple shooters in a building to the west," a squad leader reported. "They got a field of fire over anything that moves farther down the street."

Kelley tried to look out a window, but he couldn't have seen much from that vantage point. A ray of light through the cracked glass highlighted the name tag Velcroed to his vest. The tag bore his name and the Marine Corps emblem, along with other notations: 1LT, USMC, A POS. Kelley put his hands on his thighs, sighed hard. Then he stood up and, with his thumb and forefinger, pressed the push-to-talk switch clipped to the front of his body armor. Spoke into his radio again.

"See if you can get up on the roofs and put some rounds on them. Hold them where they are until I can get an AT4 up here and shoot a rocket up their ass."

"Aye, aye, sir."

Blount liked the sound of that. Try to pin us down, will you? Better watch what you wish for.

"I'll go up topside," Blount said.

"Be careful," Kelley said. "Make them keep their heads down."

"Aye, sir."

The stairwell led to parts of the house Blount could not see. He pointed his M16 up the steps, saw no threat. Charged upstairs. Nobody up there, either. The house remained clear. Just a bare mattress on a filthy floor, some scattered sheets and trash. Plastic soft drink bottles labeled in Arabic.

A ladder of rough-hewn wood led to a hatchway in the roof. Blount tested the ladder with his boot, hoped it would support his weight. The ladder sagged as he climbed, but the rungs held. Blount slammed the butt of his rifle against the wooden hatch.

The hatch slapped open. Dusty sunlight streamed in. Blount unsnapped his helmet and placed it over the muzzle of his rifle. Raised the helmet up through the hatchway. When the helmet drew no fire, he brought it back down, put it on, and climbed onto the roof. Moving in a low crouch, Blount took cover behind the low wall that rimmed the roof on all four sides.

From his elevated position, he had a view of the battle unfolding around him. A pillar of black smoke rose in the distance. Gunfire chattered and cracked both near and far. A pair of Cobra attack helicopters traversed the skyline like two lethal wasps. Several of Blount's fellow Marines lay prone on nearby rooftops, weapons trained in the direction of the house where the insurgents were barricaded.

One of the Marines, Cooper, lay next to an M40 sniper rifle. He was alone atop the next building, separated from Blount by a gap of about seven feet. A narrow alleyway ran between the two houses.

Blount wondered what was wrong; Cooper should have had a spotter with him. Perhaps Cooper's spotter, Rossini, had been wounded.

Blount knew how to help, though. He'd attended Scout Sniper School the year before, along with Lieutenant Kelley. The lieutenant didn't have to go; sniping wasn't an officer's job. But officers up through the rank of captain could take the course to better understand the skills of the Marines they commanded.

"Cooper," Blount whispered. "Coming your way, man."

The sniper motioned for Blount to approach. Something looked wrong with Cooper's eyes. He kept blinking and rubbing at them. Blount took a running start, leaped across the alleyway. He landed on the balls of his feet, rifle in his left hand. Dived for the tiles of the roof, tried to make himself as flat as possible. Crawled next to Cooper.

"Lane's hit real bad," Blount said. "The lieutenant's trying to get weapons platoon up here to take care of those hajjis. What happened to you? And where's Rossini?"

Cooper's reddened eyes streamed with moisture.

"Fucker shot at us and the bullet hit the edge of the wall right here." Cooper pointed, his hand covered by a Nomex shooting glove. "Sprayed dust and shit all in my face. I should have been wearing my goggles, but I had just taken 'em off to look through the scope. The next round went right through Rossini's hand. He wasn't no more good to me, so I sent him inside to take cover."

"Stop rubbing your eyes, bud," Blount said. "Get downstairs to the corpsman and see if he's got some eyewash. Leave your stuff up here."

"Aye, aye, Staff Sergeant."

Blount watched Cooper low-crawl across the roof and descend through a hatch. With Cooper safely down, Blount pressed his talk switch to call Kelley on the radio.

"Hammer One Actual, Hammer One Bravo," Blount transmitted.

"Go ahead," Kelley answered.

"I just sent Cooper off the roof. He's got grit in his eyes. Sir, if you're done talking to weapons platoon, we got a chance to use what we learned in school."

"Be right up."

Blount dug into Cooper's pack and found an observation scope. He uncapped the lenses and set up the optic on tripod legs extended just a few inches. That way, he could stay low while glassing the target. From the pack, he also took Cooper's DOPE book: Data of Previous Engagements. It recorded the scope settings and weather conditions for every shot Cooper had fired.

Through the mil-dot reticle of the observation scope, Blount saw the fuzzy outline of the house that shielded the insurgents. He rolled the adjustments for focus and magnification until all the edges came in sharp. Figuring by the dots in the reticle, Blount estimated the house at just under two hundred yards away.

The rear of the house gave onto an open area hemmed by a stone fence. A little urban goat pen or chicken yard, maybe. No animals in sight, though. No insurgents, either, at least for now. Blount took his eye off the scope for a moment, flipped open the DOPE book.

On the Zero Summary Chart, Blount found a row for the distance—two hundred—and a column for the temperature. The weather had been cool, typical for November in Iraq. But the sun shining on the rooftops this day probably raised the local temp to nearly seventy. He cross-referenced where the row and column met, and noted the elevation setting for the rifle scope.

Blount heard boot steps behind him. He turned to see Kelley leap over the alley and land on the rooftop. The lieutenant slid low next to Blount.

"If you want to shoot, sir, I'll spot for you," Blount said.

"That'll work." Kelley lifted Cooper's rifle, examined the scope's turrets.

"I checked his DOPE book," Blount said. "Gimme two plus one."

Kelley adjusted the elevation turret. He dialed in a two-hundred-yard setting, with one more click to fine-tune. "Set," he said.

Blount peered through the observation scope again. A door opened at the back of the house. A man crouched within the doorway. Through the lens, Blount noticed a scrap of trash, maybe the wrapper from a cigarette pack, rolling in the breeze. The drifting cellophane suggested wind at about five miles per hour.

"See that guy?" Blount asked.

"Affirm."

Kelley appeared ready to fire. He held his body straight in line with the weapon, heels down for the lowest possible profile.

But did he have a target? Blount could not see if the man in the doorway carried a weapon. What if he was just some poor, scared Iraqi?

The man eased out of the doorway. He held an AK. Propped the barrel on the stone fence. Gotcha, Blount thought.

"Spotter ready," he whispered.

"Shooter ready."

Blount felt the breeze on his face.

"Hold left lung," he said. "Send it."

Kelley fired.

Using 10X magnification, Blount saw dust fly from the insurgent's shirt. The 7.62-millimeter bullet slammed into the man's torso and exited through his back. His AK clattered to the ground. The target fell facedown, and a pool of red spread beneath him.

"Good hit," Blount said.

Kelley ejected his spent brass and chambered a fresh round. A rifle barrel appeared at the edge of the doorway where the last insurgent had come from. Whoever held that rifle remained cloaked in shadow. The weapon fired a blast, but all the rounds flew wild.

"Let's put a round in that door," Blount said. "Spotter ready."

"Shooter ready."

"Send it."

The bullet smacked into the wood. Chips flew. The rifle barrel disappeared inside the house. Blount could not tell if the gunman was hit.

Kelley worked the bolt of the M40 again. In his role as the lieutenant's spotter, Blount watched to make sure the next cartridge fed smoothly into the chamber. Blount actually preferred spotting to shooting: You glassed the target, observed the wind, checked the DOPE, fed the shooter with information. You got to think more. Talk that bullet right where it needed to go.

Blount placed his eye back to the observation scope. Nobody at the door, now punctured by a match-grade slug. But he saw movement behind a shattered upstairs window. Someone inside held a rifle, though not an AK. Blount zoomed in to 15X. The long-barreled weapon looked a little like the M40, but the forend and bipod were different. Maybe a Blaser R93, a German-made weapon. Good Lord, Blount thought, where did they get that? Must be the guy who shot Lane. All right, dude. Just come a little closer to that window.

"See that guy upstairs?" Blount asked.

Kelley shifted his rifle, peered through the scope.

"Ooooh, yeah. You thinking what I'm thinking?"

"I think he hurt a Marine."

"Then talk to me, Staff Sergeant."

The gunman crouched beneath the window. No fool, he exposed little of himself. This would require more precision than a center-mass shot. Not a problem. Aim small, miss small, Blount's instructors had taught him.

The wind picked up, swirled dust across the rooftops. The gunman slid the barrel farther over the windowsill, and his face became visible.

"Spotter ready. Hold left ear."

Kelley exhaled and spoke as he dumped his lungs.

"Shooter ready."

"Send it."

The bullet struck the bridge of the insurgent's nose. Red spray jetted from the back of his head. The force of the round threw him into the shadows, and he seemed to disappear altogether.

"Fuck you, you fucking fuck," Kelley said.

Blount smiled. His fellow devil dogs had raised profanity to a high art. Any idiot could use "fuck" as a noun or a verb. But a Marine could make it a verb, an adjective, and a noun all in the same sentence. Blount, however, seldom cursed.

"Good shot, sir."

Kelley chambered another round. Behind the two men, a hatch opened and two Marines climbed onto the roof. One carried something that looked like a large dark green tube, flared at one end.

"There's the present I ordered for them," Kelley said.

Kelley and Blount put another shot into the door, just to remind the insurgents that venturing outside was a really bad idea. The terrorists fired bursts into the street from their AKs. The fusillade hit nothing except dirt and concrete, but stopped Blount's comrades from getting beyond that house.

The two Marines with the rocket launcher pointed and talked. One of them rose up on a knee and held the launcher across his shoulder. Their chatter fell into the cadence of a well-rehearsed drill.

"Prep rocket."

The Marine holding the weapon smacked at a cocking lever.

"Rocket ready. Back-blast area secure."

"Fire when ready."

"Rocket!"

A white dart shot from the tube. Behind the Marine who'd just fired, dust spewed into the air and curled over the roof. The dart cut a straight line to the house where the insurgents hid.

Smoke and dust boiled from the doors and windows. Fire followed the smoke. The explosion created splashes of flame in almost liquid form; yellow and orange globules rolled within the dust. The rocket didn't just burn the house; it blew away part of the supporting structure. One corner sank as if made of wet cardboard.

Blount's comrades cheered. Marine riflemen emerged from behind cover, dashed from walls and ledges, descended from roofs to press forward up the street. Not a single shot came from the insurgents' former hideout.

Kelley raised his gloved palm above his head. Blount high-fived him. In the lore of fighting men, the bond between an infantry platoon commander and his platoon sergeant bordered on the mythical. At that moment, Kelley became not just Blount's commander, but also his brother.

A helo came in to pick up Lane and take him to Bravo Surgical. Lane survived, but he needed six operations to rebuild his face. Abu Musab al-Zarqawi managed to slip away from the American forces in Fallujah. Didn't live much longer, though. Karma and laser-guided bombs caught up with him less than two years later.

Fallujah had been Blount's last op with Kelley. And now Kelley was dead, killed by an enemy he never had a chance to fight.

Blount hoped his mind would settle on some final thought, a concluding coda that would bring perspective. But all the memories and images remained a disordered jumble, like checking the index of a training manual and finding nothing in alphabetical order.

He leaned his head on the window and looked down at the ocean below. The blue-rippled Atlantic stretched wide and bright. Blount liked to imagine those waves holding their form across thousands of miles of water until they broke on the shores of home.

CHAPTER 3

At the UN camp near the Libyan town of Ghat, a woman brought a child into the medical tent where Sophia Gold worked as a translator and coordinator. Gold did her best to communicate; in the U.S. Army she had built a career on speaking Pashto, not Arabic. Recent courses funded by her new employer, the United Nations, had improved her smattering of Arabic. But the modern standard Arabic of her studies differed from the Libyan Arabic spoken by these tired, wounded, and sick refugees. Gold had trouble understanding the woman.

"*Hal beemkanek mosá adati?*" the woman asked.

She wore a purple-and-white hijab and maroon robes dusty from her trek. Raw burns pocked her cheeks, and blisters bulged her skin. The sight reminded Gold of women she'd seen in Afghanistan, attacked by vengeful men throwing acid. These injuries looked a little different, though. Acid tended to eat away flesh and dig furrows rather than raise blisters.

"*Takalam beboť men fadleki?*" Gold asked. Can you speak slowly?

The woman repeated herself, enunciating each word. This time, Gold took her meaning. The woman needed help. She picked up her crying child, a boy of about five. The mother slid back his sleeve to reveal burns like her own.

"*Ahtaju tabeeban.*" She wanted a doctor.

Gold got the woman and boy to lie down on a cot under a fan powered by generators humming outside in the sand. She called over Danielle Lambrechts, a Belgian physician. As Lambrechts examined the two patients, Gold retrieved a pair of water bottles from a cooler, twisted off the caps, and gave the water to her new charges. The boy upended his bottle and gulped so quickly that water ran down both sides of his mouth. He did not stop to take a breath until he'd half emptied the bottle.

"These are chemical burns," Lambrechts said.

"That's what I thought," Gold said. Not lye burns from making soap, either.

"She came in with fifteen other people who arrived on foot. They walked from a village between here and Ghat. Ask her how it happened."

Gold formed the question in her mind and considered the Arabic words. She did not yet think in Arabic the way she could think in Pashto. As simply as possible, she asked the woman to describe what she'd experienced.

The answer came in a torrent. Gold regretted having to stop the woman and ask her to slow down and repeat herself. Eventually the story emerged—one of pure malevolence, violence for its own sake.

"Bandits moved into the old fort overlooking our village," the woman said. "In the night, booms awakened us. Two or three explosions."

As the woman spoke, Lambrechts began to treat the burns on the boy's arms. She tore open a green packet and pulled out a fabric pad impregnated with charcoal powder. The label was in French, but the pad looked a lot like the M291 skin decontamination kits Gold knew from the Army. When Lambrechts touched the pad to the boy's skin, he howled and tried to pull his arm away.

"Tell him this will help the burning stop," Lambrechts said.

Gold started to translate. When the mother caught on, she spoke quickly to her child, and the boy held his arm still. Lambrechts patted the decon pad along the length of the boy's arm.

"When the booms started," the woman said, "I hid with my child in a corner of the house." They took cover, she explained, until the danger seemed to pass. Once quiet returned, they went outside to check on neighbors.

She described how people had emerged into the night breezes. The scirocco winds had abated a little, though dust still painted the moon and dulled the stars. The villagers discovered little damage, just some shallow scarring against the mud walls of a few houses.

Then the booms began again.

This time they came endlessly; the woman had no idea how many. Her neighbors shrieked in terror, ran for whatever protection they could find. Strange odors filled the air. The woman described the stench of rotting fish floating through the village. Rotting fish mixed with gasoline, perhaps; she had never smelled such a foul and bizarre odor.

"Blister agents delivered by mortar," Gold told Lambrechts.

"Mon Dieu," the doctor said.

People began to cough and choke, the woman explained. Their eyes and noses streamed. Some appeared to drown on dry land, mouths frothing as they struggled to breathe.

"I covered my boy's mouth and nose with my veil," the woman said. "I held my breath. We hurried back inside."

In their home, they hacked and vomited. But Allah's wind showed enough mercy, she said, that they had not inhaled a fatal dose. Their skin, however, began to burn as if sprayed with scalding water. The burning came on slowly, at first barely noticeable. It worsened until painful blisters began to disfigure skin that had been exposed to the caustic mist.

"The bandits poisoned us the way one kills rats," the woman said. "We feared to leave our home, but we could not stay in our poisoned village."

She went on to tell how she tore her veil in half. One half she tied tightly over her child's nose and mouth; the other she tied across her own face.

"Some of us began to leave," she said. "Allah forgive us, we did not stop to help the dying. We wanted only to get our children out of the poison. We walked through the night to get here."

"You saved your boy's life," Gold said.

"He is all that I have left. His father died in the civil war."

The attack on civilians did not surprise Gold. Militant factions ran riot all over North Africa under banners such as al-Qaeda in the Islamic Maghreb, and the Signers With Blood Brigade. Some of the raids seemed to serve no purpose but to mark territory, and the tactic wasn't new. As far back as the 1990s, the Armed Islamic Group of Algeria carried out indiscriminate massacres. Fighters, some with henna-dyed beards to signify they'd completed a pilgrimage to Mecca, swept into Algerian towns and mowed down anything that moved. The men with orange beards deemed the villages insufficiently pious, and determined that everyone in those villages had to die.

But now the killing knew no borders. And the killers used new weapons.

Lambrechts treated other patients with blisters like those of the mother and child. Gold remained by the doctor's side, translating as best she could. One old man took every breath in agony. He coughed bloody foam, and Lambrechts said he'd inhaled enough chemical to sear the inside of his lungs. Gold tried to speak with him, but he couldn't talk.

"He needs oxygen," Lambrechts said. She gave an order in French, and a nurse wheeled over a green metal bottle. A clear hose led from a valve on the bottle to a plastic mask. The nurse placed the mask over the man's nose and mouth, and she secured the mask with an elastic band that fit around the patient's head.

The old man lay back on his cot, eyes darting from Gold to Lambrechts and the nurse. He kept one hand on the mask as if that could force more oxygen into his lungs. At first the oxygen seemed to give him relief, but as the day wore on he began to wheeze. His face took on a gray pallor, and his eyes squeezed shut when he inhaled, as if respiration itself caused pain. He died in the med tent, each breath a struggle right down to the last one.

Gold and the medical team worked long into the night, changing dressings, applying ointments, comforting patients. Before going to bed, Gold went to the admin tent to use the satellite phone. She dialed her good friend Michael Parson, an Air Force officer recently promoted to colonel. Parson worked air mobility issues and mission planning for AFRICOM, the U.S. Africa Command, headquartered not in Africa but in Stuttgart, Germany.

"I'm sorry to call you so late," Gold said.

"Sophia," Parson said, "you can call me anytime you want. It's good to hear your voice. Is everything all right?"

Parson sounded like himself, in command and straight to the point. She told him about the chemical attack near Ghat.

"Oh, shit," Parson said. "We knew they'd hit that area, but intel said the reports about chem weapons were unconfirmed. Sounds pretty confirmed now."

"First Sigonella and now this."

"Yeah, that was sarin, but you're saying you saw blister agents?"

"Yes."

Parson let out a long breath. Over the sat phone, Gold could hear the worry in his voice even as it bounced back down from space. She knew what concerned him. This showed that bad guys had gotten their hands on weapons of mass destruction, in variety and in quantity. The U.S. had once invaded Iraq over a WMD threat. Nobody in the military wanted another war, especially at a time when training and everything else went underfunded. But this time, the chemical threat presented an imminent danger.

"Where do you think they're getting this stuff?" Gold asked.

"I got some ideas, but nothing I can talk about right now. I've been trying to get some more eyes in the sky. Maybe a Predator or a

Global Hawk. Given what you just told me, I'll have an easier time with that request now."

Gold tried to think of any other help she could offer. "If the area looks safe, I think some of us will fly into the village tomorrow and look around. I'll let you know if I see anything of interest."

"That's fine," Parson said, "but for God's sake, be careful."

"We will."

Parson paused for a moment. Gold wondered whether she'd lost the connection, and then he said, "This new job of yours sounds too much like the Army. I thought you wanted something different."

Gold considered his comment; he seemed to read her mind. With the U.S. withdrawing from Afghanistan, she needed to find other ways to make a contribution. She wanted to keep doing her part to ease suffering in the world. The question was how.

"Well, it *is* different," she said. "But the mission's not always as clear. Sometimes I wake up with the feeling I'm not where I'm supposed to be."

"Where do you think you should be?"

"Wherever I can do the most good."

"Hmm," Parson said. "That might change with the seasons, but I think you're in a good place to help some people at the moment."

Gold rarely heard Parson talk about finding his own place in the world. He seemed to know his place so well: flying airplanes or leading those who fly. She had a different set of skills to put to use. And, still, the question was how.

The next morning, word came down that the insurgents had melted away from areas around Ghat. Gold put on a tan field jacket and gathered some tools: her digital camera, pens and notepad, and a canteen filled with water. Ballistic sunglasses and Nomex gloves, too. Army habits were hard to break, and in fact she remained an inactive reservist. She and Lambrechts boarded an old Soviet-built Mi-8 helicopter. The chopper—painted white to distinguish it from mili-

tary aircraft—bore lettering along the tail boom that read UNITED
NATIONS.

Wind rocked the Mi-8 at liftoff. Sand as fine and light-colored
as ground mustard enveloped the helicopter as soon as its blades
changed pitch. The brownout blocked Gold's view of the horizon,
and she began to feel a little airsick from the jolts and bumps of turbulence. Lambrechts suffered even more from the rough air; she put
her hand to her mouth as if about to throw up. But the ride grew
smoother after the aircraft climbed a few hundred feet. Above the
worst of the dust, the horizon became visible through the windows.

With the helicopter on course for the village, the desert flowed
underneath like a brown ocean. Breezes kept enough sand in the air
to blur the edges of hills and dunes, giving the terrain the appearance
of a landscape painted in watercolors. After twenty minutes of flying, paths appeared on the desert floor. Gold saw that the paths con-
verged at a village. Just outside the cluster of dwellings, a grove of
palm trees stood in a gulley; Gold presumed the ditch carried water
at least part of the year. Over the village, the pilots descended for a
closer look before landing.

Gold craned her neck to see better from her side window. Troops
patrolled narrow alleys. They wore gas masks and bulky clothing.
Under all the equipment, they plodded along like hard-hat divers
walking the ocean floor. Their gear reminded Gold of the MOPP
suits she had used in Army training for chemical environments. The
troops, Gold knew, were African Union CBRN specialists, trained
for chemical, biological, radiological, and nuclear hazards. The soldiers carried what looked like test equipment for measuring contamination.

The helicopter landed and shut down several hundred yards
upwind of the town. Two African Union helicopters were parked
nearby. A man in MOPP gear strode toward the makeshift flight
line. As he came closer, he removed his gas mask, and sweat streamed

from his face and hair. Gold and Lambrechts stepped down from the helicopter. The man greeted them.

"I am Major Ongondo," he said. "Kenya Defence Forces."

He removed two pairs of gloves—heavy rubber gloves worn over a set of white cloth gloves. Wiped his face with a handkerchief. Gold shook his hand, clammy with perspiration.

"Sophia Gold," she said. "I work with the UN High Commissioner for Refugees. This is Dr. Danielle Lambrechts."

"You may inspect the community," Ongondo said. "We detect only trace levels of blister agents. I suggest that you not touch anything."

Gold felt almost foolish showing up without any CBRN gear, but her current employer didn't equip people for chemical warfare. She wondered whether she should lead Lambrechts into the town, but it looked safe enough now. Ongondo's men had removed their gas masks and walked about with the fronts of their MOPP suits unzipped. Weaponized chemicals often dissipated quickly, especially with any wind. Sometimes weather conditions pushed the toxic cloud into places not targeted by the shooters. Shells filled with poison made for a sloppy weapon, in Gold's view. Indiscriminate by definition.

The horrors of chemical weapons used in World War I had led to a number of treaties banning them. As far back as 1925, the Geneva Protocol had outlawed first use of chemical or biological weapons. The current treaty, known as the Chemical Weapons Convention, had remained in force since 1997. But with some groups and some governments, chemicals still held a lot of appeal. The weapons could be devastating over a short duration, and they were cheap.

From the pocket of her field jacket, Gold pulled out her camera. She turned it on and took a distance shot of the village. The medina— the old residential section—looked as uniformly beige as the desert that surrounded it. Palm trees appeared as feathers of green, providing the only variation in color. From this perspective, Gold saw few signs of the horrors that had taken place just hours before. She and Lambrechts walked toward the village with Ongondo.

"More than a dozen people came to our refugee camp on foot," Gold said. Lambrechts told the Kenyan officer about the burns on the women and children, and the old man who'd died.

"We found eighteen dead," Ongondo said. "Some survivors suffer from burns, and others show no symptoms."

"Who did this?" Gold asked. "And where did they get these weapons?"

"I have no idea who and where," Ongondo said, "and I cannot imagine why." The officer's voice cracked. Until that moment, Gold hadn't realized he was struggling with his emotions.

"These things can be hard to comprehend," Gold said.

Ongondo wiped sweat from his face with his sleeve, stood with his gloves wadded up in his fists. Shook his head.

"The Baila tribe in Central Africa has a folktale to explain the inexplicable," Ongondo said. "In the time before history, a woman went to work and put down her baby by the side of the field. When the child cried, a great eagle landed and spread its wings. The woman feared the eagle would kill her child, but the bird only stopped the child's crying. The next day, the same thing happened; the eagle landed just to soothe the child. The woman told her husband, who did not believe. She took him to the field the next day. When he saw the eagle land beside the baby, he drew his bow and shot an arrow at the eagle. The eagle flapped away, and the arrow hit the child. The eagle had wanted only to soothe the child, and he placed a curse. Kindness went away from mankind, and people kill one another to this day."

"That is a very sad tale," Lambrechts said.

Gold considered the wisdom packed into such a short story: senseless violence that kills the innocent. Telling the story seemed Ongondo's way of getting his feelings under control. She wished she could talk further with the Kenyan officer. But he, Gold, and Lambrechts pressed on to matters at hand.

Inside the village, the first sign of trouble Gold noted came in the form of a dead goat. The animal lay sprawled as if struck by a car, except the goat had died in a courtyard far from any curb. Gold aimed her camera, pressed the autofocus button. The goat's black fur came into sharp clarity, and Gold took the photo.

Down the next alleyway, two AU men rolled a corpse into a black body bag. The dead person's left arm, stiff from rigor mortis, reached up from the bag as if the deceased wanted to climb out and live again. The men forced the arm down and zipped the bag closed. Gold waited before snapping another picture, to spare this unknown Libyan the indignity of being photographed in such a condition. She could not see if the person was a man or a woman.

"What an awful way to leave this world," Lambrechts said.

A dog had died nearby, a dun-colored animal of indeterminate breed. Its lips curled upward, revealing fangs shown in a final growl. Gold imagined the dog could not have comprehended this vaporous enemy that inflicted such pain. The AU troops hefted the body bag, left the dog where it was.

The sight reminded Gold of photos she'd seen of Halabja, Iraq, where Saddam Hussein's regime killed thousands of Kurdish civilians with a gas attack in 1988. The death toll hadn't climbed nearly that high here. But the randomness of this attack and the mystery of the attackers gave plenty of reason to worry about what might come next.

The AU troops carried the body bag to a square by a mosque, set it down in a row beside eight others. Gold raised her camera again and photographed the row of bags. If not for the scirocco blowing the chemicals away quickly, how many more bags would there have been?

"This could have been much worse," Ongondo said.

"I was just thinking that," Gold said.

"My medics have set up a casualty collection point. Would you like to go there?"

"Yes," Lambrechts said. "Right away."

At the three CCP tents, a Libyan doctor and two nurses worked with three military medics. In the stifling heat, Gold removed her sunglasses and wiped her sleeve across her brow. Lambrechts waded into the throng of patients; scores of people filled the tents. The coughing adults and crying children made conversation nearly impossible. Lambrechts raised her voice to communicate with one of the medics.

"I am a physician," she said. "Do you speak English?"

"No English. No English."

"*Parlez-vous français?*"

The medic shook his head.

"*Parli italiano?*"

"*Sì.*"

While Lambrechts examined patients, Gold took photos that would emphasize the first point she'd make when she e-mailed New York—*Send more doctors and medical supplies.*

The victims here appeared even worse off than those who'd reached the refugee camp yesterday. Many of their blisters had broken open to reveal red, oozing flesh underneath the ravaged skin. The sight brought bile to Gold's throat, but she forced her gut to calm and her mind to focus.

One teenage boy sat on the ground. Flaps of skin dangled from his face. He stared at the tent wall and took quick breaths. Pain, Gold imagined, had forced his mind in on itself until he could think of nothing else. She had known that kind of agony herself. Gold kneeled, opened her canteen, held it in front of the boy.

"Drink this," she said in Arabic.

The boy grasped the canteen with fingers that looked like half-cooked meat. He lifted the canteen to his mouth, drank for several seconds, passed the canteen back to Gold.

"I am sorry to do this," Gold said, "but I need to take your photograph to show what they have done to you." Governments and aid agencies needed to see this.

The boy did not answer or even make eye contact. Gold snapped a picture of his hands and one of his face. A medic came over, helped the boy to his feet, and led him to an examination table. Gold hoped the medics could give him some kind of relief.

In the crowded tent, Gold felt she was only getting in the way. She rose to her feet, put her sunglasses back on, and went outside.

The quiet of the paths and alleys contrasted with the noise inside the hospital tents. Gold checked her watch; it was just after noon. Yet the village showed no normal bustle of life. No traffic, no vegetable merchants, not even the call to prayer from the muezzin. An entire community poisoned and sick.

A calico cat stalked across the sidewalk and disappeared down an alley. Gold decided to look around some more, so she followed the animal. The cat simply vanished, as strays could do, but something else caught Gold's eye. The far end of the alley opened onto a wider street. Along the concrete wall of a home there, someone had spray-painted graffiti. The red paint looked fresh.

Gold squinted, read the Arabic. TO THE INFIDELS, TO THE SUFI APOSTATES, TAKE THIS WARNING. A NEW PASHA WILL RULE TRIPOLITANIA WITH ALLAH'S FIERCE JUSTICE.

Pasha? Tripolitania? Those words evoked the days of the Barbary pirates. Maybe some terrorist chieftain sought to cast himself in their image.

Wait a minute, Gold thought. Why would you come this far into a village you'd just hit with chemical weapons, only to spray-paint a threat?

Well, you could do it if you wore a gas mask.

That implied preparation. A dangerous enemy with a plan. Gold took a shot of the graffiti. This photo, she'd send to Parson.

CHAPTER 4

Home.

Blount sat in a high-back rocker on the front porch of his house, eight-year-old Ruthie in his lap. Priscilla, the older one, stretched out on the swing, which hung from the porch ceiling by a pair of chains. She kept the swing swaying with occasional nudges of her sandal against the hardwood floor while she read a book on an electronic tablet. The weather remained warm for October; through the screens of the open windows Blount smelled supper cooking. Bernadette, the woman who kept him sane and strong, was fixing Chicken Bog. The aromas of onion, sausage, chicken, and rice would have told even a blind man he was in the low country of South Carolina.

A violent and unpredictable world lay beyond the horizon, Blount knew all too well. But what he could see from his house looked like paradise. The front yard bordered a marsh lagoon. A pair of mergansers cut ripples across the estuary, the surface turned golden by the setting sun. Cordgrass bent with the tide. Palmettos with leaflets shaped like green bayonets stood sentry where the water met dry land. A fitting place for a Marine to make his home. The universe could have ended right then and there, and Blount would have gone out happy.

Behind him, he heard the sound of his wife's footsteps. Bernadette appeared at the screen door, a kitchen towel in her hands. Still fit after two children, partly because she ran with Blount every morning—when he was home. Skin the color of walnuts, long fingers that could stroke his back and make everything that hurt go away, she was the most beautiful thing on God's green earth.

"Y'all come on in," Bernadette said. "We're ready to eat."

"Yay," Ruthie said. Blount's youngest wriggled out of his grasp. She was getting near about too big to sit on his lap. Enjoy every minute, Blount's grandfather had told him. They'll get grown in no time.

Before Blount sat down at the table, he embraced his wife. Her freshly washed hair smelled like lavender. The evening before, she had made love to him long into the night. He'd awakened to that same lavender smell on her pillow. By then she had dressed and gone out the door to her job as the guidance counselor at Beaufort High School, over on Lady's Island.

The television blared in the background. Bernadette picked up the remote, muted the sound of the newscast, and said, "Priscilla, why don't you say the blessing?"

Blount's eldest prayed over the food, and then Bernadette began ladling the Chicken Bog. Steam rose from every spoonful. The one-dish, rice-based meal reminded Blount of the pilau they served in Afghanistan, but the seasonings tasted completely different.

"So, what did you do today, baby?" Bernadette asked. "Did you get caught up on your sleep?"

"Not really," Blount said. "My body clock still don't know where it is. I went over to the sheriff's department today to see about a job."

"What did they say?"

"They're not hiring. Budget cuts."

"Don't worry. Between all the sheriff and police departments around here, plus the highway patrol, I'm sure somebody'll take you."

"I reckon."

"But don't go with the highway patrol if they want to put you way up in District Three. You've been away from home enough."

"Yeah," Ruthie said.

Priscilla nodded, chewing.

They could afford to wait for him to find the right job. Bernadette's position paid all right, so they'd always saved most of what he made as a Marine. Gunnery sergeant pay, especially with a combat-zone tax exclusion, added up pretty good. That's how they'd got this house. But it wasn't just about the money. Blount wanted to feel like he was doing somebody some good. And he had a real specific skill set.

He picked up the pitcher of sweet tea and poured. The ice in his glass cracked and popped like distant rifle fire as the tea flowed over it. When he took a sip, his hand encircled the tea glass the way a smaller man's hand might wrap around a shot glass. He swallowed, set the glass back down on the coaster gently. Blount knew his strength, and he seldom broke anything he didn't mean to break.

As he ate, he kept one eye on the silent television. After a commercial for some video game, an anchor opened a new segment. A graphic appeared over the anchor's shoulder—a black skull and crossbones. The screen cut to images of a desert town, and a new graphic read VIDEO FROM AL ARABIYA NEWS SERVICE. Women wailed and waved their arms by a row of body bags. Blount took the remote and turned up the volume.

". . . in the second chemical weapons attack by terrorists in a week. A spokesman for the African Union says at least nineteen people died near the Libyan town of Ghat. So far, there has been no claim of responsibility. But a variety of terror groups have staged conventional attacks across North Africa in recent months, and the use of even more destructive weapons is prompting calls for international assistance. Chemical agents such as mustard gas and sarin can cause horrible injuries, and we warn you that some of the following video is graphic."

A screaming child appeared with folds of skin hanging from her arms. Blount thumbed the remote's power button and turned off the set. He didn't want his girls to see some of what he'd seen. Bernadette looked at him but didn't say anything.

After dinner, Blount worked on unpacking. He took his seabag up to the master bedroom and began to put away uniforms. Eventually he'd move them from the closet to the attic, but he needed them for a little while yet. Later this week he'd drive to Camp Lejeune up in North Carolina. He'd sit through some separation briefings and get started on outprocessing.

At the bottom of the seabag he found his old KA-BAR knife. The knife meant more to him than just an heirloom. He had carried it with him on every operation since boot camp. With this blade he had sliced parachute cord, hacked Euphrates River reeds, cut away clothing to give first aid to wounded buddies. And on one dark night in Afghanistan, he had taken a life with it. What to do with it now?

He descended the stairs, went outside, and walked across the backyard where he planned to put in that big garden next spring. An old toolshed stood under a live oak behind the house. Blount lifted the hasp and pulled open the door.

In the dim light he pulled the twine hanging from the overhead lamp, and the naked bulb winked on. The previous owner had cleared out all the tools; little remained in the shed except a bare wooden workbench. Pretty soon Blount would bring in new rakes, hoes, and probably a motorized tiller. Once he got the fence built around the pasture, the toolshed would also store tack, hay, and other things for the girls' pony. He had plenty of time for all that, though.

He could not think of a better place for the fighting knife than here in the toolshed by the garden, its fighting days done. Symbol of a long mission ended.

Blount unsheathed the knife, held the grip in his fist. Stabbed the blade hard into the top of the workbench. He slammed the knife in so deep, no one but him would have the muscle to remove it. Blount placed the sheath down beside the knife. In the aged leather he could still make out the lettering that read USMC.

The original owner, Blount's maternal grandfather, had always taken pride that his grandson carried that knife. Grandpa Buell, now ninety-two, resided at an assisted-living facility outside Beaufort. He'd outlived his wife and most of his strength, but the old Marine's mind remained sharp as ever. Grandpa had mentored Blount through some pretty tough times. A talk with the old man always helped put things in perspective. Blount decided to drive over and say hello, but first he went back into the house to tell Bernadette where he was going.

"Oh, good," Bernadette said. "You can take him these for me."

She wrapped aluminum foil over two dishes—a quart of Chicken Bog and half of a sweet potato pie. Blount carried the dishes out to his Ram and placed them on the floor of the passenger's side.

His truck gleamed; Bernadette and the girls had washed and waxed it for him before he got home. The Marine Corps sticker on the rear window shone with red lettering on a yellow background. Because Blount lived near the Beaufort air station and the Parris Island recruit depot, he saw USMC stickers on cars and trucks all over the place. Some of the stickers carried funny messages: THE 72 VIRGINS DATE COUNSELORS, TRAVEL AGENTS TO ALLAH, or HEAVEN WON'T TAKE US AND HELL'S AFRAID WE'LL TAKE OVER. Nothing wrong with a laugh, but Blount had chosen a sticker more in line with how he saw himself and his job: NO BETTER FRIEND, NO WORSE ENEMY.

But the Corps would soon become his former job. Blount felt overjoyed to return to his family. However, he'd expected to end his time in the Marines with more sense of a journey seen through, a mission accomplished. He knew he shouldn't take personally that sarin attack in Sigonella. Hard not to take it that way, though, after watching his old platoon commander die. And the news tonight brought that stuff right into his own dining room.

A sense of loss came over him as he started his truck and steered down a narrow lane lined with cypress trees, their limbs dripping with Spanish moss. Who am I going to be now? Blount wondered. But then he told himself to stop talking foolishness. Nobody stayed in the Corps forever. Hadn't he pushed his luck far enough?

Blount shut down his truck in the parking lot of Sunrise Senior Living. He knocked on the door of his grandfather's suite and found the old Marine sitting in his wheelchair. An oxygen tube wrapped over his ears and led to a cannula in his nose. The television chattered with CNN at low volume, and Grandpa held a book in his lap—a thousand-page doorstop on American foreign policy since 9/11. Even in the old-folks' home, he kept up with current events, just like the intel sergeant major he'd once been. A shadow box hung on the wall. The box contained an NCO's ceremonial sword, a row of medals, and a folded flag that had flown over the Capitol during the Ford administration.

"Hey, Grandpa. It's me," Blount said.

"Welcome home, boy," Grandpa said. He closed his book, spread his arms wide, and smiled. "I reckon this is welcome home for good."

"I guess so. Brought you some Chicken Bog and sweet potato pie."

"Come on in. I already ate, so just stick it in the refrigerator. I'll eat it tomorrow. Bernadette cooks better than the chow hall we got here, that's for sure."

Blount placed the two dishes in the small fridge and bent to embrace his grandfather. Then he sat down in a recliner beside the wheelchair.

"You're looking good," Blount said. He liked the way the old man stayed engaged with the world. What a blessing he still had his intellect. There were people down the hall who had no idea where they were or what was happening around them.

"I'm doing all right. I see y'all had some trouble at Sig."

"Yes, sir. We did."

Grandpa pulled down his glasses, furrowed his gray eyebrows, and regarded Blount as if giving him a medical exam.

"You feeling okay? That sarin's some bad stuff. I don't know how in this world you didn't get exposed when you ran inside that place. Boy, you got more balls than brains."

Well, Grandpa hadn't heard that part on the news. Bernadette must have told him everything. Fair enough.

"We didn't know it was nerve gas until we got in there, Grandpa. Corporal Fender and I got lucky, I reckon."

"You got that right."

"Maybe I won't have to deal with nothing else like that."

Grandpa took a long breath of oxygen, reached into his pocket, and pulled out two peppermints. He handed one to Blount and unwrapped the other for himself. Blount opened the foil, popped the peppermint into his mouth, and crushed it between his molars. The peppermint ritual went back to their earliest conversations. The cool rush of sugar took him decades into the past, nearly brought tears to his eyes.

"So how do you feel about leaving the Corps?" Grandpa asked. "You gon' be a deputy?"

Just like him, Blount thought. Straight to the heart of things.

"That's a good question. The department's not hiring for now."

Blount wondered what his grandfather thought about his separation from the Corps. Grandpa had made a full career of the Marines—Okinawa, Inchon, Khe Sanh. Thirty years. Blount cared little what any man thought of him, except the man before him now.

"I bet I know what you're thinking," Grandpa said. "You're glad to be home, but you're torn. It don't feel like you thought it would feel."

The last shards of peppermint melted away on Blount's tongue. How could that old man read his mind?

"I didn't think I'd feel torn. But I have been ever since I watched my old platoon commander dying outside that nightclub."

"So you knew one of them?"

"Yes, sir."

Grandpa raised his hand, crooked a wrinkled finger at Blount.

"Listen to me, boy. You got nothing to prove to nobody. I'm so proud of you I could bust. You done more for your country already than most folks could ever imagine. It's all right if you leave. It's all right if you stay. You just gotta decide how you feel. And Bernadette and the girls, too."

That was the trouble. Blount knew how he felt right up until he heard the boom that stopped the music at Route One. But with a new threat out there, the whole recipe changed. Or did it? How would his wife and kids feel if he went back into harm's way after telling them he was done?

Plenty of service members joined up, served one enlistment, then got out. Saw more in one combat tour than anybody should see in a lifetime. And no one questioned their devotion to duty. So why do you want to tear yourself up about leaving after twenty years? Blount asked himself. You've seen enough for several lifetimes.

Grandpa took off his glasses and began surfing through the TV channels. He stopped on one program, apparently at random. Four young adults—two men and two women—gestured and paced around a living room. Talked like something real serious had taken place. Grandpa punched up the volume a little, and Blount realized this was one of those reality shows where they put people together in a rent-free house and saw how they got along. These four were fighting over who would sweep the patio.

"You ever hear such nonsense in all your born days?" Grandpa asked.

"I just can't believe they pay people for that."

Blount's grandfather turned off the television and said, "I changed my mind. Let's have some of that pie."

"Sounds good to me."

Blount searched the cabinets and found paper plates, two forks, and a knife. He and his grandfather shared the sweet potato pie and said little else. Just enjoyed each other's company. The flavor of brown sugar, the crunch of the double crust, filled Blount with a sense of safety and belonging. Funny how tastes and smells could do that. The odor of sewage took him to Fallujah. Choking dust swept him into Helmand Province. Rifle smoke carried him to the ranges of Quantico. And sweet potatoes and cinnamon brought him home.

When his grandfather got drowsy, Blount asked, "Want me to help you get into bed?"

"No, I got it. Just come on back as soon as you can."

"I will, Grandpa."

Blount hugged his grandfather goodbye, went out to his truck. As he drove home, a car began to tailgate him on the two-lane highway. Blount was already doing sixty-five in a fifty-five; he saw no reason to drive faster. The car rode his bumper for two or three miles. If Blount had braked for a deer, the idiot back there would have rear-ended him. Finally, the car—it turned out to be a Camaro—zipped around him in a no-passing zone. Evidently the driver was not one of the local Marines. The Camaro displayed a bumper sticker, but one that had nothing to do with the Corps: HOW'S MY DRIVING? CALL 1-800-EAT-SHIT.

What's wrong with people? Blount wondered. You'd have to have no respect for anybody, including yourself. Relating to the civilian world, he figured, might take some getting used to.

CHAPTER 5

In the ops center at Stuttgart, Germany, Michael Parson watched a drone feed from over the Libyan town of Ghat. Funeral processions inched along streets and alleys as mourners carried shrouded bodies from mosques to cemeteries. The victims came from an outlying village, and bereaved relatives had brought them into town for burial. Though the chemicals from the attack would almost certainly have dissipated by now, Parson could understand why the mourners didn't want to hold funerals in the village itself.

The sad parades had gone on for days. Muslims tried to bury their dead by the next sunset. So Parson surmised that the funerals he was watching—there seemed to be two separate ones—were for people who died today or last night. More and more of those hurt in the chemical attack lost their struggle for life as time went on. What a damned awful way to go, he thought.

A young French officer stood beside Parson. The Frenchman wore the epaulets of a captain and the wings of a pilot. Parson had rolled his eyes when he learned he would work with allied militaries and get an assistant from the French Army of the Air. But the French had just kicked ass while fighting insurgents in Mali. This young captain, Alain Chartier, had put a hurting on some bad guys from the cockpit of his Mirage, and that made him all right by Parson.

Chartier didn't brag too much, either—unlike a lot of fighter jocks. Instead, he related stories that gave credit to teamwork. For example, he talked about the time he got so fixated on hitting his target that he let his fuel get critically low. An emergency refueling from an American KC-135 Stratotanker kept him from having to eject over insurgent territory. As he told his story, he tried to use American military slang, but he got it only half right.

"I was growing fangs and not paying attention to other things," Chartier had said. "That boom operator saved my pork."

Parson laughed and said, "Bacon. He saved your bacon."

"*Oui*. Bacon."

But they weren't laughing now. The color image on the screen tilted when the Global Hawk rolled into a turn. Then the image righted itself as the sensor suite corrected for the bank angle. The sensor operator, working from a Mission Control Element at Beale Air Force Base, California, zoomed in closer and adjusted the focus on a shrouded bundle held aloft by a dozen hands.

"*C'est dommage,*" Chartier said.

"How's that?" Parson asked.

"A pity. Too bad."

"Yeah, it's a damned shame."

Chartier watched the screen for a while, seemed lost in thought. Eventually he said, "Do you think they will send you—us—into North Africa again?"

"Hard to say. We have Marines on a ship in the Med. Did I hear you guys have your Foreign Legion on alert?"

"*Oui*. Yes, sir. And other units, too."

"I hope it doesn't come to another war."

"I would like to fly over the Sahara the way Saint-Ex did, in a simple little plane, in peace."

"The way who did?"

"Saint-Ex," Chartier said. "Antoine de Saint-Exupéry. French pilot and author."

"Never heard of him."

"Ah, you must come to know Saint-Ex, sir. He will remind you why you learned to fly in the first place. He flew airmail routes over

Africa and South America in the 1920s and '30s, and he wrote of the Sahara like a beloved mistress. But then he died in the Second World War."

"Sorry to hear that," Parson said. He looked up at the Saharan image on the screen, and he found it hard to imagine loving such a wasteland. Maybe this Saint-Ex guy had hit the Bordeaux a little too hard.

The Global Hawk flew several more orbits over Ghat, and still Parson saw nothing but the town and its mourners. He'd been working on a theory, and he decided to see if that drone could prove what he suspected. On a secure telephone, he placed a call to the drone's command center at Beale. When a master sergeant answered, Parson identified himself and explained what he wanted.

"Are you ready to initiate secure transmission, sir?" the sergeant asked.

"Sure. Going secure."

Parson pressed a button on the specially designed phone, and the handset hissed and beeped for a few seconds. Then the sergeant's voice came back, as clearly as before.

"I'll get the mission commander for you."

"Thanks," Parson said. Chartier looked at him with raised eyebrows. Parson placed his hand over the receiver and whispered to the Frenchman, "This is what we call a WAG—a wild-ass guess."

Or maybe a little better than a WAG, Parson hoped. He had never trained as an intel analyst, and he didn't consider himself much of a sleuth. But he could apply some plain old common sense. A new voice came on the phone line.

"Colonel Harris here."

"Yes, sir," Parson said. "Colonel Michael Parson. AFRICOM planning cell."

He added the *sir* out of habit. Parson still couldn't believe the Air Force had seen fit to promote him to O-6. He had pinned on his eagles just before taking the AFRICOM assignment. Never one for spit and polish, he'd had his ass chewed by colonels often enough to believe he'd never become one himself. However, he'd helped bring down terrorists ranging from a high-ranking Taliban mullah to a lowlife bin Laden wannabe who kidnapped boys to make them child soldiers. Along the way Parson also stopped a nut job who wanted to reignite the Bosnian War. Some of his citations credited him with initiative and drive. But Parson chalked it up to being in the right place at the right time with the right people by his side.

"What can I do for you, Parson?" Harris asked.

"I'm sure you know everybody's wondering where terrorists have been getting chemical weapons."

"Of course."

"Maybe the stuff comes from right there in Libya."

Parson discussed how in 2003 Muammar Gadhafi announced that he'd get rid of his chemical and biological weapons. Gadhafi saw what had happened to Saddam Hussein's government and decided to play nice. Didn't do him a lot of good; the Libyan strongman eventually suffered a fate as bad as that of the Iraqi dictator. Rebel fighters pulled Gadhafi out of a drainpipe and worked him over. Accounts varied about whether he died from bayonet wounds, gunshots, or shrapnel—but in any case, he came to an ugly, bloody end.

"But what if Gadhafi didn't really disclose all his chem and bio stocks?" Parson asked. "What if he played a shell game with the Chemical Weapons Convention?"

"And you're thinking somebody's using what he hid?"

"Yes, sir."

A frightening prospect; Parson hoped he was wrong. Inspectors had overseen destruction of part of Libya's chemical weapons and documented the location of others. But no one could say with certainty that every shell and bomb, every ton of sulfur mustard, nerve gas, and precursor chemicals had been accounted for.

"They even had some of it hidden at a turkey farm," Parson said.

"Geez," Harris said. "So there's no telling how much is left or where it's located."

"That's what worries me, sir. Old Gadhafi loyalists, foreign fighters, Islamic fundamentalists could have cached stockpiles anywhere."

So where to look now? Parson and Harris discussed logical starting places—which included every military base in Libya, along with defunct chemical production sites such as Rabta and Tarhuna. Suspicion might focus on truck convoys going to weird locations, or maybe rattletrap old cargo planes landing on makeshift airstrips. But with insurgents rampaging all over North Africa, how could you tell a truck full of conventional bombs from a truck full of chemical bombs?

"We're looking for a needle in a stack of needles," Harris said.

"I wish I could come up with something more specific," Parson said.

"Your idea makes as much sense as anything else I've heard," Harris said. "I'll see if we can dedicate more drone orbits. But it'll be up to the CFACC."

The Combined Forces Air Component Commander was a three-star general—far above Parson's pay grade. Parson could only send suggestions up the chain of command. The CFACC might be getting other suggestions, too, and Parson didn't know what priority his would receive.

When Parson ended the call, he wondered if he'd really accomplished much. How would his suggestion sound to the general? *I got it, sir. Let's search all over Libya for something we might not even know when we see it.* But it seemed better than just waiting to get hit again.

He looked around the room, saw that Chartier had disappeared. The Frenchman came back into the ops center a few minutes later and said, "Intel wants to brief us at two."

"What about?"

"They would not say, but they act like it is important."

In Parson's long career, he'd found that the quality of intelligence briefings varied widely. Sometimes a briefer, excited and engaged by his work, put together what seemed almost like a well-organized newscast. He'd gather information from classified and unclassified sources and tell you what you needed to know about your mission. Others just flipped through PowerPoint slides as quickly as possible and twisted simple concepts into ridiculously complicated acronyms. Why did a car bomb need to become a VBIED—vehicle-borne improvised explosive device?

At two o'clock, Parson and Chartier left their cell phones in their desks and went to the briefing room. The projector screen read THIS BRIEFING IS CLASSIFIED NATO SECRET. NO ELECTRONIC DEVICES. Officers and NCOs from several nations filled the thirty seats. A U.S. Army major locked the door and began the presentation. To Parson's approval, the major spoke plainly.

"We have a claim of responsibility for the chem warfare attacks at Sigonella and Ghat," he said. "Slide, please."

The major's assistant, an Army specialist, clicked a mouse. The next screen showed a bearded man in a black kaffiyeh. He had dyed his beard an off shade of orange, and a scar bisected the bridge of his nose. The man wore a green field jacket draped with pouches for AK-47 magazines—standard terrorist chic. But a much older weapon caught Parson's eye. Stuck into a bright red sash tied around his waist, the jihadist carried a flintlock pistol.

Parson leaned forward just to make sure his eyes weren't fooling him. An antique pistol? Where would a North African terrorist even get a thing like that? The Cabela's catalog?

"Whiskey tango foxtrot," Parson said.

"What is this expression you use?" Chartier whispered.

"What the fuck."

The French aviator chuckled, raised his eyebrows.

"This waste of humanity is Sadiq Kassam," the major continued.

"We believe that is his real name. He comes from Algeria, and he is forty-eight years old."

"What's with the orange beard and the flintlock?" Parson asked. "Is this some kind of punk rock pirate?"

The Americans in the room laughed, including the major.

"Sir, the beard dyed with henna means he's made a trip to Mecca," the major said. "You got me on the pistol, though. Their supply must have had that on back order for a very long time."

More chuckles, but then the major turned serious. "This guy is no laughing matter. He ran with the Armed Islamic Group of Algeria back in the 1990s. They killed for the sake of killing. Kassam emerged more recently as a rival to Mokhtar Belmokhtar, another waste of humanity who orchestrated the attack on the Algerian natural gas plant in 2013. Belmokhtar was reported dead after that; we're not so sure. But Kassam seems to want to take his place."

Probably so, Parson thought. These extremists always draped themselves in holiness, claimed they murdered civilians in the name of God and acted only as heaven's humble servants. But in truth a lot of them had the egos of rock stars. When not fighting infidels, they fought one another.

"Kassam has released a video to Al Jazeera," the major said. "I'll let the shithead speak for himself."

The Al Jazeera video began to play, and a news crawl in Arabic scrolled across the bottom of the screen. Kassam started speaking in Arabic. Someone had superimposed a graphic of English translation:

"In the name of Allah, most gracious and merciful, I bring news of His holy struggle. The Armed Islamic Group of Tripolitania seeks to bring sharia law and infinite justice to the whole of North Africa. The people long for a new pasha, a ruler who will serve as Allah's instrument on Earth. The winds of the Sahara once struck

fear into the hearts of infidels who sailed near our coasts, and those winds shall bring fear again."

Tripolitania? The graffiti in the photo Sophia had e-mailed said something about Tripolitania. Parson couldn't read the Arabic script, but she'd told him it referred to the Barbary states back in the nineteenth century. As the video continued, Kassam drew the flintlock and began waving it.

"As in the days of old, we will terrorize our enemies. We will kill and enslave nonbelievers who seek to defeat our religion. My forebears in jihad took this pistol from an American sailor more than two centuries ago. And Allah has delivered into our hands far more fearsome weapons. As we showed you on the Crusader island of Sicily and in the backsliding region of Ghat, we are not afraid to use what Allah has given us. With these weapons we will strike even at the serpent's nest in America."

Just keep running your mouth, Parson thought. Somebody's going to take that pistol away from you and shove it up your ass.

Extremists had a way of blaspheming the very principles they preached. This bastard spoke of restoring the former glory of Islamic rule—through indiscriminate use of weapons of mass destruction. Sophia would know more about the details, but Parson guessed this violated all kinds of Muslim teachings. Parson remembered her telling him about the seventh-century caliph, Abu Bakr, who established ten rules for Muslim armies. One said no killing of a child, a woman, or an aged man.

When the briefing ended, Parson and Chartier returned to the ops center. Given Kassam's threat of continued attacks, it seemed even more likely now that NATO or UN forces would get involved. As a member of the AFRICOM planning cell, Parson figured he'd better get cracking.

The new Libyan government had already given permission for military use of Mitiga International Airport near Tripoli. Parson sat at his computer, tapped at the keyboard, and brought up airfield data for Mitiga.

The field's long history mirrored the history of the country. First built by the Italians in 1923, the base was captured by the Germans during World War II. The U.S. took it over during the Cold War and named it Wheelus Air Base. Wheelus hosted the cargo planes of the old Military Air Transport service and the bombers of Strategic Air Command. The U.S. closed Wheelus in 1970 and turned it over to the Libyans, who renamed it Okba Ben Nafi Air Base.

At around the same time the Americans were preparing to shut down the base, Muammar Gadhafi deposed Libya's King Idris in a military coup. In 1986 Gadhafi got the bright idea to bomb the La Belle disco in West Berlin to kill and injure American servicemen. Payback was a bitch; President Reagan launched Operation El Dorado Canyon. Parson's own dad, as a weapons systems officer in an F-111 Aardvark, attacked the base that American fliers once called home. The elder Parson had spoken of the grueling mission from RAF Lakenheath in Britain.

"France, Spain, and Italy denied overflight," Dad had said, "so we dragged our asses all the way around the Iberian Peninsula. Refueled in the air several times." But the long flight paid off when he found that row of Ilyushin transport planes in his crosshairs.

Parson could not ask about that raid now. His father had died in the crash of his Wild Weasel during Desert Storm.

In the 1990s, the Libyan base targeted by the elder Parson converted to a civilian airport. It bore a new name: Mitiga International.

Hope Dad didn't tear up Mitiga too bad for the Libyans to repair properly, Parson thought, because I might need it soon. Parson's computer told him Mitiga boasted two runways, the longest just over eleven thousand feet. Long enough for any plane in the U.S. inventory—assuming the runway and taxiways could bear the weight of a heavy like a C-5 or a B-52. He needed to dig a little more and find the pavement classification numbers. Then he could write a proper Giant Report on Mitiga. Boring as hell, not nearly as much fun as flying. But the work needed to get done right.

As Parson worked, he glanced at Chartier. The Frenchman scrolled through e-mail. One message in particular seemed to catch his attention. Chartier's eyes widened, and he smiled faintly. Parson jotted some notes on a writing pad, then said, "What you got, a picture from one of your girlfriends in Paris?"

"No, sir. It is from my squadron commander back home."

"What's up?"

"I am sorry, sir. But they are recalling me for a possible alert. They want me back in the Mirage. No more flying a desk."

Parson leaned back in his chair, tore off a sheet of notebook paper. Wadded up the paper. Tossed the paper wad at Chartier, who grinned as it whizzed by his nose and bounced off his computer screen.

"You lucky, champagne-swilling, croissant-eating son of a bitch."

CHAPTER 6

On a Thursday morning, Blount steered his Ram onto Interstate 95 North for his journey to Camp Lejeune. The trip would take hours, but driving through the rural coastal plain of the Carolinas would give him a chance to think, to get some perspective. He hadn't realized retiring from the Corps would feel so wrenching. Once a Marine, always a Marine.

Cool wind blasted through the truck's open window. Blount's fellow South Carolinian Darius Rucker sang over the radio, something about a "come back song." Blount sighed; in his own life, he could take that line two ways. He felt pulled in two directions.

This year's tobacco crop had come in late; Halloween was only a couple weeks away, and some fields still stood studded with denuded green stalks. Pretty soon the farmers would run their Bush Hogs over the stalks, then disc the fields under and maybe plant winter wheat. Near one of the fields, Blount saw a row of bulk tobacco barns shaped like windowless, silver mobile homes. Their owner must have been curing the last of his crop; the fragrance of drying tobacco leaves wafted through the air. The aroma of curing smelled nothing like cigarette smoke; Blount had once described it to a British Royal Marine by telling him to imagine the richest tea leaves he'd ever smelled, mixed with brown sugar and bourbon.

Just past Santee, Blount reached the bridge over Lake Marion. At the water's edge, a nine-foot alligator lolled in the shallows. The middle of its tail looked as big around as Blount's biceps. Blount recalled seeing a big old gator one time while fishing with his grandfather.

"You better respect his strength," Grandpa had said, "but he won't hurt you if you don't mess with him."

Maybe Blount would get a chance to fish these waters more often. Once he got outprocessed, he'd have all the time in the world for the simple pleasures. Especially if he had to wait a while to get a law enforcement job. He sure hoped the hiring freezes wouldn't last too long.

Halfway across the bridge, he spotted a johnboat plowing across the still surface of Marion, propelled by a trolling motor. Two boys with fishing rods sat in the boat.

For Blount, that was what the counselors called a trigger.

His palms grew slick on the steering wheel. Memories and images came back of their own accord. A bright morning in South Carolina turned into the blackest night in Afghanistan. Blount saw three boys about the same age as the kids in the boat. They came out of the cave, walking toward him and the other Marines. Blount yelled at them with what little of their language he knew, taught to him by that smart Army woman Sophia Gold.

"Zaai peh zaai wudregah!" he shouted. Stay where you are.

The children kept coming at him. Blount backed up several steps and repeated his command. Sweet baby Jesus, stop right there. Don't make me do this.

He called for them to halt in Pashto and English. He'd have hollered in every language in the world if he could have, right down to caveman talk. Anything to make something different happen.

They wouldn't listen. Some other grown-ups had got to them first, taught them nothing but wrong things. He was running out of time. They were running out of time.

Blount raised his weapon, leveled his sights on the children. Cut all three of them down.

All three kids wore suicide vests. On one of them, the vest detonated.

The blast knocked Blount off his feet. His cheek hurt; something had cut his face. Maybe a ball bearing from inside that suicide vest. He felt his sweat and tears mix with the blood. He raised himself with one gloved hand. For the first time in his life, he felt like turning his rifle on his own self. Couldn't do that, though. Other Marines counted on him. He got up and pressed on.

The thump of his truck tires crossing the north end of the bridge brought Blount back to the present. That Afghanistan scene played like a movie in his head whenever it took a mind to. He didn't control the projector.

The tobacco and cotton fields, the pinewoods and trailer parks rolled by until he came to Jacksonville. Here, just like at home, many of the vehicles carried Marine Corps stickers. Familiar turns took him to the main gate, where the brick signpost read CAMP LEJEUNE— HOME OF EXPEDITIONARY FORCES IN READINESS. Blount's battalion now served with the 22nd Marine Expeditionary Unit, one of three MEUs based at Lejeune.

He showed his ID to the gate guard, who examined both sides of the card and handed it back. Blount noted that the back of the card identified him as someone falling under Geneva Convention Category II, which spelled out how he must be treated as a prisoner of war. Fortunately, that bit of information had never played a part in his career. And the Geneva Convention would have meant nothing to any of the enemies Blount had ever fought.

By now it was late in the afternoon. All the offices would close soon, and Blount would have plenty of time to outprocess tomorrow. So instead of going to personnel, he checked in at the Lejeune Inn, the base's temporary lodging facility. In the lobby he saw Corporal Fender, the Marine who'd been with him the night of the sarin attack at Sig.

"Gunny," Fender said. "Didn't expect to see you here. I thought you were getting out." The corporal, off duty now, wore faded jeans and a Carolina Panthers hoodie. Worn-out tennis shoes. His clothing might have marked him as a young delinquent if not for his buzz cut and straight posture.

"I am," Blount said. "Just running some last errands. What about you? I thought you were staying at Sig in case something kicked off."

"They sent me back here for some more chem warfare training. And now the MEU is setting sail."

"The Twenty-second?" Blount asked. "Everybody?"

"Yes, Gunny."

That meant Blount's battalion was heading out, along with a helicopter squadron and all the support sections needed to sustain an air–ground task force. In the Mediterranean, the 22nd MEU would join the Marines of the 24th, the men Blount had seen during his layover at Rota. He remembered well these pulse-quickening preparations for battle, the anticipation and the anxiety. The uncertainties of a new mission, along with the solid certainty that the Marines around him would have his back.

"Sorry you're not going with us, Gunny," Fender said. "Always felt safer knowing you were there."

The corporal meant that as a compliment, but the words knifed right into Blount's heart. Leaving the Corps came hard enough without knowing the people closest to you might soon go into harm's way. He hid his emotions as best he could, but he wanted to know more about this deployment.

"What else have they told you?" Blount asked.

"They briefed us yesterday about some new terrorist dude named Sadiq Kassam. Weird-looking motherfucker who says he wants to bring back the days of the Barbary pirates."

Blount frowned. Bring back the Barbary pirates? Every Marine knew what happened when Thomas Jefferson got fed up with the first terrorist threat against the U.S. The Barbary states had captured American vessels and enslaved the crews to extract ransom. Jefferson decided to give them another kind of payback, and the Marines still sang about the shores of Tripoli.

"Somebody needs to ask Kassam how well that worked out last time," Blount said.

"I was just thinking that. But last time, they didn't have nerve gas."

Fender had a point. Anybody with chemical weapons posed a dangerous threat. And as outlandish as talk of the Barbary pirates might seem, Blount knew terrorists dreamed of stranger things. Osama bin Laden had spoken of creating a worldwide caliphate.

Blount chatted with Fender for a few more minutes, wished him a safe deployment. With nothing to do until morning, Blount decided to drive off base for an early supper. On his way to the main gate, he met a column of military vehicles. The Humvees and Cougars bristled with weapons; some carried the .50 caliber M2, others the Mark 19 grenade launcher. Marines on their way in from some training—or maybe on their way out for a night exercise. The sight made Blount feel he was leaving a job unfinished. A big part of him wanted to climb aboard one of the vehicles, check in on the radio, offer encouragement, bark an order.

He found a barbecue joint in Jacksonville. When he ordered his pork barbecue, slaw, and hush puppies, the waitress gave him a military discount without asking for his ID. Somehow she knew, even though Blount was not in uniform.

Am I that obvious? he wondered. The Corps had become such a part of him that he exuded it. What would life become for him on the outside? Part of him felt ready to leave. Bernadette and the girls wanted him home, and he certainly needed no more nights like the one at an Afghanistan cave. At the same time, he knew he could never find this kind of camaraderie anywhere else. He knew of Marines who'd leaped onto grenades to protect their buddies. But on the outside, at least for some chumps, it was all about Number One. 1-800-EAT SHIT.

The next morning, Blount went to the battalion S-1 office to get his outprocessing checklist. The checklist would direct him to various places on base to turn in equipment, settle any debts on his government travel card, deactivate his government e-mail. But he found no one in the office to help him.

"I'm sorry, Gunnery Sergeant," a young private said. "Everybody's working on mobility processing right now."

They have their priorities straight, Blount thought. Better to spend time on Marines going to war than on one Marine calling it quits. They got more important things to do than bother with me.

The personnel people, along with folks from the clinic, the Judge Advocate General, supply, and the Navy chaplain's office, were making sure the platoons were ready to deploy.

Checking shot records, dog tags, passports, wills, and powers of attorney. Handing out refrigerator magnets from Family Readiness with numbers for spouses to call in emergencies. For Marines who wanted them, free pocket-sized Bibles with camo covers. Qurans, too. Blount had gone through that drill many times.

With his plans for the day shot down, he walked outside. An Osprey tilt-rotor from the nearby New River air station flew overhead, making its distinctive buzz and pulse that sounded like no other aircraft. At the same time, a CH-53E Super Stallion helicopter pounded above the tree line. The Stallion did not look like something meant to fly. The chopper hung in the air as deadweight, held aloft by brute force of engines and rotors. As the aircraft flew nearer, Blount recognized an M777 howitzer slung underneath the Stallion. Preparations for a fight. Probably taking the gun to New River to prep it for airlift to North Africa. Automatic-weapons fire chattered in the distance. More training going on.

To step aboard that helicopter, to catch a Humvee over to one of the ranges and supervise a combat exercise, seemed the most natural thing in the world. Blount had never felt so torn in his life. What did he owe to his family? To himself? But then, what did he owe to his country and to the Corps that had made him?

This very moment felt wrong: to find himself aboard a Marine Corps installation, in uniform, still drawing government pay, but with no task at hand. No orders to carry out, no purpose. Unsure what to do with himself, Blount stopped in to see his most recent boss, his company commander.

Captain Adam Privett rose from his desk to greet Blount, silver bars gleaming on the collar of his digital camo. Blond hair cut to stubble on the sides of his head, just enough hair on top for a comb. Papers and folders littered the desk of the thirty-year-old officer. Privett offered a firm handshake, Naval Academy ring on his right hand.

"You look busy, sir," Blount said. "I won't take up much of your time. Just wanted to say hello while I'm still here."

"Yeah, you know how it is right before a deployment. Always somebody who needs an anthrax shot or can't find his passport."

Blount's first instinct was to go find the offender. After Blount got done with him, any young eight-ball Marine would rather stand a post in hell itself than let the sun go down without his deployment requirements squared away. Instead, Blount could only ask, "When do you ship out, sir?"

"We board the *Tarawa* in three weeks. Brand-new ship. I'll miss you, Guns. Never had a worry with you beside me."

I keep hearing that, Blount thought. Hurts worse every time.

"Once you get to the Med, do you expect to get sent ashore?"

"If they can nail down a location for a terrorist base, probably. If these chemical attacks keep happening, definitely."

Blount imagined the amphibious assault ships would lurk off the coast of Libya or Algeria, maybe steam into the Gulf of Sidra. Commanders would wait for intel on the whereabouts of this Sadiq Kassam and his posse. The Marines would continue to hone their skills as well as they could aboard ship, straining at the leash like Dobermans until loosed on a target. Then they'd carry out their core mission: Locate, close with, and destroy the enemy. Blount could almost smell the sea breezes, the helicopter exhaust, the rifle smoke. Hard to believe this operation would launch without him.

"Godspeed, sir," Blount said as he rose to leave. He shook the captain's hand again.

"Go home and take care of your family," Privett said. "You've earned it."

A nice thing to say, but it didn't ease the turmoil in Blount's warrior heart. Outside Fox Company's offices he felt at sea, and not in a good way. Drifting between opposing tides with no clear, proper course. He passed by the break area, noted the ever-present smell of burned coffee, the cardboard sign over the coffeemaker: THIS COFFEE MESS APPROVED BY THE CAMP LEJEUNE FIRE DEPARTMENT. The desks and halls and lockers here felt as familiar as his own home, maybe more so. One of those lockers contained his helmet, body armor, and other gear. He needed to clean out that locker, but he just didn't feel like doing it now.

He'd accomplished not one thing today. And over the weekend he could do little but take up space in temp lodging. Blount decided to drive home, spend the weekend with his family, re-attack on Monday. A waste of gas, for sure. But maybe the open road, the night air would settle his mind. He checked out of the Lejeune Inn, filled his tank at the Marine Corps Exchange gas station, and bought a cup of black coffee.

By the time Blount drove out of Jacksonville, night had fallen. With his window down, he heard frogs singing in the sloughs just off the rural roads. He'd loved that peaceful sound since childhood. Soon cool weather would silence them for the winter. When he could hear the frogs no more, he raised his window, reached down to his cup holder, and took a sip of the bitter coffee. On 95 South he put the Ram on cruise control and turned on the radio.

The country station he'd listened to earlier began to crackle and break up, so he pressed the scan button. Pressed it again to stop the scan when he heard the buzz-saw chords of Guns N' Roses. He didn't much care for that kind of music, but this particular song brought back memories. Not necessarily good ones. Right before his Marines launched into Fallujah, somebody blasted "Welcome to the Jungle" to get their blood up. The song on the radio ended, and as if conjured by lyrics of chaos, an announcer broke in:

"This is an AP Network News live special report. The British Prime Minister's office says at least forty-eight people have died in an apparent chemical attack on the British territory of Gibraltar. Witnesses say victims fell violently ill this afternoon after an explosion rocked a densely packed street at the foot of the famed rock fortress. The Royal Air Force is flying in disaster preparedness specialists and medical teams. Hundreds of sickened residents and tourists have overwhelmed area hospitals. Authorities have not identified those responsible, but the attack looks similar to recent incidents in Sicily and Libya. In a video statement just this week, Algerian terrorist Sadiq Kassam claimed credit for those attacks and even vowed to strike on American soil."

Blount felt dread close on him like a fist. The headlights of oncoming traffic appeared as malevolent eyes. He had recently taken his family to Gibraltar; if not for timing and the Good Lord's grace the dead might have included his wife and daughters. Less than a year ago they'd hopped a space-available ride on a C-17, flown to Rota, and driven a rental car down to the rock. The girls had laughed at the Barbary apes lounging on precipices above five-hundred-foot drops. It had been a clear day; the kids had pointed at mountains across the blue strait, and Blount had told them that was Morocco.

The thought of them suffering like that Italian girl at Sig, dying like Kelley . . . Blount shuddered, blinked his eyes. No doubt that had just happened to somebody's kids. Somewhere some parents—French or Spanish or American tourists—were going through the worst thing Blount could imagine.

As he drove into the night, trying to get his mind around the horror, he thought of something he'd memorized in boot camp: the Marine Corps Rifleman's Creed. He'd vowed to master his rifle as he must master his life. To fire true, shoot straight. Until there is no enemy.

CHAPTER 7

At the breakfast table, Blount poured a cup of coffee and tried to force himself to wakefulness. He'd not slept well after getting home last night from Camp Lejeune. Bernadette wouldn't like his decision to withdraw his retirement, not one little bit, and he'd tossed and turned beside her, trying to think of a good way to tell her. At one point he'd rolled onto his side and pressed his face into her hair. The lavender scent of her shampoo had only heightened his guilt.

No good way to tell her existed. She'd feel betrayed and jerked around, after all she'd already gone through as a military wife. And, oh yeah, she'd also have to worry about him going on another combat deployment. The spouses had the toughest job in the Corps, and they didn't even get paid.

Bernadette came into the kitchen, dressed for Saturday volunteer work at the county library. Burgundy skirt and vest, heels clicking on the hardwood floor. White blouse, and over the blouse a gold necklace Blount had bought for her at a souk in Kuwait. She sat at the table, picked up a butter knife, and spread strawberry preserves on a triangle of toast.

"You get all outprocessed, baby?" she asked. "Is that a civilian sitting across from me now?" Bernadette took a bite of her toast and winked at him.

Her good mood made what he had to say even harder. On top of everything else, he would spoil that mood.

"Uh, no," Blount said. "Everybody in S-1 was working with people about to deploy."

"So you drove up there for nothing? That must have irritated you. Bet you'll be glad to get all that kind of foolishness behind you."

"Ah, well. That's what I wanted to talk to you about. I think I want to stay in a while."

Bernadette drew in a breath. Looked at him with a tightened face and eyes drained of all good humor.

"What?"

She dropped the butter knife. Loud clink as it hit the table.

"Honey, I know this ain't fair to you. But the sheriff ain't hiring, and—"

"So what? I got a job. We got savings. Did you get up to Lejeune and somebody say something to you? You don't owe them nothing no more."

Oh, Lord, she was mad. Bernadette always spoke with the perfect diction and grammar of somebody college-educated like herself. Except when she got angry. Very angry. Then the low-country farm girl in her came out.

"Bernadette, did you see the news last night? About that thing that happened at Gibraltar?"

"What are you talking about?" She shook her head like she was talking to the world's most annoying idiot—who'd just brought up something that had nothing to do with anything. "Yeah, I saw it. So what?"

"Remember when we took Ruthie and Priscilla to Gibraltar? You hear about all them people throwing up and dying? It could have been our girls."

"Well, it wasn't. Your daughters ain't in no Gibraltar. They're upstairs, getting ready to go with me to the library, thinking their daddy's finally home to stay. And you drop this on me right when I gotta go out the door."

Tears glistened in her eyes. Blount got up and put his hand on her shoulder, but she shook him off. She scraped her chair back from the table and pointed her finger at him.

"Don't touch me," she said. "And you're gonna tell this to the girls. I ain't telling them for you."

Bernadette took a tissue from her purse, blew her nose, and stomped out of the kitchen. Blount heard her calling up the stairs to the girls: "Ruthie, Priscilla. Time to go."

Two pairs of feet pattered down the stairs. Ruthie shouted, "Bye, Daddy!" The front door squeaked open, slammed shut.

Lord have mercy.

A minute later, the crunch of gravel announced his family's departure for town and the library. Blount walked to the porch with his coffee cup in his hand. At one time he'd looked forward to sitting out here and watching Ruthie and Priscilla ride in the pasture. But now, who knew when that would happen? He sat in one of the rockers and looked out over the marsh. An osprey glided over the water, wings outstretched and motionless in tranquil flight. That is, until the cawing of crows echoed across the lagoon. Blount saw a pair of crows flap over his house and begin to harass the osprey. The crows took turns diving and wheeling, mobbing the raptor. Blount couldn't tell if they got close enough to peck or claw, but at the very least they forced the osprey to dip and turn, to try to evade its tormentors. He knew crows nursed an ancient grudge against hawks; maybe hawks fed on their chicks. However, this osprey probably ate nothing but fish. Hadn't done a thing to those crows.

The aerial battle continued for a few minutes. Hawks didn't usually fight back when mobbed by crows. But eventually this osprey did something Blount had never seen before. It flapped hard to get several feet above the crows. Then it did what came natural to an osprey: The bird folded its wings and dropped toward its target like a laser-guided bomb. Struck with extended talons.

Black feathers flew. The wounded crow and its partner broke off the attack, flew away across the marsh. The osprey resumed its effortless glide, master of its own fate.

Blount drank the last of his coffee, still wrestling with allegiances to family, Corps, and country. Competing loyalties could tear a man into shreds. He decided to look in on his grandfather. Maybe the old man would offer words of wisdom.

Grandpa had finished his breakfast by the time Blount knocked on the door of the old man's suite. The room still smelled of bacon. Blount's grandfather turned down the volume on The History Channel, adjusted his oxygen hose, and said, "Come on in, boy. Always good to see you."

Blount took a seat in the recliner. He wondered why Grandpa even bothered to keep the recliner because he never used it himself. The old man stayed in his wheelchair so he could go back and forth more easily to the bookcase and magazine rack. The latest issue of *The Economist* rested in his lap.

"Grandpa," Blount said, "you see what happened at Gibraltar?"

"I sure did. Terrible thing. You and Bernadette and the girls were there, what—about a year ago?"

"Yes, sir."

"Scares me to think about what could have happened. What *did* happen to somebody's kids."

"Me, too. And that's got me thinking about staying in. The Twenty-second MEU's about to ship out."

Grandpa twisted his lips to one side, tilted his head back as he absorbed this news. Dug into his pocket.

"I see you come for a serious peppermint discussion," he said.

Blount chuckled, caught the peppermint tossed his way.

"Guess I did."

"What does Bernadette say about this?"

"Maddest I've seen her in a while." Blount unwrapped the peppermint and placed it in his mouth.

"So what makes you think you need to do this?"

Blount recounted everything that had swirled through his mind—his buddies going into harm's way, his friend Kelley dying in the parking lot at Route One, the civilians poisoned to death. He didn't say anything about the sheriff's department not hiring. Maybe that was a little part of it, too, but not nearly the main thing. So he didn't waste his grandfather's time with the money issue. The wise old sergeant major would have seen right through that one.

"What about your house?" Grandpa asked. "Would you sell it? You and Bernadette love that place. Working for Special Operations Command means either Lejeune or Pendleton. Lejeune's, what, five hours away?"

"I'll homestead the family here and get an apartment in Jacksonville if I have to. Divide the time between here and there. Bernadette's got a good job, and I wouldn't want to make the girls change schools again."

"I thought you'd had enough after that last trip to Afghanistan," Grandpa said. "That by itself would have been more than most men could take. So please don't talk like you got anything left to prove."

"No, it's not that. It's . . . hard to put it into words."

Grandpa unwrapped his own peppermint, studied it for a moment, put it on his tongue. Seemed lost in thought until he crushed the peppermint between his teeth. He chewed it, swallowed, and said, "You remember what I told you when you first enlisted?"

"Yes, sir. I do."

First and last, his grandfather had said, a warrior is a protector. You use force when you need to, and a big boy like you can do that real good. But in the main, you take care of folks. You go into a situation and think to yourself, the people here—at least the good people—are safer because I'm here.

"I can't tell you what to do about withdrawing that retirement," Grandpa said. "Nobody but you can know where your heart is and what you gotta do. But I do know this: If you go back out there to fight, don't do it for payback. You don't like it that they killed your old platoon commander. You don't like what they made you do in Afghanistan. But revenge will burn you alive, boy. It'll turn you into something you don't want to be."

Then Grandpa told a story from World War II that Blount had never heard. Blount thought that after all these years, his grandfather had related every incident, every moment he could remember about the Marines' bloody island-hopping campaign across the Pacific. But this one, he had kept to himself. And after hearing it, Blount could understand why.

As a young corporal on Iwo Jima, Grandpa Buell watched his fellow Marines raise the American flag on Mount Suribachi. Cheers went up; at first he thought the battle for that sulfurous, godforsaken chunk of volcanic rock had ended. But weeks of hard fighting remained. The Japanese had built a network of caves and pillboxes—hardened positions easily defended. Especially by troops loyal unto death to their emperor, troops who knew that with Iwo Jima in American hands, the B-29s could burn Japanese cities more easily.

"We had to dig those bastards out across every foot of that island," Grandpa said.

He explained that he had a close buddy at the time, another corporal by the name of Mason. Buell and Mason had gone through Montford Point together, had heard all the foolishness about how coloreds wouldn't fight. Mason came from Alabama. Before the war, he'd studied at Stillman, wanted to go into the ministry.

"Mason grew up poor, though," Blount's grandfather said. "He used to hunt squirrels with a twenty-two, not for fun but to help keep meat on the table. My lands, that boy could shoot. Never seen somebody so deadly with a Garand rifle."

Grandpa's eyes glistened as he spoke of his old friend. He said the brass intended for black Marines to serve only in support roles such as delivering ammo, but he and Mason wound up fighting anyway. Blount had no idea where this story was going, but he knew it couldn't be good.

One night, Mason vanished. Nobody saw him go down. Nobody heard him scream. Nothing. Just gone. Wasn't like him to run off, and on Iwo Jima, where would you have run off to, anyway?

Two days later they found him in a cave. The Japanese must have wounded him, or maybe come up behind him and grabbed him unawares. With all the caves and tunnels on Iwo, the enemy could just pop up out of the ground anywhere around you.

Mason's broken, naked body hung from ropes. They had cut off his ears. They had gouged out his eyes. They had sliced off his penis.

"You wouldn't die from none of that, though," Grandpa said, "nor from any other single wound on him."

His arms, legs, chest, and back were striped with hundreds of knife cuts. Mason had bled to death, very slowly. Missing for two days, and the body still warm.

"Back during the Depression, I seen a man who got lynched," Grandpa said. "Blood all over him. But this was worse than any lynching I ever heard tell of. After that, I kind of lost my mind."

Buell fought on with the fury of a man possessed. He even wondered if he and Mason and everybody else around him had died and gone to hell. The whole place smelled like sulfur and death, and there wasn't nothing but blood, pain, sand, and fire. How could you tell it from hell?

"There's fire in hell," Blount's grandfather said, "and by God, I brought fire."

Buell picked up a special weapon, an M2A1 flamethrower. Two tanks of jelled gasoline on his back, propelled by compressed gas. That thing could throw a stream of burning napalm fifty yards.

"Nobody said a thing to me about it, either," Grandpa said. "At that point we were all the same race: Marines. And we all wanted the same thing: payback."

The day after the Marines found Mason's body, they encountered a team of Japanese inside a concrete pillbox. From inside, the Japanese fired a Type 92 heavy machine gun. The pillbox sat atop a hummock, and the machine gun's field of fire stopped the American advance on that little section of the island.

Buell came up with an idea. If the platoon could pour rounds at the pillbox's embrasure and make the enemy keep their heads down, he could climb the side of the hummock. Under suppressing fire, the Japanese would have a difficult time bringing the 92 to bear on their flanks.

From whatever cover the Marines could find behind rocks and in depressions in the sand, the platoon opened up. With his flame-thrower, Buell charged up the right side of the hummock, the treads of his boots throwing up black sand. Another Marine went up the left side, holding a grenade.

Somehow the Japanese managed to hit the man with the grenade. He'd already pulled the pin; when he went down, the grenade exploded and tore him up. But that distracted the Japanese enough for Buell to get into position. Buell dropped to the ground only about fifteen yards from the pillbox.

With his left hand, he pointed the nozzle and squeezed the igniter trigger. With his right, he pressed the firing trigger and felt hell in fluid form course through the hose. Buell aimed the jet of burning napalm through the embrasure, and fire filled the pillbox. The four men inside began to scream, and two of them ran outside, flames in the shape of sprinting men.

"Don't shoot 'em," Buell shouted. "Let 'em burn."

The two Japanese ran right through the Marine platoon, fell to the ground twitching and writhing. No one fired a shot. The other two danced around inside the pillbox, fire stirring fire.

The platoon took two other pillboxes in the same fashion, with no mercy bullets for burning men.

"Most of the enemy on Iwo Jima wouldn't give up," Blount's grandfather said, "so they needed to die. But they didn't need to die like that." He sat silently for a while, then added, "I just wish I'd done that a little different. But I reckon you take my point. If you gotta fight, fight to protect. Don't let vengeance burn a hole in you."

There wasn't a whole lot Blount knew to say except "Yes, sir."

However, he understood exactly what his grandfather meant. He'd felt the same rage in that Afghan cave, and he'd killed his enemy with the same fury. Grandpa's story didn't mean nothing was worth fighting for. It just meant you needed to be real particular about when you did it and why. Blount wondered if the flabby, cake-eater politicians who sent him out there ever gave these things as much thought as he had during the last five minutes.

Blount went out and got some Brunswick stew to share with Grandpa for lunch. The two men ate in silence, except for Blount's words of thanks for the counsel. The younger Marine left the older one to his books and television, and as Blount drove home, he hoped to find the right things to say to Bernadette and the girls.

While he waited, he cut up an onion and three cayenne peppers. He'd also bought extra quarts of Brunswick stew to bring home. Blount figured his wife wouldn't be in a mood to cook tonight, and the fresh onion and peppers would serve as condiments for dinner.

He was warming the stew on the stovetop when he heard Bernadette pull up. The girls came in first and went up the steps without talking to him. When Bernadette entered the doorway, she didn't look angry, only tired. She went upstairs, too, and Blount wondered if he was getting the silent treatment. A few minutes later she came back down in jeans and a tank top. Bernadette walked into the kitchen, came up behind him, put her arms around his waist.

"I'll be straight with you," she said. "I don't want you to do this. But I knew what you were when I married you, and it was part of why I married you."

Blount felt her place her face against his back. He stirred the stew with one hand, put the other hand over both of hers. He felt the moisture of tears soak through the fabric of his shirt.

"You just come back to me," Bernadette said. "You always better come back to me."

He felt a flood of relief so great that he teared up, too. The stresses of deployments had broken up many a marriage, and Blount never forgot how lucky he was to have a woman this strong. He put down the spoon, turned around, and held his wife close.

"I will, baby."

The girls seemed distracted during dinner. Something was on their minds; maybe they sensed what he had to tell them. After the meal, when he started to explain his plans, they said they already knew. Bernadette had told them after all.

"I don't want you to go," Priscilla said, looking down into her bowl and sniffling.

"Me, neither," Ruthie said. "But Mama says you're like the sheepdog guarding all the other animals in the barnyard."

Blount smiled at his youngest daughter and then at his wife, and he mouthed the words *Thank you.*

In the twilight, he took his family for a walk by the water. A pair of cormorants swished by overhead, and the night insects began their concert. From across the lagoon came the sound of an alligator's bellow, a low grumble followed by a hiss and a splash. That noise might have brought fear to some folks, but to Blount it just sounded like home. Don't mess with that alligator and he won't mess with you.

When they got back to the house, Blount said, "You-all go on inside. I'll be right back."

He went into his toolshed, pulled the string for the light. Grandpa Buell's KA-BAR stood where Blount had left it, stabbed hard into the workbench. He placed his fist around the leather grip and wrenched it out of the wood. Tested the edge with his thumb.

Blount opened a drawer beneath the workbench, found a whetstone. He drew the blade across the stone for several swipes. Slid the knife into its sheath.

You and me ain't done quite yet, he thought.

CHAPTER 8

I n the AFRICOM operations center, Parson kept an eye on four separate video screens. One displayed a drone's-eye view of Libya's old chemical production facility at Tarhuna, southeast of Tripoli. That feed came from an RQ-4 Global Hawk. Two other screens showed Predator feeds—one from above an army base near Benghazi, and the other over the airfield at Ghadames. The BBC aired silently on the fourth screen.

The Combined Forces Air Component Commander—a three-star—had acted on Parson's suggestion to put drones over places that might hide uncataloged chemical weapons. Parson felt gratified that he could upchannel a recommendation and see some results. But he hardly considered himself a tactical genius; he realized he probably got his drones because nobody had any better ideas.

So far, watching the feeds was like watching grass grow, except there was no grass down there. The Predator over Ghadames recorded routine civilian traffic approaching and departing the desert airfield. The one over Benghazi showed nothing unusual for a base used by the new Libyan army. Parson made a mental note to request moving that drone somewhere else. He also considered moving the Global Hawk from over Tarhuna. So far it detected only a disused chemical plant, most of it underground. From sixty thousand feet, the facility appeared as little more than an indentation dug into the red sand at the base of a hill. Just three small buildings on the surface of the desert, with possibly more buried and invisible. Parson had seen no vehicles or personnel since the Hawk got on station yesterday.

The workload had grown for Parson since the French officer, Captain Chartier, had left. By now Chartier had returned to Luxeuil Air Base to rejoin his strike squadron and get current again in the Mirage 2000. Parson envied his young colleague's flight duty. After a long career as a navigator and then a pilot, Parson found himself deskbound much of the time as his rank and responsibilities increased.

With little happening on the drone feeds, Parson turned his attention to the news. The BBC camera showed people milling about in some kind of auditorium. Parson looked closely and recognized the well of the United Nations General Assembly. A graphic on the screen read AWAITING STATEMENT FROM UN SECRETARY-GENERAL. Parson turned up the volume. A few minutes later a balding man in dark-rimmed eyeglasses and a gray suit took the lectern. He began to speak in fluent English with a Slavic accent. The graphic changed to read UN SECRETARY-GENERAL ANATOLY BERETSOV. With a grim visage, Beretsov began to speak.

"The United Nations Security Council has voted unanimously to authorize the use of armed force against terrorist factions in North Africa. We take this step with great reluctance to put the men and women of our militaries in harm's way. However, the use of chemical weapons against civilian targets represents an affront to all standards of human decency.

"The governments of Egypt, Algeria, Libya, and Tunisia have agreed to permit use of their airspace and, in some cases, their airports and other facilities. American and French forces have begun to deploy to the Mediterranean, and they will be joined by British, Spanish, and Italian assets as needed. All the members of the Security Council hope for a quick resolution to this threat to the lives and well-being of the innocent."

Parson had already gathered and analyzed all the data on Mitiga International Airport. He'd found the field suitable for pretty much anything the allied countries might want to fly into it.

The next task would involve coordinating what went where— figuring out how to bed down aircraft at different fields to avoid a MOG problem. MOG meant maximum on ground: ramp space too choked with aircraft to accommodate any more flights. Number-crunching and logistics, basically. Parson mused to himself how a kid might look up into the sky at an airplane and think: I want to do that when I grow up. But nobody tells the kid if he does it long enough, somebody will take away that shiny jet and replace it with a damned desktop computer.

Parson glanced back at the drone feeds and still saw mainly just a lot of dirt. When his cell phone rang—his duty phone, not his personal phone—he turned down the BBC and said, "AFRICOM Operations. Colonel Parson."

"*Bonjour*, sir. This is Captain Chartier."

"Frenchie," Parson said. "How the hell are you? Do you remember how to fly that rocket of yours?"

"*Oui, mon colonel.* I was an instructor in the Mirage, so it was like going back to a longtime girlfriend. She is fast as ever."

Lucky bastard, Parson thought. Enjoy it while it lasts.

"So what's up?" Parson asked.

"I wanted to let you know my squadron has received deployment orders. We will leave Luxeuil sometime in the next few days, but we do not yet know our forward location."

I've got a pretty good idea, Parson thought, but I can't say on a nonsecure phone line.

"Well, fly safe," Parson said. "And give 'em hell."

"*Certainement.* Oh, and I have sent you something. I mailed you a book by Saint-Ex. *Wind, Sand and Stars.*"

"Thanks, Frenchie. In English, I hope."

"Of course."

Parson felt a little stupid for not speaking or reading any language but his own. Especially when he got around people like Chartier and, to an even greater extent, Sophia. He worried about her down there in the Sahara with UNHCR.

"I appreciate it," Parson said. "Let me know if I can do anything for you guys once you get in theater."

"*Merci beaucoup.* Perhaps I say too much, but we will fly out with drop tanks installed and a full load of BGLs."

Sounded good to Parson. The drop tanks would greatly extend the Mirage's range. And the laser-guided bombs—BGLs, in the ass-backward French acronym—provided devastating firepower against enemy vehicles and terrorist hideouts. Such a configuration would allow Chartier and his squadron mates to fly deep into the Sahara and strike hard, if necessary. The Mirage also carried the Damocles laser designator pod. The name amounted to a bit of Gallic poetry—the sword of Damocles over the enemy, just waiting to drop. Combined with the BGLs, the Damocles enabled pinpoint accuracy with heavy weapons.

"You boys are loaded for bear," Parson said. "I just saw where the UN gave us the green light. Kick some ass."

"*Bien sûr.* The *képis blancs* are mobilizing, too."

Parson knew that phrase from recent briefings about allied militaries. *Képis blancs* meant white kepis, the iconic hats worn by the French Foreign Legion. To Americans, at least, they were the only French troops with a reputation for busting heads. Parson considered the Legion a singular and brilliant concept for creating a fighting team: Take guys from around the world, eccentric adventurers and cutthroats who wanted a new start in life. Tell this band of brigands they could have a clean slate as long as they behaved themselves, devoted their lives to France, and passed training that could make hard men cry. Such soldiers would bear allegiance to little but their units. Hence their motto: *Legio Patria Nostra. The Le-*

gion Is Our Nation. Tough enough to get away with wearing goofy white hats.

After Chartier hung up, Parson scanned the drone feeds again. He almost dismissed them as more of the same, but something at Tarhuna caught his eye. Three vehicles sat parked next to one of the buildings. Parson felt sure the vehicles had not been there before. He looked closer and saw they were flatbed trucks.

"Son of a bitch," Parson whispered. He lowered himself into his desk chair, not taking his eyes off the screen. Men swarmed around the trucks. They entered the building empty-handed and came out in pairs, struggling with large drums or barrels.

Parson checked his computer. It remained logged in to a secure satellite-based text connection with the Mission Control Element at Beale Air Force Base, where the Global Hawk's controllers worked. Normally, Parson's duties wouldn't put him in direct connection with Beale, but his bosses granted him access because he'd made the original suggestion to monitor the potential weapons storage sites.

ARE YOU SEEING THIS? Parson typed. He didn't even know the name of the officer on the other end. The names changed as shifts changed, but the duties remained the same. His answer came a few seconds later.

AFFIRMATIVE. KASSAM AND HIS BOYS?

Parson considered his answer for a moment, then typed NOT THERE TO PICK UP THEIR WIVES FROM WORK, I'LL WAGER.

In fact, he could think of no legitimate reason for anyone to do anything at Tarhuna. He glanced up at the screen, then back down at his computer. Thought to himself: Wait a minute. He looked back up at the feed. What were those guys wearing? Parson typed as quickly as he could.

CAN U ZOOM CLOSER?

AFFIRM.

After what seemed like a long wait, though it could have been no more than a minute, the Global Hawk zoomed in. The men working around the trucks appeared to move with ant-like motions, with one mind and one accord. They wore bulky suits, and something covered their heads and faces. Whoa, Parson thought. Chem suits.

THEY'RE WEARING MOPP GEAR, he typed.

Parson's suspicions had turned out right. If those bastards were dressed like that, they were handling chemical weapons and they knew what they were doing. When it came to bad guys, Parson worried more about competence than fanaticism. You could take out a wild-eyed moron with relative ease. The job got harder if the jihadist had some skills.

As Parson considered the problem, a reply came from Beale.

IMAGERY CONFIRMS GAS MASKS.

Yep, Parson thought, I could have told you that. So who are we dealing with here? Veterans of almost anybody's military would have at least some training for work in a chemical environment. The governments of the U.S. and European countries mandated the training for fear their troops would get slimed by the other side. Other services trained because they might *use* such weapons. These dudes could have learned this drill in the old Libyan army. Or in Iraq, Syria, or Iran, for that matter. Sadiq Kassam probably recruited his motley little troop from all over.

The Combined Forces Air Component Commander needs to know about this, Parson thought. Put some steel on that target if possible.

HAS THIS BEEN UPCHANNELED TO CFACC STAFF? Parson typed. His answer came quickly.

AFFIRM. STRIKE AIRCRAFT UNAVAILABLE AT THIS TIME.

That was too damned bad. To an airman, this was a target begging to be hit. But the Air Force didn't have fighters or bombers ready at a moment's notice all over the world.

Barrel by barrel, the worker ants down there loaded all three trucks. When finished, they spread tarps over the barrels and secured the cargo with tie-down straps. Yeah, Parson mused, you probably wouldn't want a drum of concentrated mustard agent rolling off your truck and breaking open all around you. Parson typed another message:

YOU'RE GOING TO FOLLOW THESE GUYS, RIGHT?

Parson wanted to blow away the insurgents right now, but with no fighters on alert close by, that wasn't an option. The Global Hawk itself carried no weapons. But it could see where the bastards went. No reply came for a while. Parson wondered if something was wrong. Finally, the text box read BEALE MCE IS TYPING. Then the answer popped up.

WE'LL TRACK THEM AS LONG AS WE CAN.

What? Why wouldn't they stay on the trucks indefinitely? This is what AFRICOM had been looking for. Parson tapped at his keyboard.

WHAT DO U MEAN BY THAT?

This time the reply came quickly.

HAWK IS ALMOST BINGO FUEL. VERY SORRY, SIR.

You gotta be kidding me, Parson thought. His fingers hovered over the keyboard, quivering just a little because he was so ticked off. If we lost the insurgents' trail, when would we ever find them again? When these trucks blended unobserved with the flow of other traffic, they would effectively disappear. Parson stopped himself from writing his natural response, clenched his fingers into fists. "Damn it," he muttered. "Damn it, damn it, damn it." Other officers in the room glanced up from their computers. Parson shook his head. Mind your own damned business.

He took a deep breath, calmed himself enough to write something reasonably professional. Parson typed HOW MUCH MORE TIME ON STATION?

FIFTEEN MINUTES AT BEST, came the answer.

We're going to lose them, Parson thought. He tried to come up with a way to salvage the situation.

CAN WE REDIRECT THE PREDATORS TO TARHUNA? he typed.

He got the answer he expected.

THEY CAN'T GET THERE IN TIME.

Parson massaged his temples, sighed hard. He pushed his chair back from his computer and looked up at the feed. One of the trucks began to roll.

"We had you," Parson whispered to himself. "We had you dead to rights."

Nothing left to do but suggest the obvious. Parson typed again.

FOLLOW AS LONG AS YOU CAN. AT LEAST WE'LL KNOW WHAT DIRECTION THEY WENT.

His answer came quickly this time:

YES, SIR.

The first truck began moving along a narrow paved road, and the other two vehicles followed. Parson checked the data displayed along the edge of the video screen. The information included altitude, speed, heading, and other flight information. Based on the Global Hawk's heading and sensor orientation, he determined the trucks were rolling south.

So that narrows it down, Parson told himself. South into the vastness of the Sahara.

The Hawk followed the trucks for a few miles but then veered away. The vehicles disappeared in the upper left corner of the screen as the drone broke off its surveillance.

Figures, Parson thought. I have millions of dollars' worth of high-tech hardware at my disposal. But I'd settle for a Piper Cub and a pilot with a Kodak if I could put them over those trucks.

Lacking even that, Parson decided he'd ask if the CFACC could send an eval team to the site later on to see what evidence might remain there. But more than likely, he knew, the team would find nothing to indicate where the chemicals had been taken.

Once terrorists took weapons from a central location, they could hide them so easily. Back during the Iraq War, the bad guys broke into stocks of hundreds of shoulder-fired antiaircraft missiles. Damned things plagued coalition airplanes and helicopters for the entire conflict. Parson could recall spiraling down to landings in Baghdad and Balad, wondering when the next rocket would come burning up from the ground.

Parson decided to give himself a break from all this frustration. He got up, left the ops center, and walked down the hall to the snack room. Took a Dr Pepper from the refrigerator, cracked off the cap. A few sips of the cold soft drink settled his nerves just a bit. His eyes wandered across a poster from Dassault Aviation that someone— probably Chartier—had taped to the wall.

The poster showed a Mirage in flight. The delta-wing jet banked hard to the left with its afterburner lit. Cool.

Parson took the Dr Pepper bottle with him as he returned to the ops center door and punched in the security code. He swung the door open and returned to his desk.

In the short time he'd been gone, a new e-mail had popped up on his computer. He opened the e-mail and saw the attachment was a set of orders. When he read the orders, his mood improved immediately. The text read:

MEMBER IS DIRECTED TO PROCEED AT EARLIEST OPPORTUNITY FOR TEMPORARY DUTY AT MITIGA INTERNATIONAL AIRPORT, LIBYA. . . . TDY PERIOD NOT LESS THAN 90 DAYS. . . . DUTIES ENTAIL COMMAND OF 401st AIR EXPEDITIONARY GROUP. VARIATIONS IN ITINERARY NOT AUTHORIZED. . . . MEMBER WILL CARRY WEAPON. GOVERNMENT TRAVEL CARD USE MANDATORY.

Parson clicked to print the orders, sat back and smiled. This wouldn't get him back into the cockpit, but at least it would get him out into the field. This day didn't suck so bad after all.

CHAPTER 9

Sea breezes washed over Blount on the flight deck of the new USS *Tarawa*. The amphibious assault ship foamed through the Med at about twenty knots, steaming toward the Gulf of Sidra, off the Libyan coast. On the vessel's superstructure, a sign painted in three-foot-high yellow lettering warned BEWARE OF JET BLAST, PROPS, AND ROTORS. But the *Tarawa* would conduct no flight operations today. Its armada of helicopters and Osprey tilt-rotors sat silently on the eight-hundred-foot deck, so the Marines took advantage of the long steel beach to conduct some training.

A squad stood around Blount and Corporal Fender. The men wore desert combat boots and digital camo trousers, but above the waist they'd stripped to green T-shirts. Fender held a nonfiring handgun made of yellow plastic.

"Y'all might see me use moves a little different from what you've been taught," Blount said. "Don't get me wrong; I like the Marine Corps Martial Arts Program just fine. But I also studied Krav Maga and some other styles on my own. Bottom line—use what works for you."

Blount and Fender stepped onto a rubber mat. Fender pointed the pistol at Blount.

"Fender, the gunny is gonna feed you that pistol for lunch," one of the Marines called out. His buddies laughed.

"Nah, I ain't gon' hurt him," Blount said.

In fact, he had never injured a fellow Marine in training. That would have harmed a brother devil dog, shown bad form, and displayed a disregard for government property. Blount went on with his lesson.

"Now, more than likely you'll shoot him before it ever comes to this," he said. "But suppose you got no weapon of your own, for whatever reason. You'll want to disarm him quick as you can."

Blount stood about five yards from Fender. He raised both hands to shoulder level.

"This is about the worst place to be," Blount said. "At this range, I can't reach him and he can't miss. I might say 'whoa' or something, and with my hands up maybe he'll think I'm surrendering. I just want him to hesitate for half a second. And I want to get off his centerline and close that distance right *now*."

Blount paused, eyed Fender's hand. With a lowered voice, he addressed the corporal: "Hey, bud. Make sure you got your finger outside that trigger guard. I don't want to break it."

"Aye, Gunny."

"All right," Blount continued. "I'm gon' use my whole body to get control of that weapon and knock him off his feet."

In two strides, Blount sidestepped, advanced on Fender. Blount's right hand shot upward, grabbed the pistol by the barrel, and pushed it away. His left hand curled around the other side of the weapon and he cupped it over the hammer. Arms outstretched, Blount pushed Fender off balance. He delivered a kick toward Fender's groin, but he pulled his foot back before he made contact. Otherwise, the blow surely would have crumpled Fender to the deck.

Then Blount yanked with his left hand and pushed with his right. The motion put Fender on his knees and forced his wrist at such an angle that he could do nothing but let go of the pistol. If he hadn't, his wrist would have broken. Fender kept his finger away from the trigger as warned. He released the handgun and stood up, rubbing his wrist.

"I didn't use a lot of strength here," Blount said, holding the yellow pistol. "You little guys can do this, too. Now, in the real situation, you'll do this so fast you'll break his wrist no matter what he does. And you can expect that gun to go off, whether he means to fire or not. Don't worry about it; you got control of the muzzle. And it'll be the last thing his trigger finger does before it breaks, too."

More laughter. Blount enjoyed instructing in the Marine Corps Martial Arts Program—"semper fu," as they called it. The program's motto: *One Mind, Any Weapon.* Just an ancillary role to his main job as a special operations team chief. Though he missed Bernadette and the girls already, it felt good to teach and lead Marines again.

Still, something about this mission seemed different from all his previous deployments. The chemical weapons threat had a lot to do with it; anybody who said he wasn't scared of nerve gas was either lying or stupid. But the chem threat alone did not explain why this trip felt . . . otherworldly. Maybe it was because the enemy this time—that new terrorist leader Sadiq Kassam—was such a weirdo. Orange beard, stolen flintlock, and all that. Maybe it was because Blount couldn't get that image of Kelley's last minutes out of his mind. Or maybe things felt strange because Blount had nearly settled into home for good, then made a real conscious decision to venture into danger again. As the *Tarawa* pitched through blue swells, the journey seemed almost mythic, as if he were crossing a threshold into some new realm with hazards and trials he could not imagine.

The very sky seemed to threaten. To the east, off the bow and in the direction of Libya, thunderheads loomed over the sea. The clouds strobed with internal lightning. The effect made Blount think of watching a distant battle at night; you couldn't see the mortars exploding, but you could see the flashes reflected against a mountainside. Godlike threshold guardians seemed to give Blount one last warning to turn back.

Stop thinking nonsense, he told himself. You wanted this.

Blount watched the squad of Marines practice the moves he'd shown them. Then he dismissed them; he'd give another lesson to a different squad tomorrow. No use trying to teach this stuff to too many guys at one time. If they couldn't see what he demonstrated with his hands and feet, they couldn't learn much. He loved this part of his job. You never knew when you'd give a Marine a tidbit of information that would save a life or win a battle.

He gave the yellow pistol back to Fender to put away. Then Blount buttoned on his uniform blouse and made his way to the TACLOG, the Marines' shipboard nerve center. He found Captain Privett monitoring radio and computer traffic. Coffee mugs and sticky notes littered a room filled with electronic gear. A map of North Africa hung on one wall. The other walls displayed topographical and aeronautical charts of various sections of the Sahara. Shades of brown and gray depicted the terrain; almost no green appeared anywhere. The isogonic lines and contour markings implied an ordered world, a direct contrast to the mayhem that existed on the ground. Above the North Africa map, some Marine with a literary bent had posted a quote from a Roman poet, a line that rang true for the Corps: *What coast knows not our blood?—Horace, 23 B.C.*

"Anything new, sir?" Blount asked.

"Yeah, check this out." Privett turned up the volume on one of the speakers. "An African Union patrol is going into a village somewhere in Algeria. Sounds like the bad guys got there first."

Blount listened hard, easily imagined the scene as troops entered an urban hostile fire zone. Their weapons at the ready, each man would scan his sector, primed to make instant decisions on whether to fire. Their radio procedures differed slightly from those Blount knew, but the cross talk sounded like squad leaders checking in with a platoon commander. The signals came in weak but readable.

"Simba," a voice called. "This is Piranha One. I have eight bodies on the western edge of the town. Each one has been shot in the back of the head." The soldier spoke English with an accent, maybe that of Kenya or Nigeria.

"Roger, Piranha One. Do you see enemy activity?"

"Negative. But these wounds look fresh. The bodies are not cold. Whoever killed these people cannot be far."

"Acknowledged. Keep me advised."

Monitoring foot-mobile troops from a warship in the Mediterranean might have felt odd to some folks, Blount realized. But to him it seemed perfectly natural. Fit right in with the role of the Marines: to come in from the sea and project power ashore. Those men on the radio weren't Marines, of course, but he hoped they knew what they were doing and stayed safe.

Several minutes ticked by with no more radio traffic: just the hiss and whine of an open channel, along with occasional crackles caused by the distant lightning. Then the first voice came back, this time speaking much more quickly.

"Simba, Piranha One. We are—" The man held down his talk switch but paused for some reason. Gunfire sputtered around him. "We are under fire. Enemy in a row of houses to our east." More staccato pops in the background, along with shouted orders too indistinct to make out.

"Roger, Piranha. Shark will link up with you."

Another stretch of silence followed. Blount looked at Captain Privett, who tapped a pen across his palm. Nervous energy caused by frustration, Blount figured. Tough to listen to friendlies in contact and have no way to help them.

"Do they have air cover?" Blount asked.

"None that I've heard about."

Too bad. A gunship or attack jet might have helped those guys a lot. But American, French, and British aircraft were still moving into the region. Without all the pieces in place, troops who got into a scrape just might have to fight by themselves.

The radio squelch broke again. The shooting sounded louder this time. "Simba—" The soldier let go of his transmit switch. Privett shook his head, glanced up at Blount. The soldier on the radio called once more: "Simba, where is Shark?" The boom of a grenade or mortar round rattled through the tinny speaker.

More seconds of silence passed. The next time the squelch broke, Blount heard more shooting, a scream, and shouts in Arabic.

"They're getting overrun," Blount said.

Privett nodded, pressed his lips together, looked at the radio.

"Piranha, what is your status?" a voice called.

No answer.

"Piranha, what is your status?"

The static streamed unbroken for a moment, until a click brought back the sounds of battle. No words, but more shooting.

Then some voices off mike. They sounded close, and they spoke in Arabic. Someone responded in English.

"Please."

A burst of automatic fire sounded over the air.

Click.

Silence.

Privett stared at the map in front of him. "Damn it," he whispered.

Every time Blount lost one of his brothers in arms, a little piece of him died, too. He didn't know this AU troop just executed by terrorists. But he'd followed the losing battle, listened in on the man's final moments. Just hearing the voice speak that last word formed enough of a bond for Blount to connect with this unknown soldier. Whatever the guy's training or skill, he'd used what he had to try to fight the madness in his world. And if he had a family, they would soon know their worst fears had been realized.

Blount left the TACLOG and went outside to the rail. The thunderclouds to the east glowered closer now. Their darkness blocked the sun and turned midafternoon to dusk. Needles of rain spat from the sky, flung sideways by rising wind. In his marksman's mind, Blount made an instinctive calculation: that wind felt like twenty-five to thirty miles per hour. The ship's forward progress complicated the math a little. But with the wind quartering off the bow, you'd correct for half-value wind speed if your target lay straight ahead. Dial in the setting. Spotter ready. Shooter ready. Fire.

Sailors scurried around on the flight deck. Blount didn't know their duties; perhaps they were preparing the *Tarawa* to face the storm. The ship heaved through rising waves; Blount felt that first little gut-turn of seasickness. The crests of the swells frothed white. Ahead, the clouds roiled and rose in what looked like a conscious display of menace.

Lightning speared the surface of the ocean. Blount happened to be looking right where it struck; he thought he actually saw steam rise where fire hit the water. The bolt burned his eyes. When he closed them he could still see the lightning's jagged imprint on his retinas.

As he waited for his eyes to recover, he heard a shout from somewhere behind him.

"Man overboard! Port side, man overboard!"

The word passed quickly. A few seconds later an order came over the loudspeakers of the 1 Main Circuit, the shipwide public address.

"Man overboard, port side. Launch the alert helo."

A flight crew ran to a waiting Seahawk: two pilots, a crew chief, a pair of rescue swimmers. Farther down the deck, a sailor grabbed a smoke float, yanked the pull ring, and tossed the float over the side. Orange smoke churned from the float and streamed downwind.

Despite the crew's quick action, Blount supposed the float marked only the general area to search. The *Tarawa* might have traveled several hundred yards between the moment the man fell overboard and when the smoke float hit the water.

Six blasts sounded from the ship's whistle. Overhead, someone ran up the Oscar flag, a square signal panel divided diagonally into triangles of red and yellow. The Oscar snapped and fluttered against a sky as slate-gray as the *Tarawa* itself. Sailors mustered in groups so their chiefs could determine who was missing. Blount reported to the TACLOG; all Marines were accounted for.

When he went back outside, the Seahawk's rotors were turning. In the gusting wind, the helicopter rose unsteadily. Its wheels left the deck, touched down again. The rotor blades slapped a louder rhythm, and then the Seahawk climbed away and lowered its nose.

Blount wanted to help, but he had no role in the procedure. Rescuing a man overboard was one of the most basic naval skills; he knew the sailors would have trained until this drill became second nature. Still, he scanned the water. Spotting the dot of a man's head would prove difficult in these conditions. Sailors working on the flight deck wore a vest with an emergency light, but even that could be hard to spot on a day like today. Spiderwebs of foam sizzled across the ocean's troughs and peaks. Rain fell steady and dimpled the surface of the water. Gusts blew harder and kept shifting direction— now off the bow, now quartering, now off the beam.

The helicopter turned and passed off the port side, just meters above the sea. The aircraft flew alongside the *Tarawa*'s wake, the crew probably hoping the path of churned water would lead them to their lost sailor.

The smoke float receded in the distance. As the smoke spewed into the air, wind snatched and scattered the wisps like sails torn from a yardarm.

Blount thought that if he were a superstitious man, he might have seen this accident as a kind of test, some challenge from a Neptune angered by the ship's presence: *You men of the* Tarawa *may pass no farther until you prove your worth.* He wanted to reply in defiance, to shout into the wind: *I got a score to settle and nothing's getting in my way.* Then he remembered his grandfather's words. Fight to protect, not to punish. Act from love instead of hate.

Try as he might, Blount could not see anything that looked like a man in the water. The Seahawk turned, crossed the wake, turned again. Then the aircraft slowed and hovered. Its main rotor whipped the surface and slashed spray into a microstorm boiling beneath the helicopter.

Thank God, Blount thought. They found him. Just hope he ain't drowned.

A metal basket swung from the Seahawk's hoist. One of the rescue swimmers rode the basket to the ocean's surface, and the man kept looking down and pointing. The basket descended, disappeared into a trough. A few moments later Blount spotted the basket sliding up the shoulder of a wave, two men inside. Blount clapped and cheered along with the sailors around him.

The cable tightened, and the basket rose into the air, dripping. The rescue swimmer worked on the figure splayed beside him. Not a good sign. Blount wondered if the swimmer performed CPR.

The hoist reeled the cable until the basket dangled just outside the helicopter's starboard-side door. Gloved hands reached for the basket and cable, pulled the rescue swimmer and sailor inside. Closed the cabin door.

Sweet, Blount thought. He found it a pleasure to watch folks who knew what they were doing, whether they flew a helo, shot a rifle, or built a barn. A man could get real good at something and use that skill to make the world a better place, even if only for a little while in a little area. Blount worried about the condition of the sailor, but at least the guy was in good hands.

Rain stung Blount's cheeks. Gusts whipped the Oscar flag in new directions, and what looked like white stones began bouncing on the steel expanse of the *Tarawa*.

Hail, Blount realized. He'd seen a hailstorm strip a field of tobacco right down to the stalks, and he wondered what the ice rocks would do to the helicopter's rotors. The shearing wind wouldn't help, either. Those pilots sure had their hands full; old Neptune was in a real bad mood.

The Seahawk accelerated out of its hover, dipped its nose, flew straight on toward the *Tarawa*. Blount felt the ship turn a few degrees; maybe the skipper wanted to put the bow into the wind to make it easier for the chopper to land. Blount's Air Force friend, Colonel Michael Parson, had once told him everything that flies lands into the wind, from a sparrow to a space shuttle. Trouble was, the wind kept shifting.

The helo clattered alongside the ship, crossed overhead, turned and flew astern. Blount guessed the pilots were trying to get a feel for the wind. The aircraft lined up on final approach, grew larger as it descended toward the deck.

Gusts rocked the Seahawk. It banked, corrected, bounced some more. Wipers ticked a rhythm across the windscreen. The helo crossed over the stern and lowered itself toward the yellow and white lines painted along the flight deck. Almost home free.

Blount felt the wind against his face die away completely. Then a gust hit him from behind. Rain and hail lashed down in a torrent.

The Seahawk banked hard. Dropped to the deck like it forgot how to fly.

Rotor blades struck steel plating and shattered into shrapnel. The helo rolled onto its port side, tail rotor and stubs of the main rotor blades still spinning. Flames erupted from the engines. Cracks clouded the windscreen, but Blount could see the crew inside struggling with harnesses, pulling at latches.

Sailors ran for the downed chopper. Hoses appeared from everywhere, and a blast of foam doused the fire. Blount expected to see fliers piling out of their stricken aircraft, but all the doors remained closed. From outside the helo, sailors yanked at handles, but the Seahawk remained sealed.

Blount wondered why in the world they couldn't get that thing opened. Then it dawned on him. The chopper had hit just hard enough to bend the frame. The doors were jammed.

He charged toward the Seahawk, boots splashing through pooling rain. Maybe the sailors had a hydraulic tool to tear into that thing like a can opener. That could take several minutes, though, and in the meantime Blount could lend them some muscle.

The fire was out, thank the Good Lord. But if that boy they'd plucked from the water had suffered cardiac arrest, he needed to get to the medical bay right this minute.

Blount pushed three sailors out of the way, climbed up on the side of the helicopter. Rain streamed over the airframe, made for slick footing. The chopper's cabin door—aft of the cockpit—had two windows; he could see crewmen inside struggling with some sort of handle.

"Can you jettison these windows?" Blount shouted. He didn't know all the particulars of the Seahawk, but he knew every military aircraft was designed so you could get out of it fast.

A muffled voice inside answered, "We can't get the jettison lever unlocked."

Blount placed his hands on the cabin door's exterior handle, turned it away from the position marked CLOSED & LOCKED. He braced one boot against a landing gear strut and pulled.

Every fiber of his muscles burned. His teeth gritted. He uttered a growl as he pitted bone and tendon against buckled aluminum. The door scraped open about two inches. More voices called from inside the aircraft.

"We're gonna lose this guy if we can't get him out of here."

"Pop out that front door."

A fist smacked against the window of the small cockpit door in front of Blount. The door detached and slid to the flight deck. Two gloved hands appeared at the edges of the door opening, and a pilot pried himself from the chopper, still wearing his helmet. All right, that was progress. Able-bodied men could scramble free that way pretty easily. But the cockpit door made a mighty small hole for pulling out an unconscious patient. Blount still needed to get the main door open.

He adjusted his footing, shifted his handhold. A sailor climbed up beside him and looked for a spot to brace himself. The landing gear strut offered the only good point for leverage, with room for just one man. Blount appreciated the help, but he'd have to do this alone.

"I got it, bud," Blount said. "Just make sure this thing don't catch on fire again."

"Aye, aye, Gunny."

The sailor slid off of the helicopter, and Blount set himself for another try. He adjusted his feet. Gripped the edge of the door and pulled not just with his arms, but with his entire body working as a crowbar. A simple matter of raw strength multiplied by mechanical advantage.

Blount's whole frame tensed with effort. He felt his spine compress, the cartilage in his elbows stretch. Another growl escaped his open mouth, and raindrops flecked his tongue. The metal began to cut into his fingers, and he wished he'd worn gloves. The muscles in his face squeezed hard enough to force his eyes closed.

Just as he sensed his back had taken all it could withstand, the door screeched open about a foot. The sailors cheered.

"Hit it one more time, Gunny," one of them cried.

Blount relaxed for a moment, took two deep breaths. Thought to himself, Please just gimme strength for another minute. Stiffened his body, and pulled again.

The bound-up rollers in the door tracks broke free. The door slid fully open with such force that Blount lost his balance and fell from the aircraft. Instinct took over, and he used a martial arts move to break his fall: he slapped his forearms onto the ship's deck just as his hips and back hit the wet metal. Banged his elbows, and that hurt something awful, but better than cracking his head.

Two sailors climbed inside the helo and helped the rescue swimmers lift their patient out of the aircraft.

"Will he make it?" a sailor asked.

"I think so," one of the rescue swimmers said.

Blount lay on his back in the rain, spent. Blood trickled from shallow cuts in his fingers. Fender came over to check on him.

"I'm good, bud," Blount said.

The men lowered the patient to the deck and took him away on a litter. A sailor ran up with a Hurst tool.

"Don't need it," one of his shipmates called. "The gunnery sergeant kicked that helicopter's ass."

Sailors laughed. Blount sat up and smiled, his uniform soaked. He thought of one of the stories his grandfather had read him when he was a child. Something about steel-driving John Henry outworking the steam hammer, but then dying of a heart attack. I beat the Hurst tool before it even got here, Blount thought, and all I got is cut fingers. He felt the pounding of his heart begin to slow to a normal rate. Fender helped him to his feet.

Blount rubbed his elbows. They still stung. Behind him, two petty officers spoke as if he weren't there. Perhaps they thought the wind covered their words, but Blount heard it all.

"That's one of the biggest dudes I ever seen in my life," one of them said.

"Yeah," his shipmate answered. "Seems like a real nice guy, but you don't ever, ever want him mad at you."

CHAPTER 10

Sophia Gold worried as soon as the helicopters thudded overhead. The United Nations refugee camp expected no visitors today. Outside the UNHCR tents, she squinted, shaded her eyes with her palm, and recognized three old Soviet-designed choppers of the Kenya Defence Forces, flying on behalf of the African Union. The aircraft carried the red, green, and black roundel of Kenya's air force, along with the emblem of the AU: a gold-colored map of Africa that showed no national boundaries.

The aircraft approached to land at the camp's makeshift helipad, a few hundred yards away from the camp. Rotors churned the warm air, and the helicopters seemed to crawl through the sky. As they descended, dust erupted beneath them, kicked into the air by downwash. The sand swirled against the billowing tents, and Gold clamped her eyelids shut. When the gritty gale subsided, she opened her eyes to see Major Ongondo emerge from the lead helicopter.

The Kenyan officer did not have on a MOPP suit today. Instead he wore camo fatigues in the British style for temperate weather: a green-dominated pattern of black, beige, and brown. Not ideal for the desert, but certainly more comfortable than full chem gear. His shoulders sagged under the weight of a flak jacket stiff with ceramic plates, and he carried a Heckler & Koch G3 rifle on a sling over his shoulder.

The helicopters shut down, and men jumped from the crew doors. They opened the rear clamshell doors at the back of the choppers, and Ongondo and his men began unloading patients. Nurses and medics ran to help, and Gold went with them. Wounded men, women, and children lay on stretchers. Some of the men wore uniforms; the others were civilians. They seemed to have been evacuated hurriedly; a few of the injured had not even received first aid. A small boy in a blood-spattered Pokémon T-shirt uttered moans that sounded more like the screech of an animal than any sound a human would make. Something, probably a high-velocity bullet, had torn through his hand and left a bleeding mass of tendons and splintered bone.

Gold climbed aboard one of the helicopters and took one end of a stretcher by its wooden handles. Ongondo lifted the other end, and they carried an injured woman out through the back of the chopper. A bandage filthy with blood and dust covered the woman's shoulder.

"Ah, Ms. Gold," Ongondo said as they shuffled toward the medical tent. "I remember you."

"Yes, sir," Gold said. She looked down at the woman, who called out in Arabic and pointed to the boy with the mangled hand. Her son, perhaps? "What happened to these people?" Gold asked.

"The bandits attacked a village on the Algerian side of the border," Ongondo said. Keeping both hands on the stretcher, he blew a droplet of sweat from the end of his nose. "Here is the result," he continued. "One of my patrols was wiped out before the bandits withdrew. Your camp was the nearest hospital."

"I'm so sorry about your men," Gold said.

Though the Kenyan officer spoke with command presence, his eyes glistened.

"I am, too," Ongondo said. "And it pains me just as much to see more civilians hurt. What wrong have they done?"

"Nothing," Gold said, "except live in territory the terrorists want."

"My people have a saying," Ongondo said. "'When elephants fight, the grass suffers.'"

An important moral in a very few words, Gold noted. Ongondo

seemed to fall back on his learning whenever he struggled with emotion—just the way Gold did.

Lambrechts met Gold and Ongondo when they entered the med tent. The doctor wore light blue scrubs, and a stethoscope hung from around her neck. The woman on the stretcher did not speak, but after looking around, she closed her eyes and breathed in deeply. Relieved, apparently, to find herself at a hospital, however primitive.

"This woman has suffered a gunshot wound to the shoulder," Ongondo said. "Most of these people have been shot. Some have stab wounds. There are eight of my own men. And one prisoner."

"Prisoner?" Lambrechts asked. She kneeled to examine her new patient.

"Yes. We wounded and captured one of the bandits."

"Is this the same group that attacked the village outside Ghat?" Gold asked.

"We believe so," Ongondo said. "Sadiq Kassam's terrorists."

Lambrechts looked up from the wounded woman. "Are there injuries from chemical weapons?"

"None that we have seen."

Gold looked out through the tent flap and saw medics and soldiers bringing more patients. Some of the wounded cried out in pain; others stared with dull eyes at things far beyond the horizon. Gold had seen all this before, too many times. But she never got used to it.

On the makeshift flight line, soldiers who'd flown in on the helicopters gathered around one of the aircraft. They formed a knot at the back of the chopper and began escorting a walking patient. Gold could tell from the way the men handled him that they felt little sympathy about his wounds. Two soldiers pulled him by the front of his shirt, and the man stumbled to keep up. He wore green cargo pants that looked vaguely military, along with a checkered scarf around his neck. The man's hands were tied behind him. Blood soaked one sleeve.

"Our prisoner," Ongondo said.

"What will you do with him?" Gold asked.

Ongondo placed his hands on his hips, regarded the captive, bit his lower lip. "Not kill him, if that's what you mean," he said. "As much as he deserves it."

"We will treat him here," Lambrechts said. "You must promise you will not abuse him in any way."

"You have my word, ma'am. Technically, the Geneva Convention does not apply to terrorists. But my orders are to treat him as a legitimate prisoner of war."

"Please do."

Gold understood Lambrechts's concern. A UNHCR camp must remain a place of refuge and relief. Ongondo had just lost men under his command; such a situation would test anyone's judgment and professionalism. But perhaps an officer who quoted proverbs about the ravages of fighting would think before pulling a trigger or swinging a fist.

The medical staff triaged the patients. The prisoner, suffering from an arm wound, had to wait because his injury wasn't life-threatening. Lambrechts asked Gold to keep an eye on the AU soldiers and their captive.

"Make sure no one does something I'll regret," Lambrechts said. "We can't let a war crime happen under our noses."

"I'll stay with them," Gold said.

Lambrechts turned her attention to the wounded soldiers and civilians. The most seriously injured troop had taken a round at the bottom edge of his body armor, and the bullet had ripped through his lower abdomen. Others suffered from embedded shrapnel, and one had lost an eye.

Ongondo and his men stayed in the rec tent, waiting for word on their wounded comrades. They glared at their prisoner, seated on the floor. Three soldiers kept rifle barrels trained on the man, and Gold could see how this could go very bad very quickly. Just one undisciplined troop with an itchy trigger finger could murder the prisoner and claim the man tried to escape.

Gold tried to think of what she could do to ease the tension. Food and drink, perhaps? At least that would give the men something to focus on other than vengeance. She went to the mess tent, which offered little between meals. But she found cans of Pepsi and Sprite labeled in English and Arabic, along with apples and oranges. She took the soft drinks and fruit from the refrigerator case and brought them to the soldiers. The soldiers cracked open the cans, which dripped with condensation. They ate and drank, and they glared but offered no protest when Gold held a can of cola to the prisoner's lips. He drank in deep gulps, foaming liquid running from his mouth.

The scirocco subsided, and scattered puffy clouds scudded over the desert. Late in the day, as sunset reddened the clouds, a medic called for the wounded prisoner. Gold and Ongondo helped the man to his feet and escorted him to what passed for the camp's operating room—just a smaller tent off the main medical tent, staffed by Lambrechts and an anesthesiologist.

The Swiss anesthesiologist, a female physician in scrubs identical to Lambrechts's, clipped away the flex-cuffs that bound the prisoner's hands. Then she helped him remove his shirt and lie down on the table. Blood soaked the pressure bandage around his arm. But the bullet had not struck bone, and Gold supposed the man would keep the limb. Still, the wound looked ugly enough when the bandage came off. The round had left a ragged tear in the muscle tissue; a gobbet of flesh hung down from the bicep like a misplaced tongue.

With a small hypodermic, the anesthesiologist injected something just under the skin of the prisoner's good arm. After a few minutes, she inserted a large-gauge needle at the injection site and connected an IV drip. Ongondo watched with little apparent emotion.

"He does not warrant such care," the Kenyan officer said.

"Our oath requires us to help anyone in need," Lambrechts said. Blood had spattered her scrubs. A smeared red handprint marked her sleeve. Gold wondered whether the print came from Lambrechts herself or from the flailing hand of a patient.

"I understand. And I thank you for treating my men."

"All of the wounded you brought here will survive, if luck is with us."

The prisoner began to mumble. Gold leaned in close to listen.

"Ash-hadu anla ilaha, Muhammadan abduhu wa rasuluhu."

"You can understand him?" Ongondo asked.

"Yes, sir," Gold said. "I speak Arabic, though not as well as Pashto."

"What does he say?"

"The Muslim profession of faith."

"In case he does not wake from surgery, I suppose," Ongondo said.

"Perhaps."

Ongondo thought for a moment. "If you speak his language," he said, "then perhaps you can help us. We will need someone to interpret when we question him."

Gold hesitated before answering. She did not relish the idea of taking part in another interrogation; she'd done more than her share of that in the Army. As Gold considered how to respond, the anesthesiologist opened a valve on the IV drip. The prisoner's eyelids fluttered, and he went unconscious.

"Let's talk outside, sir," Gold said.

Gold and Ongondo left the operating tent, stepped out under a dusky Saharan sky. The sun had slipped below the horizon.

"I gather that you are reluctant to take part in the questioning," Ongondo said.

"I am," Gold said. "I'm not sure it's appropriate for me to do that."

"I will respect whatever you decide. But we may have to wait a while for another interpreter. And the prisoner could have time-sensitive information."

A good point, Gold had to admit. After all, if this guy was involved with Kassam, maybe he'd have information about the chemical attacks.

"All right, sir," Gold said, "I'll help. But please promise me you won't put the prisoner under any duress. I'll have to walk away—and report it—if you do that."

"I gave my word before," Ongondo said, "and it still stands now."

When the prisoner came out of surgery, Lambrechts insisted that they let him sleep through the night. That suited Gold. It gave her a little more time to prepare herself mentally.

The next morning, Ongondo and three of his men woke the prisoner. Gold watched them emerge from the sleeping tent and march him to a storage shelter. In the shelter, surrounded by crates of canned food, Ongondo made the man sit on a folding chair. The soldiers pointed their weapons at him. No one moved to strike him, but Gold wondered what would have happened if Ongondo hadn't been there. One soldier took out a set of flex-cuffs.

"He's not going anywhere," Gold said. "May we leave him untied?"

Ongondo waved his hand, and the soldier put the cuffs away. Gold hoped the small kindness might make the prisoner more likely to talk. The man wore the same bloody shirt and cargo pants he'd had on yesterday, except a sleeve had been cut away from the shirt before surgery. The blood had dried and darkened on the wrinkled clothing. Gold found a bottle of water, twisted off the cap, handed the bottle to the prisoner.

A breeze carried the coolness of dawn and flapped the blue polyethylene of the shelter walls. Still, sweat trickled down the man's brow. He fingered his pockets and sipped from the bottle. From time to time he squeezed his eyes shut as if he were concentrating on some mystery, working out some puzzle in his head.

"Are you in pain?" Gold asked in Arabic.

"A bit," the man said.

"Should I call the doctor?"

"No. I can bear it."

That surprised her. Most people facing interrogation, even without the threat of torture, would take any opportunity for delay. But Gold had long since given up trying to fathom the terrorist mind. At best, she could recognize certain patterns, anticipate typical attitudes.

"What is your name?"

"Ahmed."

"And family name?"

"Bedoor."

"Ahmed Bedoor," Gold said. "Where are you from?"

"Egypt."

Hmm. Gold pondered the answers, given promptly, conversationally. Ahmed Bedoor, if that was really his name, veered from the typical in more ways than one. She had seen men in his place spit and curse, call her an infidel harlot. Vow retribution and hellfire. Or refuse to speak at all.

"And you are one of Sadiq Kassam's men?" she asked.

"I serve the pasha of Tripolitania."

The title Kassam claimed, the one Gold had seen in graffiti in the village hit with the chem attack. Gold translated the statements for Ongondo, then regarded her strange charge and considered how to proceed.

"In what capacity do you serve him?" she asked.

"I am a mere foot soldier."

Bedoor's bearing puzzled Gold. He seemed almost . . . professional. He had to know, or at least suspect, that he faced long imprisonment or execution. Perhaps this was a kind of resignation; Gold had seen unexpected attitudes displayed by prisoners on a few occasions, sometimes when they were under the influence of narcotics. Insurgents often went into battle stoned out of their minds to bolster courage or dampen pain. Some American soldiers told stories of putting five, six, eight rounds into a jihadist to take him down, and they attributed such superhuman resilience to PCP or LSD. But if Bedoor had taken anything, it had probably worn off by now.

"What does your group hope to accomplish?"

The prisoner drew in a long breath, studied Gold as if she had asked a foolish question.

"The pasha has made that clear in his recent statements. We will return this region to sharia law, to true Islamic rule, as in the days of old."

Gold paused to fill in Ongondo on the questions and answers thus far. Bedoor spoke fairly standard modern Arabic, so she had an easier time understanding him than some of the refugees from the Ghat region.

"Ask him how many men Kassam has," Ongondo said.

Gold put the question to the prisoner. At this point in interrogations, some low-level jihadists professed innocence and claimed they'd been forced to fight against their will. She wondered why he didn't try that.

"I do not know how many men there are," Bedoor said.

Gold repeated Bedoor's statement in English. Ongondo sat on a box of canned pears, placed his elbows on his knees, steepled his fingers.

"Ask him what weapons they possess."

Gold repeated the question in Arabic.

"I do not know. I had a rifle."

Ongondo rolled his eyes, stood up, motioned for Gold to come with him. They stepped outside the shelter tent.

"Do you believe anything he's saying?" Ongondo asked, arms folded.

"I can't get a feel for this guy," Gold said. "I don't necessarily think he's lying, because he could just deny everything. But he's pretty well spoken for a terrorist foot soldier."

"These bandits come from all walks of life. Try asking him where Kassam has based himself."

Back inside, Gold formed the question into Arabic. Bedoor looked out the tent's opening into the desert. He'd made little eye contact with Gold during the questioning. His distracted manner almost made her feel she was communicating with a ghost, one made to appear against its will through a forceful séance.

"I cannot tell you that," he said.

The answer rendered into English did not please Ongondo.

"Tell him he will answer that question, or he will have a very unpleasant day."

This sounded a little too familiar, a little too much like interrogations Gold had interpreted in the past.

"You promised no mistreatment."

"I will keep that promise. But we need that information if we can get it."

Gold considered how to pose the question without threatening. She never shied from using her own judgment when it came to choice of words.

"These men want very much to know where Sadiq Kassam is now," Gold said in Arabic. A true statement, certainly, without any venom.

"I am sure they do," Bedoor said.

Now what to do? Gold did not need to maintain neutrality; the United Nations did not pretend terrorists had equal standing with the new governments of North Africa. Once again, time for a judgment call.

"If you answer their questions here, with me, you will fare better than if they take you elsewhere." Another true statement.

Bedoor looked out into the desert again. He stared at the horizon, which brightened as the sun rose higher. He put Gold in mind of a specter again, waiting for the séance's spell to break and let him cross back over to the spirit world.

"Very well. The pasha's headquarters is an abandoned village near the town of Ubari."

"Ubari, Libya?"

"Yes, it is on the Libyan side of the border."

Gold updated Ongondo in English.

"Excellent," he said. "Excellent work, Ms. Gold." He gave a command to one of his troops: "Get me a map."

A soldier hurried from the tent and came back a few minutes later with a chart marked in military grid zones. Numbers and letters marked the zones, with numerical designations for point coordinates.

"Can you read a land navigation chart?" Gold asked in Arabic.

"Some," Bedoor said.

She spread the chart before him. Bedoor hesitated, looked up at the soldiers glaring at him. He pointed to a spot.

"Here," he said. "Your map does not depict the village because it is so small. But it is here."

Gold peered at the place Bedoor had indicated. As he said, the chart did not show a village. Was he lying? Not necessarily. Nomads moved around; villages grew and crumbled. He'd pointed to one of the strangest environments on earth, at the edge of the Ubari Sand Sea. The chart's contour lines appeared as irregular circles. A rolling expanse of dunes, interrupted only by a few saline lakes. Ongondo noted the grid zone, wrote down the coordinates.

"Do you think he's telling the truth?" Ongondo asked.

"Impossible to say," Gold said.

Ongondo folded the chart and glanced at one of his soldiers.

"Take him back to the medical tent," he said. "Let him rest."

At that moment, Bedoor placed his hand into the waistband of his cargo trousers. He fished around for a moment, took out his hand, and placed something in his mouth. Bit down, chewed, swallowed.

"What did he just do?" Ongondo asked.

"He took a pill," a soldier said.

Already suspecting the worst, Gold kneeled beside Bedoor's chair. She put her hand on his good arm and asked in Arabic, "What did you put in your mouth?"

Bedoor shuddered, gathered himself as if it took great effort to speak.

"There is no God but God," he said, "and Mohammed is his prophet."

Bedoor began to take rapid, shallow breaths. He slumped in the chair. His lower lip took on a blue cast.

Gold ran to find Lambrechts. When they returned, Bedoor was lying on the storage shelter's floor. Lambrechts and two medics helped carry him into the med tent. They laid him on an examination table, and Lambrechts pulled open one of his eyes and shone a penlight into it. She ripped open his shirt. Put the eartips of her stethoscope into her ears, listened to his chest. Immediately she tore away the stethoscope by its tube, placed the heel of her right hand on his breastbone and the heel of her left hand over her right. As Lambrechts started chest compressions, one of the medics drew a curtain around the table. Gold and Ongondo waited outside the med tent.

"I thought we searched him thoroughly," Ongondo said.

"It would be easy to miss something as small as one pill in his waistband," Gold said.

In the first several seconds, Gold heard Lambrechts firing off instructions in French, along with the clink of medical instruments—perhaps vials and syringes. Then the med tent grew quiet. A few minutes later Lambrechts came out, her expression clouded, hands in the pockets of her lab coat.

"He's dead," she said. "Cyanide, I think."

CHAPTER 11

At Mitiga International Airport in Tripoli, Parson saw lots of work to do. The Libyan government provided ramp space alongside the main runway, well away from the passenger terminal and civilian gates. But now he needed to put up tents and temporary shelters to house maintenance teams and aircrews, intel briefers and medics, cooks and cops. All the tents and shelters required phone lines and computer cables, sandbags and sand-filled HESCO barriers, electricity and air-conditioning.

An Air Force Red Horse squadron—Rapid Engineer Deployable, Heavy Operational Repair Squadron Engineers—arrived in C-5 and C-17 cargo jets. Parson watched the engineers offload pallet after pallet of equipment needed to set up a forward base. He intended to bed down French Mirages here, along with the Pave Hawk helicopters and HC-130 tankers of an American rescue unit. The Mirages could provide air support for forces on the ground, the Pave Hawks could rescue downed pilots or troops in trouble, and the HC-130s could refuel the choppers in flight.

Vestiges of the airport's days as a military base remained. Old asphalt hardstands for parking fighters dotted the field; Parson found some of them still usable. Others had cracked up and were sinking into the soil. A few of the older buildings hinted of a 1960s air base. Parson couldn't tell which structures were built by Americans, and which had been put up by the Soviets or the Libyans.

Whenever he looked up into the sky at Mitiga, he thought of his father. Dad had been here once for just a few seconds, a few hundred feet off the ground in the right seat of the Aardvark: Target acquired. Weapons away. Target destroyed.

Parson still hated not flying, but he decided this assignment wasn't too bad. Uncle Sam had entrusted him with a chunk of pavement borrowed from the Libyans and told him to turn it into a place to project power and kick some terrorist ass. Quickly.

Thanks to the Red Horse guys, it did happen quickly. By the end of the first week, three long rows of tents sprouted a safe distance from Runway 11/29. A deployable hardshell ops center fronted the tents. As soon as the operations center went up, a comm squadron began installing radios, computers, and antennas.

Parson walked into the ops center, found it stifling. He wiped sweat from his face with the sleeve of his beige flight suit as he considered where to put his desk. He heard an electric motor start outside. The cloth plenums for air-conditioning ducts swelled with airflow, and coolness began flooding the room. A Red Horse master sergeant came into the operations center, tested the air-conditioning by placing his hand in front of a duct.

"Damn, you boys are fast," Parson said.

"Just part of the J-O-B, sir."

Parson chose a corner for his own office, which amounted to a folding table, a folding chair, a laptop computer, and the pens he'd carried with him in his pockets. Bare bones, but enough to get started. He booted up his computer, logged in to his e-mail, and saw that he had 143 new messages. Since yesterday.

"Sometimes I wish I was still a butter-bar lieutenant," he muttered under his breath.

"What's that, sir?" the master sergeant asked as he checked an electrical outlet.

"Nothing."

Most of his e-mails concerned the endless little fires he had to put out to get this operation rolling. One of them confirmed his suspicions about what he'd seen from the drone cameras over Tarhuna: a coalition team sent to the site found it empty. The men he'd watched loading the trucks had cleared out all the chemicals that had been stored there. God only knew where those chemicals were now.

Another of the e-mails came from Gold. It read:

HOPE THINGS SMOOTH ON YOUR END. THOUGHT YOU SHOULD KNOW THE UNHCR CAMP TREATED VICTIMS FROM ANOTHER RAID. MAINLY GUN-SHOT WOUNDS, NO CHEM THAT WE KNOW OF. ALSO WANTED TO GIVE YOU A HEADS-UP THAT I HELPED INTERROGATE AN ENEMY PRISONER OF WAR. EPW NOW DEAD, APPARENT SUICIDE. DON'T KNOW IF HE PROVIDED ACTIONABLE INTEL, AND I CAN'T DISCUSS FURTHER ON NONSECURE E-MAIL. IF IT'S WORTH ANYTHING, YOU'LL HEAR THROUGH CHANNELS.

Well, that was interesting. An EPW who sang, then killed himself? Sophia always seemed to find herself in the thick of things, in or out of uniform. Parson wanted very much to know what the guy said before he died. But she was right: If the intel counted, and if he needed to know, he'd find out soon enough.

Another of Parson's e-mails brought good news. A C-5 coming in tonight would deliver a pair of crash trucks and a team of firefighters. With crash response in place, he could start bringing in aircraft.

The other non-annoying e-mail came from Frenchie. More correctly, Captain Chartier. The e-mail read:

MON COLONEL,

I AM PLEASED TO REPORT I WILL ACCOMPANY MY SQUADRON TO MI-TIGA AS SOON AS WE RECEIVE A SLOT TIME. THANK YOU FOR SETTING UP OUR HOME AWAY FROM HOME. PERHAPS I SHALL TAKE YOU UP IN THE MIRAGE, NO?

MERCI BEAUCOUP,
ALAIN CHARTIER
CAPITAINE, ARMÉE DE L'AIR

A jet ride sounded like a fine idea to Parson. A flight made operational sense, too. The Mirage pilots would need to get familiar with the local area and the approaches to Mitiga before flying combat missions. And since Parson had the responsibility for running the base, a local hop would improve his own situational awareness. But for an American officer to get a ride in a French jet, approval would have to come down from the two-star level. Parson replied to Chartier's e-mail:

I'LL HOLD YOU TO THAT IF IT GETS APPROVED, FRENCHIE. MANY THANKS. GOT PARKING SPOTS WAITING FOR YOU GUYS. HAVE A SAFE FLIGHT OVER THE MED.

MP

Parson spent the rest of the day responding to e-mails, issuing instructions to staff, and checking on schedules for arrival of personnel and equipment. When a C-5 Galaxy arrived that evening, Parson noticed the letters WV painted on the tail. An Air Guard crew, he realized, out of Martinsburg, West Virginia. The mountaineer fliers conducted an engines-running offload. They kneeled the jet, lowering the airframe on the landing gear's jackscrews to place the cargo deck closer to the ground. A loadmaster opened the aircraft's visor, tilting the entire nose up and away from the fuselage. That exposed the cavernous cargo bay, which contained not just two fire trucks but a fuel truck, as well. As Parson watched the crew offload their cargo, he thought of his own days as a C-5 pilot—and a mission from hell that took him more than halfway around the world with an airplane falling apart around him. Even that experience had not spoiled his love for flying, and he hoped to return to the cockpit soon.

Drivers steered the trucks down the Galaxy's forward ramp. The crew closed up the airplane and unkneeled it. After spending less than an hour on the ground, the big jet thundered away into the darkness.

Parson could have spent the night in a hotel in Tripoli. But he decided if tents were good enough for the troops and fliers deploying to North Africa, they were good enough for him. He unrolled a sleeping blanket over a cot in a twenty-man tent occupied by no one else. The tent would fill soon enough, but for this one evening, the solitude under the canvas felt nearly as comfortable as an upscale hotel room.

He took off his boots and placed them in a plastic bag to keep scorpions out. Took his pistol out of its holster and placed it on a metal bookshelf beside his cot. Unzipped his flight suit and hung it on the corner of a locker. In his boxer shorts and Air Force–issue T-shirt, he stretched out on his cot. By the light of a naked bulb, as Saharan winds billowed the tent walls, Parson opened the book Chartier had sent him, *Wind, Sand and Stars*, by Antoine de Saint-Exupéry.

Frenchie had sent the 1939 American edition. Parson noticed the author had dedicated that edition to American pilots and their dead. Good on him for that, Parson thought. Frenchie had explained how Saint-Ex started flying back when planes were made of cloth and pilots were made of steel. The author's life ended far too early, while flying a P-38 Lightning on a recon mission out of Corsica in 1944. The Mediterranean became his grave.

Parson began reading and he immediately related to the tales of fighting through violent weather, navigating across jagged mountains. He'd experienced the same challenges, only in more modern machines. But he never could have described flying in such precise and poetic words. One line in particular caught his attention: "*. . . below the sea of clouds lies eternity.*"

Damn straight it does, Parson thought. He knew too many people who had proved it, beginning with his father.

The book drew him in so deeply that he had a tough time deciding where to stop. But he had plenty of work to do tomorrow, so with reluctance he dog-eared a page, dropped the book to the floor, and turned out his light. The rhythm of flapping canvas put him to sleep almost immediately.

The next morning, the rescue squadrons landed with their Pave Hawk choppers and HC-130 Combat Kings—specially equipped C-130s that could refuel helicopters, conduct searches, and drop pararescuemen. Parson spent much of the day on the flight line, greeting crews and helping their maintenance teams set up shop. The work got him away from his desk and put him in a good mood.

That afternoon, the Mirage 200Ds arrived with Gallic flair. Chartier called in on the ops frequency, and the tower approved a low pass. Eight jets came in two elements of four aircraft. The first element made a pass over the field in close formation. To Parson's aviator's heart, the sight was a thing of beauty, representing the height of engineering talent, mechanical craftsmanship, and piloting skill. One by one, each Mirage peeled off, leveled its wings onto a downwind leg, and dropped the landing gear. Turned base, banked on final approach. Descended the glide path with engine hushed. Settled onto the runway amid puffs of tire smoke, and rolled along in a nose-high attitude for aerodynamic breaking. The second element landed in similar fashion. Newly arrived ramp crews marshaled the French planes into parking, and the pilots and backseat weapons systems officers raised their canopies and shut down their aircraft. Chartier sat in the lead aircraft, French tricolor patch on his left sleeve, oxygen mask disconnected from his helmet. He waved a gloved hand when he saw Parson.

"*Bonjour!*" Chartier shouted. He pulled at fittings inside the front cockpit; Parson figured he was unplugging the interphone and G suit connections. In the rear seat, Chartier's weapons systems officer removed his helmet. Chartier jerked his thumb toward the rear cockpit. "This is Captain Giraud. He is so deadly with the weapons on the Mirage that we call him the Sniper."

"Pleased to meet you, Sniper."

"Good day, sir."

"Sniper scored some good hits back during Operation Harmattan," Chartier said.

Parson had to search his mind for a second, but then he remembered. Back in 2011, when allied forces teamed up to stop Muammar Gadhafi from slaughtering Libyan rebels, the French took part with their Mirages, Rafales, and Super Étendards. Operation Harmattan was named for a West African trade wind. Americans knew the mission better as Operation Odyssey Dawn.

The backseater appeared a few years younger than Chartier. Dark hair, sweaty and matted from the helmet. Each flier's face still bore the imprint of an oxygen mask. The aviators climbed down from their jet and stretched.

"It gets a little cramped in the Mirage," Chartier said. "I will be glad when our masseuse arrives."

Parson laughed. "Yeah, right."

"No," Chartier said. "I am serious."

"The hell you say."

"Our Air Force gives us a masseuse. Hours in a cramped cockpit can lead to orthopedic problems and blood clots in the legs. If her time permits, your American crews can also visit the masseuse."

Parson shook his head. "You boys know how to live; I'll give you that."

"*Vive la France,*" Giraud said.

Parson surprised himself with the way he warmed to his French colleagues. He recalled with embarrassment his attitude when the French opposed the U.S. invasion of Iraq. Freedom fries with my Big Mac, thank you. The failure to find large stocks of chemical weapons in Iraq put a different spin on things. Meanwhile, the froggy bastards had done good work in Afghanistan, and now they were helping in North Africa.

More C-5s, C-130s, and C-17s came in over the next few days. They delivered, among other things, an Air Force Emergency Management team to set up a contamination control area. If fliers came back from a mission with gear and clothing exposed to chemical agents, they could decontaminate at the CCA. The transport aircraft also brought fuel teams, intel officers, maintenance crews, chairs, tables, a complete field kitchen, and a beautiful raven-haired masseuse named Michèle.

"Now we are ready to fly," Chartier proclaimed.

"Veev luh France," Parson said as he watched Michèle descend the steps of a C-5.

"Your accent needs work."

Chartier made good on his promise to take Parson up in the Mirage. When the local-area familiarization flights began, the French approved Parson for a backseat ride. He borrowed Giraud's helmet and G suit, and he climbed into the Mirage's rear cockpit with the eagerness of a new flight student. He had spent his career in the heavies—first as a navigator in the C-130 and then as a pilot in C-5s. During pilot training Parson had flown spin recoveries and aerobatics in the T-6 Texan II, but life in the C-5 consisted mainly of straight-and-level flying, point A to point B. Critical missions, to be sure, but no turns hard enough to gray your vision, no rolls to swap sky and earth.

The French pilot briefed Parson on emergency procedures for problems such as engine failure and rapid decompression. All pretty standard stuff, except Parson wasn't used to flying with an ejection seat. Parson buckled himself in, connected his interphone cord, G suit, and oxygen mask. A radarscope dominated his main panel. Apart from that, the cockpit seemed built in the usual fighter configuration. A center stick for flight controls, throttle on the left side. Up front, Chartier turned on the battery switch, and inverters and avionics fans began to buzz. Annunciator lights illuminated both cockpits, and Chartier's voice crackled in the headphones of Parson's helmet.

"Stand by for engine start."

Parson pressed his talk switch on the side of the throttle and said, "Roger."

Chartier reached to press buttons and flip switches Parson could not see from his seat. But Parson could hear the Snecma M53 engine when it began turning, and the huff when the igniters lit the fuel mixture in the combustion chamber. Annunciator lights winked out as oil and hydraulic pressures climbed.

The whines and hums of an airplane coming to life made Parson feel like a young lieutenant again, newly enamored of the sky and the machines that conquered it. He'd always loved aviation, but for most of the last decade, airplanes had taken him to war. He had transported the wounded, brought home the dead. He had seen blood splashed across instrument panels. But this sortie, he anticipated, would bring only the sheer joy of flight.

Both canopies lowered and closed, and cool air from the air-conditioning and pressurization system began filling the cockpits. Parson pulled on his gloves, kept his hands off the control stick and switches. Chartier called ground control for his flight clearance and permission to taxi, and the Mirage began rolling out of a hardstand where an American F-100 Super Sabre or a Soviet MiG might once have parked. A second Mirage, Chartier's wingman, taxied from the next hardstand.

The canopy offered great visibility. Parson instinctively scanned for other air traffic and saw nothing but an Emirates airliner climbing for departure. When he looked behind him, he noticed the hot exhaust gases shimmering from the Mirage's tailpipe. As the two jets neared the runway's hold-short lines, the tower called. The Libyan controller spoke accented but practiced English.

"Dagger Flight, cleared for takeoff, Runway Two-Niner."

"Cleared for takeoff, Runway Two-Niner," Chartier answered. Then he added on interphone, "Here we go, *mon colonel*. Afterburner takeoff."

Chartier eased the throttle forward and turned onto the runway. He stopped and waited for the second Mirage to taxi into the wing position. Next, Chartier pumped his brakes, held them, and twirled his index finger to signal his wingman to run up engines. Parson's own interlinked throttle moved as Chartier pushed up the power. Chartier gave the engine gauges a quick final scan and looked back toward his wingman.

The man in the front cockpit of the second jet gave a thumbs-up. Chartier moved his head back against the headrest—then moved his head forward to signal the wingman for brake release. The throttle clicked into the afterburner detent. The burner lit off with a roar, and the rapid acceleration pressed Parson back against his seat. In seconds the airspeed indicator scrolled well past one hundred knots. Chartier pulled back on the stick just slightly, and the Mirage knifed into the blue Saharan sky. Just after the aircraft broke ground, Chartier brought up the landing gear.

Ahead, Parson could see downtown Tripoli shrinking to a sand-table miniature of itself as the jet rocketed for the heavens. Across the urban landscape, rusting cranes stood like skeletons over abandoned construction projects. Beyond the city, the Mediterranean glowed a deep azure. Chartier leveled off at seventeen thousand feet above the water, then turned left.

Not the kind of airlifter turn Parson was used to: acknowledge the controller's vector, dial in the heading on the horizontal situation indicator, press a button on the autopilot, sit back and watch it happen. Instead, Chartier slammed into nearly a ninety-degree bank, stood the Mirage on its wingtip. The horizon tilted, and when Parson turned his head to the left he looked straight down at the sea. The second Mirage followed close behind.

"Rock. And. Roll," Parson said.

"Quite a little vixen, is she not?"

"Damn straight."

Chartier leveled the wings and set a course for a designated practice area over the desert. South of Tripoli, the sands flowed beneath the aircraft like a butterscotch ocean. The jet's speed imparted motion to the dunes, transformed them to waves. Parson thought of his fellow aviator Saint-Ex, and he began to understand how a pilot might come to admire the Sahara's terrible beauty. And oh, how Saint-Ex would have admired this airplane. If he'd lived a little longer he might have flown jets, commanded machines that outraced sound.

"We are in the practice area," Chartier announced, "so let's practice." Then he spoke on the radio in French. The pilot of the second Mirage answered, chuckling. Parson could not understand the words, but he still knew what they were talking about. Uh-oh, he thought. They're going to show off.

"All right, Frenchie, bring it," Parson said. "Let's see what you got."

"Here comes a roll," Chartier said.

Sunlight glinted across the canopy as Chartier raised the nose several degrees. Then the horizon rotated, and Parson found himself looking *up* at the expanse of dust. Chartier continued the roll until the Mirage flew straight and level again, right back on its initial heading. Sun and blue sky above, ground below, in their normal positions once more.

"Now you try one," Chartier said.

Parson placed his fingers around the stick, tried to remember how he'd last done this years ago during pilot training at Columbus Air Force Base, Mississippi. The muscle memory had left him; he needed to think his way through: Start with back pressure. Elevators neutral. Full aileron deflection. This delta-winged jet had elevons instead of the standard flight controls, Parson knew, but the pilot inputs would remain the same. He took a breath of oxygen: Here goes nothing.

Again the world turned about the aircraft. Parson glanced at the attitude indicator, watched the horizon tilt. Earth up, sky down. He kept the stick pushed to the right, added a little back pressure. The Mirage's fly-by-wire control system felt as natural as the stick in a Piper Cub. Sky above, now, level it out. Parson completed the maneuver slightly nose-high and about five degrees off heading. A little sloppy, but competent.

"Not bad for a trash-hauler," Chartier said.

Parson laughed. Damned fighter jocks were all alike.

"Hey, Frenchie," Parson said. "How many fighter pilots does it take to change a lightbulb?"

"I have no idea."

"One. The fighter pilot holds the bulb, and the world revolves around him."

"Ah, very funny. Shall we try a loop?"

Oh, hell, Parson thought. This would be harder. All right, he decided. No way I'll let him see me wimp out. A loop inflicted strong G-forces and required more delicate flying than a roll. The jet would trace a giant circle in the air, with flight controls and engine power needing adjustments all the way around.

"Go for it."

Without hesitation Chartier pulled up hard. Parson felt G-forces close in, tripling his weight against the seat. The G suit squeezed his legs to help keep blood from rushing out of his brain. The force of the loop caused Parson's oxygen mask to slip down just a bit on his sweat-slickened face. His vision remained clear, though, and he watched the horizon rock up and over him. Near the top of the loop the G-forces vanished, and he floated weightlessly. Parson looked up at the earth. Then the jet scorched through the vertical and the world returned to its accustomed place beneath the sky. Chartier pulled out of the dive and leveled the Mirage back on its initial altitude as if he'd flown the loop on rails.

"Your turn," Chartier said.

"I was hoping you'd say that."

Parson put his hands on the stick and throttle, thought for a moment. Damn, how did I used to do this? Pull up; judge your attitude by the horizon. Ease off the back pressure past the vertical, go over the top and pull again. Simple, just fly in a circle. Yeah, right.

The earth rolled away as Parson brought the stick back and added thrust. Parson glanced to his left side and saw the horizon go perpendicular to the wings. He relaxed pressure on the stick too early. The Mirage wallowed into the top of the loop, and airspeed began to bleed off. With his hands full of an unfamiliar airplane and the fluids of his inner ear sloshing in strange directions, Parson suffered a touch of vertigo. Disoriented, he failed to notice the drop in speed until he heard the whooping tones of the stall warning system.

Air no longer rushed over the wings fast enough for the jet to fly. Parson shoved the throttle farther, pulled back on the stick to complete the loop. Too late.

The Mirage rolled to the left, broke from controlled flight. Parson felt himself tumbling through space, then it seemed the whole universe began to twist. More beeps and tones sounded, perhaps warning of an engine compressor not getting enough air, an unflyable angle of attack, or an excessive rate of descent. What started as an inverted stall developed into a spin. The desert floor rotated in the windscreen. The altimeter began unwinding as the fighter corkscrewed toward the ground. Parson couldn't believe he'd let an airplane get away from him like that. Before Parson could start the spin recovery, Chartier took over.

"I have the airplane," the Frenchman said. Calm voice of an instructor.

Parson fumbled for the interphone switch. "You have the aircraft," he said. Sweat ran into his eyes. His heart pounded.

Chartier kicked full right rudder, pushed the stick forward, brought the thrust back to flight idle. The earth quit spinning. The

Mirage dived toward the sand. Chartier pulled up, added power. Parson felt the Gs press on him again, then ease off as the jet leveled and flew straight.

"Shit, I thought I was better than that," Parson muttered under his breath. He pressed his talk switch. "Damn, Frenchie. Sorry about that. Rookie mistake."

"No problem, sir," Chartier said. "My fault for throwing a loop at you. You need more time in this vixen before you max-perform her."

Still, Parson continued to curse himself. That's what I get for thinking with testosterone instead of brain cells, he thought. Should have had sense enough to say no thanks. This is a war machine, not a damned toy.

"Would you like to see a split-S?" Chartier asked.

Would I like another hit of crack? "Uh," Parson said, "you fly it. I'll watch."

"*Bon.*"

Chartier flew a few more aerobatic maneuvers, all flawlessly. A natural aviator, Parson judged. Frenchie carried on the heritage of his countrymen who'd made important advances in aviation.

Parson knew the old joke about European heaven and European hell. In heaven, the Brits were the cops, the French were the cooks, and the Germans were the engineers. In hell, the Brits were the cooks, the Germans were the cops, and the French were the engineers.

But in truth the French had improved early aircraft design enough to lend their own words to important parts: aileron, empennage, fuselage. Veev luh France.

On the way back toward Tripoli, Chartier swung out over the Gulf of Sidra, his wingman just behind and to his right. The two jets turned west, and Parson watched the coastline scroll by the left wing. A little past the town of Misrata, a strange sight appeared. A forest of stone columns rose up from the rocky earth. Whatever roofs they once supported had long since crumbled. The half circle of an amphitheater dominated the site, concentric arcs of seats waiting for patrons. Rock walls enclosed an ancient market. A tiled street led to the sea.

"What's that ruin down there?" Parson asked.

"If memory serves," Chartier said, "that is the Roman city of Leptis Magna. The emperor Septimius Severus was born there."

Gold would love this, Parson thought. Not the aerobatics but the aerial history lesson. Too bad this plane doesn't have three seats.

Leptis Magna receded behind the tail, and Chartier began his descent.

Back at Mitiga International, the French pilots flew a couple of instrument approaches, just to get familiar with local procedures. When Chartier came in to land, Parson thought the descent rate felt too steep. Chartier caught it by adding a little thrust. Then he pulled up the nose to flare, settled to the runway with hardly a bump. The jet rolled along on its main wheels, and Chartier kept the nose high for aerodynamic braking until gravity took over. After a few seconds, the nosewheel dropped to the pavement, and the aircraft slowed to walking speed. The second Mirage landed after Chartier turned onto the taxiway.

"Swing low chariot, come down easy," Parson said.

"*Pardon?*"

"Nothing. Old American song. Nice landing."

"*Merci.*"

When Chartier opened the canopies and shut down the Mirage, Parson climbed from the aircraft. He felt chastened after stalling the airplane; the tools of war were serious business, not carnival rides. But he also felt flush with exhilaration, and he hated for the flight to end. He needed to get back to his real work, though. He removed the borrowed helmet, peeled off the G suit, and thanked Frenchie for the ride.

After Parson walked across the tarmac in a sweaty flight suit, the air-conditioned ops center felt like a refrigerator. At his desk, he found the comm people had set up his classified computer for receiving secure e-mail and taskings from AFRICOM.

He had received three classified e-mails. The first of the messages informed him that Marines on a ship in the Med had been placed on alert. Human intelligence, which meant somebody's eyes and ears on the ground, indicated the likely location of an HVT. High-value target. Intel from Gold's interview, perhaps?

The second message, time-stamped an hour later, described an assault on the HVT that would involve members of the 22nd Marine Expeditionary Unit and elements of the French Foreign Legion. The Marines would arrive by helicopter and the Legionnaires would parachute to a location known as Objective Thomas Jefferson—a Libyan village on the edge of the Ubari Sand Sea. Parson didn't know much about Marine Corps doctrine and procedure, but he did know this mission could get ugly. The assault force would fly straight into a fight with an enemy that had demonstrated more than once its ability to use chemical weapons. Presumably the Marines and Legionnaires would at least have the advantage of surprise.

When Parson read the third message, the exhilaration he'd felt since his Mirage ride drained away. Though the local-area familiarization flight had legitimate military purposes, he felt guilty for having enjoyed himself when matters of life and death loomed so close. The e-mail copied him in on a two-word order to the Marines:

EXECUTE TONIGHT.

CHAPTER 12

Aboard the USS *Tarawa*, the order Blount had waited to hear came over the 1 Main Circuit speakers:

"Call away, call away."

The signal for Marines to board helicopters.

Two CH-53 Super Stallions sat ready to launch. Exhaust fumes rolled from their turbines and got snatched away by rotor wash rolling in gales across the flight deck. Dull gray paint coated the helos, and lettering on the sides in only slightly darker shades read MARINES. Refueling probes jutted from the noses of the CH-53s. The flight crews sat at their stations, running last-minute checks, communicating via the boom microphones on their helmets. Beyond the helicopters, the Mediterranean heaved in waves the color of iron. Blount carried his M16 as he led twenty other Marines to the rear of the second aircraft, and they walked up the helo's open ramp. He noticed the crew chief's helmet bore a sticker that read NO FEAR.

Good attitude, Blount thought, but not good advice. If you didn't feel fear, you were stupid and dangerous. But you pushed through that fear like a runner pushes through pain to finish a marathon.

Blount took his place on a seat made of nylon webbing, one up front near the pilots. As stick leader for this flight, he needed access to the cockpit, so he strapped on a gunner's belt. The gunner's belt connected to a tether that would let him move around and still have fall protection. He also needed to hear the pilots' interphone and radio traffic. For that, he took a headset from the crew chief and plugged it into an interphone jack. Blount removed his ballistic helmet, which bore a bracket that held his night vision goggles, and donned the headset.

Weird beeps and tones sounded in the headset. The copilot was running some sort of test, and he didn't seem to like what he saw.

"I'm getting a fail on MWS," he said.

"We need that," the pilot said.

"Lemme try it again."

The copilot flipped through a checklist binder, ran his finger down a page sleeved in clear plastic. With two fingers, he pressed a pair of buttons on the panel in front of him.

Lights on the panel winked and cycled, and most of them flashed off. One of the lights remained illuminated.

"Shit."

"Try turning it off and back on."

"Rog."

The copilot pressed another button, and all the lights on the box he was testing went out. What the heck was MWS, anyway? All the military loved acronyms, but aviators took it to a crazy level. Blount tried to think. MWS? Missile warning system. Yeah, we do need that.

When the copilot powered up the system again, he pressed the test buttons once more. The beeps and flashes started anew, and this time the man looked satisfied.

"Good check."

"Cool beans."

Blount turned his attention to settling into his seat, if his equipment would allow. He wore a full charcoal-impregnated MOPP suit. Over the MOPP suit, he'd donned a Kevlar vest. His bayonet and IFAK—Individual First-Aid Kit—dangled from the left side of the vest. The IFAK contained the usual combat gauze and pressure bandages, plus a few additional things Blount liked to add. A gas mask carrier hung at his hip. Other pouches contained ammunition for his

M16, pen gun flares, nerve gas antidote, a radio, butyl gloves, and M8 test paper for detecting the presence of chemical agents.

A Velcro strap secured the sheath of his grandfather's KA-BAR. On top of everything else, the odd lumps of an inflatable life preserver bulged in uncomfortable places. If the chopper ditched at sea, he could pull tabs to fire CO_2 cartridges that would inflate the life preserver's cells.

Over the troop seats, Blount noticed a placard that made him smile. The placard read WARNING—DO NOT STOW FEET OR EQUIPMENT UNDER SEAT. No problem. He carried everything on his back and shoulders, more than sixty pounds worth of gear. He kept his feet right in front of him, a dog tag laced into the left boot. An aircraft crash or IED explosion might blow dog tags from around your neck and make identification that much harder. But boots tended to stay intact—even if nothing remained of their owner but the feet inside.

The pilots called the ship's Primary Flight Control for their take-off clearance.

"Musket flight cleared for takeoff," came the answer.

The Super Stallion swayed into the air. Blount felt a rolling motion as the gusting Mediterranean wind rocked the helicopter. The Marines around him began a war chant that sounded more like barks than words—devil dogs primed for a fight. *"Oo-rah, oo-rah, oo-rah!"*

Corporal Fender gave a thumbs-up. The kid looked a little nervous, but he kept pursing his lips and looking around at his buddies. Blount took that as a good sign: Resolute. Feeling trust in the others and from the others.

Blount wondered what Bernadette, Ruthie, and Priscilla were up to at this moment. Maybe having lunch; it was the middle of the day back home. For just an instant, the scent of Bernadette's lavender shampoo came back to him as if she were right there. That memory would have to do; he carried no pictures of his family, no memento like a scarf from his wife.

He had two reasons for that. One: If he were captured, God forbid, he wanted his enemy to know nothing about Bernadette and the girls. Two: Unlike a lot of servicemen, he'd never pocketed a challenge coin, a rabbit's foot, or any other good-luck charm during missions. He'd made it through his first deployment years ago without any sort of talisman, and after that he hadn't wanted to change anything. He admitted to himself he'd become superstitious about not being superstitious.

Though he didn't believe in trinkets, he did believe in prayer. Please let me get back home to them, he thought. And in the meantime, please help me do right.

The Super Stallion climbed and turned onto a southerly heading. Out the cockpit windows, Blount could see where sun, sea, and sky met at the horizon. Ragged clouds scudded along, growing pink with the dying day. Only a thin rind of sunfire remained above the water, and even that shrank by the second. Mission planners had timed this flight to arrive at the objective just at EENT—the end of evening nautical twilight. In other words, full dark.

On course and on speed, the helo hummed along, fairly pulsing with power. At this moment, the machine and the men inside it seemed invincible, but Blount knew how quickly fortunes could change in combat. Waves flashed by below, dark and undulating. The Marines grew quiet now. The Stallion flew with all exterior and most interior lights off, so the gloom deepened inside the aircraft as night closed in. The dull-green glow of NVG-compatible instrument lighting emanated from the cockpit. On the radio, Blount heard the lead helo check in with an Air Force AWACS bird orbiting overhead.

"Monticello, Musket flight is off the deck and en route."

"Roger that, Musket. Safe flight."

Blount considered what advice or encouragement he could offer to the men around him. All of them knew what they were doing, and he didn't want to patronize. So he kept his words simple and specific to the mission.

"Double-check your antidote kits," Blount shouted over the helicopter's roar. "Make sure they're in your left cargo pocket, so your buddy knows where to find them. Don't use your own on somebody else."

Standard procedure. If you feel symptoms, the Marines had been taught, pop yourself with your own injectors. If you see somebody doing the funky chicken, as the instructors put it, they're too far gone to treat themselves, so you'll have to treat them. With *their* kits, not yours. You might be next.

Marines patted their pockets, shouted, "Aye, Gunny!"

Looking out the windows, in the last visibility of twilight, Blount discerned a line across the sea. Beyond it the light played differently, as if the water stopped at a giant sheet of cardboard. Across the cardboard, scattered lamps twinkled.

The North African coast.

"We're about to go feet dry," the pilot said. "You can come out of your LPUs in thirty seconds."

Blount repeated the order, shouting over the engines and wind noise. The men waited a few moments, then began unhooking the clasps of their life preserver units. The crew chief collected the LPUs and placed them in a stowage bag. No sense carrying a piece of gear you didn't need anymore. With the LPU gone, Blount had better access to another piece of equipment clipped to his vest, an infrared chemical light. The chemlight consisted of a plastic cylinder with an inner vial that separated two chemicals. When you bent the flexible plastic, the vial would break, and the chemicals would mix to emit a glow—but not one in the visible light spectrum. The chemlight would appear only to someone wearing night vision goggles and would help distinguish friend from foe.

Mentally, Blount reviewed the op plan. The helicopters would land just outside the village, and the Marines would conduct a small-scale movement to contact. A platoon of French Foreign Legionnaires would arrive by parachute to provide a ring of security around the village.

Fire discipline was critical. Classic doctrine said you used a movement to contact when the tactical situation was vague. That sure held true tonight, Blount realized, since no one knew how many civilians remained in the village and what their loyalties might be. Yet again, he faced an enemy that hid behind the innocent.

Blount thought of something he'd read in high school. His language arts teacher had assigned a story about some dude who took a tour of hell. The guy went through all these different circles of hell, and as he went deeper, the sins of the damned got worse and worse. At the very bottom, there was old Judas himself, forever getting eaten by Satan for betraying Jesus.

Though young Blount had always thought of literature as something you had to put up with to get to play football, that story got his attention. It was sure more interesting than books about white English ladies worried about who they were going to marry. But now, aboard a Super Stallion bound for a target, Blount thought the writer got it a little bit wrong. Yeah, Judas belonged where he was. But right beside him ought to be anybody who ever used civilians as shields. On God's green earth and whatever world lay beyond, there couldn't be nothing lower than that.

He thought of the child suicide bombers he'd been forced to shoot in Afghanistan. Blount wished a surgeon could just cut that memory out of his brain. The only comfort came in knowing he'd sent to hell the terrorist responsible for all that—on the blade of Grandpa's knife.

Over land now, Blount tried to follow the pilots' navigation to maintain his own situational awareness. He dug his land nav map from a leg pocket and clicked on the green beam of a penlight. The topographical depiction differed from the aeronautical charts used by the pilots, and he had trouble orienting himself.

"Where exactly are we now, sirs?" Blount asked.

"I'll mark it for you, Gunny," the copilot said.

The copilot borrowed the land map, took a pencil from the sleeve of his flight suit. On Blount's map, the flier drew a tiny circle amid a brown expanse. Then the copilot pointed to numbers on a screen.

"This is distance to go," the copilot said. "This one is time remaining."

Forty minutes.

Blount looked aft, considered the young faces with set jaws, determined eyes. Each man held his weapon between his knees with the muzzle down. That way, an accidental discharge wouldn't pierce an engine or rotor blade. In less than an hour these men would face combat, some for the first time. Blount hoped for a quick, surgical strike with no Marine casualties, but he knew some of these guys might not see another sunrise. He vowed he'd do everything possible to bring them back safe. He felt grateful to fly in as stick leader; he could see this thing done right.

The helicopter droned for another fifteen minutes, and Blount heard chatter on the radio.

"All stations," an accented voice called, "Mother Goose is at the baker's."

Blount consulted his comm card, a laminated sheet with call signs and frequencies on one side, classified brevity codes on the other. Mother Goose was the airlifter carrying the French paratroopers. "At the baker's" meant the plane was at the initial point for the run-in to the drop zone.

"Twenty-five minutes," Blount shouted to the Marines. "The Legionnaires are on time."

He half expected some wise-ass comments about the French, but somewhere over the black desert, the men had left joking behind. A minute or so later, the same voice spoke over the aircraft radio again.

"All stations, Mother Goose bought a loaf of rye."

Silliest brevity codes Blount ever heard, but they worked. Jumpers away.

The parachutists needed to hit the ground before the choppers arrived. For obvious reasons, troopers couldn't float down in parachutes with helicopter blades spinning somewhere in the dark beneath them. The military had a word for avoiding such calamities: deconfliction. So far, so good, Blount thought. We're deconflicted and on time.

At this moment, he knew, the Legionnaires were free-falling in a high altitude/low opening jump. The plane that carried them flew so high the bad guys would never hear it. The troopers would land silently and wait, get eyes on the target.

Blount watched the numbers count down on the cockpit screens. Anticipation and fear rose inside him, the fear harnessed and transformed into focus. Take something bad and make it work for you, he thought, the way a poison in small doses can become a medicine.

Another accented voice came on the radio, weak but readable, speaking almost in a whisper. A man on the ground.

"All stations, soft rain on the millpond."

More brevity codes. Safe HALO jump, nothing to report on the status of the village.

Ten minutes to go. Blount called out the time remaining, and added, "Charge your weapons. Bust your chemlights. Turn on your radios and NVGs."

On his M16, Blount pulled the charging handle to chamber a round—*shack!* Shacking reverberated through the aircraft as other Marines did the same. He switched on his PRC-148 and cracked the chemlight hanging from his body armor. On his helmet, which he still held in his lap, he switched on the night vision goggles. But he decided to keep the headset on until just before the CH-53 touched down.

A few minutes later, he lifted his helmet in front of his face at an angle to peer through the NVGs. He looked at the men behind him to see if the infrared chemlights worked as advertised. Sure enough, on each Marine, a cylinder of illumination glowed like redemption. In addition, everyone wore squares of glint tape on their helmets and shoulders to help identify them as friendlies. Viewed through the goggles, the glint tape sparkled like quartz under a black light. The Marines appeared transfigured, transformed, and purified for some mystical journey.

But when Blount lowered his NVGs, the back of the helicopter went dark as a crypt. He raised them, took another look at his men, lowered them again.

If a modern artist wanted to render a twenty-first-century ride to the underworld, Blount thought, this scene would do just fine. Lord knows we are bound for a dark, dark place.

"Five minutes," the copilot said.

Blount repeated the time hack. "Five minutes," he shouted. "Look alive, boys. Welcome to the shores of Tripoli."

"Oo-rah, Gunny!"

A couple minutes later he heard a call from the lead aircraft.

"Musket One-One has target in sight."

"Musket One-Two has negative contact," the pilot of Blount's helo answered.

Both Musket One-Two pilots, scanning with NVGs, looked through all quadrants of their windscreen. With the naked eye, Blount saw nothing out there but night.

"I got it," the copilot said finally, pointing.

"All right. I see it," the pilot answered on interphone. Then he pressed the transmit button on his cyclic and said, "Two has a tally."

Blount took off his headset, donned his helmet, and looked out through his NVGs. Weird sight. From an altitude of a few hundred feet, he could make out irregular shapes, the angles and polygons of a village in the night desert. But he saw not one speck of cultural lighting. Even during the small hours in the remotest hamlets, you'd normally catch the glow of one or two electric lights or at least an oil lamp. NVGs could even pick up the reflection of banked embers from a cooking fire. However, everything that burned or shone in that village had been extinguished.

Had the place been abandoned? Had the intel been bad?

Blount didn't get a chance to ponder his questions. Without warning, the hamlet below erupted with gunfire.

Tracers slashed the night. A stream of bullets arced up from the village, cut parabolas toward the other helicopter out in front. The helo banked to evade the rounds. On the desert floor, a light source bloomed so bright it nearly washed out Blount's NVGs.

The ignition signature of a shoulder-fired missile.

A dart of light shot upward from the pool of glow on the ground. The heat-seeker corkscrewed toward the lead chopper. The aircraft's defensive systems reacted faster than a human hand could push a button. Flares, hotter than the CH-53's turbines, spewed from the helicopter. Burning magnesium set the night afire.

The missile flew wild, confused by multiple hot things all around it. Musket One-One banked, turned, punched more flares.

When the tracers erupted again, they lasered toward Blount's aircraft. The pilot yanked the chopper hard right, danced away from the bullets. Blount could do nothing but hold on.

"Two taking fire," the copilot called.

On the ground, light spilled from another missile launch. Something bright came up, a spiral of smoke behind it. The object seemed to hang in space, with no relative motion to the aircraft.

That meant a collision course.

Blount expected to see flares spawn from his helicopter. Nothing.

"Punch 'em," the pilot ordered as he whipped the cyclic for another turn.

Maybe somebody squeezed the trigger for a manual flare launch. But Blount did not feel the soft thumps of igniting flares. Instead came the crack of something striking the side of the helicopter.

And the boom of detonation.

CHAPTER 13

The night seemed to rotate around the helicopter. Earth and sky in night vision green twirled as if creating a vortex to pull Blount and his Marines out of this world and into some shade dimension. Men groped for handholds, shouted curses.

The CH-53 spun wildly. In the cockpit, tones blared, warning lights flashed: *Low pressure. High temperature. Low voltage. Fire.*

Smoke, sharp with the odor of burned oil, filled the cabin. Somebody shouted, "Brace!"

The chopper struck the ground so hard Blount's NVGs tore from his helmet. Now he knew only darkness and collision, as if the aircraft were a torpedoed submarine sinking to crush depth. The helo impacted as it swung in a circle, and the torque threw him from his seat.

The tether on his gunner's belt was meant to stop someone from falling from the chopper—not to restrain more than three hundred pounds of muscle, bone, gear, and body armor converted into a flying object. The tether parted, and Blount felt himself hurled into space.

Disorientation, darkness, and concussion distorted his perceptions. He sensed that something dropped him a great distance, threw him down a mineshaft. Motion and violence defined his existence. Things struck him—perhaps other men, perhaps aircraft debris or body parts. Blount wondered for an instant whether he was already dead, swept up with the damned and cast into Hades.

He landed on his back.

His entire skeleton rattled with the shock of impact. The pain seemed too specific, too purely orthopedic, for the eternal suffering of the lost. Still alive, then. His mind began to form linear thoughts again, to sense the events around him. Men screamed. Gunfire chattered. Metal burned. Dear Lord in heaven, he thought, we just got shot down.

Blount rolled onto his side, felt the fine sand of the Sahara underneath him. Somehow the force of the crash had thrown him out of the helo, but he could not remember the crew opening the ramp. He hurt everywhere, but everything seemed to work. Time to get back in the fight. Where was his rifle? He sat up, reached for his NVGs, remembered they'd disappeared, too. He had planned to rely on chemlights and glint tape to tell bad guys from Marines, but the loss of NVGs robbed him of that.

His mind registered two priorities: find a weapon, and take cover. Everything else flowed as unprocessed background noise. He scrabbled to his feet, stumbled toward the biggest chunk of helicopter wreckage.

Something tripped him. In the darkness he realized it was a body. Alive or dead he could not tell. But he kicked a rifle as he staggered along. He groped for the M16, smacked the forward assist with the heel of his hand to make sure the weapon was locked. The injured needed attention, for sure. He hoped to God the Navy hospital corpsman had survived, and Blount planned to help him as soon as he could. But in combat, the first step in first aid was to kill the enemy.

The injured were already calling for help:

"Corpsman up!"

"Doc? Where's the doc?"

"Doc up!"

Blount crouched behind a tangle of aluminum. Next to him, a plate of steel rose from the ground like an obelisk. A rotor blade, stuck in the sand. Above him in the night, the other helicopter thudded overhead.

The village lay only a couple hundred yards away. Cloaked figures sprinted among the houses. The enemy wore what looked like shemaghs or balaclavas over their heads, but the darkness made it hard to tell. Blount flicked his fire selector to BURST and watched for a good target.

A boom sounded from between two of the buildings, accompanied by a spray of sparks. A glowing dot coursed toward the downed helicopter. Some sort of grenade, fired through a launcher? Blount squeezed his trigger, loosed three rounds at the shooter.

A second boom echoed when the grenade—or whatever it was—exploded. Blount expected to feel the sting of shrapnel. No stings came.

He smelled an odd odor. Almost like something you'd smell in a hospital. Camphor, perhaps.

Oh, sweet Jesus, Blount thought. Help us now.

"Gas, gas, gas!" he shouted.

Blount dropped the M16. Held his breath, squeezed his eyes shut. Threw off his helmet. Tore open the Velcro enclosure of his gas mask carrier.

With the mask in his right hand, he dug his chin into the mask's chin cup and pressed the whole assembly tight against his face. Blount had been taught to don a gas mask in nine seconds or less. Now, nine seconds seemed far too long.

Still holding his breath, he pulled the mask's harness over the back of his head. Yanked at the neck straps to cinch it all down. He cleared the mask by placing his hand over the outlet valve and exhaling. The edges of the facepiece fluttered with the escaping air.

Next, he covered the filter canister's inlet port and inhaled. The facepiece collapsed against his cheeks. Good seal.

Quick. But not quick enough.

A sickness came over Blount like he had never known. His mouth filled with saliva. He could not remove the mask to spit, so he swallowed hard. His chest tightened as if a chain had looped around him.

Off to his left, a red pen gun flare spat upward. As Blount's body betrayed him, his mind struggled. What did that red flare mean? He should know.

Emergency extraction.

One of the squad leaders must have assumed Blount was dead and fired the signal to abort the mission.

More spit, foam, and vomit forced its way into Blount's mouth. He could not let himself throw up into his mask, so he forced himself to swallow. Some of the vomit escaped his lips anyway and began to gurgle in the mask's inlet valves. So this was what it felt like to get poisoned to death, how those people had died in Gibraltar and Sig. How Blount's old friend Kelley had suffered in his last moments.

He sank to his knees, felt his bladder let go. The warm liquid ran down his thighs.

Ain't nobody can help me now, Blount realized. Even if they see me, they're probably poisoned, too. Time the other helicopter touches down, I'll have crossed over to Beulah Land.

He groped for his auto-injectors.

Blount carried four of them. Three were the newer ATNAA injectors that contained doses of atropine and pralidoxime chloride in one syringe. The fourth contained diazepam as an anticonvulsant. His trembling fingers found one of the ATNAAs. Blount hoped he'd keep enough control of his central nervous system to get this done. In the stress of combat, some folks had trouble even with gross motor skills like slapping a bolt release with the heel of your hand. But self-treatment with hypodermics required *fine* motor skills, working with your fingertips.

Blount felt for the injector's safety cap. Which end was the cap and which was the needle? Working blind, straining to focus despite nausea and panic, he fumbled with the injector. He knocked off the safety cap, then dropped the whole thing. Lord in heaven. He swept his hands through the sand around him. His fingers closed around a cylindrical object. Blount grabbed the ATNAA by what he thought was the safety end, cap now gone.

Wrong end. The pressure-activated spring punched the needle through his glove. Through his palm, and between his metacarpal bones. All the way through his hand. The antidote squirted uselessly into the air.

Blount let out a growl of pain, frustration, and anger at himself. The foul liquid sloshing inside his gas mask entered his mouth. He coughed and spat. Jerked the needle out of his hand and threw it to the ground.

He tore off his gloves. That put him at risk of absorbing chemical agents through his skin. But he already had enough of that mess inside him to make him deathly sick, and the poison would kill him if he couldn't get medicine into his bloodstream. He had only two tries left. As stick leader and team chief, he needed to get himself straightened out and functioning.

Tracers flashed around him. Some incoming, some outgoing. He dug into his pocket for another injector.

Sweat slicked his fingers, ran down his back. Breathing came harder, like somebody was twisting and tightening that chain around his ribs. How long before he couldn't breathe at all?

Blount clutched a fresh ATNAA. He'd just learned the hard way that the needle end was a little more narrow than the safety end. He ran his middle finger along the barrel of the injector, found the safety cap. Pulled off the cap. Jammed the other end against his left thigh.

The hypodermic slammed home. Felt more like a knife than a needle. The cords of Blount's leg muscles clamped around the cold stainless steel and heightened the pain. The antidote coursed into his flesh like liquid fire.

Every instinct screamed for him to pull that thing out and make it stop hurting. But he held the needle for a ten-count. Then he withdrew the injector, dropped it to the desert floor. Procedure called for him to pin the spent ATNAA to his clothing, but he didn't have time to fool with that now. Blount jammed his hand into his pocket for the last ATNAA.

He didn't feel any better yet. Bile rose in his throat. He swallowed hard. Least I got something to do while I'm dying, he thought. He found the injector and popped off the cap. Pressed the business end to his left thigh.

This time hurt even worse. Pain blazed the length of his entire leg. Blount found the discipline to leave the needle in for ten seconds only by taking his hand completely off the injector. He let the needle hang embedded in his thigh for what felt like ten seconds—he forgot to count—then yanked it out and dropped it.

Then he realized he had another problem. Every breath came with more effort. Blount suspected the difficulty had more to do with the mask than with his lungs. Though he'd tried to swallow the vomit and spit, the fluid clogged the mask. He tried to pull in another drag of air. Got nothing in his nostrils but his own bodily fluids. He coughed hard, and that cost him the last of the air remaining in his lungs.

With the mask off, he'd likely die of chemical poisoning. With the mask on, he would surely suffocate.

Blount tore the mask from his face. Vomit splashed onto his head and neck. He shut his eyes tight and held his breath until his lungs shrieked for air. Maybe if he could delay breathing for just a few seconds the poison around him would dissipate more. He remembered an instructor's credo in water survival: *Breathing is a luxury.*

Not anymore.

He opened his mouth, took in a breath, deep and ragged. That started a spasm of coughing, but at least if he was coughing, he was getting air. He didn't smell any chemicals now, but with his nervous system in this state he didn't trust any of his senses. Oh, God, did he feel sick. More fluid forced its way up from his stomach and into his mouth. He spat out the vomit. Groped for the anticonvulsant injector.

The CANA injector—Convulsant Antidote for Nerve Agent—flared wider near the safety end than the ATNAAs, so it felt different in Blount's hand. But it worked the same way. He removed the cap and touched the CANA to the back of his thigh.

Blount cried out, shouted words he never wanted people to hear him say. He'd always thought he possessed high pain tolerance, but this poison and these stabbing needles were breaking down his self-control. He didn't like that at all. You had to master your own self all the time, he believed. Sick was no excuse.

He counted to ten out loud. Removed the needle and threw the injector as far as he could. Found his rifle on the ground. Picked it up and shook it, muzzle down, to clear any sand that might have entered the bore.

The M16 seemed so heavy. He felt so weak, and Blount never felt weak. The night grew brittle around him, as if he would need to crack through a barrier to move forward. Was that the poison talking? Or the medicine? And why wasn't the medicine working any better? He tried to shoulder the rifle, make somebody pay for doing this to him and his Marines.

But he couldn't make the weapon do what he wanted. The signals between his brain and his hands got all gummed up, like a computer about to crash. The fingers of his right hand spasmed, hit the trigger. Loosed three rounds up into the darkness. Not aimed fire but an accidental discharge.

Lord. Blount had never, ever let a weapon go off by accident. And he'd have given the devil's own wrath to any eight-ball private who did.

His vision went grainy. A few hundred yards to his right, the other helicopter settled toward the ground. Dim figures ran toward him from several directions. Friends or foes? Hard to say. Some of them were shooting. Were they shooting at the helicopter? The poison that made him so sick also made it hard to think. The men coming at him must be Marines. He'd let them help him into the chopper. In a minute he'd feel better and then he could do something useful.

He tried to move to the men running toward him. But his feet and knees would not take orders from his head. Blount swayed, fell down hard. He let go of the rifle so he wouldn't shoot his friends. Tried to sit up but could not.

Four men reached him. He raised his arm, expected an extended hand to bring him to his feet.

Instead he got a kick in the side.

"What the . . ." Blount said.

He saw that the men wore gas masks. Different model.

A boot slammed him in the head. The men grabbed at his arms and legs. He started to bring up the rifle but another boot kicked the weapon away. He clenched his fists, tried to swing. No use; he could generate no force. One of the men began to shout orders to the others.

The gas mask muffled the words. But in Blount's last moment of consciousness, he recognized the language. Arabic.

CHAPTER 14

arson realized something was wrong as soon as the STU phones lit up. The ringing of one secure telephone unit might mean routine communication. But when all three secure lines rang nearly at once, as computers pinged with flash traffic and the VHF and UHF radios buzzed, you knew you had a problem. The noise level in the ops center rose. Two duty officers, both of them captains, answered the first two calls; each held a receiver to one ear while using a fingertip to close the opposite ear. Parson did the same when he grabbed the third call.

"Kingfish ops," he said. "Colonel Parson."

"Sir, this is Captain Adam Privett. I'm in the TACLOG of the USS *Tarawa*. We just lost a helicopter at Objective Thomas Jefferson."

Parson scanned a room full of junior officers and NCOs. The worst had happened, the Marines needed help, and the lives of a lot of good men might depend on what happened in this operations center in the next few minutes.

"I got pararescue on Alpha Alert," Parson said.

"We'll take whatever you got, sir."

"Gimme your nine-line."

Parson slid a pen from the sleeve of his flight suit. Flipped open a writing pad to take notes on the nine standard elements of information for a rescue. He already knew the coordinates of the site, as well as the frequencies and call signs of the aircraft involved. But when Privett came to line four, Parson knew this was no ordinary rescue. As the Marine officer spoke, Parson jotted on his pad:

4) Special equip—MOPP gear

5) Number patients—unknown

6) Site security—unknown

The worst news came at line nine, for nuclear-biological-chemical contamination.

9) Chemical contamination confirmed

Parson had never faced anything quite like this: ordering crews into a mission so bad that rockets and bullets were the least of their problems. Suit up, boys; you're flying into a cloud of poison. He had no time to agonize over it. He cradled the phone on his shoulder and called out to one of his captains.

"Tell Pedro they're alerted," Parson said. "I want 'em in here in two minutes."

"Yes, sir."

Within ninety seconds, two Pave Hawk rescue helicopter crews— call signs Pedro One-One and Pedro One-Two—showed up for a quick mission brief. Four pilots, six pararescuemen, two flight engineers, and two aerial gunners awaited orders. The pararescuemen— also known as PJs—lugged medical rucks and wore kneepads over the legs of their flight suits. All the crew members carried M4 carbines, the weapons' rails bristling with optics, flashlights, and forward hand grips. The men also carried M9 pistols in thigh holsters.

Everyone seemed alert but not tense. One crewman had a tin of Skoal stuffed behind a pair of medical shears on his tactical vest. None of them sat down. They crowded around Parson to listen for instructions, arms folded across pouches bulging with spare magazines and handheld radios.

"Guys, you gotta go in MOPP Four," Parson said. "Alarm Black at the crash site."

"We're ready to suit up, sir," one of the pilots said.

Like all his crewmates, the pilot looked to be in his late twenties. He wore a black patch on his sleeve that read PEDRO 66. Parson recognized that call sign; the flier wore the patch in honor of five members of a rescue crew killed in a 2010 crash in Afghanistan.

"Two Marine CH-53s assaulted the objective," Parson went on. "Musket One-One and Musket One-Two. Musket One-Two got shot down. One picked up all the survivors they could carry. They had to abort the mission, and they did confirm the presence of chemical weapons."

"Enemy personnel still at the site?" another pilot asked.

"Unknown," Parson said.

Parson printed out a weather sheet for the pilots while the enlisted crew members ran to their aircraft. Setting up to fly with chem gear would delay takeoff for a few minutes, but that couldn't be helped. At least the weather cooperated, sort of. No cloud ceiling, visibility four miles in dust. Not ideal, but the Pave Hawks could look for survivors with infrared imaging as well as night vision goggles. A man on the desert floor—at least a living man—would appear as a warm object contrasted against a cooler background. Much of the night remained, so the crews still had the advantage of operating in darkness.

The pilots jogged across the ramp to their waiting Pave Hawks. Parson stayed close to his computer, radios, and secure phones, but he stepped outside for a moment to see the helicopters take off. The ramp's floodlights gave off a glow softened by the dust in the air. A few of the brightest stars burned through, and in the haze, they glittered with the uncharacteristic colors of amethyst and garnet. The evening seemed almost pleasant, as if nature itself beckoned crews into the night, only to suck them into a toxic trap.

The Pave Hawk fliers had already suited up with helmets, gloves, and masks. The hoses of their chem gear snaked from the masks to electric blowers that supplied the men with scrubbed air to breathe. They closed their doors, manned their guns, and taxied across the tarmac, rotors kicking up grit, strobe lights flashing underneath the tail booms. At the departure end of the runway, the Pave Hawks levitated into the darkness.

As soon as Parson got back to his desk, a call came over the UHF radio. He recognized the call sign of the AWACS plane monitoring the battle space and coordinating all the air assets.

"Kingfish, Kingfish," the voice said. "This is Monticello."

A master sergeant on Parson's staff lifted the hand mike of the Thales radio. Thumbed the transmit button and said, "Monticello, Kingfish. Go ahead." The sergeant was talking to an AIO, an airborne intelligence officer aboard Monticello. The secure-voice radio lent a warbling sound to the AIO's words as the system decrypted the signal.

"Kingfish, be advised the Marines report four missing. The French Foreign Legion reports two paratroopers missing. Names to follow."

Six missing? Parson wondered what the hell was going on out there. He slid his notepad closer, took out his pen.

"Kingfish ready to copy," the sergeant said.

Parson wrote down the names as the AIO spoke.

"Missing personnel are as follows: Legionnaire First Class Ivan Turgenev, Adjutant José Escarra, Corporal Tony Fender, Corporal Mark Grayson, Sergeant Daniel Farmer, Gunnery Sergeant A. E. Blount."

Parson stopped writing after scribbling *Farmer*. Had he heard that last name right?

Please don't let it be him, Parson thought. No, that's not the right attitude, he told himself. No matter who it is, he's somebody's son or father. But please don't let it be Blount. The big Marine with the big heart had gone through enough already. Parson had seen Blount's great compassion for Afghan orphans. He'd also witnessed Blount's wrath unleashed on a terrorist in Afghanistan—one of the most frightening things Parson had ever beheld. He remembered thinking it was a damn good thing that kind of strength got tempered by Marine Corps discipline and a strong moral compass.

"Ask him that last name again," Parson said.

The sergeant relayed the question.

"Gunnery Sergeant A. E. Blount," came the answer.

Parson held his pen over the page, as if not writing it down would stop it from coming true. He knew Blount had a family, and he thought he'd even heard something about Blount getting out of the military. Why did this have to happen now?

He closed his eyes for a second, wrote down the name.

CHAPTER 15

Blount was riding.

His mind, passing in and out of consciousness, registered that he was rolling along, lying on the ridged bed of a pickup truck. He knew little else with certainty. In a muddled state of awareness, he could not distinguish between reality, dream, and memory. The metal furrows of the truck bed made it hard to find a comfortable position, but in his fatigue he did not care.

The ride felt familiar, and he thought he recognized his situation. Exhausted from pulling ground leaves, he had fallen asleep in the back of his grandfather's truck on the way from the tobacco field. They'd get back to the house in a few minutes. He'd need to use Gojo to scrub the tobacco gum from his hands, because Grandpa wouldn't let him sit at the supper table until he'd washed up. The gritty pumice of the hand cleaner would grind off the black gum, but only time would remove the stains. If he was this tired, he must have earned his meal of hoecakes, butter beans, stewed tomatoes, string beans, and peach pie.

He started to raise up to see if Digger was in the truck with him. Why was it dark out?

A boot slammed him in the chest and knocked him back down onto the truck bed.

Voices shouted in Arabic. Through his squinted eyes Blount made out indistinct figures leaning over him in the night, spitting and yelling. He felt so weak. Not from work but from sickness. His weapon was gone. But maybe he had enough strength . . .

He let instinct and muscle memory take over. Glow from inside the cab gave him enough light to see. When the nearest enemy leaned a little too close, Blount sprang to a sitting position. He grabbed the man by the shirt, yanked him down. The man twisted as he fell and landed with his back against Blount's chest. Blount slid his right arm under the man's chin, encircling the neck. To create a choke hold, Blount grabbed his own left bicep with his right hand. Great ropes of muscle now locked the terrorist's throat. Blount leaned forward, squeezed hard. Let out a long growl as he clamped down, his arms functioning as a vise. The death embrace seemed almost intimate. The odor of the man's sweat filled Blount's nostrils. Up close, Blount noticed acne underneath the man's beard, the rat-like tilt of his nose.

The man began to gurgle and kick, as blood no longer flowed to his brain and air no longer reached his lungs. And if Blount could get the angle right, maybe he could send this son of a bitch to hell a little faster by breaking his neck.

"You wanna be a martyr, Rat Face?" Blount hissed. Clamped tighter.

The butt of an AK-47 smacked the side of Blount's head. A foot stomped his leg. Still he held on to his prey, squeezing the life out of it. The man gurgled louder. His tongue lolled from his mouth. His eyes bulged.

"I ain't playing," Blount growled. "You going over the river with me."

The rifle butt struck Blount again and again. He felt his jaw crack.

He also felt his prey start to go limp. When you get where you're going, boy, you tell Satan to kiss my ass.

So tired. So very tired. God, that AK stock hurt when it hit.

Blount let go.

The terrorist scrambled away from Blount, buried himself in the far corner of the truck bed. Placed his hands around his neck, coughed and jabbered in Arabic. Blount savored his victim's look of fear for just a moment.

You and me ain't finished, Blount thought.

Another boot kicked him in the chest.

A wave of nausea hit him. Bile came up in his throat, probably the last fluid in his stomach. He rolled onto his side and vomited. He heard distant laughter, though it came from only feet away. His fingers found a sticky substance. Blood and spit. He rolled onto his back.

Only then did he realize other men lay in the back of the truck. Two remained motionless, and two jerked their legs in a spasmodic pattern. Dying from nerve gas, maybe.

In the starlight, Blount could make out a plume of dust rising from behind the vehicle. More dust swirled beside the pickup, and Blount realized he was riding in one of at least two trucks speeding across the desert. Why hadn't they just killed him? And where were they taking him?

Please, Jesus, just give me my strength back, Blount thought.

He clenched his fists, waited for another opening. Normally he could deliver a hammerfist hard enough to break bones. But now he felt so weak. Weak as a cat, like the old folks used to say. But at least a cat could leap from this pickup and outrun everybody. Blount lacked the energy to sit up again, much less run.

If I can't fight, he thought, just let me die. Don't want to let them make me do or say something I don't want to, then slaughter me like a hog.

He put his hand to his face, opened his mouth, worked his jaw. Cracked but not broken. Hurting something awful.

Through the fog in his mind he became aware of another pain. Why did his legs hurt so bad? Oh yeah, puncture wounds from the heavy-gauge spring-loaded needles. A skilled nurse or corpsman could slide a hypodermic into a vein with hardly any sting at all. But those auto-injectors had punched into his muscles like the spikes of an iron maiden.

No wonder I feel awful, Blount thought. Got hit with poison so vile the only thing that could save me was another kind of poison.

Maybe the Good Lord kept me alive for a reason, he reckoned. And these dirtbags are keeping me alive for a different reason.

Blount knew from his training that now presented his best chance for escape. The deeper the enemy took you into his system for holding prisoners, the harder to get away. Best to make a break while they moved you. But at the moment, chemical warfare raged inside Blount at the cellular level. Compounds worked against toxins; other medicine worked against the compounds' side effects.

Providence had blessed him with a strong body that he kept fit and healthy. But now, healing required all his strength and will. He'd just spent all his reserves trying to choke one bad guy. Nothing else remained.

One of the dirtbags hoisted a camera and took a photo. The flash blinded Blount. He wanted to slap the camera out of the dirtbag's hands, but he lacked the strength. As he lay in the bed of the truck, he felt himself slip away into unconsciousness.

CHAPTER 16

Parson looked around the ops room. This wasn't the glittering command center depicted in the movies: banks of computers, walls lined with video screens, the president and the joint chiefs at the other end of a red phone. This deployed operations center consisted of plywood and sandbags, a dozen folding chairs, eight laptops, some telephones and radios, stacks of bottled water, extension cords crisscrossing the dusty plank floor, and a couple of mice nobody could catch. But it was what he had, and by God, he'd use it all to get Blount and those boys back. Assuming they were still alive.

He considered what else his resources at Mitiga could contribute. No other crews had been placed on an official alert status to launch at a moment's notice. But if the French could get airborne in their Mirages, they could help look for the missing. He called Chartier's cell phone.

"Sorry to wake you, Frenchie," Parson said, "but we got a situation." He told Chartier about the loss of Musket One-Two and the missing Marines.

"*Zut alors,*" Chartier said. "That is not good. I will call my crews and see what we can do."

"Thanks, Frenchie. I owe you one. We'll call to get a frag order cut for you by the time you get here."

"*Bon.*"

An overall NATO air tasking order assigned the Mirages to the expeditionary air wing at Mitiga. Parson called AFRICOM air ops to request a frag—a fragmentary order appended to the larger tasking order—directing the French jets to assist the search in any way possible. Even in the direst of emergencies, the military required its paperwork.

As Parson clicked a computer mouse a few minutes later to print out the frag, he heard the door swing open. He turned to see Chartier, Sniper, and two other French fliers come in. A beard shadow darkened Sniper's face. Chartier wore no T-shirt under his flight suit. The other Mirage crew—Diderot and Valois, according to their name tags—had the same look of fliers roused unexpectedly from their cots. Diderot had not yet zipped on his G suit. He carried the suit over his shoulder, its pneumatic connection dangling. Valois toted a helmet bag too stuffed to close. In addition to his helmet, the bag contained a pair of flight gloves, a kneepad for scribbling notes in the cockpit, and a bottle of water. Like Sniper, the man wore a growth of stubble. Parson knew they could be in for an uncomfortable flight. An oxygen mask chafed a lot less when you had a fresh shave. He printed out two more copies of the weather sheet, then rose to greet the Mirage crews.

"I know this is a little out of the ordinary," Parson said. "I appreciate your help. We have six personnel missing. Two are Legionnaires. Four are Marines."

"Tonight," Chartier said, "they are all our brothers."

"Damn straight, Frenchie. Here's your weather." Parson handed Chartier the papers. "I really don't have much else for you. Their last known position was Objective Thomas Jefferson. We got two Pave Hawks en route. Check in with AWACS once you get airborne. Their call sign is Monticello."

Chartier gave a thin smile.

"What?" Parson asked.

"Someone has a sense of history. And it so happens Jefferson was once your minister to France."

"Cool," Parson said. He held up his right fist, and Chartier bumped it with his own fist. "Now, get your asses in the air."

"*Oui, mon colonel.*"

Outside, sleepy French ground personnel in camo shorts and combat boots pulled away boarding ladders after the Mirage fliers climbed into their cockpits. The ground crewmen stood fire guard during engine start, and the jets' turbines whined to life. Parson saw the helmeted aviators run through their before-taxi checklists, and then both fighters began rolling.

Kick some ass, Parson thought. Find our guys and kick some ass.

On the runway, the Mirages lined up for takeoff and held in position for a moment. Dappled with shadows thrown by runway edge lights, the fighters looked even more intimidating—sharp angles poised to launch, laden with fuel and fire, the ultimate expression of potential energy. In the lead jet, Chartier pushed up his power. He released brakes and began hurtling down the strip. The afterburner kicked in with the sound of a sustained explosion, a continuous blast of burning kerosene. A few seconds later, number two began rolling. Both fighters sliced into the night, the thunder of their engines pealing across the desert, spikes of flame blazing from their tailpipes.

Parson's staff maintained a listening watch by the radios as the night wore on. He knew they could do their jobs, and he should have tried to get some sleep. But he could not bring himself to leave the ops center and go to bed. He kept himself awake by sipping Red Bull and bitter instant coffee made with packets scrounged from MREs. The caffeine left a rank taste in his mouth but did little for his alertness. As he grew more tired, he found himself forcing thoughts through his mind like an aircraft pump forcing oil through a clogged filter. High pressure, low results.

He considered what else he could do for Blount and the other missing servicemen. Not much at the moment, but once the sun came up the Marines would probably fly out to the crash scene and look for clues. A call to Captain Privett in the *Tarawa*'s TACLOG confirmed his hunch.

"Yes, sir," Privett said. "We plan to fly out there when it gets light."

"You can refuel here at Mitiga if you like," Parson said.

"Thank you, Colonel. We'll see you then."

Parson hung up the phone, tried to think of any base he'd not covered. An old flight instructor had once told him that in an airplane, if you're not doing *something*, you're probably screwing up, even during a long cruise. You could always give the gauges an extra scan, recalculate fuel burn, call for updated weather. Stay on top of everything; don't just sit there.

So, what else could he do? Well, Sophia would want to know about Blount. Maybe she could keep her ear to the ground for any information about missing Americans. Parson logged on to an unclassified computer to send her an e-mail. He would need to write around any sensitive information, which for now included even the names of the missing. But she would know who he meant. He began tapping at his keyboard:

SOPHIA,

BY THE TIME U READ THIS YOU'LL PROBLY KNOW ABOUT CRASH OF THE MARINE HELO. I'M SORRY TO TELL U OUR BIG FRIEND IS MIA. WILL KEEP U ADVISED.

Parson paused a moment, blinked his eyes to make the letters on the screen get a little less blurry. Then he added:

PLZ B CAREFUL.

MP

For a moment, he debated whether he should share this information so soon with someone not in the chain of command. Finally he clicked SEND. Sophia was no longer in the active-duty Army, but her knowledge—and her current location—made her an intelligence asset. Who knew what she might pick up? The more she remained in the loop, the more she could help. And Parson felt he owed Blount every ounce of help he could muster.

As dawn approached, Parson's wired-and-tired exhaustion grew. Despite all the caffeine, he found himself drowsing. A call on the radio woke him from microsleep.

"Kingfish, Dagger flight. Do you read?" Chartier's voice.

Parson shook his head as if that would throw off the cobwebs. He listened as one of the duty officers picked up the mike.

"Dagger flight, Kingfish has you five-by-five."

"Kingfish, be advised we are ten minutes out. Code one, no maintenance required. Request parking."

"Uh, Dagger flight, use hardstands Delta and Echo."

Parson heard the jets streak overhead as they rolled into the break for landing. A while later, Chartier and the other Frenchmen came into the operations center. Parson could tell from their expressions they had no good news for him.

"Any contact at all with the missing guys?" he asked.

"*Rien,*" Chartier said. "No voice. No beacon. How do you say? Not a peep." He ran his fingers through his black hair, left matted and sweaty by his helmet.

"Damn it," Parson said. Blount would have made emergency calls at prebriefed intervals if he could have done so. No contact meant he and the others were dead, badly hurt, or captured. One of their radios could have broken, but not all of them.

"Nothing visual, either," Chartier added. "No strobe or glint tape." The French pilot slumped into a chair, rubbed his eyes, and unzipped the constrictive bands of his G suit from around the legs of his flight suit.

"You guys look beat," Parson said. "You should visit that masseuse of yours and then take a nap."

"Maybe," Chartier said. He showed no mirth over the possibility of a back rub.

He's as upset about this as I am, Parson thought. Good.

Parson needed rest, too, but he would not allow himself that luxury, at least not until the Pave Hawks returned. The Mirage crews went to their quarters, and a new shift came to work in the operations center, but Parson stayed on duty. When the sun lightened the horizon it only deepened his fatigue. He ordered a cot brought into ops. Before settling on it to nap, he left instructions for someone to wake him if anything happened.

He got twenty minutes of sleep, and then a sergeant shook him.

"Choppers coming back, sir," the sergeant said. "They just checked in with the tower."

When Parson sat up, he heard the distant thumping that signaled the approach of the rescue helicopters. The lead chopper called the ops center on UHF.

"Kingfish, Pedro One-One and One-Two inbound. ETA five minutes."

"I'll talk to 'em," Parson said. He groaned as he rose from his cot and went to the radio. He lifted the mike, pressed thumb and forefinger to the bridge of his nose, spoke with his eyes closed: "Pedro flight, expect parking on alert ramp."

"Roger that, Kingfish. Be advised both aircraft are Alpha Four, we will need the CCA, and we have two Hotel Romeos."

Parson's muddled mind processed the codes and acronyms. Hotel Romeo?

A new kind of tired came over him, more like a feeling of defeat. Hotel Romeo meant human remains. Damn it to hell. And the crews wanted the contamination control area. That meant they'd been exposed—or thought they'd been exposed—to chemical agents. Alpha Four meant the helicopters themselves were contaminated. Maintenance crews in full MOPP gear would have to scrub down the aircraft. What a fucking mess.

"Kingfish copies all," Parson transmitted. Then he called out an order to a duty officer. "Get Mortuary Affairs out to the flight line, and tell Emergency Management to man the CCA. And nobody gets near those helicopters except in MOPP Four."

"Yes, sir."

Parson watched the helicopters return in the morning light. He wore no chem gear, so he kept a safe distance. Both HH-60s swung low over the field, descended toward the ramp. They settled to the pavement and began to taxi, their rotors pulsing counter to each other like the drumming of a tribal dirge.

Once on the alert ramp, their turbines hushed and their rotors slowed, replaced by the whine of auxiliary power units. Eventually even the APUs fell silent, leaving only the scrapes, thuds, and muffled curses of suited crew members dismounting their machines.

A van from Mortuary Affairs pulled up next to the helicopters. Two men in chem gear emerged from the vehicle. A pair of crewmen in the first helicopter lifted something from the aircraft's cabin. One of the pilots—still swathed in helmet, hoses, and blower—stepped down from the cockpit. He stood very still. Slowly, with as much formality as his equipment would allow, he rendered a salute. Parson saluted, as well. The crewmen carried a body bag from the aircraft and placed it in the van.

In the same way, with the same salute, another body bag came out of the second helicopter. The Mortuary Affairs men drove away. The bodies would have to suffer the indignity of decontamination before being processed for burial. Parson did not know what that entailed, and he did not want to know.

The Pave Hawk crews walked across the ramp to a row of three large tents set up two hundred yards from any other tents or buildings. The tents were open at each end, and inside them, a half dozen Emergency Management troops prepared to receive the fliers. The aviators lined up and waited for instructions. Parson noted that a few of them wore ground MOPP uniforms with arms and legs encircled by M9 tape. The brown tape would change color to indicate exposure to certain toxins.

One of the EM guys pointed to an open box outside the first tent. The box, about four feet square, contained a dry substance that looked a lot like cat litter. The box also held a long-handled scrub brush.

"Step into the shuffle box, sir, and scrub down your boots."

The first crewman took his place in the shuffle box as the others waited behind him. When he'd cleaned his boots to the satisfaction of the EM troop, he stepped out of the box and moved over to a trash barrel. The crewman removed his outer gloves and dropped them into the trash.

Parson longed to ask them what they'd seen and if they knew the identities of the dead. But he had to leave the men alone as they decontaminated.

In stages, the fliers went through the processing lines in the tents. At each stop they removed another piece of gear or clothing, taking care not to touch bare skin to anything exposed to poison. They hung blowers and hoses on racks, doffed helmets, peeled off flight suits. At the end they wore only their underwear, and an EM troop directed them to a shower. While the men showered, Parson talked to an EM sergeant.

"Did they get slimed real bad?" Parson asked.

"Looks like it, sir," the sergeant said. "I checked the M9 tape on one of the pararescue guys. It had green specks all over it."

A positive test for nerve gas. Thank God I told them to suit up, Parson thought. At least I've made one good call today—or last night, or whenever the hell it was.

Air Force fliers routinely practiced flying and working in chem gear, and every few years they got tested on those procedures in operational readiness inspections. Many crew members despised ORIs as having little to do with real-world combat. In recent years, at least, more service members had passed out from heat exhaustion in MOPP suits than had ever been hurt by chemicals.

But now, because of Sadiq Kassam getting his hands on some of Muammar Gadhafi's and Bashar al-Assad's hand-me-downs, ORI scenarios were coming true.

Parson didn't consider himself a brilliant tactician or a masterful leader of men. Instead, he thought of himself as a crew dog who got promoted high enough to get stuck with heavy responsibilities. So he tried simply to make decisions that would keep guys safe while they did their jobs. Take care of the people, he believed, and as long as they're good people, they'll take care of the mission.

The Pave Hawk crews emerged from the showers in clean but ill-fitting flight suits, and Parson finally got to pose the question that nagged at him most.

"Did you get an ID on the bodies you found?" he asked.

"Yes, sir," a pararescueman said. "One was a Legionnaire, and one was a Marine corporal."

"Thanks for all you did, guys. I know this mission sucked. Get some rest."

"Yes, sir."

Parson didn't know how to feel about what he'd just learned. He couldn't let himself take any relief from the news. Two families back home were about to receive that knock on the door they'd always dreaded. But Parson's old friend Blount was still out there. Some-where.

CHAPTER 17

Blount had no idea how much time had passed when the truck finally stopped, but the sun had risen. He came to awareness like swimming up from the bottom of a muddy farm pond with weights around his waist. He felt a tugging sensation; because he was so big, his enemies pulled him by his arms and legs. He decided not to sit up and make it easy for them. He lay limp as one terrorist took his wrists. Two others took him by the ankles, and they carried him like men struggling with a huge bundle of cured tobacco sheeted in burlap.

They brought him inside a stucco-walled building, put him down on a concrete floor. The air hung close and hot.

The terrorists brought in two more prisoners. Blount recognized Corporal Fender. The captors dragged Fender by the arms, dropped him on the floor to Blount's right.

Blount raised up, tried to get to Fender.

"Hey, bud," Blount said. "You all right?"

One of the captors shouted something in Arabic and kicked Blount in the chest. Another lowered the muzzle of an AK-47 toward his head. Yet another clamped shackles around his wrists and locked them with a key.

Each shackle connected to a separate chain. Not a light chain like you'd use to tether a dog, either. More like a logging chain, maybe ten-thousand-pound test. The other end of each chain connected to a metal ring embedded in the wall, just a few inches above the floor.

Blount looked over at Fender. They chained him up the same

way. Fender sat against the wall with his chains coiled around him. He stared up at the ceiling with his mouth open.

Dried vomit stained the front of Fender's MOPP suit. But he seemed to breathe steady, and Blount didn't see any blood.

On Blount's left, the dirtbags chained another man. The man did not wear MOPP gear, just fatigues in an unfamiliar camo pattern. A subdued-color patch on the soldier's sleeve featured vertical bars in three different shades of beige. Above the bars the patch read FRANCE. A Legionnaire, then. The Legionnaire was not as big as Blount, but he was almost as stocky and muscled. Shaved head. A white guy, but dark from lots of time in the sun. Tattoos spiraled the length of his arms. Some of the tattoos depicted nude angels, large-breasted and winged. One of them wielded a sword. Other images included a bear, mainly teeth and claws. A rifle cartridge. A flaming skull.

And lots of lettering. Blount couldn't read any of it, but he knew it wasn't French. It wasn't even regular ABCs.

The man had taken a bullet in the thigh. A bloody pressure bandage circled his leg. Didn't seem to be bleeding now, though, so the slug must have missed the femoral artery. At least so far, the Legionnaire acted as tough as he looked. No trembling or crying. He just met Blount's eyes and nodded.

Blount still felt weak. Feeble, even. And his jaw ached from getting slammed with the butt of that rifle. But his mind had cleared enough to try to take stock of his situation. The enemy had carried him to what looked like an abandoned house. A table made of unfinished wood stood in a corner. The rings that anchored his chains had been installed recently; someone had chiseled holes in the walls, spaded in wet cement, and inserted heavy bolts before the cement dried. The rings hung from circular heads on the bolts. The clanking of chains in the next room told him the dirtbags had prisoners in there, too.

His captors had robbed him of most of his equipment. He still wore his tactical vest, but the pouches for his radio, GPS receiver, grenades, ammunition, and everything else lay empty and slack. They'd even taken his watch and his grandfather's KA-BAR. They'd piled a bunch of equipment on the table in the corner, far out of reach. Blount recognized two M16s, along with other American gear. He had no idea what had become of his gas mask and his pistol.

One of the dirtbags entered the room with three galvanized pails. He set down a pail beside Blount, and he placed the other two next to Fender and the Legionnaire. Our toilet buckets, Blount realized. So they plan on keeping us here for a while.

And then what? Dear Lord up in heaven, he thought, you know what. A machete and a camera. These things don't ever end well. Not unless a rescue force gets here in time. And for that to happen, they gotta know where we are.

Regret came over Blount like a cloud of nerve gas. What would it do to Bernadette and the girls to know he had come to an end like this? And he could have avoided it so easily. Just a few days ago he'd been sitting on his porch with his family—mission accomplished, home again, done with it all. There had been no rush about finding a job. But he couldn't let go of the action, the camaraderie, the sense of belonging.

Selfish, selfish, selfish, he thought. I brought this on myself. But not just on myself. I brought it on my family. Dear God, forgive me for what I've done to them.

Blount felt his eyes brim. He forced his eyelids to stay open to let the tears dry up rather than fall. These sleazeballs would not see him cry. He would die well, without screaming and carrying on. That was the last thing he could control. These motherfu—these men—would not take away his self-control and dignity.

I'll take at least one with me, Blount resolved. Sooner or later they'll unchain me to take me to my execution. And if this poison don't make me any weaker, if I get better instead of worse, I'm gon' slam somebody's head into this wall. That'll probably make the others shoot me instead of sawing through my neck. Kill an enemy and die quicker? You gotta put that in the win column.

Fender didn't look so good. He sat on the floor with his chained arms around his knees, rocking back and forth. The chains stretched six or seven feet long. Blount guessed the dirtbags wanted their prisoners to have enough freedom of movement to piss by themselves. That eliminated the need to unlock shackles every time somebody had to go to the bathroom.

"Fender," Blount whispered. "You all right?"

Now why did I ask that? Blount wondered. Of course he ain't all right.

Fender looked up, pale-faced and drawn, like his mind had seized up and couldn't process things straight.

"We're done, Gunny," Fender said. Voice not much more than a squeak. Then he began to murmur to himself as he rocked: "We're done, we're done, we're done."

"You belay that foolishness," Blount whispered. "We ain't dead yet. Boy, I know you're a good Marine. You keep your game face on."

Fender quit muttering. Buried his face in his knees.

Blount didn't know why he'd tried to give any kind of pep talk to Fender. Things looked about as hopeless as they could get. But at least Blount and his fellow captives could show these terrorists how strong men died. For all their talk, these filth didn't know from strong. To Blount, they amounted to the very soul of cowardice. For years he'd seen them use civilians as shields, throw acid on women, hang suicide vests on children.

That last part ignited a special fury every time Blount thought of it. And his captors came from the same breed that put bombs on those boys in Afghanistan. Made him pull a trigger on kids.

He felt his pulse rise. He clenched his fists around his chains.

For Blount, fury brought focus. A warrior's mind worked that way; you channeled your anger into your mission. And Blount had a mission: take out one more terrorist.

Now, how to go about that? Well, he could start with a little tactical deception. I ain't feeling any worse, he realized. Might even get better. But the dirtbags don't need to know that.

Blount thought of Samson, way back in the Bible. Praying to God to give him his strength back one more time so he could kill his enemies. Blount didn't know if his strength would come back, but he'd find a way to use it if it did.

He lay flat on his back. He worked his tongue around in his mouth to stimulate his salivary glands. When his mouth filled with spit, he waited for one of the enemy to come back into the room.

Soon enough, one of the dirtbags returned. Happened to be the same guy Blount had nearly choked to death, Rat Face.

Blount rolled onto his side. Retched as loudly as he could. Made a great show of vomiting onto the floor.

Rat Face laughed. Walked over and kicked Blount in the back.

That's right, chump, Blount thought. See how messed up I am. Sick as a dog. Just threw up all over your floor. It's only clear spit, but you done got so overconfident you didn't notice that.

CHAPTER 18

Gold sat down to breakfast in the refugee camp's mess tent with a troubled mind. She still struggled with her choice of a role in a world changing quickly around her, and an interrogation ending in a prisoner's suicide didn't help. She'd always hoped that as a linguist and interpreter, she could make it easier for people to communicate, to examine ideas. Exchange thoughts over tea instead of bullets over barricades. But this morning she'd awakened again with that feeling she wasn't where she was supposed to be.

The powdered eggs on her cardboard tray didn't look very appetizing. Gold tore open a packet of pepper and sprinkled it over the eggs, and she chided herself for complaining, even if only to herself. A lot of people displaced from North African villages would have loved to get this meal. She took a sip of the coffee in her Styrofoam cup, found it weak and bitter at the same time. Gold ripped open more packets—this time of sugar and creamer—and they made the coffee even less drinkable.

This chow hall reminded her of mess tents in some of the more remote forward bases in Afghanistan. Cooks toiled over stainless steel vats heated by propane. Greasy nylon passed for tablecloths. One table offered a mound of assorted snacks that wouldn't spoil: packaged granola bars, bags of chips, crackers wrapped in cellophane. Someone had placed a shortwave radio on the snack table and left it tuned to the BBC. Gold half listened while she ate; the segment about international stock indexes did not interest her. Hard to believe that comfortable life went on with so much suffering happening in places like this. She thought of a line from the Russian writer Anton Chekhov: Behind the door of every contented man, someone should stand with a hammer and remind him with a tap that there are unhappy people.

Lambrechts entered the mess tent and looked over the offerings. The Belgian doctor wore a MÉDECINS SANS FRONTIÈRES T-shirt. She came to Gold's table carrying a bagel and a plastic knife, and from somewhere she'd scrounged a single minitray of cream cheese.

"*Bonjour,*" Gold said.

"*Bonjour,*" Lambrechts replied, smiling at Gold's use of what little French she knew. "You look pensive," Lambrechts added as she sat down.

"Maybe so," Gold said. "I want to try to do some good here, but I feel like I'm always O-B-E."

"You're what?"

"Sorry, Army talk. Overtaken by events."

With her plastic knife, Lambrechts spread cheese across the bagel. She appeared to ponder Gold's dilemma for a moment.

"Anyone would be upset after seeing someone take his own life," Lambrechts said, "You can't hold yourself responsible."

"It's not that. It's—"

Before Gold could elaborate, something on the radio caught her ear. The program broke away from business news for a special broadcast:

"The Reuters and Associated Press news services both report a disastrous military raid in North Africa last evening. The news agencies' sources say a joint U.S. and French operation involved an assault on a suspected hideout of terrorist leader Sadiq Kassam. The attacking forces encountered unexpectedly fierce opposition, which may have included use of chemical weapons.

"Information remains sketchy, but sources say one Marine helicopter crashed. Officials confirm at least two dead, several wounded, and as many as six missing. The names of the dead and missing have not been released, pending notification of relatives."

"Oh, my God," Lambrechts said. "That's awful."

Parson might have had something to do with that mission, Gold knew. She needed to find out more. Now.

"Excuse me," she said. "I'm sorry to rush off, but I have to check my messages."

"Of course," Lambrechts said. "Tell me if I can do anything."

"Pray."

Gold stood up, gathered her tray, cup, and plastic fork. She dumped her half-eaten meal into the trash and ran to the admin tent. When she logged in to her e-mail account, she saw a message from Parson. To her great relief, it was only a few hours old. So Parson had not found an excuse to fly out with the Marines and get himself killed. But when she opened the e-mail, it brought no good news.

Our big friend is missing? No, Gold thought. *Please no.*

That could only mean A. E. Blount. Gold remembered a night when she, Parson, and Blount's Marines entered a village terrorized by a Taliban splinter group. They found a little orphaned girl, already traumatized, who looked up at Blount with wild-eyed fear. The girl had almost certainly never seen a black man, and had probably never seen any man even close to Blount's size. No wonder she was afraid of him.

But without speaking her language, and aided only by a chocolate bar, Blount put the child at ease. In the days that followed, the girl became drawn to him as a protector.

God didn't make enough people like Gunny Blount, Gold thought. *We can't lose the one we have.* Suddenly Gold knew where she needed to be, at least for today: Mitiga.

She picked up the sat phone, thinking to call Parson and then her bosses in New York. But before punching in a number, she put the phone back down. No phone calls, she decided. She'd just go. As Parson would say, sometimes it's easier to ask forgiveness than get permission.

She left the admin tent and walked out to the refugee camp's helipad. The UN's Mi-8 helicopter had seen better days. Its crew chief, a mechanic retired from the Royal Canadian Air Force, busied himself wiping grease smears from the chopper's white paint. Oil cans lay on the ground beside the aircraft. The whole machine smelled like the engine of an old used car.

"Good morning," Gold said. "Are you guys flying today?"

"Yes, ma'am. We're heading up to Tripoli."

"You don't have to call me ma'am. I was enlisted, too."

The crew chief rubbed his fingers with the oily rag, smiled at Gold. "I knew there was a reason I liked you," he said.

"Thanks, Chief. Are you landing at Mitiga International?"

"Nope. Going to a helipad near the docks to pick up a load of food."

"Do you think the pilots would drop me off at Mitiga?"

Gold explained the situation. She gave no names, but she told him about the shoot-down and the missing personnel. The crew chief's expression changed as soon as he heard the word *missing*.

"We'll take you anywhere you want to go," he said. "We all did tours in Afghanistan."

"Thank you for your service, Chief."

"And for yours."

While she waited for takeoff, Gold dropped by the medical tent to tell Lambrechts she was heading to Mitiga. She did not give the doctor a chance to object or ask questions.

Unsure when she'd return, Gold packed for several days. Her gear included a GPS receiver, desert boots, a Surefire flashlight that ran on lithium batteries, and a green-and-black shemagh, or Afghan scarf, that she'd worn on her last military deployment. Good sandstorm protection in any desert. When she wrapped the shemagh around her neck and pulled on her boots, she felt almost like a soldier again. Nothing missing but the M4.

At departure time, Gold inserted a set of foam earplugs, donned her ballistic sunglasses, and hoisted a dusty duffel bag long faded from deep olive to light green. Gold boarded the helicopter, buckled into a troop seat, put on a headset, and the helo lifted off.

The refugee camp dropped away beneath her, blue United Nations flag fluttering from a makeshift pole. The Sahara unfurled below the Mi-8 as an endless expanse of dunes and plains. As the aircraft rattled toward Tripoli, Gold could not help but wonder if Blount was lying dead somewhere—or if he'd become a prisoner. Terrorists would probably consider it a badge of honor to behead such a big and powerful Marine, to wield the knife at his execution. Would some gruesome video show up online at any moment?

The answers to her questions lay down there somewhere. Perhaps Blount was in that tiny village at the two o'clock position. Or perhaps at the end of that sand-covered hint of a road off the eleven o'clock. No way to know now.

After a while, the horizon to the north changed texture. The pencil line where the earth met the sky turned darker. The pencil line gave way to a blue incandescence as the helicopter made progress, and eventually the Mediterranean revealed itself. The desert stopped abruptly at the shoreline, and the cluster of shapes on the shoreline came into focus as Tripoli.

"We'll land in about ten minutes," the crew chief said on interphone.

"Roger that," Gold said. "Thanks."

A few minutes later, as the helicopter flew over Mitiga International, Gold saw that Parson had been busy setting up his forward air base. A row of fighter jets perched on hardstands along a taxiway. Prefab clamshell hangars dotted the tarmac. A pair of HH-60 rescue helicopters sat on the parking ramp in front of what looked like an air ops center. A few other assorted aircraft rounded out the collection: a C-130 transport, a KC-135 tanker jet, and an AWACS plane with a rotodome mounted on top of the fuselage.

The pilots began talking with Mitiga's control tower. Gold couldn't follow all the flyboy lingo, but she gathered that the UN helicopter was number two for landing behind another chopper. She looked forward through the windscreen and saw a tremendous helo painted in the slate gray of the U.S. Navy and Marines. The military chopper trailed dark gray exhaust as it flew.

The big helicopter descended through the haze, and the UN aircraft followed it. When a turn pointed the Mi-8 toward the Med, the water shone so brightly Gold had to shield her eyes, even though she wore sunglasses. Freighters dotted the surface, presumably awaiting anchorage at Tripoli. Another turn placed both helicopters on final approach.

"What's that other helicopter?" Gold asked.

"That's your Marine Corps," one of the Canadian pilots said. "It's a CH-53."

Gold tried to picture the Navy ship from which the CH-53 would have launched. She'd seen no carrier or any other kind of military vessel among the freighters, and she found it vaguely reassuring that something as fearsome as that Marine helo, bristling with guns and flare magazines, could swoop in from a steel deck somewhere in the ocean beyond the horizon.

The 53 settled to the tarmac near the rescue helicopters, and the UN chopper landed behind it. As the Mi-8 shut down, Gold pressed her talk button to thank the crew.

"I owe you one, guys," she said.

"No, you don't," the crew chief said. "Least we can do."

Gold removed her headset, released the clasp of her seat belt, and lifted her duffel bag by one of its shoulder straps. She hopped down from the helicopter without waiting for the crew chief to put the boarding steps into place. All the sensations of a middle-latitudes air base hit her at once: heat, dust, exhaust fumes, and the never-ending whine of engines.

The structure with the most antennas and satellite dishes must be the operations center, Gold assumed. She made her way past the first line of sand-filled HESCO barriers, showed her United Nations ID to an Air Force security policeman, walked around another line of HESCO barriers, and pulled open a plywood door.

The scent of dusty sandbags, the beige glow of fluorescent light reflecting off clamshell walls, the stacks of bottled water transported her. This scene could have passed for Kandahar airport in 2002. But the world had changed since then, and not always for the better.

However, her lasting friendship with Parson counted as one good change. She heard his voice before she saw him. His back to the door, he was talking about fuel with someone on his cell phone. Ops center staff, some in flight suits and some in fatigues, worked at desks around him.

"That Marine Corps helo just landed," Parson said. "They're gonna want to fill up with JP-8." He turned, phone still to his ear, and saw Gold. His eyes widened with surprise. "Yeah, thanks," he said, still maintaining eye contact with Gold. "Don't worry about the billing." He terminated the call with a press of his thumb. "Sophia," he said. "Great to see you, but how did you get here?"

Parson wore his usual desert flight suit with a name tag that displayed his rank and his pilot's wings. Beside the wings Gold noticed something new: a round badge that consisted of a star adorned with wings and a wreath—the Air Force commander's insignia.

"I caught a ride on a UN helicopter. Got here as soon as I could. I want to do whatever I can to help you find Gunny Blount."

Gold put down her bag and embraced him. The brief display of affection in front of other military personnel felt strange, but it violated no regs. She worked in a civilian status now.

After the hug, with her hands still on his arms, she leaned back and regarded him. He looked like he'd worked through the night.

Skin sagged under his eyes, and he needed a shave. He still appeared reasonably fit, though. If anything, he'd lost some weight. Maybe subsisting on the food of a deployed chow hall for several days had done that to him.

Before Gold could say more, four Marines came into the ops center. Gold recognized two of them as pilots from the CH-53; they wore flight equipment that included horse-collar-style flotation gear in case they ditched at sea. The other two looked like ground officers and wore digital camo: a captain and a lieutenant colonel. The golden wings of the Navy and Marine Corps Parachutist Insignia gleamed on their uniforms. The lieutenant colonel made introductions.

"I'm Bill Loudon and this is Captain Adam Privett," he said. "Twenty-second MEU off the USS *Tarawa*."

"Yes, I talked to Captain Privett on the phone," Parson said. "I'm Michael Parson and this is Sophia Gold. She's with the UN, but she was a sergeant major in the Army, and she's still in the Reserve."

"Pleased to meet you, Sergeant Major," Loudon said.

"You, too, sirs."

"Guys, we'll help do anything possible to get your men back," Parson said. "Sophia and I know one of them, so we have a personal stake in this, too."

"Who do you know?" Privett asked.

Parson told them how they'd met Blount in Afghanistan. He left out the worst parts, but he made it clear how the big gunnery sergeant had impressed him.

"Yeah, we all love Gunny," Privett said. "I pray to God he's not dead. If he's not, those terrorists don't know who they're messing with."

"You got that right," Parson said.

"So, where do things stand now?" Gold asked.

"These guys are flying out to the crash site today," Parson said. Loudon frowned and looked toward Gold. Parson added, "Don't worry; she's cleared."

"Where did it happen?" Gold asked.

Parson went to an aeronautical chart taped to the wall and pointed to an X written in pencil. That spot on the map looked familiar to Gold. It was the same location the prisoner had identified during his interrogation, just before he took the cyanide.

Realization came over Gold like the fever of a sudden illness. The prisoner, Ahmed Bedoor, or whatever his name really was, had played the central role in an elaborate ruse. He'd let himself get captured so he could, with seeming reluctance, give up Kassam's hiding place. But it hadn't been a real hideout. It had been a well-prepared ambush with heavy weapons and chemicals.

"Oh, my God," Gold said. "This whole thing was a setup from the start." She told them about Bedoor's capture, interrogation, and suicide.

"Wait," Privett said, holding up his hand. His eyes narrowed at her, and his expression turned cold. "You mean this is your fault? Some hajji comes in with a bullshit story and you send it right up the chain?"

"Captain—" Loudon said.

"Sir," Privett said, "due respect, but our guys got chewed up because of bad information from this woman?"

"Captain Privett, you will stand down," Loudon said.

"You're damned right he'll stand down," Parson said. He took a step toward Privett as if to start a bar brawl, shook a finger in his face. "You have no idea who you're talking about. She was getting her fingernails pulled out by the Taliban when you were ironing your little white milkman's suit at the Naval Academy."

Typical Parson, Gold thought. You didn't go off half-cocked with an accusation about someone close to him, especially when he was this tired and had so much responsibility on his shoulders.

Privett backed away from Parson, held out his palms almost as if in surrender, but he cut his eyes again at Gold.

Gold could understand Privett's anger because she shared it. His was misdirected; he didn't realize she'd only interpreted Bedoor's words—not analyzed them and judged their worth. Those decisions had been made elsewhere. The circumstances had allowed little time to consider all the possibilities; actionable intelligence came with a very short shelf life. Commanders often had to give orders quickly and without full information. And this time the Marines had paid a high price.

"Captain Privett," Gold said, "nobody likes how this has happened. I'm just an interpreter, and I'm as angry about these terrorists as you are. If you'd seen what I've seen—what those chemicals do to people—you'd know what I mean. And I want you to know I came here to help find Gunny Blount."

Privett still seemed resentful. "Thanks," he said, "but I don't see how you can help."

"I do," Parson said. "I'd like to send somebody out with you to take photos, but I don't have any Air Force people I can spare. If you'll take her with you, I'll get AFRICOM to put her on the flight orders."

"We'll take plenty of photos," Privett said.

"I know, *Captain*," Parson said, emphasizing Privett's lower rank. "But the Air Force will want some of its own, and another set of experienced eyes on the site won't hurt."

"Fine with me," Loudon said, "but she'll need chem gear."

"That, we have," Parson said. He picked up the phone and made a call.

In a storage tent, a supply sergeant helped Parson find chem gear for Gold. While they searched through stacks of cardboard boxes, Gold said, "Thanks for taking up for me, but you didn't have to be so hard on the captain."

"Yeah, well, he didn't have to be so hard on you."

"He's lost some of his men. That would put anybody on the edge."

"I know."

The stocks of extra gear included only one gas mask in Gold's size, which was small. She tried on the M45 mask, and it seemed to fit reasonably well. But a guess of "reasonably well" wouldn't cut it in a chemical environment. With Gold still wearing the mask, the sergeant connected a hose from the mask to an electronic test box. The test box's readout confirmed the mask's seals fit tightly enough to keep out toxins.

Next, they found a Chemical Protective Overgarment. Parson pulled out his boot knife and sliced open the vacuum-sealed bag that contained the overgarment. The bag hissed as air rushed into the cut made by Parson's fancy Damascus steel knife.

"Now that I've opened this, it's good only for a hundred twenty days," Parson said.

"I hope I won't need it for that long," Gold said.

"Me, too."

Parson shook out the CPO coat and trousers. Gold pulled on the trousers and placed the suspenders over her shoulders. The carbon-treated fabric left a chalky residue on her fingers. She adjusted the suspenders for better fit, then tugged at the hook-and-pile fasteners on the waistband. Donned the coat, zipped it, closed the drawcord at the waist. Her new gear also included overboots and rubber gloves.

She began sweating immediately. A day in this suit would test anyone's physical fitness. She did not look forward to the misery of wearing this thing in the sun. But it sure beat the agony of death by nerve gas.

CHAPTER 19

Blount woke to strange surroundings and strange pains. He didn't know the time of day or how long he'd slept. Why did his jawbone hurt? And what were those sore places in his leg muscles? But then awareness flooded back into his mind like the toxins flooding his bloodstream, and he remembered his life was over.

Was he already in hell? He deserved it, he figured, for leaving Bernadette and the girls after telling them he'd returned to stay. But despite the misery of chemical sickness and capture, Blount judged that he remained among the living, at least for now. The scene around him, awful though it was, didn't strike him as a proper representation of hell. Hell would be more crowded.

His clothing felt different. As his mind took stock of his situation, he realized his captors had pulled off his tactical vest and MOPP suit. They must have had to cut the sleeves unless they unfastened his chains while he was out. Now he wore only his combat utility uniform in desert digi-camo, and his desert combat boots.

He needed to piss something awful. He pulled his galvanized pail toward him, unbuttoned the fly of his trousers. Urinated into the pail. His urine flowed dark.

That usually meant dehydration. Blount had no doubt he was dehydrated, but he'd been dehydrated before. And he'd never seen urine that dark—like homemade cider. It smelled bad, too. Was there blood in it? No telling the ways that poison had jacked him up. So maybe he had some kind of kidney problem.

Doesn't matter, he thought to himself. They're gon' kill you a lot sooner than kidney failure will get you, and they'll do it in a much worse way.

The sound of piss gurgling into the pail woke the tough-looking Legionnaire to Blount's left. The man grunted, opened his eyes. Winced and placed a chained hand to the pressure bandage on his leg. No one else was in the room except Fender, chained to the wall to Blount's right, so Blount decided to risk conversation. He buttoned his fly and spoke in a whisper.

"Hey, bud. What's your name?" The cracked jaw made it hurt to talk.

The man frowned like he didn't understand. Blount wondered if the guy spoke English at all. But then the man said, "Ivan. Legionnaire First Class Ivan Turgenev."

Thick accent. English obviously wasn't his first language, and probably not his second, either. Blount figured his second would be French.

"You a Russian?"

The man nodded.

"I'm Blount. Gunnery sergeant, U.S. Marines. This boy here is Fender. They got more of our guys in the next room."

Before Turgenev could reply, one of the dirtbags came running in. The dirtbag aimed an AK-47 in Blount's general direction and shouted, "Quiet! No talk! Pasha coming."

Blount braced himself for a boot to the ribs or a rifle stock to the face. But the terrorist just turned and went back into the other room. Started yammering in Arabic with the other terrorists.

Now what had the dirtbag just said? Pashcoming? Some Arabic word, maybe. No, he wouldn't talk Arabic to me, Blount thought. Pash—pasha coming. Somebody was coming. Somebody named Pasha? Whatever it was, it was a big deal to these scumbags. Blount got it: The boss was coming.

So what could that mean? Probably nothing good. Think, Blount told himself. Maintain appearances. Let 'em believe you're too weak to do anything when they come to take you away to kill you.

Not a hard thing to do, either. Blount still felt weak. His muscles had stiffened as if gummed up with molasses. He hoped they let him live at least another day; he thought he'd need at least that long to get better—assuming he got better at all. Taking one of them with him when he died remained his goal. But if they came to get him now, he wouldn't have enough fight in him. Just like old Samson, he thought, please give me my strength back in the last five minutes of my life.

From outside, Blount heard the sound of a vehicle pulling up. Maybe more than one vehicle. Lots of babbling in Arabic. How did they understand one another when they all kept talking at the same time? He sat up, slid on his hips across the floor to the farthest reach of his chains, tried to look out a window.

The chains would have allowed Blount to stand; they had enough length for that. But he didn't want his captors to know he had the strength to get up. Truth to tell, he didn't know for sure whether he *could* get up. Maybe tomorrow.

Blount could see nothing except the red fireball of the sun low in the sky. He didn't even know which way was east or west, so he couldn't tell with certainty whether the sun was rising or sinking. Without his watch, he could only guess. The scumbags didn't act like they'd just gotten up, so maybe it was late afternoon. He'd find out in a few minutes as he watched the sun come up or go down.

The sun settled lower. So he'd slept—or remained unconscious— all day. Or at least a day. He had no idea.

Fender began to stir. Blount half crawled, half pulled himself by one of his chains to return to the young Marine's side. The sweat on Blount's arms felt slimy, not like the healthy perspiration of a work- out but the fever sweat of sickness. Dust and grit clung to his wet skin, adding to the general sense of filth and illness. Fender opened his eyes, and Blount noticed the corporal's expression of horror. No, Fender, Blount thought, this ain't a bad dream. It's real. Blount had just experienced the same kind of awakening several minutes earlier.

"Don't talk or make a lot of noise," Blount whispered. "Some kind of boss man just got here."

Fender's expression turned quizzical. Blount had no more answers to give. He wished he could tell Fender to remember his training, his Code of Conduct. For that matter, Blount hoped he himself could live up to the Code. He couldn't remember the whole thing, but Article III, the section most relevant to him now, stuck in his mind: *If I am captured I will continue to resist by all means available. I will make every effort to escape and help others escape. I will accept neither parole nor special favors from the enemy.*

Well, that last part didn't count for much here. A special favor from this enemy would mean dying by a bullet instead of a blade. But the Code's overall points still held. Blount considered that he, Fender, and every other allied serviceman here remained on duty. Just because you got captured didn't mean you didn't have responsibilities.

Fender unbuttoned and pissed into his pail. Blount couldn't see the color of the urine. After Fender finished, Blount decided to risk talking one more time.

"You sick?"

"Kinda. You?"

Blount held out his hand, palm down. Waggled it side to side, chain clanking. So-so. I'm feeling just so-so. Fender nodded.

At least he wasn't blubbering. That's right, boy, Blount thought. Resist. Even if that means nothing except not letting them see you break down.

The chattering in Arabic continued in the next room, but now one voice addressed the others. Evidently the boss was telling them what was what. Blount wondered what the other three prisoners in there were seeing and hearing. Whatever they were doing, they weren't talking. Blount had never heard them speak.

After a while, Blount smelled something cooking. At first he thought his chemical-addled senses fooled him, but the smell grew stronger. Maybe the scumbags were about to feed the prisoners. Blount didn't feel like eating; under these circumstances he could certainly take no pleasure from a meal. But he decided to eat whatever they gave him. He wanted one last burst of strength, and for that he needed nourishment.

Boss man in there kept on yakking. Blount had attended mission briefs that didn't take that long. Probably prattling on about some jihadist kill-the-infidels foolishness.

The sermon finally ended. One of the terrorists, Rat Face, brought in two clay bowls of something that steamed. He put one bowl down beside Fender and the other beside Ivan. Blount wondered if out of spite Rat Face was going to starve him, but the terrorist came back with one more bowl and set it down beside him. Rat Face plunked it to the floor so quickly that some of the contents sloshed out. Then he danced backward to get out of Blount's reach.

Yeah, you're scared of me, Blount thought.

Rat Face brought no spoons or any other kind of utensils. Blount looked into the bowl. Boiled lentils, cooked down almost to a soup. He dipped three fingers and a thumb into the bowl and scooped out some of the lentils. Put them in his mouth and tried not to think about the dirt on his hands. Chewed. Swallowed.

Didn't taste very good, but Blount decided to eat all that he could force down. No, he'd save just a little bit. Ivan started eating with his fingers. Fender just stared at his bowl.

"Eat," Blount whispered.

Fender nodded, dipped his fingers into his bowl. That's right, Blount thought, maintain your body. Here, for all intents and purposes, it ain't nothing but government property.

Blount ate as many of the lentils as he could with his hands. Then he lifted the bowl to his lips and slurped. Some of the broth ran down his chin. He stopped drinking when only a mouthful of the liquid remained.

A few minutes after he finished eating, three dirtbags came into the room: Rat Face, a terrorist Blount decided to call Monkey Ears, and one of the strangest-looking characters Blount had ever seen. The boss, apparently, or the pasha, or whatever they called him. The dude had a great big orange beard, like some meth-addicted redneck, and he wore a flintlock pistol stuck in a sash around his waist.

A *flintlock.*

So this was Sadiq Kassam himself, with that ancient pistol supposedly taken from an American serviceman a couple hundred years ago.

Where on this broad earth would a North African terrorist get something like that? Had it really been passed down by generations of Muslim fighters? You certainly wouldn't depend on it as a weapon in this day and age; a zip gun made in prison would be more reliable. You'd carry it only as a symbol.

Blount decided to ponder all that later. Now looked like a good time for some tactical deception.

He sipped the last of the broth in his bowl. Swished the broth around in his mouth to mix it with saliva. Put his hand to his waist like his stomach hurt. Actually, his stomach *did* hurt, but not that bad. Jerked his legs a little bit, and breathed in and out fast through his nostrils. Leaned over his piss pail, which gave off a stench foul as any hog pen. Spat into the pail like he was vomiting.

The dirtbags started talking their abba-dabba talk. Monkey Ears said, "The pasha says Allah's justice has laid you low with illness."

So one of them spoke English. All right, Blount told himself, think. Keep consistent. Take your time. Use your training for this, and don't say the wrong thing.

He opened his mouth like he wanted to answer, then held his face over his pail like he might throw up again. Yeah, Blount thought, I'm trying to be polite and answer you, but dag-nabbit, I'm just sick as a dog. And buying time. We'll just see how this plays out.

Before Blount could decide what to say, Ivan spoke up.

"You have poisoned him nearly to death. He needs a doctor. I need a doctor."

Ooo, Blount thought, Ivan's figured it out. Not stupid, that one. Got a little teamwork going here. A tiny victory. Let's roll with it.

Monkey Ears started speaking Arabic, and then Kassam jabbered for a while.

"You will get a doctor only when your governments meet our demands," Monkey Ears translated.

Ivan seemed to think for a moment, considering his words with care. Bet this guy started in the Russian Spetsnaz, Blount thought, then got into some kind of trouble and had to leave the country. No telling what kind of high crimes and misdemeanors led him to join the French Foreign Legion. Who'd have thought this would be the fellow watching my back?

"What are your demands?" Ivan asked.

Monkey Ears spoke in Arabic, Kassam answered, Monkey Ears translated.

"That all your forces leave this continent and never return. If any foreign troops remain in Africa after tomorrow, we will behead one of you each day."

A wave of nausea came over Blount. Not from any chemicals inside him but from a kind of fear he'd never experienced before.

He'd known from the moment of capture that they faced impossible odds. But perhaps some part of his mind had held out crazy hope that this would turn out different. Maybe the captors would want to bargain for something reasonable. However, foreign troops leaving tomorrow was deliberately unreasonable. These dirtbags had no intention of making a deal. They planned to behead everybody. One a day, for six days. Command the headlines for the better part of a week.

Blount's fingers began to tremble. He recognized this as a loss of fine motor skills, a physical manifestation of terror. Not familiar territory for Blount; he was more used to making his enemies shake with fear. He'd faced danger before, but nothing like this. The fight-or-flight instinct kicked in hard, but Blount could do neither. He found himself on a level of fear beyond anything he'd imagined. His breathing grew rapid and shallow, and this time it wasn't an act.

Fender began to rock back and forth on his hips like he'd done before. A strange whine escaped from between the corporal's closed lips, a long, one-note keen. Ivan closed his eyes tightly, as if a halogen lamp were shining in his face. Chains clanked in the next room; the prisoners in there had heard the threat, too. One way or another, everybody entered some kind of panic response.

Rat Face smirked. Monkey Ears looked at Kassam as if waiting for instructions. Kassam drew the flintlock, began waving it around and yammering in Arabic.

Blount didn't worry about getting shot with the old pistol. Kassam probably didn't have the black powder it needed. And if the weapon did actually fire, dying by gunshot would be a mercy compared to what was coming.

After lots of gesturing and posing, Kassam placed the pistol on the table with the weapons and equipment taken from the prisoners. Blount tried to force himself to concentrate through his terror and keep a semblance of situational awareness. Understand what's happening, he told himself.

Kassam gathered Rat Face and Monkey Ears at the table, and they moved the gear around. They put the flintlock in the middle of the table, surrounded by modern M9 handguns and M16 rifles. Then Kassam barked what sounded like an order, and another dirtbag came in from the next room. The new dirtbag held a camera.

He conferred with Kassam for a moment, and then snapped photos of the table.

Oh, I get it, Blount thought. One of those photos will go up on some jihadist website: *Captured infidel weapons then and now.* Cute.

Kassam stepped away from the table. The terrorist chieftain began hectoring Blount and his fellow captives. Blount could not understand a word until Monkey Ears came over and translated.

"How do you like your shores of Tripoli now, Marine?"

CHAPTER 20

Gold looked out over the Sahara from the CH-53. The setting sun lent a rose-colored glow to the sands. She hoped enough daylight remained to get a good look at the crash site and find some clues. Since leaving the Army, she had struggled with finding the best way to make a dent, to ease the misery that plagued the world around her. The U.S. drawdown from Afghanistan had forced her to reevaluate how to use her talents. But now those talents had been misapplied because of a terrorist ploy, and Gold wanted to find those scumbags and stop them. Anger seldom motivated her, but it motivated her now. The burn of it felt strange down in her chest.

In the back of the helicopter, she sat on a troop seat near the two Marine officers, Captain Privett and Lieutenant Colonel Loudon. The officers carried rifles, but Gold had only a digital camera, a canteen, a booklet of M8 paper, and a supply of M291 decontamination pads. All wore headsets connected to the aircraft's interphone system.

A lot of questions rattled around in Gold's mind, but one remained foremost: Where are you, Gunny? He had to be somewhere out in that vast desert, dead or alive—and if alive, captured or trying to evade capture. Would all of Gunny's strength and compassion, his love of kids, his devotion to his Marines, his competence as a warrior decay down to dust somewhere in those trackless dunes? The thought of losing him turned up the heat simmering inside Gold. She cautioned herself to focus that rage, keep it under control. Wrath ranked among the seven deadly sins—for a reason.

"That's a whole lot of nothing out there," Privett said on interphone as he gazed outside.

"You got that right," Loudon said. "Colonel Parson has the Mirages and the HH-60s going up again, and there's a drone up there most of the time. But they got a shitload of territory to cover."

It would help, Gold knew, if one of the missing Marines or Legionnaires would make a radio call or at least turn on a beacon. But so far, nothing. No electronic signature of any kind. She looked out the windows, too, and let several minutes pass without saying anything. When she finally spoke, she tried to offer a sliver of hope.

"You know," she said, "Gunny Blount's pretty resourceful."

At least she'd thought of something truthful to say. Not "He'll be all right." He probably wouldn't. Not "We'll find him." In the unlikely event Blount was ever seen again—except in a slaughter video—he'd probably be found dead.

Privett and Loudon both looked over at Gold, and Loudon nodded. Yes, Gunny Blount was resourceful. They seemed to like the truth of that statement. No point in offering false encouragement to Marines.

"Ten minutes," came an announcement from the cockpit. "Better finish suiting up."

They had delayed putting on gas masks for as long as possible. The darn things were pretty uncomfortable. During chem exercises, Gold had seen people go into claustrophobic panics and rip the masks off their heads. The exercise inspectors would, of course, immediately mark them down as dead.

Gold had no issues with mask-induced claustrophobia, though she certainly didn't enjoy wearing chem gear. She peeled open the Velcro enclosure of her mask carrier, removed the mask. She checked the filter to make sure it was screwed in tightly, and she placed the mask over her face. Pulled the retaining straps over her head and tugged at the tabs. Covered the filter with her hand, inhaled to check the seal. Good test.

Wordlessly, she unbuckled her seat belt and turned to Privett. She checked the security of his suit, the tightness of the drawstrings, the overlap of his sleeves around the wrist sections of his gloves. It always helped to use the buddy system to suit up for a toxic environment, to make sure no skin was exposed, no clothing had been left loose enough to admit chemical agents. As she examined Privett's gas mask, she found a loose retaining strap. The loose strap allowed part of the mask's seal to come away from his skin when he exhaled.

"Hold still," she said. Tugged the strap tight.

When she finished, Privett placed the hood of his chem suit over his head, then checked Loudon's mask and suit. Gold buckled her seat belt for landing. The helicopter descended, and when it rolled into a turn, she looked out to see the crash site. The scene nearly made her physically ill.

Below, she saw the hulk of a CH-53 Super Stallion, just like the one she was riding. Debris lay around it, probably parts the chopper had scattered as it hit the ground. Darkened sand surrounded the wreck, although the aircraft did not appear to have burned. Maybe spilled oil, hydraulic fluid, or fuel accounted for the discolored sand.

The Marine pilots kept the CH-53 in a turn, and a couple of orbits over the area revealed no sign that any bad guys had come back. The pilots landed several hundred yards away from the crash site. A good idea, Gold figured. Otherwise the rotor wash would have disturbed whatever evidence remained. The HH-60s that had recovered the bodies earlier, as well as the surviving CH-53 from the initial mission, might have already compromised evidence.

The helo shut down, and Loudon and Privett climbed from the aircraft, gloved fingers over the trigger guards of their weapons. Gold followed. Their bulky suits slowed their movements, and in the barren terrain, she could not help but think of a moon landing. She felt like a space traveler encased in protective gear, surrounded by an environment that could kill her if her suit suffered so much as a pinhole.

Parson had briefed her on how to document a crash scene. He wanted lots of photos, and he'd said to begin with a wide shot of the whole area. Get an establishing shot, he'd said, just like a filmmaker would use to open a scene. Gold fumbled in a leg pocket for the camera. The butyl gloves made it a challenge even to turn on the thing, but she eventually pressed the power button and heard a faint zing as the camera came to life.

She aimed the camera, took a shot of the wreckage and the abandoned village behind it. Moved closer to the crash site. Shell casings littered the ground, most of them the 5.56 millimeter of Marine M16s. Gold also saw the shorter brass of M9 pistol ammunition, along with the 7.62 millimeter of AK-47s. The Marines had given a hell of a fight; no doubt about that.

Few bootprints indented the sand. Gold imagined rotor wash or desert winds had erased them.

The temperature hovered in the upper eighties, and Gold began to sweat inside her suit. She hated to stop work to drink water, but she knew if she didn't hydrate she might pass out and become a danger to the others. She put her camera away, dug into another pocket and found a decon pad.

In a chemical environment, the simplest tasks became complicated. Her gas mask included a drinking tube that mated with a receptacle on the canteen cap. She could insert the tube without ever exposing the water to toxins. But the cap might have become contaminated. Gold opened the decon pad and rubbed it across the canteen cap. Felt the outside of her mask for the tube, but couldn't quite find it.

Even drinking water required the buddy system. Loudon walked up to her, peered at her mask, and detached the drinking tube coupling from her mask's outlet valve cover.

"Thanks," Gold shouted, knowing the gear muffled her words.

Loudon took her canteen, decontaminated the tube coupling, and seated the tube in the canteen's cap. He turned the canteen upside down to let gravity do its job. With her teeth, Gold took hold of the end of the tube inside the mask. Then she began to drink from the tube like sipping soda from a straw.

The water was warm and tasted like a canteen that had sat in storage for five years. Gold wished she'd thought to bring Gatorade or at least put ice in the water. But the foul-tasting water would keep her from keeling over.

She took her teeth off the tube and yelled, "You need to drink, too, sir."

Loudon nodded, and Gold took his canteen. Set him up to drink just the way he'd done for her. When he finished, they replaced their canteens on their web belts and continued the survey of the crash site. Privett was already at the wreck of the helicopter, snapping his own photos. Something on the ground caught his attention, and Privett motioned with his arm for Loudon and Gold to come take a look. Loudon trudged over, walking heavily in the rubber boots that covered his combat boots. Gold followed close behind.

At Privett's feet lay a gas mask—one of the American models, an MCU-2 like Gold's. Something had stained the sand around it with discoloration a shade different than the petroleum stains near the helicopter. Blood from a gunshot wound, perhaps, or the result of someone vomiting his guts out while dying of chemical exposure. The wreckage had shielded the discolored sand from wind that might have covered it with more sand. Gold tried to stay in an analytical frame of mind and not get angrier, not think about the suffering that had happened on this very spot.

She wondered how contaminated the area remained. The M9 tape on her suit showed no color change, but she wanted to check more closely. Gold opened an outside pocket on her gas mask carrier and found her M8 test paper. The sheets of M8 paper came in booklets of twenty-five. She flipped through the booklet, and with her rubber-clad fingers tried to grab hold of a single page. The gloves robbed her of all dexterity; she felt like a surgeon operating with oven mitts. When she thought she'd grabbed a single sheet between her thumb and forefinger, she made a tearing motion and ripped away four sheets.

Gold let three sheets flutter away while she held on to one. She placed the booklet back inside the mask carrier, then kneeled beside the discarded gas mask on the ground. Touched the paper to the gas mask's face shield. Held up the paper to examine it.

No color change.

M8 paper reacted immediately in temperatures above freezing, so Gold would have seen the evidence if chemicals remained on the mask. Most chemical agents dissipated quickly, but the absence of nerve gas in one spot didn't mean the whole area had cleared. She walked a few steps, placed the test paper against the ground. Still nothing.

She moved to the front of the wrecked helicopter and touched the paper to the aircraft's refueling probe. Examined the paper, saw no reaction.

"Everything I've checked so far is clean," Gold shouted.

Loudon gave a thumbs-up. Gold debated declaring the area safe and removing her mask; it certainly would feel good to take off the thing. But she decided to test a few more surfaces.

Gold reached up to one of the cracked windscreen panels of the CH-53, wiped the test paper across the dirty glass. The effort left a clean streak on the windscreen, and the M8 sheet seemed to have picked up only dust. But a corner of the paper changed color. The difference was so subtle Gold nearly missed it: beige to yellow.

Yellow indicated G-series nerve gas.

A different variety. Parson had told her the M9 tape worn by the pararescuemen who first responded to the crash indicated V-series gas. The terrorists possessed an assortment of chemical weapons, and they didn't seem to be running out.

"Got a positive," Gold yelled.

She showed the M8 paper to Loudon and Privett. Loudon took the paper and held it up in the light of the setting sun.

"Yeah," Loudon said, "that's definitely yellow."

A few things could cause a false positive, Gold knew. Wasp spray, for one. Not likely anyone had wandered through here with a can of Raid. So the area remained hot.

Gold covered the inlet port of her gas mask filter and inhaled, just as she'd done when she first donned the mask. The resulting vacuum squeezed the mask against her face, reconfirming a tight seal. A needless gesture at this point, but now that she had hard evidence of contamination, the extra check made her feel safer. Loudon and Privett rechecked their suits, tightened drawstrings. Gold pulled out her camera again and hunted for more clues.

She didn't quite know what else to look for. But amid the shell casings and bent metal, she found something that would certainly interest the chain of command and the intelligence community.

A dud round lay at her feet, most likely from some sort of mortar. The round carried the tail fins typical of an ordinary mortar shell, but its middle section looked a little longer than normal. Propellant had scorched the fins, but for whatever reason, the warhead had not exploded. Only part of the shell remained visible in the sand; the nose had buried itself. Did that thing contain a load of sarin or some other witch's brew just waiting to go off?

Gold felt pretty confident her chem gear would protect her from trace exposure to toxins. But she didn't care to see how the mask and suit would perform if she got hit with a concentrated dose. She snapped a photo and backed away.

If a dud round had turned up after an attack on an Army base, Gold would have followed the five Cs: Confirm presence of unexploded ordnance. Clear personnel. Cordon the area by at least three hundred feet. Check for other UXOs. Control the area and let only emergency services inside the cordon.

Those emergency services would have included explosive ordnance disposal, to disarm or destroy the damned thing. Lacking all those resources for now, she could only warn the others.

"Got a UXO," she shouted.

"Where?" Loudon called.

Gold pointed.

"I still don't see it," Privett said.

Gold could understand. Perhaps in training exercises the young officer had directed searches for unexploded rounds following a mock attack. But in those exercises, UXOs were usually easy to spot. Instructors might place an intact, inert shell right on a sidewalk. But real mortars falling in real combat zones looked different. Gold had learned to recognize them despite their tendency to hide.

With her heel, she dug a long line in the sand to mark the UXO as best she could. She added short diagonal furrows at the front of the line to form an arrow pointing to the shell. A lame effort that would soon get blown away by wind, but the best she could do at the moment. Loudon took pictures of the UXO, as well.

After surveying the crash site, they moved to the abandoned village where the terrorists had hidden. The casings of expended AK-47 ammo littered the ground in greater numbers. Doors of mud-brick homes stood open. Inside the buildings, rough furniture sat broken and overturned. Smashed crockery crunched underfoot. In one kitchen, spilled flour dusted the floor.

All these signs suggested to Gold a settlement vacated recently and quickly. Not the first time jihadists had taken over and destroyed a village. Strangely, no animals wandered the alleyways—not a single cat, goat, or chicken. Gold suspected the blowback from chemical weapons had driven them away.

She found it curious that she saw no people, dead or alive. Had everybody evacuated? Or had the jihadists killed everyone and buried the bodies? She'd never known terrorists to go to the trouble of digging graves for their victims. As Gold and the Marine officers searched the dwellings, she entertained a fleeting thought that with no death odor in the air, there must be no corpses.

Then she remembered no odor would get through her gas mask filter. During her Army training, she had once worn a mask in a bunker filled with tear gas. The air she inhaled carried no stench or sting at all. After a few minutes the instructors ordered the trainees to hold their breaths, remove their masks, and run from the bunker. Once Gold got outside the bunker, the mere traces of tear gas that drifted from her clothing made her eyes and nose stream. Each breath felt like inhaling thorns. Private Gold fell to her knees, hacking and groaning but marveling at how the mask had let her breathe with no discomfort in a room filled with that awful stuff.

So now, instead of following a stench through the village, she followed flies. Through the broken window of a cinder block hovel, black flies buzzed, lit on shattered glass, flitted in and out of the building. Their presence surprised her; she'd have thought the chemicals would have kept them away. But perhaps the poisons were dissipating enough for the flies to survive.

Gold looked through the window. At first she thought she saw piles of laundry. Then she recognized feet and hands, bloated bellies, exposed skin with an unnatural green tint. Perhaps two dozen bodies had been tossed into that room: men, women, children. Apparently the terrorists had dragged all the bodies into that room to get them out of sight as they waited for the Marines.

Now her anger boiled. Her hands sweated inside her double set of gloves. All these innocents, murdered because they got in the jihadists' way. Gold closed her eyes for a moment, grappled with the fury within her.

She had seen other massacres, in Afghan villages attacked by the

Taliban. Facing such horrors never got easier. If anything, each incident tore at her heart worse than the one before. She had long ago stopped asking why a higher power allowed such things to happen; the answer to that question would not come in this mortal life.

Gold gestured to Privett and Loudon.

"Sirs," she shouted through her mask, "you need to see this." Bit off each word as if it had a caustic taste.

The Marine officers joined her at the window, peered inside.

"Oh, God," Privett said.

"I wondered where everybody had gone," Loudon said. He pushed open the door. Flies rose inside the room, swarmed around, settled again. "We gotta document this," he said. He took out his camera, and Gold did the same.

She took a photo of a boy lying on his back, sweatshirt bunched under his arms, chest exposed, dried blood around his mouth and nose. She snapped an image of a man atop a heap of other bodies, a gunshot wound to his head. She captured another shot of a woman wearing an olive headscarf. The woman's body showed no obvious sign of injury, and her mouth remained frozen open. Gold could imagine the agonized final breaths, pain eased only by death's final release.

"Looks like they shot the ones who didn't get slimed," Privett said.

"Those might have been the lucky ones," Loudon said.

The village yielded still more evidence. The houses protected some of the alleys from wind and rotor wash, and in those pathways Gold found bootprints and blood spatters. Some of the blood, dried to a rust color, had smeared across the outside wall of a home. Perhaps someone had fallen against the wall after taking a bullet. Other bloodstains streaked the stones of a walkway and suggested a body dragged across the stones.

Gold wondered what was going through the minds of Privett and Loudon. They knew all the Marines who'd fought here. As Loudon snapped more photos, Gold could not discern his expression underneath his gas mask.

"What do you make of all this?" she asked.

"Hard to say," Loudon said. "Can't tell which of the blood and shell casings came from the firefight with our guys and which of it happened when the insurgents first entered the village."

And some of the blood might have come from wounded terrorists, Gold supposed. Maybe the Marines and Legionnaires had given as good as they got. She just wished she knew where Gunny Blount was now. Gold had once found herself in the hands of terrorists. If anybody could handle that kind of stress, Gunny Blount could. As Gold's mind strained to find excuses for hope, she thought of a *National Geographic* article she'd read about the brain chemistry of explorers and adventurers. According to the article, the brains of explorers and their like—pilots, sailors, soldiers, and Marines—produced large amounts of dopamine. Dopamine, a neurotransmitter, helped process anxiety and control motor skills. In other words, it had a lot to do with functioning under pressure.

In Gold's long career, she'd seen people with varying ability to handle dire stress. Some could hack it and some could not. She didn't know if you could break it down to organics; to her, courage and skill were spiritual things. But if dopamine would help, then she wished Blount all the dopamine in the world.

Gold examined the bloodstains and drag marks more closely. Someone appeared to have been pulled to a vehicle; the drag marks ended at a set of tire tracks. The tire tracks stood out clearly in the fine sand of an alley between two houses.

"Looks like they put somebody in a truck or an SUV," Gold said.

"Or several somebodies," Loudon said.

She tried to imagine the scene: wounded and poisoned men thrown into vehicles, voices shouting in Arabic, rifles jabbing and pointing. Sick and injured prisoners taken . . . where?

Gold followed the tire tracks, hoping to get a direction of travel. Only one dusty road led through this village; maybe she could at least learn which way down that road the insurgents had fled.

But as soon as the tire tracks reached the end of the alley, they disappeared. The blast of helicopters and the rush of the wind had left the desert as desolate as if no man had ever crossed it.

CHAPTER 21

Blount had always enjoyed good health; he could count on one hand the times he'd been really sick. One of those came during seventh grade when a flu bug put him down for two weeks. During that illness, strange and vivid dreams haunted his sleep. Lost in deep woods that formed a maze. Charged by a bull with steel horns. Attacked by a buzzard that wouldn't let him alone until he picked up a dead tree limb and knocked the bird out of the air.

Such vivid dreams came to him now, with all the stark colors of the flu dreams. But the new dreams did not take him into fights with monsters. Instead they took him into his past.

He found himself standing on yellow footprints painted on pavement—his first day of boot camp at Parris Island. Not far from his home, but an entirely different world. His grandfather had tried to prepare him for the rigors of basic training. Physically, he was ready. The running, the obstacle course, the heat all challenged him, but he met each challenge. The difficulty came with the mental stress: the yelling, the impossible-to-please drill instructors, the stuff he had to memorize.

One day a DI demanded that he recite the first general order of a sentry. Blount drew a blank.

"Sir," he said, "this recruit's first general order is—" Nothing. No words would come.

"What's your problem, there, recruit?" the DI shouted. "Got

vapor lock in that mush brain of yours? How are you gonna think under fire?"

"Sir," Blount yelled. The DIs wanted everything loud. "This recruit—"

The DI moved in for the kill. His sweating face, veins bulging, came within an inch of Blount's nose.

"This recruit blah blah blah!" the DI screamed. "You can't even tell me your first general order? You gotta be shitting me!"

"Sir, no excuse, sir."

"Damn right there ain't no excuse. I bet every other recruit in this platoon can tell me their first general order." The DI barked at the boy standing at attention next to Blount. "You there. Dunnigan. Tell me the first general order."

Dunnigan recited it flawlessly.

"See how easy it was for him," the DI yelled at Blount. "I think I know what you are, Recruit Blount. You're our first FTA."

Blount's heart nearly shattered. Failure to adapt. Not good enough for the Corps. Not good enough for his grandfather. Recruit Blount resolved not to let that happen.

He studied whenever they let him stand still. He studied while standing in the vaccination line, while waiting his turn at an obstacle, while drinking the lukewarm water they gave him. He memorized the general orders, the chain of command, the assembly and disassembly of the M16 rifle. He awaited the challenge of the next time a DI demanded to hear the first general order.

That moment came back to him now in a dream so real he could feel the Parris Island humidity.

"Recruit Blount, what is your first general order?"

"Sir," Blount shouted as loudly as he could, "this recruit's first general order is to take charge of this post and all government property in view."

The DI took a step back.

"All right, Blount," he said. "Tell me your chain of command."

Blount recited the names, all the way from his drill instructors to the Navy secretary to Defense Secretary William Perry and President Bill Clinton.

"Well, maybe Recruit Blount has finally managed to unfuck himself." The DI walked away to harass somebody else.

Blount came to wakefulness in his chains and filth with the words of the first general order ringing in his ears as if he'd just shouted them.

This recruit's first general order is to take charge of this post and all government property in view.

He looked around, tried to take stock of things. Ivan lay on his side, with his hand over the pressure bandage on his leg. The Russian appeared to sleep. Fender sat awake with his back to the wall, chains coiled on the floor beside him. The corporal nodded when Blount looked into his eyes. Shackles partially covered Fender's tattoo, the one on his left wrist that read *Anne*. You had something to live for, too, Blount thought. Too sad to ponder, especially with a boy that young. At least Blount had enjoyed a good life for a while, with a fine family and home. Until he threw it all away. Nothing left now but to die a good death.

As if reading Blount's mind, Rat Face came into the room. He wore a leering grin, which made his acne and rat nose all the more ugly. Rat Face looked at Blount and made a slashing motion under his throat with his finger. Then he held up the finger as if indicating a one.

Yeah, I know, Blount thought. One day till the executions start. Unless the coalition leaves all of North Africa today, which ain't gonna happen.

Rat Face retreated into the adjoining room and returned with a tray carrying three bowls. Breakfast time, then. Blount guessed Rat Face resented his job of helping feed the prisoners, so he needed to start his day by taunting them. When Rat Face brought Blount's bowl, he spilled part of it on Blount's legs. He walked away with a smirk.

The bowl contained lentil gruel again, this time cold. Blount tipped the bowl to his lips and forced down several mouthfuls of the sorry excuse for food. Tasted like congealed lard. He wanted very much to wash it down with some water. Couldn't hurt to ask.

"Water," Blount said. "We need water." Maybe Monkey Ears was in the next room and would understand the English. Blount had no idea if any of the other dirtbags spoke his language.

Blount heard some abba-dabba talk next door. Some of it sounded like bitching. Then came the sound of pouring. Good, then.

Rat Face came in with two tin cups. He sat one down beside Ivan and one beside Fender. Left and came back with one more cup, and brought another dirtbag in tow.

Standing over Blount, Rat Face made a hawking sound at the back of his throat and brought up a gobbet of mucus. Spat into Blount's cup. Put down the cup and walked off laughing with the other dirtbag.

So you got your worthless little ass kicked by a man half-dead from poison, Blount thought, and now you want to save face.

That was all right. Blount had resolved to kill one more enemy before they killed him. And he hoped it would be Rat Face.

Blount picked up his water cup. The ball of snot and spit floated on top. He shook the cup until the gobbet floated to the edge, and he poured it onto the floor. The rest of the water looked clean enough, so he put the cup to his mouth, drank it all down with one long pull. He needed to stay hydrated to get his strength back, and he didn't expect to live past the incubation period of whatever germs he ingested.

Fender shuddered when he saw Blount drink the water. Blount shrugged and whispered, "How do you feel, bud?"

"Like shit. But it don't matter, does it?"

Blount wished he could form some encouraging reply, but he

lacked the words. Maybe it didn't matter how any of them felt if they were about to die anyway. Blount just hoped he, Fender, and the others could focus long enough to go out the right way. If you accepted that you were already dead, you could function so much better.

But Blount found that acceptance hard to maintain. His mind seemed bound to seek hope, to think of home, to want to return to Bernadette and the girls. Those thoughts could lead to nothing but despair. He forced himself to think only of the here and now and his final mission of taking out one more bad guy. Channeling his mind down that single narrow path felt like walking a fallen pine log to cross a creek, balancing with each step.

From time to time Blount would see a mental image of his wife or one of his daughters. That only sapped his concentration and made his eyes brim. So he tried to work on mission planning. When they came to get him, what combatives could he use?

More than likely, one dirtbag would unlock his shackles while another held a rifle on him. When he made his move, the dirtbag with the weapon would open up for sure. Blount could expect to have only a second or two. He'd have time for one explosive blow, and he'd need to make it count. So, what type of blow?

That depended. He could strike as soon as they unlocked the first arm or wait until they freed both arms. Both arms would give him more options. But if he acted as soon as they freed the first one, he might have more element of surprise. Maybe get an extra half second to work.

And what would that work involve? A punch to the throat to crush the windpipe? That would put the dirtbag down right now but not necessarily kill him. A palm strike to the nose? Blount had heard of that blow killing by driving bone fragments into the brain, but he'd have to get the angle just right. Put the guy's head in a Muay Thai clinch and knee him in the gut? That would take too long and probably not inflict lethal damage.

How about just snapping the neck? Hmm. If he did it just right, he could pull that off with one quick, violent twist. One hand on the enemy's chin and the other over the back of his head. Push with one hand; pull with the other, hard and fast. Dirtbag would probably die before he hit the ground. Blount liked that plan. Kinda elegant.

Alternatively, he could grab Rat Face—or whoever—by the head with both hands, pivot, and slam his skull into the wall. Might could do that even with both hands still chained, if he stayed close enough to the wall to provide some slack. Dig thumbs into Rat Face's eyes in the process. That way, if Rat Face happened to survive the head injury, he'd live the rest of his miserable life blind.

Planning helped occupy Blount's thoughts, but his plan would have to stay flexible. He couldn't know the way they'd unlock him, the postures and angles the situation would present. He'd have to rely on instinct. And speed. The moment would require a clear mind and a recovered body.

In the meantime he could only rest, eat, drink. And observe. You could never have too much intel and situational awareness. What was the strength of the enemy force?

Well, there was Rat Face and Monkey Ears, along with one other unnamed dirtbag Blount had seen that morning. Judging from the voices speaking Arabic next door, there was at least one additional guard, for a minimum of four. No sign of their boss, Sadiq Kassam. Apparently he came and went. Probably spent most of his time in a more comfortable place. Why would he stay in this hovel if he didn't have to?

Their weaponry? They all seemed to have AKs, though Blount thought he remembered seeing at least one pistol during his ride in the back of the truck. And of course, they had all the weapons they'd taken from the Marines and Legionnaires.

Blount looked at the table across the room. His own M16 remained there, along with all the other gear. Funny thing—Kassam had left his flintlock pistol there, too. Why would he do that? Because he planned to come back soon.

Naturally, he planned to come back soon. He'd return to video the first execution tomorrow. Dear Lord, who would it be? Blount allowed a selfish thought: Please let it be me. Lemme take one down and then get shot. Let's just get it over with. Don't let me have to hear somebody else screaming, and then another one, and then another one.

He forced those thoughts away. Grabbed hold of his mind like he'd put a sparring partner in a choke hold. You better man up, Recruit Blount, he told himself. Stop this, stop this, stop this.

Take whatever comes, and deal with it. Focus.

Chains clanked as Fender reached for his water cup. He drank until he emptied it, but he never touched his food. Blount took in a deep breath, reminded himself the best way to fix yourself was to help somebody else.

"Eat that," Blount whispered. "You need the calories."

"For what, Gunny?"

"For you don't know what. You're still on duty, Marine. Just get yourself ready to resist any way you can."

"Aye, Gunny."

Blount wanted to add a thought or two, to tell Fender he had a responsibility to feed his body. At this point that body no longer served as a vessel for his hopes and plans, the mortal coil to take him into old age. There would be no old age. His brain and bones, muscles and blood now retained only one final function—to serve as a weapons system.

But Blount didn't get to follow up. Before he could whisper another word, Rat Face came running in with an AK, shouting the only English he seemed to know.

"No talk! No talk!"

He pointed the rifle at Blount's face, kicked him in the side. Sent a stab of pain through Blount's ribs.

"No talk!"

Rat Face stomped Blount's right shin with a glancing blow. That brought a different kind of hurt. Felt like it scraped off some skin.

"Leave him alone," Fender said.

What was this? Fender bucking up? Good on him, Blount thought.

Rat Face kicked Fender in the face. Fender's head jerked back, and blood streamed from both nostrils. Blount would have loved to grab Rat Face right then, but he still felt pretty weak. So he bided his time. And groaned as if badly hurt.

That seemed to encourage Rat Face. He turned from Fender with a smirk on his face and directed his attention back to Blount. Held the AK in his right hand. With his left, he reached down and picked up one of Blount's chains. Snatched hard.

The yanking motion flailed Blount's arm and torqued his shoulder. Made Blount mad more than it hurt. Blount snapped his wrist back and ripped the chain from Rat Face's hand.

The rusty links scraped Rat Face's fingers and drew blood. Infuriated, Rat Face stalked to the corner of the room, propped his rifle against the wall. Came back and grabbed both of Blount's chains.

He jerked both chains rhythmically, forced Blount's arms to fly around like a marionette's. At first Rat Face's expression was twisted in fury, but then he found Blount's torment amusing and began to laugh. And jerk harder.

Blount could feel his rotator cuffs beginning to hurt. He moved with the yanks and pulls like he'd weave in anticipation of a sparring partner's punch. The dancing motion minimized the damage to his shoulders but made Rat Face laugh all the more.

So you wanna pull my chain for real, Blount thought. Just you wait.

The rings that anchored Blount's chains squeaked as they twisted with the motion Rat Face's yanking imparted. With each pull, they flipped away from the wall and then dropped back down with a metallic clink.

The commotion woke Ivan. The Legionnaire levered himself with his arms to a sitting position. Wearing a puzzled expression, he regarded the scene for a moment. Then he barked out a phrase like he was giving an order.

"*Ça suffit!*"

Blount didn't know the words, but whatever the meaning, it had the effect of making Rat Face drop the chains. He stepped over Blount to kick Ivan's wounded leg. Through gritted teeth, the Legionnaire let out a combination of a groan and a hiss, leaned forward and put his hands over the bloody pressure bandage. Then he spewed a string of words that could only be Russian profanity.

Monkey Ears came from next door. He spoke in Arabic. Rat Face shrugged, laughed, left the room. Monkey Ears watched him go, fingered a cigarette from a shirt pocket, lit the cigarette with a butane lighter. Returned to the other room, left a swirl of blue smoke in his wake.

Blount turned to Ivan and mouthed the words *You okay?*

The Legionnaire raised his eyebrows in a questioning manner. Muscles stretched tight across his jaw, and he pressed his lips together so hard they turned pale. Must have hurt pretty bad, then. Hell of a way to start his day. Blount didn't like the color of the blood seeping through Ivan's bandage, either. He was no medic, but he thought the blood should have flowed brighter red than the wine-colored stain spreading through the fabric.

Old Ivan had guts; Blount gave him that much. The dude had to know if he said anything he'd bring abuse on himself. Good thing we never had to fight the Russians, Blount considered. Though they served an awful system, they generated a tough breed of man. Blount had heard of Russian firefighters who parachuted into forest fires and battled flames for days while living on little but what they could hunt, catch, and forage.

Blount slid back against the wall and tried to settle his mind. In a way, Rat Face's effort to torment and humiliate him made his job easier. Anger motivated a man much better than despair. Thoughts of vengeance came in straight lines and tight channels, where sadness got all fuzzy. Yeah, Blount remembered his grandfather's advice about not letting hate take control. That guidance applied most of the time, Blount thought, but I'm hating right now and I ain't ashamed of it.

And Blount's thinking was getting clearer all the time. Maybe that poison was wearing off.

He leaned on his left elbow, just where his left chain hooked into the wall. The floor felt grittier than before. He looked at his arm and saw light-colored granules sticking all over his skin. Now where did that come from?

Underneath the metal ring cemented into the wall was a circle of what looked like white sand. Blount touched the sand with his index and middle fingers.

It was not sand at all but abraded cement fallen away from where it had been troweled into the wall to secure the rings. As Rat Face had yanked the chains, the motion had forced the rings and the bolts that held the chains to wear against the cement.

Blount put his hand on the ring and pulled. Nothing. Still anchored. Then he twisted it. The bolt holding the ring moved ever so slightly. Blount could not pull out the ring and bolt, but he could twist the bolt about a quarter of an inch. Maybe a flange or something on the other end of the bolt kept him from extracting it altogether. At any rate, the poor-quality cement had chafed and ground away while Rat Face played his little game.

Interesting. Blount had never worked construction, but he knew there was a little bit of art to building with cement. He remembered back when he was little and all the tobacco farmers modernized their operations. They stopped curing their leaf in log barns. In place of the log structures they installed big metal bulk barns, which sat on cement slabs. A farmer expected to use a bulk barn for decades, so he didn't want it sitting on sorry, crumbling cement. He'd have somebody who knew what they were doing pour that slab. The men would wait for the proper temperature and humidity, and they'd mix the cement just right. They'd put some know-how into it.

But these jihadist thugs probably mixed cement the way they did everything else: hurriedly, stupidly, in the roughest manner possible. And that gave Blount an idea.

CHAPTER 22

Parson sat on a cot in a rec tent the French had put up in their section of the base at Mitiga. The Americans had already dubbed that area the French Quarter, and the French masseuse, Michèle, had set up shop in the rec tent. Michèle's iPod, connected to a speaker, played Edith Piaf at low volume. Chartier lay on a padded table, wearing only shorts. Hot stones lay across the small of his back. Michèle pressed her fingers against the blades of Chartier's shoulders, kneaded his muscles. Parson remained fully clothed in his flight suit and boots, and he fidgeted as he chatted with Chartier.

"You really should try this, sir," Chartier said. "It will help you think."

Parson shook his head. "No, thanks, Frenchie. Got no time."

The very suggestion annoyed him. How could he relax and get a massage, for heaven's sake, while Blount and the others were still out there, going through God only knew what? The rational part of his mind didn't resent Chartier having a massage. The man had just returned from a long sortie, and other Mirage crews would soon take to the skies. But part of Parson wanted to grab Chartier's flight suit—now draped across the back of a chair—wad it up in a ball, throw it at him and yell *Get your ass back in the air!*

Instead, Parson controlled his frustration and said, "Frenchie, we got everything from Libyan puddle-jumpers to satellites looking for those boys. The Joint Personnel Recovery Agency is coordinating all that now. But if there's anything else we can do on our end, I want it done. If you have any ideas, let's talk about them."

Michèle removed the black stones from Chartier's lower back, worked the base of his neck with her thumbs. She wore a white pullover that highlighted her figure, and she smelled vaguely of coconut. Massage oil, perhaps, or sunscreen to protect her skin from the Saharan sun. The scent put Parson in mind of beaches and bikinis, an image all out of accord with the problems at hand.

He liked attractive women as much as the next guy, and Michèle was as hot as the igniters in a Pratt and Whitney. At the moment, however, he saw her as a distraction. He even wished she were off his base, but the French had their ways. As long as the Mirage drivers got things done, he had no right to object.

"Hmm," Chartier said. "Perhaps I have an idea."

That piqued Parson's curiosity. He wanted to hear any input that might help. The Air Force had taught him to lead that way; the Crew Resource Management program encouraged aircraft commanders to listen to suggestions from even the lowest-ranking loadmaster or gunner. You never knew who might have noticed something or thought of something that would prevent disaster. Parson considered CRM just plain old common sense, and he tried to apply it not only in the cockpit but in everything he did.

"Then let's get back to ops for a little conference," Parson said.

"Yes, sir," Chartier said. He spoke in French to Michèle. She gave a mock pout as he sat up. She tied her black hair in a ponytail, went over to the chair, and handed him his flight suit.

As Chartier got dressed, Parson thought of the book the Mirage pilot had given him. The author, Saint-Ex, had once crashed in this same desert, miles from where anybody would have looked for him. He described the ordeal in a chapter titled "Prisoner of the Sand." Saint-Ex and his mechanic, Prévot, wandered the Sahara for days before getting rescued by a Bedouin. The French airman wrote of the thirst that swelled his tongue, the visions of water sources that broke his heart as they evaporated into vanishing mirages. And now Blount had become a prisoner of the sand, one way or another. Was he going through something similar to Saint-Ex's ordeal, or worse?

Parson recalled when he'd rescued Gold years ago in the mountains of Afghanistan. He'd used a combination of blunt force and precision. Strong will, and violence of action. But he'd started with a trail to follow, a set of footsteps in the snow. Parson remained a navigator at heart; he attacked problems in terms of getting from point A to point B. That required data, a fix on point B. But now he had only hundreds of miles of sand, and complete radio silence from the missing men.

What if Blount and the others turned up far away from where they'd gone missing? They could be anywhere by now. No solution but to keep as many aircraft aloft as possible, over the widest range possible.

In the ops center, Parson found that the comms people had continued making improvements. They'd set up a satellite dish and installed a video screen. Parson could use the screen for teleconferences, but for now someone had tuned it to CNN. A crawl at the bottom of the screen caught his eye: *Search continues for Marines missing in action.* Parson sighed, led Chartier into his office. Parson took the folding chair, and Chartier sat on a stack of Meals Ready to Eat. One MRE lay on Parson's desk. He unclipped his boot knife and sliced open the meal pouch.

"Not exactly French cuisine," Parson said, "but I'm hungry. You want part of this?"

"Sure," Chartier said. *"Merci."*

Inside the pouch, Parson found a packet labeled MEDITERRANEAN CHICKEN. Oddly fitting. Parson raised his eyebrows, handed the chicken packet and a plastic spoon to Chartier. The Frenchman tore open the pouch and started eating the chicken cold. Parson opened a packet of dried fruit for himself. Ate the contents one item at a time, like eating from a bag of peanuts.

"If I could," Parson said, chewing a raisin, "I'd put up enough planes over North Africa to make an aluminum overcast."

Chartier thought for a moment. "Well," the French pilot said, "I think I know where to start with that."

Parson stopped chewing. "I'm all ears, Frenchie," he said.

"We have eight Mirages we can send up as four pairs, one pair at a time. With tanker support, we can fly six-hour sorties. We're already flying a lot, but if we can get the tankers, we can keep jets up twenty-four hours a day."

The idea improved Parson's mood immediately. He fished a dried cranberry from the packet and popped it into his mouth. Talked as he chewed.

"I like the way you think, Frenchie. Let's tell the joint recovery folks we can offer that if the tankers can support it."

"D'accord."

The 24-7 Mirage flights would supplement the AWACS bird, the Pave Hawks, and all the other aircraft on the lookout for the MIAs. The jets might get pulled away for other missions from time to time, but that was okay with Parson. The pilots would still keep their eyes peeled, they'd still monitor the emergency freqs, and they'd hear if somebody called. And of course, they'd always go out armed, in case the chance presented itself to put fire and steel on bad guys.

Parson opened his secure e-mail. He tapped at his keyboard for a few minutes, considering how to word the idea to send it up the chain of command. Finally, he addressed the message to AFRICOM headquarters and to Chartier's bosses in the Armée de l'Air, and he copied in the Joint Personnel Recovery Agency. Clicked SEND.

"Can't promise anything, Frenchie," Parson said, "but I imagine they'll approve it. Your idea makes a lot of sense."

Parson knew the old joke about Air Force Regulation 1-1: Common sense equals insubordination. But over the course of his career, he'd found his Air Force superiors usually put politics aside when things got this serious.

Chartier left to brief his crews on the change in their mission. Parson got up from his desk and went to the newly installed refrigerator for a soft drink. He found Gold at the front of the operations center, watching CNN.

"Didn't want to interrupt your meeting," Gold said. "What's new?"

She wore the khakis that had become her new uniform, along with her ever-present green-and-black Afghan scarf. Tiny tassels dangled from the edges of the scarf. Though blondes usually had light complexions, her face had taken on an almost permanent tan. Sophia still kept herself Army fit, and she looked like a woman who'd spent so much time afield that deserts and mountains had become her natural element. She was in her early forties now, and Parson thought she actually became more attractive as she aged.

He took two Dr Peppers from the fridge, gave one to Gold. He told her about Chartier's idea for round-the-clock flights in the Mirages.

"Sounds like you guys have things covered pretty well from the air," she said. "I'd like to think of something more I can do from the ground."

"Just staying available as an interpreter helps a lot. Maybe we'll capture one of these bastards and ask him a few questions."

"That worked out well last time." Her eyes glinted with an unusual coldness.

Never once had Parson heard Sophia speak sarcastically. She must really feel duped or used, he thought, though nobody could reasonably blame her for what had happened. Maybe she was blaming herself.

Parson put down his Dr Pepper and placed both his hands on her shoulders. Gold leaned in, let him hold her for a moment. Her body relaxed against him as if to let go of all her tension for just an instant.

On the television, a map of North Africa appeared over the anchor's shoulder. Gold pushed away from Parson's grasp. She hunted for the remote and found it on a flight scheduler's desk among half-empty water bottles, Styrofoam coffee cups, and a booklet of approaches for Mediterranean and North African airports. She aimed the remote at the screen and pressed a button with her thumb until the newscast became audible:

"Terrorist leader Sadiq Kassam says he is holding the six Marines and French Foreign Legionnaires who have been missing since Thursday. In a statement delivered to Arab news agencies, Kassam vows to begin executing the prisoners one per day unless coalition forces withdraw from North Africa immediately. Kassam's group, now calling itself Holy Warriors for the Caliphate of Tripolitania, released a photo purportedly showing one of the missing Marines."

The television switched to a full-screen image of the photo. Though video editors had blacked out the prisoner's face, Parson immediately recognized Blount. The gunnery sergeant lay in the back of a Toyota pickup truck, bloodied and beaten. Insurgents sat around him, wielding pistols and AK-47s. He appeared to have vomited down the front of his MOPP suit, and he looked unconscious.

"Oh, God," Parson said, "that's Gunny Blount."

Gold's back straightened and her mouth dropped open. She placed the fingers of her right hand across her lips as she watched the video.

"No," she whispered.

Parson tried to process everything he'd just learned. First, the six missing men were in the hands of an enemy who intended to kill them. Second, the vomit suggested Blount had suffered from chemical exposure. And if Blount had gotten slimed, the rest probably had, too. All this bad news came straight from the news media instead of intel channels because Kassam had delivered the statement and photo directly to media outlets. Everybody was seeing it, both here and back home.

Apparently, a similar thought occurred to Gold.

"I hope Blount's family doesn't see that," she said.

"They almost certainly will."

Parson had known Blount and the others faced dire circumstances. But the visuals brought home the horror in the starkest way. Parson's Marine Corps friend now rode the thinnest edge of existence, with a life expectancy likely measured in hours. The leering captors in the photograph filled Parson with rage. If not for your damned poison toys, he thought, that man would have broken all of you in half with his bare hands.

Before Parson could finish getting his mind around what he'd seen, the newscast cut to a related story:

"The captured military members served with a coalition battling jihadist insurgencies across North Africa. The fighting has created a humanitarian crisis as villagers flee towns attacked by terrorists. The United Nations says its refugee camps have become crowded, and officials are opening new camps in Libya, Algeria, and Tunisia. Our correspondent visited one of those camps. . . ."

The screen displayed a row of blue tents set up in the desert. After the story ended, the anchor interviewed an analyst who discussed the difficulties in supplying remote camps, and the risk of disease caused by overcrowding. Parson wondered how much TV analysts got paid for pointing out the obvious.

"Looks like your UN people have their work cut out for them," Parson said. "We all do."

He didn't know if Blount and the rest of the captives stood any chance at all, but he'd marshal every resource at his disposal. One of those resources stood next to him now. At the moment, Sophia looked more pensive than horrified. Parson's first instinct called for him to keep her out of harm's way. But she had come to help, not stay safe. Once she took on a mission, you couldn't stop her; he'd seen that before.

"I'm almost afraid to ask this," Parson said, "but what are you thinking?"

"I'd like to tour all of those camps. Talk to as many people as I can. Maybe somebody saw something or knows something about where the insurgents hide between attacks."

Parson liked that idea. With Gold looking for human intelligence on the ground and the aircraft watching from the air, it amounted to a two-pronged stab at the problem. Though he'd spent his career as an airlifter, he knew enough about battle to understand the concept of combined arms: Bring to the fight as many different ways to hurt the enemy as possible. A task force might hit them with naval gunfire as well as airplanes. A division might hit them with attack choppers as well as mortars. A platoon might hit them with a .50-cal as well as an antitank rocket. A single infantryman might hit them with his rifle or a grenade. When one thing didn't work, another might. Maintain your options.

"Just tell me when and where you want to go," Parson said.

CHAPTER 23

Once when Blount was a kid, he saw a man dying of snakebite. Frump, the county drunk known only by that nickname, had wandered along a dirt road, thumbing for a ride. When nobody picked him up, he kept going until the road crossed a creek. Frump stumbled down the creek bank instead of walking across the bridge. Maybe he'd already downed a bottle of that cheap apple wine he bought at country stores.

As he waded the creek, Frump stepped on a water moccasin. The snake bit him on the calf. Poor old Frump was too drunk or ignorant to put a constricting band above the bite. Back then, first-aid books still said to cut Xs across the fang punctures and suck out the poison. Frump didn't do that, either. He might have fared better if he'd just sat there and waited for the next farmer to drive by.

Instead, he ran. When he couldn't run anymore, he walked. He traveled three miles to where the dirt road met a paved highway, with Phil's Grocery and Mercantile at the intersection. By the time he got to Phil's, his heart had pumped that venom all over his system.

Blount and his grandfather saw Frump lying under a pin oak back of Phil's, and he was one pitiful sight. Frump kept throwing up, and his calf swelled up bigger than his thigh. Grandpa tried to give the old drunk first aid with a snakebite kit from Phil's shelves, but it was too late. By the time Grandpa scissored open Frump's pant leg, the skin around the bite had discolored to an unnatural shade between blue and gray, as if that part of Frump's body had already turned corpse.

"It burns, it burns," Frump kept saying. His breathing came quick and shallow. The last thing he said that anybody could understand was "My mouth taste all rubbery." Phil tried to give him an RC Cola while they drove him to the hospital in the back of a flatbed, but Frump couldn't even sit up to drink it. Before they reached town, old Frump's sad sojourn on this earth had ended.

"You don't normally die of a cottonmouth bite," Blount's grandfather said later, "unless you're real young, real old, or you got something else already wrong with you. Frump's been poisoning himself with alcohol for years."

Now, as a grown man with military training, Blount knew what killed Frump was a hemotoxin, or what chem warfare specialists would call a blood agent. Blount suspected something different had poisoned him and the other Marines and Legionnaires: a neurotoxin, or nerve agent.

Such idle thoughts occupied Blount's mind as he worked at the bolt that suspended the ring that anchored his left chain to the wall. He gripped the ring and bolt with his left hand held behind his back. Shoulders and head against the wall, Blount stared up at the ceiling with his mouth open like he was sicker than he felt. He could rotate the bolt for about a quarter turn, and he kept grinding it back and forth. At first he thought he made no progress. But his fingers kept getting all powdery, and he'd wipe them on his trousers until the dust blended in with the general filth. Each time, he knew the dust meant that much less cement securing the bolt.

Blount had no idea of the hour except that it was dark outside. Fender and Ivan remained asleep, and from time to time Blount dozed, too, but never for long. At one point, in the netherworld between sleep and wakefulness, he thought he heard the ocean. But then he realized it was only the surf of wind through the desert. He shook off the drowsiness and got back to work. He balanced his need for rest with his lack of time. How long would he have to free himself?

Even if he succeeded, he still expected to die. But this way, he could choose his moment of action instead of just waiting for them to come and get him. A slight tactical advantage.

The sound of shuffling and footsteps came from behind the door. Someone in that room flicked on a light. A shaft of white light angled through the doorway and lit up a slice of the floor. Blount wondered about that; he wouldn't have thought this hovel had electricity. A few minutes later, Rat Face came in with a battery-powered lantern. The lantern threw harsh light and stark shadows, and the glare made Blount squint.

What brought this dirtbag at this hour? Rat Face walked around the room, stopped over Blount. The lantern's twin fluorescent tubes burned Blount's eyes, but he forced himself to look up at his tormentor. Blount's hand remained on the bolt. If he'd worked it free by now, this moment would have presented a golden opportunity. Instinctively, Blount studied the distance and angles. And the targets: Rat Face's head, neck, ribcage, groin, knees, shins.

Rat Face just kept staring. That made Blount worry. Had he been discovered? Had the guards heard the grinding? He dared not move his hand now. He just held his body position, took in long breaths and tried to make them sound ragged. Yeah, dirtbag. I'm still sick and weak. You can come close as you want, and I can't do nothing.

Without a word, Rat Face kicked Blount in the side. Didn't hurt much; Rat Face delivered the kick with poor technique and little power. A hateful and brutish act should come naturally to a terrorist, Blount thought, but this guy is so stupid he can't even get that right. Still, Blount groaned and allowed himself to fall over. He let go of the bolt; he didn't want to look like he was hiding something. He knew Rat Face wouldn't notice the concrete dust. Somebody too dumb even to kick properly wouldn't catch a thing so subtle, especially in dim light.

Blount guessed correctly. Rat Face stood over Blount with a smirk on his face, babbled something in Arabic. Turned and strode into the other room. Victorious again.

So why would that lowlife come in just to deliver a kick? Blount pondered for a moment, then came up with a theory. If the terrorists made good on their threat, the coming day would bring the first execution. Rat Face was too excited to sleep.

A flush of heat came over Blount. The heat of terror, he realized. He began to sweat, and he sensed the salty odor of his own body. The old folks used to say dogs could smell fear, and he wondered if this was how that happened.

Through his nose, Blount drew in a big chestful of air and let it out. This time he did it not to exaggerate sickness but to try to control his body and thus his mind. Stave off panic. He vowed he would not descend into abject fear. Recruit Blount would master himself as he had mastered his rifle.

He pushed himself back up to a sitting position, chains clanking. Placed his hand on the ring and bolt. Twisted back and forth, a quarter turn each way. After several repetitions, Blount rotated the bolt clockwise as far as it would go, then applied all the torque he could muster. The gristle of his hand stretched and tightened so hard he feared he would pop a tendon or break a bone. The binding force traveled all the way up his arm to his shoulder. He gritted his teeth. Held his breath.

Something gave.

The bolt lurched in his hand. Metal scraped against cement with such force that Blount just knew Rat Face heard it. Sounded like when you were plowing tobacco and a plow point struck a rock. But the noise drew no reaction.

And now Blount could rotate the bolt a half turn. He tried pulling it out of the wall. The bolt came out about half an inch, then stopped. Clearly he'd knocked away some of the cement that had secured the bolt. That cement must have broken away in a solid chunk that fell inside the wall. Real progress.

Blount forced his mind to focus on this little victory, and it improved his spirits. Kind of like the time back in high school when his team was losing real bad, and he caught an interception and ran forty yards with it. Didn't win the game, but he made the other side's quarterback look like a chump. Took away some of the pain of defeat.

To Blount's right, Fender snored. He lay curled in a fetal position, chain draped over his hips. Good that the boy can get some rest, Blount thought. To his left, Blount felt eyes on him. He turned to see Ivan awake. The Russian leaned on his side, weight supported by his elbow. In the pale light cast from the battery lantern in the other room, perspiration gleamed on Ivan's bald head. Ivan looked at Blount's hand gripped over the ring and bolt, and he gave a nod with a thin smile. Blount considered telling Ivan and Fender to work on their bolts, too, but decided against it. Triple the risk of detection. Ivan looked too weak to apply much torque anyway.

The next twist of the bolt came easier. The flange on the other end dug deeper into the cement; Blount could feel the bite of the metal. The more play he had, the more damage he could do to the cement. He sat awake, twisting, torquing, until the sky lightened to the east. By then the bolt rotated nearly a full turn, and it came out of the wall about two inches. So how long was the darn thing? Three inches or a foot? Only one way to know. Keep cranking on it.

A vehicle pulled up outside. Bustling sounds came from the next room, yammering in Arabic. More lanterns and flashlights clicked on. One of the prisoners in the other room said, "What's happening?"

"Silence," someone hissed. Monkey Ears.

More abba-dabba talk.

So Kassam has come back, Blount thought. Not a good sign at all. Blount had held some small hope that the talk of executions was bluster, that somehow this time would turn out different. The history of these extremists gave no reason for that hope, but the mind sought hope the way lungs sought air. A drowning man could not stop himself from one last attempt at breathing, even if he inhaled water.

Kassam entered the room where Blount, Ivan, and Fender lay chained. Rat Face, Monkey Ears, and two other dirtbags came behind. Monkey Ears shone a flashlight on each of the prisoners. Rat Face held an AK.

Blount froze. Kept his hand behind his back, on the bolt. Had his time come? He still hadn't freed the bolt, so his options remained limited. His palm grew slick as it gripped the iron.

He felt fate rush at him with mind-numbing speed. The walls blurred. He'd sometimes wondered what date would appear as the second date on his headstone. Today's date.

Stop, Blount told himself. Stop, stop, stop. Think tactically. You're back in the dojo for pads-on, full-speed, full-force sparring. Just let it come natural. Muscle memory and training will do their job. This ain't nothing. If they come for you, get up, present your shackles to be unlocked. And shift your feet to assume a fighting stance.

They didn't come for him.

Kassam went over to the table, picked up his flintlock, and stuck it in his sash. He and all the other dirtbags left the room. Ivan and Fender sat up, awake now, part of their chains coiled in their laps.

So I get a little more time, Blount thought. Gotta use it well.

Blount heard the terrorists talking in the next room, and then their voices grew even fainter. Perhaps this building had a third room for a kitchen or something. Blount couldn't be sure; when they'd brought him in he'd been too disoriented and sick to process his surroundings well.

It made no difference. Blount's mission remained the same: get that chain out of the wall. With the dirtbags' eyes off him now, he resumed working at the bolt. Twisted it to the left. Twisted it to the right. Pulled at the same time, for more friction against the cement.

Fender stared at the floor. Ivan looked straight across the room, gazing at things beyond visual range. Blount imagined they'd both thought what he'd thought: This is the end.

Well, this *was* the end. But not this very moment. In the meantime, he wanted them to stay alert. He decided to take a chance on talking.

"Y'all okay?" he whispered.

Fender looked over at him, shrugged. Ivan cut his eyes toward Blount but made no other response.

"Stay loose," Blount whispered. "Be prepared for anything."

He figured Fender, at least, ought to know what that meant. At pretty much any deployed Marine Corps combat ops center, you could find a dry-erase board or a computer file labeled BPT. *Be prepared to do the following.* Be prepared for a convoy. Be prepared for an assault on a high-value target. Be prepared for a recon patrol. Depended on the mission.

In this case, be prepared to follow my lead, whatever that may be.

Through the walls, Blount could hear Kassam and his henchmen talking in excited tones. That didn't bode well; Blount supposed they debated which prisoner to kill first. But for now, it offered a chance for some rare communication.

"Say, Ivan," Blount muttered. "You all right over there?"

Ivan wiped his bald head with his sleeve. In the oddly delicate morning light, the move gave Blount a view of the voluptuous sword-wielding angel inked into Ivan's forearm. Maybe that was the Russian's idea of his guardian.

"Leg hurts," Ivan whispered.

"I know it does. Could you move if you had the chance?"

Ivan watched Blount turning the bolt, seemed to understand.

"I will try."

Sounded good. Now keep him engaged, Blount thought.

"So what's your story, bud?"

Ivan narrowed his eyes, regarded Blount. Seemed to wonder why he'd been asked such a question. Blount hoped he hadn't pissed off the Russian. Just trying to tighten up the team here. Sweat gleamed on Ivan's arms and face, perhaps from heat, perhaps from pain. Ivan's eyes returned to that beyond-the-horizon stare, and then he spoke.

"Fought in Chechnya," he whispered. "Saw bad things. Did bad things."

Blount could imagine. He remembered intel briefings about atrocities committed on both sides in that war: villages bombed, prisoners with their fingers chopped off and throats slit, murders and rapes. One briefing included video of a downed helicopter pilot found lying in a field. Insurgents ordered him to stand up, then cut him down with a burst of rifle fire.

Brutality fed on brutality until it seemed the militants would do anything. Blount recalled watching news reports about an Islamist attack on a school in Beslan, Russia, that left hundreds dead, mainly kids. With his soft spot for children, Blount could not begin to imagine the mentality behind such a thing.

Ivan shifted himself, bent his good leg at the knee, propped one arm on the knee. The chain dangled from his wrist. He looked at Blount again.

"Got out of army, got out of Russia," he whispered. "But life of soldier was all I knew." Shook his head, gave an ironic smile. "Thought with Legion I could serve with best but maybe not have to kill again."

So the life of the soldier was all he knew. Yeah, Blount could relate. And Ivan had lived that life for a pretty good while if he fought in Chechnya. An experienced fighter, then. He sure looked the part.

"You?" Ivan asked.

"Same thing, bud," Blount whispered. "Saw bad things. Did bad things. Got out—well, almost. Got back in."

"Too bad for us."

Yeah, too bad for us, Blount mused. He could have avoided this fate so easily. He *had* avoided it, and then he'd stepped back into its path.

But he stopped that line of thought as if he'd stomped the brakes of an old farm truck on a dirt road. Down that road lay self-pity, a thing that would make him combat-ineffective.

He still had a mission.

Blount gave another twist to the bolt, felt more cement grind away. His final mission might change a little bit, depending on whether and when he could free at least one arm.

He still had his orders, given to him long ago.

Sir, this recruit's first general order is to take charge of this post and all government property in view.

CHAPTER 24

Aloft in a sky the color of a robin's egg, far above desert dust, Parson crouched in the boom operator's pod of a KC-135 Stratotanker. Beside Parson, the boom operator lay at his crew station in a prone position, chin on a padded chin rest, left hand near a control stick for the refueling boom. The tanker jet had taken off from Mitiga on a mission to refuel the Mirages on patrol over North Africa. Somewhere out there Chartier and his backseater shared the sky with the tanker, along with a second Mirage flying as wingman.

The Mirage crews searched for targets of opportunity, listened for distress calls, watched for any signs of the missing Marines and Legionnaires. So far they'd reported nothing. Parson pulled back the sleeve of his flight suit to check his aviator's watch. Pretty soon the French jets would reach bingo fuel. Time to gas up and resume the hunt.

Parson wore a headset so he could follow the tanker's radio traffic and interphone conversations. He rode along on this flight as an ACM, an additional crew member. At Mitiga, he'd set all his resources into motion, given every order that could possibly help Blount. If he just sat at his desk now, sick worry would consume him. He wouldn't even have the solace of talking to Gold; she was so busy setting up her itinerary for visiting refugee camps that she didn't have time to chat. And he'd probably spend time worrying about her, too. Here in the air, he could at least see part of his plans in action.

As a pilot in the C-5 Galaxy, Parson had taken gas from Stratotankers many times, but he'd never seen an aerial refueling from this point of view. Amid UHF hiss, he heard Chartier call the tanker.

"Crude Eight-Seven, Dagger flight has you in sight."

"Roger that, Dagger. Clear to join," the tanker copilot called.

The tanker's left-seat pilot, the aircraft commander, gave an order on interphone.

"Okay, folks, let's knock out the preparation for contact checklist."

Clipped commands crossed the interphone. When the checklist called for the sighting door, the boom operator opened the door to uncover the boom pod window. Beyond the boom pod lay the expanse of the Sahara glaring in the desert sun.

Parson adjusted his sunglasses, peered through the glass. Searched in vain for two specks that would represent a pair of Mirage fighters. The boom operator, a staff sergeant in his early twenties, did the same.

"Tallyho on the Mirages," the boom operator said.

Parson examined the ground and sky. Nothing.

"Where?" he asked.

"Seven o'clock, sir, right at the horizon."

Young eyes, Parson thought. He squinted, scanned in a sideways-8 pattern.

There.

Right where beige ground met azure sky, a pair of dots hovered in the haze. At first they appeared to show no relative movement with the tanker. But after a few seconds, they grew larger and took the shape of arrowheads. The Mirages flew a thousand feet below the tanker; in a few minutes they'd climb up to the refueling altitude of 24,000 feet.

The tanker crew finished the checklist. The boom operator lowered the refuel boom. The boom dropped into the slipstream, steered by small winglets, or ruddervators. On the ruddervators, Parson saw the designation: 134 ARW. These guys came from the 134th Air Refueling Wing, Tennessee Air National Guard. Knoxville folks.

The refueling drogue, which looked like a large basket at the end of a hose, extended from the boom. Most USAF aircraft refueled by inserting the boom into a latching receptacle, but the Mirage gassed up by the probe-and-drogue method. Chartier would have to maneuver his aircraft so that his receiving probe fit into the drogue. Then valves would open and fuel would flow. The job called for precision flying and flawless teamwork between the tanker and receiver.

"All right, I'm in tanker manual override," the boom op said. "I got comm one."

"It's your show, boom," the aircraft commander said.

"Roger, sir."

The boom operator moved the selector on his comm box to UHF1. With that, he became the director of an aerial ballet conducted at more than two hundred fifty knots. The two Mirages drew nearer but widened their formation. One of them remained a thousand feet below, and the other began climbing toward the tail of the KC-135. As the fighter rose toward formatting altitude, Parson got a better view of its delta wings, its refuel probe jutting from the right side, the weapons mounted on rails under the wings.

The Mirage flew so precisely that it seemed to lock itself into position just below and aft of the Stratotanker. Parson heard Chartier's voice on the radio:

"Dagger One-One is stable."

"Dagger One-One is cleared to contact," the boom operator answered.

The Mirage floated toward the drogue. Parson could see Chartier and his backseater, Sniper, in the tandem cockpits. Their helmets became clearly visible, and they flew so close Parson could have seen their eyes if not for their smoked visors. Chartier kept his right hand on the control stick and his left hand on the throttle. He seemed not to move either hand, but Parson knew the French pilot was making adjustments so minute they required only the slightest pressure from his fingers.

The fighter jet's probe eased into the basket, clicked into place with a momentary mist of fuel. The hose shimmied with the impact.

"Contact," the boom operator radioed.

"Latched," Chartier said.

Parson watched Chartier and Sniper with professional interest. A lot of pilots had little rituals for flying this delicate maneuver. In the C-5, Parson liked to lower his seat full down for a better view of the tanker. Some guys called for cool temps on the air-conditioning to avoid sweating. Some chewed gum. A few talked to themselves: "Hold what you got, hold what you got, hold what you got."

The boom operator monitored his panel, watched the pounds of fuel count down on his gauges. Parson noticed the boom op's unofficial morale patch on his right shoulder. The patch read KC-135 BOOM OPERATOR, and it featured an image of Bart Simpson. Beside Bart, the lettering read PUMP THIS, MAN! Parson chuckled to himself. As an officer, he knew he should tell the boomer to put on an official patch, but he had more important things to worry about. So did the boomer.

The airplanes reached a turn point on the refueling track, and both began a gentle bank to the right, still connected and fueling. The desert scrolled by below, lakes of sand interrupted by the spiderwebs of dry wadis and the ripples of dunes. A belt of dusty air hugged the ground, but up here on the track, the winds flowed clear.

A couple of minutes went by without any traffic on the radio, so Parson asked the boom operator if he could use comm one.

"All yours, sir."

"Thanks," Parson said on interphone. Then he transmitted, "Hey, Frenchie, this is Parson. You comfortable enough to talk?"

The radio hissed for a moment, then Chartier answered. The French pilot could transmit by pressing a button on the throttle assembly without removing his hands from stick and throttle.

"I am as comfortable as if my head were on my *chérie*'s lap on a beach towel on the Riviera."

The remark made Parson smile despite his worries. "Yeah, right. You guys see or hear anything?"

Another pause. When Chartier spoke again, his tone was serious.

"I am afraid not. We have monitored the guard frequency, listened for beacons, anything. Nothing visual on the ground, either."

Parson watched the Sahara unrolling beneath him. Blount and the others were down there, at a given set of coordinates, at a certain distance along a radial from a navigational beacon. Just a question of learning the numbers. But how? The fighters, tankers, and drones at Parson's disposal might eventually find his missing friend—or they might accomplish nothing except boring holes in the sky. Parson had to try everything.

He pressed his transmit button and said, "Thanks, guys. See you back at Mitiga."

"Roger that, sir," Chartier said. "I am almost full now." A few seconds later he called, "Dagger One-One requests disconnect."

"Dagger One-One, Crude Eight-Seven disconnect."

Once again a mist of residual fuel puffed from the drogue, and the Mirage's probe withdrew. Chartier and Sniper slid farther aft of the tanker and drifted to a slightly lower altitude. The other Mirage eased up into the pre-contact position, called stable, received clearance from the boom operator to move into contact.

The second jet took on its fuel as quickly as the first. Parson noted how aerial refueling in the real world never involved as much time behind the tanker as the AR training missions. On any given training flight, he'd spend an hour or more in the wake turbulence of the KC-135, latching and unlatching. Plugging with the tanker's autopilot on. With the autopilot off. Flying the AR from the left seat, and then from the right seat. Parson had plenty of beefs about policy, but he felt the Air Force did at least one thing well: When the training made the real-world mission seem easy, you were doing something right.

However, no amount of training could prepare him for his next task, and he dreaded it. He'd decided he owed it to Blount to call the big Marine's wife, just to check in. Parson's official duties did not require it; he was not in Blount's chain of command. But their shared experience in Afghanistan had formed bonds and obligations that transcended rules and regs. A fight to the death against a common enemy had a way of doing that. He had checked with Headquarters Marine Corps earlier in the day, and they'd told him he could contact the family.

When the Stratotanker landed back at Mitiga, Parson thanked the crew for letting him ride along, then climbed down the boarding ladder. The tanker's air-conditioning had cooled the lenses of his aviator's glasses enough that they fogged over when touched by the warm desert breeze. He pulled off the shades, wiped them on the sleeve of his flight suit. The Nomex fabric had frayed along the cuffs; he'd kept this particular suit for years. Parson tended to hold on to flight suits until they wore out completely; he liked the feel of flight gear well broken in.

In the ops center, he opened a Dr Pepper and checked his watch. Two in the afternoon. That made it eight in the morning back in Beaufort, South Carolina. Was that too early to call? No, Blount's people came from salt-of-the-earth farmer stock; they'd probably been up since dawn. Would a call from a colonel scare Bernadette worse than she was already? Probably not. As an experienced military wife, she'd know officers brought the worst news in person, not over the phone. A knock would terrorize her, but not a ring.

With no more excuses to procrastinate, Parson took a swallow of his soft drink and turned on his cell phone. Thumbed through his contacts until he found Blount's home number. Turned on his satellite phone, cross-referenced the number, punched it in.

A world away in South Carolina, the phone rang four times before someone picked it up. Parson was surprised to hear a male voice say, "Blount residence."

Who was this? Blount didn't have a son.

"Ah, good morning. This is Colonel Michael Parson. Air Force."

The person on the other end paused for a moment, then said, "Good day, sir. This is Sergeant Major Thomas Buell, retired Marine Corps. I am Gunnery Sergeant Blount's grandfather."

The voice sent chills up Parson's back. What pain must this man feel right now, with his grandson in enemy hands? Yet Buell found the strength to speak clearly and strongly, and to observe military courtesy to boot. The voice carried the gravel of age, but Buell sounded like someone with a sharp mind who had taken command in a crisis. This Sergeant Major Thomas Buell must have made one formidable Marine in his day. Yeah, Blount would have come from a line like this.

"Sergeant Major," Parson said, "I am a friend of your grandson's. I'm not in his chain of command, but I'm helping coordinate air support for his recovery."

"We appreciate your efforts, sir. Do you have any news for us?"

"Only that we're doing all we can. We're keeping manned aircraft and drones up around the clock. Crews have instructions to listen for beacons or voice calls, and watch for any visuals on the ground."

"I'm familiar with the procedures," Buell said.

"I just got down from a flight to refuel some fighters on patrol. They're looking and listening for your grandson even as we speak."

"That's good to hear."

Buell did not sound relieved or impressed. Parson doubted he had told the man much he didn't already know. Certainly Buell knew the odds, the history of incidents like this.

"Sir," Parson said, "I won't kid you about what we're facing. But I can't imagine anyone better equipped for this than your grandson."

Long pause. Parson wondered if the old man had to compose

himself, to fight to maintain his professional bearing. No longer in the service, Buell had no obligation to "sir" anybody or to conduct himself like a senior NCO. But it seemed part of his nature.

"I thank you for the respect you've shown this family with your phone call," Buell said.

"How's Mrs. Blount doing?"

"As well as you can expect under the circumstances."

"May I speak with her?"

"I'll see. Stand by, sir."

Buell put down the receiver. Then came what sounded like wheels across a hardwood floor. Maybe the old man used a scooter or wheelchair. Parson drew in a long breath. Did he really want to do this? No turning back now. At least he knew Blount's wife and kids had a rock to depend on in the gunny's absence. After a couple of minutes, someone picked up the phone.

"This is Bernadette Blount."

The woman sounded hoarse, tired. Of course she did, Parson thought. He introduced himself and said, "Ma'am, I'm calling from Libya. I'm a friend of your husband's."

"What are you doing to bring him back?"

Parson told her the same thing he'd told Buell.

"You bring him back to me," she said, enunciating each word as if a period followed it. A command if there ever was one, with all the moral authority of the most just military order. Fair enough, Parson thought.

"Ma'am," he said, "we're going to do all we can."

"And just what is that?" she asked. "Just what is all you can? Fly a bunch of airplanes around so you can say you tried? Maybe kill some terrorists after my husband is gone? What good does that do me and my children?"

If Blount's grandfather had sent chills up Parson's spine, Blount's wife turned his bloodstream to ice water. Yes, of course he'd do all he could. But, as she said, what good would that probably do in the end?

She had him dead to rights. What could he possibly say to bring this woman any comfort?

"Ma'am," Parson said, "I can't imagine—"

"No," she interrupted. "You cannot. You cannot imagine what I'm going through. You cannot imagine what his children are going through. My husband was *home*. He was here, just days ago. And now they're about to cut his head off."

Bernadette Blount's voice trailed off. Parson heard a stifled sob and the muted background noise of a hand over a receiver. He had no idea what to offer next, and he berated himself for making this call to begin with. Had he only made things worse? Could he seriously tell her it would be all right? Because it wouldn't, almost certainly. Bernadette Blount surely knew about all the people around her untouched by war, intact families safe at home and taking it for granted. But because she'd married into a line of those who chose to serve, she bore a unique burden. Before Parson could think of anything to say, she spoke again.

"My husband has done more than his share for this country," she said. "He has done more than you people had any right to ask. My husband has earned his peace and his home. Do you understand what I'm saying?"

Parson already knew there was no point bullshitting Marines. Same thing applied to their wives. He had nothing to fall back on but truth.

"Yes, ma'am, I do," he said. "I saw him earn it in the space of ten minutes in a cave in Afghanistan. I've seen him at work, Mrs. Blount." Parson paused, unsure what to add. Then he said, "He deserves to come home."

The sat phone connection hummed wordlessly so long that Parson wondered if Blount's wife had hung up. When she spoke again, her voice cracked with emotion.

"Yes, he does," she said. "Make it happen."

CHAPTER 25

I n the late afternoon the terrorists made up their minds. Kassam led his band of dirtbags into the adjoining room. Blount heard yammering in Arabic, chains clanking. Kassam must have pointed to his chosen victim. An American voice began to speak.

"No," the man said. "No, please. Just wait a while. They might give in. Just wait a while."

The man's voice trembled with fear but did not sob. Blount recognized him by sound: Sergeant Daniel Farmer. All along Blount had wondered who lay in the other room.

Fender and Ivan both sat up, looked at Blount. They understood what was happening. Fender's face took on an ashen cast.

Farmer. Dear Lord up in heaven. A boy who had a good future ahead of him, whether he stayed in the Marines or not. Skinny white guy who didn't look like your typical Marine. Hair short enough for regulation but not shaved or high-and-tight. Bookish type. Two years at UNC–Wilmington before joining the service. Biology major or something. Just got engaged.

Blount's mind raced. What could he do? How could he stop this? He twisted the bolt, ground it against the cement. Still not free yet. Forget it. Get them in here close enough, Blount decided, and just do what you can.

"Hey!" Blount shouted. "Leave that boy be. What's wrong with you people?"

Maybe Rat Face would run in and give Blount a kick. But in the other room, no one responded.

"Is your God telling you to do this?" Blount yelled.

Still no response. More clanking of chains. They were probably unshackling him. Now Farmer's voice spoke in a murmur: "Oh, God; oh, God; oh, God."

"You want to mess with somebody," Blount called, "come in here and mess with me."

No response.

Something horrible was about to happen and he could do nothing about it. His grandfather's words about a warrior's attitude seared in his memory now: "You go into a situation and think, everybody here is safer because I'm here."

But not this time. Blount burned with impotent rage. Yanked hard against his chains. More dust fell from the cement, but not enough.

He could offer nothing but words. Pitiful, but he'd do the little he could do. Let Farmer hear a friendly voice on the way out.

"Semper fidelis, Farmer," Blount shouted.

"Semper fi!" Fender yelled.

Even Ivan repeated the motto in his Russian accent. Maybe he knew the Latin for *Always faithful*, or maybe he just repeated the syllables to add his voice to this show of unity.

The other prisoners in the next room did the same. Monkey Ears shouted, "Silence!"

"Tell my fiancé I love her," Farmer said.

Oh, Jesus, Blount thought. Somebody gotta stop this. A Delta team or some SEALs need to blow through that wall this instant. Stop this, stop this, stop this. Couldn't there be a last-minute miracle? Stranger things had happened.

No miracle came. They led Farmer away; Blount heard the chains drop, the feet shuffle. Farmer evidently kept his composure; Blount heard no crying or begging.

Several minutes went by in silence. But then from another room or maybe from outside, Blount heard a harangue in Arabic. Then he heard a harangue in English, from Monkey Ears:

"To imperialists, Zionists, and infidels who have chosen to ignore our warnings: This is the fate that awaits all crusaders. The pasha of Tripolitania, slave to God, wields Heaven's sword. He will drive you from the lands of the faithful and he will strike you in your own dens of infidelity. You must convert to the one true faith, or you will die by the sword, the bomb, or the chemicals of a mighty God. Let the death of this pig serve as your notice."

Blount shook with fury. He put his hands over his ears, then put his hands back down. He must hear everything. He must gather intel, remain aware. If nothing else, the sounds would motivate him to greater strength.

Ivan stared straight ahead. Fender buried his head in his arms. Chains clanked in the other room.

And the screams began.

Dear God, they went on forever. The analytical part of Blount's mind tracked the screams for maybe half a minute. But that half minute stretched across all time. As Farmer was killed like an animal at slaughter, Blount pulled and turned the bolt. Torqued it harder than he had imagined possible. Heard the grinding under the cries of agony.

His fist trembled as it gripped the metal. Cement cracked, gave way.

As the screams died, the bolt came loose. Blount pulled it out of the wall, held it up and examined it. The thing was a shaft of iron as big around as his little finger, with a barb-like flange on one end. The other end, of course, held the ring to which his left chain was attached. Fender and Ivan looked at him, eyes widened. Blount put his finger to his lips.

"Shhh," he whispered. "Don't say nothing. I'll see if I can loosen the other one."

"I'll work on mine," Fender said.

"Nah. Just play it cool. Don't want them to catch us. Pay attention to everything, and stay ready for anything."

"Aye, aye, Gunny."

Several minutes later Kassam and Rat Face came into the room. Blount thought he'd descended into the lowest trenches of rage and disgust, but his anger deepened further when he saw the terrorist leader. Blood soaked his sleeves. Blood had spattered all over his shirt and sash. Blood flecked his flintlock pistol. Blood dripped from the machete in his right hand.

Blount glared at Kassam. Kassam placed the machete on the table with the weapons and equipment, wiped his hands with a towel. Placed the flintlock on the table, too. Rat Face carried a video recorder and a still camera. He took a photo of the objects.

Every cell in Blount's body wanted to lash out right then. But he bided his time, swallowed his fury. When he made his move, he expected to get only a few seconds to work before an AK cut him down. He needed to choose that moment with cold calculation, not hot emotion. The dirtbags had said they'd kill a hostage a day. With one chain loose, Blount figured he had about twenty-four hours to grind away at the other one. The more freedom of motion he had in his last seconds, the more harm he could visit on his tormentors.

Kassam and Rat Face left the room. Blount supposed their next task would involve posting their murder porn online, sending their message out into the world. Go ahead and post your message, he thought. Pretty soon you're gonna get one from me.

With his head leaned back against the wall, Blount closed his eyes and began to twist the bolt connected with the chain on his right. He found that one a little harder to move; the cement held it more firmly. No matter. Whether he got it loose or not, he already had one arm free. He'd make do with that if he had to.

Blount let his mind drift as he turned and twisted the shank of iron. He knew he'd meet his Maker in a day or so. What would that be like? He'd always tried to live a good life, but he still found the prospect of judgment daunting. What would the Good Lord have to say about the lives Blount had taken? Each one had been what guys called a "righteous kill," justified in combat, legal under the laws of war. But man's law held no sway where Blount was going.

He decided not to worry about that. He could not change the past; he could only act in the present. And he harbored no doubt that his last kill—or kills—would be righteous.

Something he'd heard from his minister back home came to mind. At the A.M.E. Zion church one Sunday, the preacher read the Prayer of Saint Francis. Blount remembered only the first line: *Lord, make me an instrument of your peace.* He liked that idea, though he knew some folks might find it ironic coming from a Marine. But to him, it made perfect sense. In the quest for just peace, you needed force when all else failed. And in Blount's last moments, he wanted to serve as an instrument of peace. Remove from the earth one of these men who delighted in the murder of innocents in the name of God.

He let a long stream of consciousness flow through his mind in the form of meditation. People found all kinds of ways to get close with the higher power; Blount had seen many right in his home community. He recalled one Sunday when his mother—a troubled woman who'd married an abusive man—took him to a Praise House over on St. Helena Island. Some of the Gullah folks there still danced the ring shout.

A ring shout didn't actually involve shouting—just singing, clapping, and stomping while moving in a circle. The ancient tradition had crossed the Atlantic in slave ships, its roots in African dance. Even as a child, Blount had been touched by the dancers' sincerity and the way they enjoyed the company of their fellow worshippers. This tradition had seen his people through the darkest days imaginable, when all they had was one another.

And that's all we got now, Blount pondered. Here in these chains, surrounded by enemies, we got nothing but one another.

Around sunset, Blount heard his captors murmuring in Arabic. Praying, maybe? Funny thing; he knew Muslims prayed five times a day, but he could not remember having heard these dirtbags do it before now.

He wondered how they could even think about praying after the despicable act they'd committed. What kind of thinking could lead you to believe in a God of long knives? Even if you wanted to kill somebody, why would you saw through the neck of a living, breathing, screaming fellow human being? Especially when you had a gun and you could kill the man less brutally.

This mystery he would never understand. From his training and reading, he knew all normal people of all races and creeds carried a natural aversion to killing their own species. Healthy minds just clicked that way. In the military, you needed to condition people to overcome this natural aversion. On the rifle range, you made them fire not at a round bull's-eye but a torso in silhouette. In the shoot houses, you had pop-up dummies that looked like a real enemy. You worked to create a trained response so a guy wouldn't hesitate at a critical time on the battlefield. Because even after all that training, a normal person *still* hated to take a life.

But not Kassam and his henchmen. Something in their souls had died, twisted, turned black. Blount did not consider them soldiers; he counted them psychopaths and sadists, fringe elements of humanity without that normal disinclination to murder and cruelty. Their talk of jihad only offered religious excuses for things they wanted to do anyway. In Blount's travels he had met plenty of peaceable Muslims whose only jihad took place within their hearts as they strived to do the right thing day to day.

As the sky outside began to darken, Rat Face brought food to the prisoners. Same garbage—boiled lentils. Same smirk. And the same gesture, a slashing motion across his throat.

Blount fought the urge to react. Kept his eyes downcast. Jerked his foot like he didn't have good control of his nervous system. Tried to look still sick.

He lifted the bowl of lentil mush. Sat with his back to the wall so his chains had plenty of slack, and the loose one would not pull out of the masonry. The food was slightly warm this time. Blount brought the bowl to his mouth, drank, slurped, chewed. Nothing except tasteless calories, but that's all he needed.

"You guys eat as much as you can," Blount whispered.

Ivan winced as he reached for his bowl; his leg wound clearly pained him. Likely infected by now, Blount guessed. If a machete didn't take the Russian's life, gangrene probably would.

Fender drew in long breaths as if eating took a great measure of focus. Maybe it did; who knew how different people would react to this kind of stress? Fender's bowl shook as he picked it up with both hands, but he took a fairly big gulp of the mush. Swallowed without chewing, slurped another mouthful. After a few minutes, the three men had eaten all their lentils. Blount allowed himself about two seconds of satisfaction over this tiny tactical success. Get stronger, boys, he thought. We're still on a mission.

In the early evening, the dirtbags seemed to relax. Apparently their boss man had departed; Kassam never came into the room again. But once more, he left his flintlock pistol on the table. Yeah, Blount thought, he's coming back tomorrow. Same reason.

The dirtbags began eating their own suppers, and they enjoyed fare that looked right much better than lentil mush. Monkey Ears brought a wooden chair into the room, set it down a few yards away from Blount. Sat in the chair and opened a yellow pouch containing American-made humanitarian rations. Taken, no doubt, from some village these terrorists had raided. In the dim light Blount could not read the lettering on the package, but Monkey Ears began spooning something that looked like chili. As Monkey Ears ate, he regarded Blount. Not with Rat Face's impudent smirk, but with a look of contentment. Like he'd traveled some long road, climbed some high peak, and now found himself within reach of triumph.

Monkey Ears ate in silence. He got up and left, came back and sat down with a steaming cup of what smelled like tea. Blount wondered if Monkey Ears was trying to torment him with the sights and aromas of better food and drink. Didn't work; Blount had eaten enough of the mush to satisfy his hunger, and he didn't care for hot tea, anyway. Like most folks from the Deep South, he liked his tea very cold and very sweet. He pushed away that thought so he wouldn't dwell on small pleasures he'd never taste again.

The dirtbag sipped until he finished the tea. Then he fingered a shirt pocket until he came up with an unfiltered cigarette. Struck a match and lit the cigarette, shook out the match and dropped it on the floor. Blew out a long plume of tobacco smoke.

You still ain't getting to me, Blount thought. I like cigars instead.

Why was this fool playing these games, anyway? Men about to lose their lives don't care about tea and cigarettes.

The ash on the end of the cigarette grew long. Monkey Ears took another drag, and the fire within the ash brightened and faded. The ash dropped into his lap. Monkey Ears brushed away the ash, held smoke in his lungs for a moment, then exhaled and began to speak.

"This is only the beginning, you know."

Blount didn't answer. Ivan and Fender said nothing.

I ain't got time for your foolishness, Blount thought. I got work to do. Go sit with your dirtbag buddies so I can get to this other bolt.

"We have stocks of chemical weapons bigger than you imagine," Monkey Ears continued. "We have some left over from Gadhafi. We have others sent to us by brothers in Syria. Bashar al-Assad should have remained an ophthalmologist. He could not even control his own arsenals."

Blount shrugged.

"I tell you this because I want you to die with the knowledge of what we have in store for America. What we did in Sicily, what we did in Gibraltar, came only as practice for what we will bring to your cities."

The terrorists had said this before. In intel briefings, Blount had heard of threats like that from Kassam. But to hear it straight from one of the bad guys gave it a new ring of authenticity. Kind of like on a Marine base when rumors flew about a coming deployment: You might dismiss the first murmurings. But when you heard it from someone on the commander's staff, it became more real.

Blount denied Monkey Ears the satisfaction of a response. He just stared at the floor like he was too sick to listen. Ivan and Fender gave no reaction, either. But Blount burned inside. These lowlifes had long dreamed of a strong follow-up to 9/11, a dream spoiled by a combination of luck, good anti-terror ops by the U.S. military, and good policing. The combination had worked fairly well for years. The Boston Marathon bombings, awful as they were, didn't compare to the mass casualties of 2001.

However, terrorists had now figured a way to get chemical weapons into Europe. Who knew how? Container ships or speedboats, maybe. Didn't matter; if they'd done it in Europe they could do it in America. They might not get Blount's little girls, but they'd get somebody's children, somebody's spouse.

Fury rose within him like a fever. The shackles themselves angered Blount. Chained to a wall in Africa, he felt the rage of his ancestors. His people had suffered under a different brand of evil, but one just as vile as the one before him now. The preacher man back home knew what he was talking about when he said evil was real. Evil flowed in the world on a daily basis, and a great big gout of it had pooled and started to smell bad right here in this place.

CHAPTER 26

Gold strode up the ramp of the C-130 Hercules waiting on the tarmac at Mitiga. She carried an overnight bag—an Army duffel packed with a satellite phone, her camera and GPS, a change of clothes, a notepad and pens, two MREs and four bottles of water. The worn duffel still bore a cloth strip with her old title: SGT. MAJOR S. GOLD. Beside her name, a patch in the subdued colors of camouflage showed a set of jump wings and lettering that read AIRBORNE. She might have been boarding this plane for a military mission— except that she boarded alone, and instead of a uniform she wore a safari shirt, civilian tactical trousers, and an Afghan scarf.

The airplane's four turboprop engines thrummed in ground idle, the black exhaust smoke whipped by spinning propellers. The Herk had flown in from Sigonella with five pallets of rice bound for a refugee camp outside Illizi, Algeria. As Gold took her seat made of nylon webbing, she noticed lettering on the rice bags: UN WORLD FOOD PROGRAMME.

The C-130 crew had originally planned to shut down engines to board their passenger; their regs allowed engines-running onloads only for military personnel trained to avoid dangers such as prop arcs. But Parson had radioed to them that their civilian guest was a free-fall-qualified parachutist and a veteran of the 82nd Airborne Division. Gold had stood beside Parson in the operations center as he made the call. The pilot just laughed and said, "Yeah, we'll do an ERO."

Inside the cargo compartment, Gold took in the sights, sounds, and smells as if returning home. Burning jet fuel fumes combined with grease and mil-spec paint to form a metallic odor common to all warplanes. She eyed the two steel cables that stretched from the forward bulkhead to the troop doors near the tail. How many times had she clipped a static line to those cables—maybe in this very airplane—and waited for the green light?

Gold's past informed her present, gave her the qualifications for her current job. But now she felt a strong sense of the passage of time. It seemed just yesterday when she'd first received the order to stand up and hook up. She'd exited the airplane with feet and knees together, looked up to the reassuring sight of a fully inflated canopy. That sight had become so familiar, yet she knew she'd never see it again.

The loadmaster closed the ramp, and the Herk began to taxi. Fog spewed from the air-conditioning plenums; from experience Gold knew C-130s did that while on the ground in warm, humid air. The cargo compartment filled with mist until the flight engineer found the right setting.

She looked out the small porthole-style window as the aircraft lined up on the runway. The sound of the engines magnified, and so did the vibration throughout the cargo compartment. The C-130 began to accelerate. Distance markers ticked past, and the aircraft lifted into a smooth desert sky.

After the aircraft had cruised for only a few minutes, the loadmaster shouted over the engine noise.

"Ma'am," he said. "There's a call for you on the radio. It's from Kingfish. You can use my headset."

Kingfish? Oh, yes, Gold thought. The call sign for Mitiga operations. Probably Parson himself. The loadmaster took off his headset, unplugged it from one interphone cord and connected it to another. Gave the headset to Gold.

"Our call sign is Reach Eight-Six," the loadmaster told her. "You're on secure voice."

Gold donned the headset, pressed the talk switch, and said, "Kingfish, Reach Eight-Six. Gold here."

"Sophia," Parson said, "we just got some bad news, and I didn't want you to hear it thirdhand. They've executed one of the prisoners."

Gold closed her eyes, drew in a deep breath. Despite all her hopes, she'd known this was likely. And she could well imagine all the horrors Parson's words implied. Static sizzled over the channel as Parson released his mike switch. Gold pressed her own switch to ask a question. But she wasn't sure she wanted to know the answer.

"Who was it?"

"Sergeant Daniel Farmer. A Marine."

Gold offered a quick and silent prayer for Farmer and all those who loved him. Sorrow churned within her amid all the anger she carried. She tried to focus on her job; that was the best thing she could do for Blount and the others in enemy hands.

"Any changes in the mission?"

"Negative," Parson said. "I thought you should know. Sorry to have to tell you this way."

"It's okay, Michael."

"Be careful, Sophia. Kingfish out."

Gold gave the headset back to the loadmaster. She tried to hold back the brimming in her eyes, but lost the battle and had to wipe tears. A short time later, the loadmaster spoke up with another announcement.

"You might want to buckle in tight, ma'am," the crewman said. "We're gonna do a tactical arrival."

Gold pulled her seat belt tighter, nodded.

"I've done them before," she said.

After a few minutes, the engines hushed as the pilot pulled back the throttles. Clanks and hydraulic hisses signaled the gear and flaps deploying. The Herk rolled into a steep bank, and Gold felt the airplane spiraling down. Thousands of feet below, the blue tents of the refugee camp rotated in the window.

The plane completed one turn, then two and three before the wings leveled. The ground loomed close, and then came the soft bumps of touchdown on a dirt airstrip.

When the propellers entered reverse pitch, Gold felt her torso yanked forward by the rapid deceleration. Dust enveloped the C-130, beige powder obscuring the view out the windows. The airplane slowed to walking speed. The dirt maelstrom cleared immediately when the prop blades returned to a pitch setting for forward thrust.

After taxiing off the rough strip, the Herk crew opened the ramp and shut down the engines. The smell of the desert rolled into the airplane: dust baked by the sun, and air oddly laden with moisture. The loadmaster pushed the pallets of rice one at a time onto a waiting forklift, aided by African Union troops. Gold recognized Major Ongondo supervising the effort. She thanked the crew for the ride, hoisted her overnight bag, and hopped out of an open troop door. Ongondo noticed her, came over with an outstretched hand.

"Ah, the ubiquitous Ms. Gold," Ongondo said.

From his sunny demeanor, Gold supposed he hadn't heard the news.

"Major," Gold said, shaking his hand.

"I presume you came to help run this camp. This one is quite new."

"Actually, no. I'm looking for any kind of information that might help us find our missing personnel. This is not a good day." Gold told him about Farmer's execution.

Ongondo placed his hands on his web belt, lowered his chin. Behind him, his men broke down the pallets of rice. One by one, they carried each bag into a mess tent.

"I am very sorry to hear this," Ongondo said. "I imagine you have come searching for facts."

"You could say that. I need to see if anyone has seen or heard anything that might lead to Kassam."

Gold wiped her face with her checkered scarf. The morning sun had risen higher now, and the temperature climbed with it. The day promised to be warm for fall in North Africa.

"I'll try to identify some refugees willing to speak with you. We do have some clans here that have done business with Islamists. Things are a little tense, in fact."

The major led Gold into one of the blue tents. The temperature inside felt only slightly cooler than outdoors. No air-conditioning units, but an industrial fan whirred in a corner. An orange electrical cord as thick as Gold's thumb curled between the fan and a generator that hummed outside. The fan's breeze flowed across a row of empty cots, and the tent's interior glowed with the watery light of sunshine filtered through blue fabric.

"Perhaps you can use this as an office for a few hours until more refugees arrive," Ongondo said. "Some of the other tents have already filled."

"Thank you."

Gold opened her duffel. She had packed clothes and toiletries on the bottom, tools on top. She sat on a cot, pulled out her notepad and pens, her sat phone, and two bottles of water. Placed everything beside her on the canvas. Ongondo left and came back several minutes later with two refugees: a man and a boy.

Each wore a blue *cheche*, the traditional headgear of the Tuareg people. The headgear looked much like any other turban, except its wrappings also covered the lower part of the face. The presence of Tuaregs surprised Gold. In some of the conflict that had seared North Africa in recent years, the nomadic Tuaregs had allied with Islamists. Together they had fomented a rebellion in Mali, and Tuaregs had also fought on behalf of Gadhafi in Libya. Mixing Tuaregs with other refugees fleeing jihadists seemed like a recipe for trouble. No wonder Ongondo had spoken of tension.

Why had these guys fled here, anyway? Perhaps the new brand of Islamist represented by Kassam did not respect old alliances. Also, many Tuaregs' interpretation of Islam did not support the strict sharia law that jihadists imposed. No telling how alliances were shifting in the chaos all around.

A more immediate problem occurred to Gold. She did not speak their native language. She tried a greeting in Arabic.

Blank stares.

She seldom felt stumped, but she felt that way now. She wondered if she could find an Arabic speaker out here who also spoke one of the Tuareg dialects.

"I speak some Tamahaq," Ongondo offered.

Gold turned toward him, mouth open slightly.

"Ah, that's helpful, sir. Where did you learn that language?"

"University of Nairobi. I majored in African Studies."

Well, that explained his broad knowledge of folktales, proverbs, and languages. On a better day she would have asked Ongondo more about his schooling, but now was not the time.

"Can you ask them how they wound up here?"

Ongondo nodded and began speaking. His questions and the Tuaregs' answers carried vowel sounds that sounded vaguely like Arabic. That made sense; the Tuareg dialects were part of the Berber languages—which were part of the Afro-Asiatic languages. And the Afro-Asiatic tongues included Arabic.

Understanding the classifications was one thing; understanding the conversation was quite another. Gold had to wait for Ongondo's translation. She could, however, read the fatigue and fear in the Tuaregs' eyes.

"Their clan had camped south of here," Ongondo said. "I am not sure exactly how far south. Some of the Tuaregs still spend a lot of the year on the road as traders."

Ongondo and the two refugees continued speaking in the Tuareg dialect. While they talked, Gold twisted open the two bottles of water she'd placed on the cot and handed them to the Tuaregs. The refugees paused in their chatter to take long swallows and to make hand gestures Gold interpreted as thanks. The boy closed his eyes and let the fan's breeze flow over him as if someone were rubbing his face with satin. Gold wondered how often he'd felt a fan, let alone air-conditioning.

"Bandits raided their camp," Ongondo said. "Burned their tents, stole goats and bags of millet. Shot anyone who resisted. These two are father and son. The mother and another son were killed."

Gold regarded the two. She had seen that glazed look of grief and suffering too many times, mainly in Afghanistan, and she never got used to it. She didn't want to get used to it. To become emotionally calloused could lead to accepting violence and abuse as normal.

"Please tell them I am so sorry for what happened to them," Gold said. "Do they know who did this to them and why?"

More conversation in Tamahaq. Tears ran from the boy's eyes, down his mocha-colored skin until they disappeared under the folds of his face covering.

"They say the bandits called them *kafir*, unbelievers," Ongondo said.

These are Muslims, too, Gold thought, but jihadists would declare *kafir* anyone who got in their way. These people had supplies the terrorists wanted. That made them unbelievers.

"Pretty ironic, since some of the Tuaregs once aligned themselves with jihadists," Gold said.

"Like aligning with an adder," Ongondo said. "If you let it into your house it might kill the rats. But it would just as soon bite you."

"Can they identify any of the attackers?"

Ongondo translated the question. The refugees shook their heads.

"Do they know where their attackers came from?"

Same answer.

Gold considered what else to ask. These two seemed to know nothing that might lead to Kassam. Or if they did know, they were afraid to talk. A dead end either way. She hoped conversations with other refugees might prove more helpful.

The Tuareg father began speaking. Not in response to a question from Ongondo, but something he volunteered. His eyes brimmed as he talked. Ongondo nodded slowly, as if moved by the words. While he listened, Ongondo crooked a finger and pressed it to his lips. Gold thought she recognized the situation: The Tuareg man was expressing a complicated idea, and Ongondo had to put some thought into how to translate it.

When the Tuareg finished, Ongondo paused for a moment. Then he said, "This is hard to convey in English, but he says earth and heaven and hell have spun out of their orbits. Demons from hell have been flung to earth."

So it seemed. Gold had received evidence of that over the radio a short time ago.

"Wow," she said. "That's poetic and heartbreaking at the same time."

The poetic part didn't surprise her. Though she did not speak this language, she knew the Tuaregs had a strong oral tradition: adventure poems, love poems, war poems, folktales and legends passed down for uncounted generations. Recent events would give them more stories to recount, and not the good kind.

Before Gold could think of any words of solace, a commotion interrupted her thoughts. Shouts came from outside, angry voices in at least three languages. Was this a terrorist attack within the refugee camp? But she heard no gunfire, no explosions.

She and Ongondo raced from the tent. The Tuaregs stayed put, the man shielding his boy with his arms.

Outside she found a melee. Young men ran between the tents, armed with whatever they could find to throw. Some carried rocks and water bottles. One yanked at a tent stake, perhaps to use it as a spike.

"Stop!" Gold yelled. Then she shouted in Arabic for him to leave the stake alone. Unaccountably, he obeyed and ran on.

African Union soldiers sprinted toward what seemed the nucleus of the fight, a knot of men and boys at one end of a row of tents. Inside a circle of bystanders, fists and elbows flew.

"Hold your fire," Ongondo barked to his men.

A good call, Gold thought. So far this looked like only a fistfight, but it could turn into a full-blown riot in an instant. If the AU troops resorted to deadly force, a bloodbath might result. This could get ugly if not defused quickly, Gold knew. Along with the troops, she waded into the scuffle, grabbed a boy by his right arm just as he cocked back to throw a punch.

The boy whirled and flung his other fist. Gold tried to block it but the blow caught the side of her head. The whack disoriented her for a second, and silver dots swam into her vision. The kid looked about fifteen, and he swung almost as strongly as a man. Gold grabbed him by the left arm, too.

Apparently the boy had thrown the punch blindly. He looked confused when he saw a blond woman had hold of him. He let Gold pull him away from the scuffle.

"*Khalass,*" she said. That's enough.

He started to jerk away, but he stopped struggling when he saw the AU troops breaking up the fight. Most of the refugees offered little resistance, though one of them slammed the heel of his hand into a soldier's jaw. Bad move. The soldier responded with an elbow strike that bloodied the man's nose. Reddened mucus streamed from the refugee's nostrils.

Gold noticed no injuries worse than that. As the troops extracted men and boys from the fight, they found a teenage boy at the bottom of the pile. A Tuareg, evidently. His *cheche* lay on the ground, blue fabric smeared with dirt and a few bloodstains. The teen had suffered a split lip; blood dribbled down his chin. One of his eyes appeared swollen. Two soldiers helped him to his feet, brushed sand from his shirt.

Thank God nobody pulled a knife, Gold thought. This could have become so much worse. Even without guns and knives, rioters could have stabbed with tent stakes, wrapped a tent rope around someone's neck, crushed a skull with a rock.

Ongondo moved among the refugees and soldiers, speaking in English, Arabic, and Tamahaq. He seemed to lecture some of the males who'd been fighting. He shook his finger at one boy, who folded his arms and lowered his eyes to the ground. The sight put Gold in mind of a school principal dressing down a student involved in a hallway fracas.

Ongondo turned to one of his soldiers and said, "Very good. I was so afraid someone would shoot unnecessarily."

"Thank you, sir."

Third World soldiers were not known for their fire discipline. Gold figured these served under better leadership than usual.

Gold turned her attention to the teenager rescued from the center of the fight. He shook grit from his *cheche*, wound the fabric around his head with a look of wounded pride.

"Let's take him inside," Gold said. "I'll see if a nurse can look at his lip."

Ongondo steered the boy into the tent where they'd interviewed the first two Tuaregs. Gold found a medic who said he came from Italy. Inside the tent, Gold pointed to the injured teen, and the medic pulled away the boy's face covering. The medic dabbed a damp washcloth at the teen's injured lip as the other two Tuaregs looked on. The white washcloth came away with red stains.

"He needs sutures," the medic said, "but I have no anesthetic to deaden his lip. Not all of our supplies have arrived yet."

The medic opened a tube of Brave Soldier. He took a cotton swab from a first-aid kit and squeezed some of the antiseptic ointment onto the cotton. "Tell him I will put medicine on his lip. It may sting."

Ongondo spoke in Tamahaq. The teen cut his eyes toward the officer and nodded. The medic used his thumb and forefinger to pull the bloodied lip into an exaggerated pout, and he rubbed the swab over the gash.

"If you can take him into Illizi," the medic said as he worked, "the clinic there should have lidocaine or something like it. They can sew his lip."

The teen held still. When the medic released his lip, the boy covered his mouth with his hand, spat out blood.

The three Tuaregs began to talk among themselves.

"What are they saying?" Gold asked.

"The man wants to know how the boy got into a fight. The boy says other refugees accused him of helping terrorists."

"Did he?"

Ongondo raised his index finger as he listened. He wore a look of intense concentration while he followed the chatter.

"The boy's uncle was a grain merchant," Ongondo said. "The uncle has sold lentils and millet to—someone. To 'foreigners,' I think they are saying. Foreigners up to no good, I suspect. The uncle has already been killed."

"Did the Tuareg man and his son know this other boy before now?"

Ongondo translated the question, and the man answered with several words.

"They are distant cousins," Ongondo said. "The man suspected the boy's uncle had some dangerous customers."

Gold found her writing pad where she'd left it on the cot. From inside its spiral binding she withdrew a ballpoint pen and clicked the end of it. The effort made her think of thumbing the fire selector on an M4; she could handle a rifle well enough, but she felt she'd always done her most important work with her mind and her pen. She jotted down the date and time, made notes on what she'd heard. Looked up from her pad and regarded the Tuaregs.

"We need to get them out of here," she said.

CHAPTER 27

Blount woke in the early morning, before light. During the night, between periods of fitful sleep, he had worked at the bolt securing his right chain. Now he could twist the bolt all the way around, but he had not yet freed it completely. The bolt on his left remained loose, and Blount kept it inserted in the wall to fool his captors.

He guessed no one else had yet awakened. No sounds came from the next room. Ivan snored to Blount's left. To Blount's right, Fender lay curled on his side. Dim light from an oil lantern spilled through the doorway. The dirtbags tended to leave at least one lantern burning all night.

The predawn stillness reminded Blount of childhood mornings back home. When you harvested tobacco—primed tobacco, as the farmers called it—you started work early to avoid the iron-press heat of afternoon. You walked to the field as soon as you had light enough to see. In those quiet minutes before the tractor arrived, you could hear a drop of dew fall from the tip of a leaf. Sometimes you'd find a stray morning glory vine entwined around a tobacco stalk, pink and purple blooms spreading open to greet the dawn. Off in the distance, from down in the woods, you might hear the *ka-ka-ka-koo-koo-koo* of a rain crow.

A good memory for Blount's final moment of solitude.

He decided to act. Now.

The dirtbags would be groggy, their reaction times slow. With a whole lot of luck, Blount might even kill *two* of them before they cut him down. He nudged Fender with the tip of his boot.

"Hey, bud," he whispered. "Wake up."

Fender groaned, rolled over. Opened his eyes, squinted at Blount.

"Time to go to work, Marine," Blount hissed. "You understand?"

Fender stared at Blount for a moment. Then he nodded slowly, set his lips tight together.

"I'm gon' act sick and bring 'em in here. Just stay loose and ready. Follow my lead."

"You got it, Gunny."

Fender sat up. Blount turned to Ivan. The Russian's eyes were open.

"Nice knowing, you, bud," Blount said. "You ready for what I told you about?"

Ivan gave a wry smile.

"Do svidaniya," he said.

Don't overthink this, Blount told himself. You can't really plan it; you can just rely on your training and muscle memory and what the Good Lord gave you.

Blount placed his left hand on his left chain, near the loose bolt in the wall down near the floor. Placed his right hand farther up on the same chain. Slid himself up against the wall for more slack in the chains. Kneeled on one knee, his right. Kept his left knee up with his foot flat on the floor. Adjusted his left heel so that it contacted the wall. Better leverage that way. Now he could pull the loose bolt out of the wall, spring upward, and use the freed left chain as a weapon. Only the right chain held him, and he could move within its full arc.

"Boys," he whispered. "If either one of you gets out of this alive, tell my wife and kids I love 'em." He wished he could have one more whiff of Bernadette's lavender-shampooed hair.

His eyes misted. His throat caught. He blinked hard, took in a full chest of air, shut down his emotions.

No longer a husband. No longer a father. No longer a son or a grandson. Gunnery Sergeant A. E. Blount, he told himself, nothing remains of you but weapon.

He coughed hard, hacked, spat. Shook his chains like a malevolent specter.

"Oh, God, I think I'm dying," he shouted. "Somebody help me."

Coughed again, snorted.

"He's having a convulsion," Fender yelled. "Help!"

"I can't breathe," Blount bellowed. Retched like someone vomiting.

Sounds of commotion came from the other side of the wall. Chains clanking.

"Help him," one of the Americans shouted from the other room.

Rat Face came through the doorway. Oh, yes, Blount thought. He slowly slid the loose bolt and eyelet out of the wall. Coughed and wheezed. Shook his limbs as if suffering a seizure. Rat Face pointed an AK-47. When he saw Blount in apparent distress, he lowered the rifle and held it in his right hand. Blount bowed his head, opened his mouth, and retched. Rat Face stepped closer and raised his foot for a kick. He never delivered it.

Blount pushed off on his left boot, exploded upward. Unfolded himself quick as a switchblade. Circled the chain around Rat Face's throat and wrenched hard.

In that instant of speed and strength, Blount felt a sense of mastery. He would spend his last moments in action, at the height of his skills.

The steel links crushed the terrorist's windpipe. Blount pulled him close, glared into the bulging eyes. Heard the rattle of constricted breath.

"I ain't playing with you no more," Blount hissed. Pushed with one fistful of links and yanked with the other, tightening the chain further. Popping and squishing noises came from under the chain.

Rat Face tried to bring up the AK. Feeble motion of a dying man.

He dropped the weapon; the AK clattered across the floor. Blount felt his prey go limp, and he unwrapped the chain. Rat Face collapsed at Blount's feet. The dirtbag lay on the floor with his mouth open as if he wanted to ask what lethal force had overtaken him so swiftly.

"What's happening?" an American shouted from the next room.

Blount did not answer. He dropped his knee, with all his weight behind it, onto Rat Face's chest. The ribs and breastbone made popping sounds like during hog killing in the fall when you open up a carcass.

"Yeah!" Fender shouted. He crouched with his back to the wall, waiting for orders from Blount.

Sure that Rat Face would never rise again, Blount stood and tried to reach the AK. Couldn't quite get to it.

Monkey Ears charged into the room, pistol in one hand. He stopped for half a second about two paces in front of Blount. Glanced down at Rat Face's body. With a look of horror, he brought up the pistol and fired.

The bullet slammed into the wall behind Blount. Peppered the back of his head with flying grit just as he flung the left chain like a whip.

Blount aimed for his enemy's gun hand. Instead the chain struck Monkey Ears in the face. It tore skin from the bridge of his nose, knocked him off balance. The terrorist tried to take aim. Blount lashed with the chain again.

Reflexively, Monkey Ears used both arms to shield himself from the slinging steel. He fired his pistol, but the bullet went into the ceiling. Monkey Ears stumbled, tried to point the handgun at Blount. The weapon's muzzle trembled.

At a heart rate above a hundred fifty beats per minute, Blount knew, most people lost fine motor skills. Fingers got in the way of one another. Perhaps the dirtbag's loss of motor skills gave Blount the half second he needed.

Blount weaved to his left to get off his enemy's centerline. At the same time, Blount's right hand came up and grabbed the pistol, fingers over the slide. The weapon fired, but Blount now controlled the muzzle. The slug flew wild. Blount ignored the pain as the slide cycled underneath his fingers, tearing skin. He squeezed down harder on the weapon.

"What's going on?" a voice called from the next room. "Who got shot?"

The chains weighed down Blount's wrists, slowed his movements. Dangled around his legs and interfered with his footwork. He'd have taken the pistol easily with unencumbered hands, but now he had to improvise.

Blount clutched his enemy's wrist with his left hand, kept his grip on the pistol with his right. Yanked with the left, shoved with the right. Wrested the weapon away from Monkey Ears. The break-and-take popped the terrorist's trigger finger; Blount heard the snap even though his ears rang from the pistol shots.

Monkey Ears shrieked and stumbled to the floor, his wrist still in the grip of Blount's left hand, pulling Blount off balance. Blount stumbled, lost his hold on the pistol, and dropped it. He kicked the weapon toward Fender, and Fender grabbed it. Monkey Ears shouted something in Arabic, no doubt calling for help. The terrorist wriggled within Blount's grip like a catfish caught on a trotline.

Urgent voices babbled from outside. Blount knew Kassam stationed at least two more guards somewhere. If they had to come in from outside, Blount might have three or four more seconds to work.

Fender fired. The bullet struck Monkey Ears in the middle of his torso. The terrorist fell onto his back, twitching.

"We got two of 'em," Fender shouted to the other prisoners.

"Get ready for somebody to come through the doorway," Blount said.

"Aye, aye, Gunny," Fender said. He sat with his back against the wall, pistol held in both shackled hands. He kept the muzzle trained toward the doorway, steadied by his elbows against his knees.

Blount had already lived longer than he expected. Somewhere in the recesses of his mind, he thought of the first general order: *Take charge of this post and all government property in view.*

Blount tried to get the AK-47 Rat Face had dropped. He lowered himself to the floor, slid to the limit of his right chain, strained to reach with his boot. The AK remained about a foot too far away.

"Ivan," Blount said, "can you get to that weapon?"

The Russian groaned, crawled as far as his chains allowed. Reached out his arm. Needed six more inches to grab the stock.

The clatter of bootsteps came from the next room. "It's cool, man," an American voice shouted. "I ain't got a gun. Be cool, be cool, be cool."

Outstanding. The minds of the other guards would have to process those words, whether they understood English or not. Maybe buy another few seconds.

Blount changed his plan. Maybe he could free himself entirely.

He grasped his right chain with both hands. Stepped closer to where the bolt and eyelet remained cemented. Planted one foot against the wall, pushed off with all his strength. Twisted to his left to increase the power of his body weight in motion.

The masonry cracked but held. The links between Blount's fingers snapped tight and dug into his skin. He ignored the pain and set himself for another try.

A skilled martial artist, Blount used leverage and mechanical advantage instinctively. You didn't punch just with your forearm; you put your shoulder behind it to multiply the force. You didn't kick with only your foot; you brought up your knee and unloaded your hips to strike so much harder. Though Blount possessed the strength of a Hereford bull, he considered form more important.

This time he placed his back to the wall with the right chain over his right shoulder. Braced one foot against the wall, grounded the other foot on the floor. Blount gritted his teeth and let out a deep growl. Burst forward like a sprinter leaving the starting block.

He bent at the waist and rotated his shoulder as the chain extended.

"They're coming your way, Gunny," someone shouted from the next room.

The eyelet ripped from the wall. Blount crashed to the floor. The muscles of his upper body felt torn and strained as if racked. But he was free.

Blount scrambled to his feet, looked around for Rat Face's rifle. Where was it?

A terrorist came through the doorway, rifle in his hands. Fender fired and the man went down. Another guard rushed in with an AK. Pressed the trigger and started blasting.

In the close confines of the room, the automatic weapon roared like hell's gates thrown open. The rounds tore into the opposite wall. The air filled with bullets, bullet fragments, flying brass, chunks of masonry, and dust.

Blount dived to get low. He grabbed the ends of both chains, held them like two steel whips. One mind, any weapon.

For an instant Blount saw the look of confusion on the shooter's face. Perhaps in the dim light the dirtbag's brain had too much to analyze: *Who shot my buddy? What are the prisoners doing? Where did the big one go?*

Blount whirled from the floor and sprang to a crouch. As he moved, he flung his right chain. The chain knocked the rifle from the dirtbag's hands. Blount flailed with the left chain and missed entirely.

"Shoot him!" Blount barked. Why wasn't Fender firing?

From the corner of his eye, Blount saw the young Marine pulling at the handgun's slide. Clearing a jam.

Blount let go of the chains, launched himself at the new enemy.

Grabbed the back of the man's head with his left hand. Cupped the enemy's chin with his right. Pulled with his left hand. Pushed with the other, almost like throwing a straight punch. Snapped the neck.

The life drained from the dirtbag's eyes, which froze into a look of incomprehension and fear. Blount let go of the dead man. The body slumped to the floor.

More pounding of boots from outside.

"Here comes another one, Gunny," shouted a prisoner in the next room.

Another one?

Blount had confirmed only four. But it was hard to gather good intel when you were sick and chained up. He scanned for Rat Face's AK. There it was, in the corner.

His chains tangled, slowed his arms. Blount had converted his bonds to weapons, but now they fettered him again. Before he could grab the rifle, a fifth dirtbag charged in, firing.

The burst caught Ivan across the thighs. Blood from the leg wounds spattered the Russian's face and chest. He did not cry out, but he slumped against the wall and watched helplessly.

Fender finished clearing the jammed pistol. Chambered a round, pulled the trigger. The bullet struck the terrorist in the arm. The man flinched. His weapon's muzzle dropped, sent rounds blasting into the floor.

Arms burdened by tangled chains, a rifle two seconds away when he needed it now, Blount made an instant calculation: The weapon he could employ fastest was his feet.

He spun on his left heel, raised his right knee to load for a round kick. Only then did he register that his new opponent was almost as big as he was. Blazing eyes, bulging arms, black beard. One arm bleeding.

Blount snapped his hips, sent all his weight behind the kick. Aimed for the bundle of nerves that runs down the upper leg. Let his breath explode out with a *"Shssss!"* as he landed the blow. Struck with the top portion of his combat boot, along the laces. Felt the solid impact of a well-thrown kick.

The enemy staggered but did not go down. Brought up his rifle barrel, but the bullet wound slowed his movements.

Blount followed with a side kick. Knocked the weapon from the dirtbag's hands. The AK clattered to the floor and slid to where Ivan lay hemorrhaging.

The big terrorist lunged at Blount.

The chains had left Blount with his center of gravity askew; he remained a little off balance from his last kick. When the dirtbag shouldered into him, both men tumbled to the floor.

Blount broke his fall, slapping the floor with his forearms. Landed with his head up to prevent cracking his skull. But that gave the terrorist an opening. The man fell on top of Blount, grabbed a length of chain and wrapped it around Blount's neck.

Blount wrenched his head to the side. That moved some of the pressure off his trachea, changed his predicament from an airway choke to a blood choke. Still, a blood choke could rob his brain of oxygen and put him out in seconds.

He clawed at his enemy's face. Put the heel of his hand against the terrorist's jawbone. The beard felt like steel wool.

Blount's vision began to dim. A snarl of rage died in his throat. A python seemed to tighten coils around the arteries of his neck.

The enemy twisted harder with the chain, used his good arm. Let out a howl of exertion and pain.

With all the power that Blount could muster, he pushed up on his enemy's head. Before he passed out, he hoped to give Fender a target.

His triceps burned. Vision grew darker. Shoot, boy, Blount thought. In a second or two it won't matter if you hit me.

A thump sounded from the corner of the room. After so much gunfire in close quarters, that's all Blount's ringing ears could sense from one more shot.

The dirtbag's head came apart in Blount's hand. Blount found himself holding on to a face but little else. Blood and brains splashed him. His wrist stung. The terrorist went limp, became deadweight.

Blount pushed the corpse off him. Rose up on one elbow, pulled the chain from around his neck. Slowly, his surroundings came into focus.

Ivan sat against the wall, blood pooled beneath his legs. With both hands, he held the AK the big terrorist had dropped. Smoke curled from the muzzle.

CHAPTER 28

At a clinic in Illizi, Algeria, Gold waited while a doctor treated the Tuareg boy who'd suffered a split lip during the camp brawl. She sat with Major Ongondo and the other two Tuaregs in a small kitchen. For security reasons, Ongondo had asked to keep Gold and the refugees out of sight instead of in a public waiting room.

One of the clinic attendants made tea for the group. The man lit a gas burner under a pot of water. While he waited for the water to boil, he spooned shredded tea leaves from a foil pouch into two glass bowls.

The white-tiled kitchen looked well worn but spotless. Algerian folk music played on an old transistor radio. After the awful news about Sergeant Farmer, Gold tried to settle her mind, to focus on something else. She could tell the music came from some sort of stringed instrument, though she could not identify the instrument precisely. She asked Ongondo about it.

"That is a mandole," he said. "Very similar to a mandolin."

"Beautiful," Gold said.

When the water came to a boil, the attendant poured it into the bowls containing the dry tea leaves. He stirred the mixture in the bowls, and the aroma of green tea filled the room. Then he poured the contents of both bowls through a strainer, leaving behind the steaming, soggy tea leaves. The liquid ran down the sink drain.

It smells so good, Gold thought, so why did he pour it out? The man must have noted her puzzled expression. He communicated as best he could in what English he knew.

"Only to clean, ma'am. Only to clean tea."

Gold smiled, nodded. Ongondo chatted amiably with the Tuaregs in their language. He sat with his legs crossed, and he wore his sidearm, the only weapon he'd brought with him. Gold could not understand the conversation, but it flowed so casually that they might have been discussing music, food, or soccer. Excellent, Gold thought. Keep them at ease.

The attendant took fresh mint leaves from a small icebox. He washed the leaves and placed them in a pewter teapot. Added cold tap water from a spigot, dumped in the wet tea leaves and two cubes of sugar. Placed the teapot on the burner.

After the teapot began boiling, the attendant poured the tea into four cups. Steam curled from each one, and a pleasant aroma of mint filled the room.

Before leaving the refugee camp, Gold had called Parson about the three Tuaregs, one of whom might know something about where to find terrorists—or at least where terrorists had ordered food delivered. She hadn't pressed the boy for specifics yet; she wanted him in a place where he felt safer. But Parson needed time to get approval from AFRICOM to send an aircraft and allow billeting for three Algerian nationals and an AU officer.

She lifted her cup and took a sip. The balance of the delicate flavors surprised her. Gold tasted the mint, the sugar, and the tea almost separately. She'd had tea across much of the world, in countless variations, and she appreciated the care the attendant took in brewing this batch. It was sweet and . . . clean, just like the man had said. This small act of kindness, his meticulous preparation of the tea, showed a respect for his own culture and for his visitors. Gold closed her eyes for a moment and savored the civility of this moment, in its contrast with the violence and hatred beyond these walls.

The man put on a cloth mitt, opened a tiny oven, and removed an iron skillet. He let the dish cool for a few minutes, and cut three slices of something that looked like quiche. He put the slices on ceramic plates and poured honey over the food. Then he found forks in a drawer and served his guests.

"Thank you," Gold said. She forked a mouthful of the food. Found it still quite hot, but she chewed anyway. Much like quiche but sweeter.

"You like?" the man asked.

Gold swallowed the mouthful, took a sip of tea.

"Yes, sir," she said. "Very good. What is it?"

"*M'shewsha*. We call *m'shewsha*."

"Thank you very much."

The Tuaregs seemed to like it, too. The boy smiled, ate with his fingers. When Gold finished eating, she tied on a head scarf to cover her blond hair and went outside to her vehicle. She and Ongondo had transported the Tuaregs from the refugee camp to Illizi in the UN's Nissan Armada.

They had parked on a sandy street next to the clinic. A layer of desert dust covered the new vehicle. Good. That would show signs of tampering all the better. Even though they had stopped at the clinic for only a couple of hours, Gold wanted to take every precaution. If people at the camp suspected one of the Tuaregs knew something about terrorists, who else might suspect? She stepped around the SUV, looking for handprints, stray wires, or anything else that suggested someone had installed something that didn't belong. Terrorists knew how to plant a bomb so that the opening of a car door or the turning of an ignition switch could send the driver and passengers to oblivion. She took her time with the inspection so anyone watching her might see. If the bad guys noted her caution, she reasoned, they might decide she presented too difficult a target.

She saw no signs of a bomb, no evidence of anyone staking out the Nissan. A few meters down the street, a brown dog of indeterminate breed skulked from behind a building. Hairless scar tissue marred its hindquarters, and the animal carried its tail between its legs. Two blocks beyond the dog, a white Toyota pickup started its engine. The vehicle pulled away from the curb, motored past the clinic, and disappeared in a left turn down an alleyway. The bearded driver did not seem to notice Gold.

Gold opened the Nissan's door and sat down behind the wheel. The interior still smelled like a new car, a sensory input all out of accord with the dust and heat of a Saharan town. She found her satellite phone under the seat, rotated the phone's antenna from its stowed position until it clicked into place at a forty-five-degree angle. The antenna—a black cylinder about the length of a pen—slid out a few inches when Gold extended it. She pressed a button at the bottom of the keypad to power up the device. The word "searching" appeared on the screen until the phone found its connection in space. Gold punched in Parson's number. When he answered, he sounded like he spoke from next door.

"Hello, Michael," Gold said. "Any luck getting approval to bring these guys to Mitiga?"

"Yeah. Had to take it to the two-star level, but I'm sending an aircraft for you now."

"Any idea when we should expect the plane?"

"The nearest airport to you is Takhamalt. That's just a few miles away. Can you get there by five?"

Gold checked her watch. "Yes," she said. "We borrowed a vehicle from the UN camp."

"Sounds good. I'm about to launch a Herk."

"Great. Maybe we'll see you by tonight."

"Major Ongondo can come to Mitiga with the refugees," Parson said. "We don't have anybody else who speaks their language."

"That's a good idea," Gold said. "You can fly him back here when he's done, and the vehicle will be waiting for him at the airport."

"That'll work."

Gold could imagine the horse-trading and lobbying Parson must have gone through to get all this approved. His unorthodox style of command bent rules and interpreted regs in a way that strained the English language. She'd known Parson to get away with things that might get other officers canned, but his bosses tolerated him because he got things done.

After Gold terminated the call, she went back inside the clinic. The doctor had finished sewing the injured boy's lip. The boy sat in the kitchen with Ongondo and the other Tuaregs. His lip was swollen, and Gold could see a stitch of thread at the edge of his mouth.

"He is sore," Ongondo said, "but he will survive."

"What do I owe the doctor?" Gold asked.

"Nothing. I already took care of it."

"Very kind of you, sir. Colonel Parson is sending a plane to Takhamalt to pick us up. I'd like to go ahead and get to the airport now."

Gold felt a little exposed, escorting refugees who might have sensitive information. She wanted to return to the relative safety of Mitiga as quickly as possible.

"Agreed," Ongondo said.

"I'll drive."

In the Nissan, Gold started the engine and turned on the air-conditioning. A mixture of dust and mist spewed from the vents for a couple of seconds, and then the AC's output cleared. Ongondo sat in the front passenger seat. The Tuaregs climbed into seats in the back and began talking among themselves.

Gold consulted a map she'd left in the console, studied the route to the airport. A habit she'd retained from driving around Afghanistan: Know where you're going. Don't get lost and have to spend extra time meandering through a hostile area.

A plainer vehicle would have been better, she knew, or at least an older one. Something that blended in more. Savvy Americans driving in Kabul often chose rattletraps, the dirtier the better. But Gold would make do with what she had. She moved the shifter for the automatic transmission, stepped on the gas, steered into the street.

She drove past the office for Sonelgaz, the state natural-gas and electricity company. The Algerian flag flew atop the roof: half green, half white, with a red crescent and star in the center. The business district gave way to a residential area. Trees that resembled the palmettos of the southern U.S. dotted the courtyards of bigger homes.

Men in linen cloaks, or *gandouras*, strolled the neighborhood. Gold saw few women. One man eyed the Nissan as it passed, a cell phone to his ear. Nothing unusual about that; North Africans loved their mobile phones and other devices as much as anyone else.

The Tuaregs continued chatting. "They have never flown before," Ongondo said. "The boys are excited about getting on an airplane. The man is just worried."

"I hope they enjoy the flight," Gold said.

She didn't want to seem rude, but she limited her small talk to stay focused on her surroundings. In the unfamiliar town, she didn't want to miss a turn, get lost, or blunder into the wrong area.

The paved streets led to a dirt road at the edge of the town, and the dwellings turned to hovels made of mud and stone, with thatched roofs. Dust rose off to her right. Gold looked closer and saw a white Toyota pickup—perhaps the same one she'd seen back at the clinic—rolling along a side path. The path intersected the road ahead of her, and she eased off the accelerator to let the truck get ahead.

The truck matched her speed.

From the left, two more vehicles approached. A beat-up taxi and a Land Rover bounced through ruts. It appeared they would meet the Toyota at about the same spot. Gold slowed just a bit more to avoid the momentary congestion.

She checked her mirror. An SUV approached from behind, perhaps an American-built Jeep, its white paint coated with dust. The vehicle gained on her.

Gold's palms began to sweat as she gripped the steering wheel.

"I think we have a problem," Gold said. She placed her right hand on the shifter, scanned around to look for options.

There weren't many. No more side streets between her position and the intersection ahead. Ditches on both sides of the road, too deep to cross even in four-wheel drive.

If you wanted to set up a vehicle ambush, she realized, this is where you'd do it.

Ahead, the Toyota, the taxi, and the Land Rover met in the intersection. All three slid to a stop.

The vehicles blocked the road.

Men emerged from them. Bearded figures holding rifles. Bandoleers across their chests sagged with magazines for their AK-47s.

Ongondo drew his pistol.

"Hold on tight," Gold shouted. She saw only one chance for escape: back away from the roadblock, reverse course and get past the Jeep now behind her.

She stomped the brake pedal. The Nissan ground to a halt, dust enveloping it.

The men raised their weapons. Gold shoved the shifter into reverse, placed her left hand on the steering wheel's three o'clock position.

"Get down," she yelled.

Hit the accelerator.

Gold had not practiced tactical driving in a long time, and never in a vehicle like this. With the ditches on either side, she had no room for error. And no time for hesitation. Every two-tenths of a second in a kill zone meant another bullet coming her way. She fell back on her training.

The Nissan sped backwards. Over her shoulder, Gold watched the Jeep loom larger in the rear window. It had stopped to block the road behind her.

Inside the Nissan, the Tuaregs shouted and screamed. Ongondo pointed his sidearm, fired shots through the windshield. The bullets punched white-rimmed holes in the glass. Gold couldn't tell if he hit any of the attackers.

When she came within about eight car lengths of the Jeep, she whipped the steering wheel to begin a Y-turn; she meant to swerve ninety degrees in reverse, shift into drive, then twist the wheel in the opposite direction to peel out and escape.

The Nissan's rear wheels backed to within inches of the ditch. Gold slammed on the brake, shifted into drive. Dust shrouded the vehicle.

Gold wheeled to the right to complete the Y-turn. Planted her foot on the gas. Keep it moving, she told herself. If they stop your car, it becomes your coffin.

Momentarily blinded by the dust, Gold heard pops of rifle fire from the Jeep. Two bullets slammed through the windshield from outside. Gold felt the pricks of flying, pulverized safety glass.

The Nissan blasted through the dust cloud. The view cleared to reveal the Jeep parked in the middle of the road, both doors open. From behind both doors, men aimed AKs.

Gold ducked as low as she could. Steered for the right of the Jeep. Ongondo kept firing.

More gunfire cackled from outside. Bullets slammed into the body of the Nissan. Flying glass stung Gold's cheek. She didn't see where the shards came from. In one of the back seats, someone shrieked.

Don't look at the obstacles, Gold had been taught. Look at the escape path. She gauged she had just enough room to slip between the Jeep and the ditch—if she hit the Jeep's door and the man behind it.

Gold braced herself for what she had to do.

The corner of the Nissan's front bumper smashed into the Jeep door with a crunch of metal. She drove the door—and the man behind it—against the side of the Jeep. The Jeep's window shattered with such force that the exploded granules looked like splashing water. Scraping steel joined the sounds of rifle fire and screams.

The bearded face flashed by in an openmouthed grimace. Blood and viscera smeared across the sides of both the Jeep and the Nissan. Specks of red appeared on Gold's side window.

The Nissan tore free of the trap, pieces of its side mirror bouncing in the roadway. In the rearview mirror, Gold saw the Jeep's door—torn from its hinges—roll across the ground and come to rest in a ditch. The terrorist's body collapsed beside the Jeep, white *gandoura* soaked crimson. Gold noticed something unnatural about the way he fell. The scraping motion of the door had torn the body in two.

Gold raced back toward Illizi, tried to come up with a plan. She could think of nothing better than to put as much distance as possible between her and the attackers. Maybe they wouldn't try to strike again in town with witnesses all around.

Or maybe they wouldn't care where they struck.

Either way, Gold saw no option except to head back through Illizi and find another route to the airport.

The Tuaregs shouted in Tamahaq. Gold glanced behind her and saw blood all over one of the windows. The Tuareg man moaned and held on to his bleeding right wrist. A bullet—or maybe a couple of bullets—had pierced it. Blood dripped from the torn muscle tissue, ran down the arm and into the man's sleeve. Blood spattered onto his lap, spilled across the seats.

Gold steered around a child driving a little herd of four gray-and-black goats. The animals bleated as the Nissan charged past.

"He needs a bandage," Ongondo said. Then Ongondo spoke in the language of the Tuaregs. The older boy—the one who'd been in the fight at the camp—unwrapped his headdress and gave it to Ongondo. The younger boy—the Tuareg man's son—looked on in wide-eyed fear.

"I want to take him to the clinic, but they might spot this vehicle and hit us again," Gold said.

She checked her mirror. Nothing behind her at the moment. But the gunmen could have gone anywhere.

"We should get to the airport," Ongondo said. "Get all of us out of here and back to Mitiga. I am sure the American medical people can treat him there."

"Let's do that," Gold said.

The Nissan rocked through potholed streets as it returned to Illizi. Inside the town, more traffic sputtered along the roadways. Gold asked Ongondo to check the map for another route to Takhamalt airport. As she drove, she scanned for triangular road signs bearing the silhouette of an airliner. She also kept glancing in her mirror, looking for a Toyota, a taxi, or a Land Rover. So far, none of them appeared.

Even if they never did, Gold still had a problem. She'd have to talk her way through whatever gate security existed at Takhamalt—in a half-wrecked, shot-up SUV with a wounded man inside.

CHAPTER 29

With the agility of a big panther, Blount came to his feet in a fighting stance. He glanced at the doorway, saw no more enemy. Lunged for the AK-47 Rat Face had carried. Pulled back the bolt just enough to see that a round was chambered. Clicked the fire selector to the semi position. Posted himself by the door frame to check the next room, chains dragging from his arms.

From that position he caught a glimpse of another Marine, Corporal Mark Grayson. Grayson saw Blount, too, and yelled, "Clear! It's clear in here, Gunny."

Blount's heart swelled. Hot damn, he thought, these men are acting like Marines.

"Clear!" Blount yelled. He entered the room to see Grayson chained next to a Legionnaire. Both men looked up at Blount with expressions of pure wonderment. A pair of slack chains lay next to the Legionnaire. Must have been where they'd held that poor boy Farmer.

Another doorway opened into a third room. Blount posted by that entrance, saw no one in there. Only a pool of black blood in the middle of the floor. A green flag with squiggly writing on it hung from the wall. Two blood-soaked towels in a corner. Bloody drag marks. To Blount's mind, a scene of such evil that it almost surprised him not to see Satan himself standing there smirking.

"Clear," Blount said.

He peered through the windows, checked outside. The desert extended to infinity. No sign of any people.

Blount had never expected to live this long. To kill a bad guy, two at the most, was the best he'd dared to expect. But now the mission changed: Get out of here and get moving. Find a safe spot and call for help.

He handed the AK to Grayson.

"This weapon's in condition one," Blount said. "Light up anybody who comes inside. I'll look for the keys to these shackles. Got a man in there shot real bad, too."

"Aye, aye, Gunny," Grayson said. He turned to the Legionnaire beside him and said, "On your feet, dude. Help me watch the doors and windows."

The Legionnaire pushed himself up from the floor, chains dangling. "Watch window," he said. Funny accent. Not French. Spanish, maybe?

Blount ran back into the room where he, Fender, and Ivan had been held. Fender stood, pistol gripped with both hands in the Weaver ready position. Scanned the windows as best he could at the limits of his chains. Tipped his chin toward Ivan.

"I think he's bleeding out, Gunny," Fender said. "I can't reach him."

Ivan lay against the wall. Eyes heavy-lidded, rifle across his blood-soaked lap. Left arm slack by his side, palm upturned. Right hand on the weapon, index finger across the trigger guard.

Blount kneeled beside Ivan, the Russian's blood sticky all around. He pulled the AK from Ivan's hand, set it down in the widening red puddle. A faint smile crossed Ivan's face.

"Magnificent," the Russian whispered.

"That was a mighty good shot, bud," Blount said.

As he spoke, he unbuckled his belt of black webbing, yanked it from the loops of his uniform trousers. Ivan needed a tourniquet. Right this instant. Two of them, in fact. Blood gushed from wounds in both thighs.

"Anybody got a CAT?" Blount shouted. Marines carried combat

application tourniquets, but with everyone's gear scattered or stolen, Blount had no idea where to find his.

"Negative, Gunny," Grayson called.

"Afraid not," Fender said.

"Gimme your belt," Blount told Fender.

Fender grasped the pistol with one hand, stripped off his belt with the other. His belt was gray rather than black like Blount's, indicating a lower proficiency level in the martial arts program. Fender tossed the belt.

Blount caught it with his left hand, the loose chain swaying. As gently as he could, he raised Ivan's knees. Felt warm blood flowing through his fingers. Ivan's eyes were closed now. Blount looped the belts around the Russian's upper legs, pulled the belts tight, fastened the open-face clasps.

If the movement caused Ivan any pain, he did not show it. His head lolled back against the wall, a look on his face of . . . serenity. The bear tattooed on his arm still snarled and slashed at all enemies.

Blount put two fingers on the Russian's neck, searched for the carotid artery. Ivan's heart beat so rapidly it felt like the fluttering of a bird's pulse. Trying to pump up the blood pressure, Blount realized, without enough fluid to get the job done. He thought maybe he could use a pressure point to help slow down the bleeding. He placed the heel of his hand against the front right side of Ivan's pelvic bone. Tried to press down on the femoral artery. The effort seemed to have no effect.

Ivan wasn't going to make it. Blount had seen this before. Too much blood loss already.

"You done good, bud," Blount said. "You can be one of my riflemen any day."

"You can be . . ." Ivan breathed.

Blount tried to think of words to ease Ivan's passing. Nothing came to mind. A shame to watch a man go forth to his judgment and not have anything to say to him.

For Ivan's part, he seemed satisfied to see victory in his last moments, and to play a part in that victory. A man of action, he didn't need any words. Blount could relate.

He felt the carotid artery again: *Thump. Thump-thump-thump . . . Thump-thump. Thump . . . thump.*

Blount shifted the position of his two fingers on Ivan's neck. Nothing.

"He's gone, Fender," Blount said.

"Tough son of a bitch."

"You done good, too."

"Thank you, Gunny."

"You just cover me while I find some keys."

After the tremendous spike of adrenaline, Blount suddenly felt exhausted. So very tired, like he'd primed tobacco all day. But he couldn't rest now. Time to take charge of this post, get these Marines moving.

So which one of the dirtbags would have had the keys? Five dead enemies lay across the floor, some of their clothing sodden with blood. The room smelled a lot like when you open up a deer to gut it. He stepped over to Rat Face, left three bloody tracks. The crushed trachea gave Rat Face's throat an unnatural contour; the steel links had torn away enough skin and gristle to expose part of the windpipe. Rat Face wore that milky stare of the dead, looking into the next world. Blount wondered what those eyes saw now. Not seventy-two virgins, he imagined.

Blount tried to search Rat Face's clothing. The shackles made it difficult for Blount to place his hand all the way inside the pockets. Instead, he used his fingers to turn the pockets inside out. He found nothing but a folding knife.

Maybe Monkey Ears had the keys. Blount searched Monkey Ears in the same way, turning the pockets of the man's trousers. On the left side he found half- and quarter-dinar coins. On the right he found a key ring.

"Got some keys here, boys," Blount said. "Y'all see anybody coming?"

"Not yet," Fender said.

"Negative, Gunny," Grayson called from the next room.

So which key? Blount examined his shackles. They looked a lot like double-lock handcuffs, only heavier. He knew of Marines and SEALs who carried universal handcuff keys, but a universal key wouldn't have worked on these damned things. The key slot was bigger than standard. Lord only knew where these shackles came from and how old they were.

Blount jangled the keys, fingered each one. Car keys, door keys, keys to whatever, maybe this dirtbag's stash of porn. But a rusty iron key caught Blount's eye.

The key had a short blade and a large round bow, like a misshapen skeleton key. Blount inserted it into the key slot on his left shackle.

The key fit. But it wouldn't turn either way.

Frustration burned in Blount's chest. Bad way to finish if he couldn't get everybody's chains off. If all else failed, maybe they could shoot the eyelets and free themselves that way. But they couldn't shoot the shackles off their wrists; it would be too easy to slip and blow off a hand. If the keys wouldn't work, the men might have to drag chains across the desert as they fled. A trek into the Sahara would be hard enough as it was.

A drop of oil would have gone a long way. Damned terrorists couldn't even maintain their equipment. Blount slammed his left shackle against the wall. The impact stung his wrist.

He tried the key again.

No movement. The locking mechanism was rusted. What Blount needed now, of all things, was a can of WD-40 or Break-Free. But all he had was muscle.

Blount swung his wrist once more—a little like throwing a roundhouse punch, except he bent back his hand to strike with the shackle. He scraped the heel of his hand. The iron dug a gouge into the masonry.

He brushed the dust from his bleeding hand, inserted the key. Twisted it left. Nothing. Tried it again. Felt the mechanism click. Twisted the key to the right. Something else clicked. One click for a ratchet lock, Blount presumed, and another click for a pin lock. The shackle opened, dropped from his wrist, and clanged onto the floor.

"All right," Fender said.

"What's happening in there?" Grayson called from the next room.

"Gunny unlocked his chain."

"Cool."

Blount placed the key into the other shackle. Maybe that one was less rusted; the key turned more easily, and the right shackle fell away. He rubbed his wrists, went over to Fender.

"Gimme your left hand, bud."

Fender shifted the pistol to his right hand, offered up his left.

Blount inserted the key. He had the same trouble with Fender's shackle.

"Smack it against the wall," Blount said. "It's all rusted."

Fender hit the wall with his shackle.

"Ow!" Fender cried.

"All right, hold still."

Blount tried the key again. This time it worked. Fender's left shackle and chain fell away.

"Yeah!" Fender shouted. He held up his right hand. That shackle unlocked on the first try.

Fender stepped toward Rat Face's body. Stomped the side of the head. One of the lifeless eyes bulged out.

"Fuck you, motherfucker," Fender said.

"Take it easy, Corporal," Blount said. "He ain't gon' get any deader."

Fender placed his hands on his hips, looked down at the dead ter-rorist, breathed hard. Rubbed his wrists, looked up at Blount.

"Aye, aye, Gunny."

Blount held out the key ring.

"Go unlock Grayson and that other guy," Blount said. "I'll see what gear I can find."

Fender took the key and went to the other room. Blount could hear him talking with Grayson.

"Never expected to see you again," Grayson said.

"You shoulda seen Gunny Blount kicking their asses. It fucking scared *me*."

Blount heard their chains clanking, more conversation.

"Get this shit off me."

"Who's this guy?"

"Says his name is José Escarra. He don't speak much English."

Across the room from where Blount had been chained, he examined the equipment the terrorists had placed on the table. He found his watch, his grandfather's KA-BAR knife, two Marine Corps M16s, his radio, a GPS receiver, a CamelBak hydration pack, and other gear. Kassam had also left his flintlock. Blount lifted the antique pistol by its wooden grip.

Dried blood speckled the lock and the barrel. Sergeant Farmer's blood. For a moment Blount wanted to fling the pistol against the wall. Instead, he pulled his handkerchief from his pocket and wiped the blood away.

The pistol's cock jaws still contained a chunk of flint. Blount wondered if that flint came from a field somewhere in America a couple hundred years ago. The grip bore fine checkering; somebody had put some pride into the making of this thing. Letters stamped on the side plate read PERKINS. Another stamp read SALISBURY 1799. Was Perkins the owner or the builder of this weapon? Was that Salisbury in North Carolina, Maryland, or England? No time to think about it now. Blount stuck the pistol in the cargo pocket of his trousers. He looked around for ammunition and found only enough for one extra magazine for each weapon. For both the M16s and the AK-47s, the magazines carried thirty rounds.

In the next room, chains and shackles fell to the floor.

"When you guys get loose," Blount called, "you need to get some water to take with us. Food, too, if there's anything fit to eat. Look around."

"Aye, Gunny," Grayson answered.

Each breath Blount took, each step, seemed a miracle. Training, luck, and fire support from Fender and Ivan had given him a new life. But he and the others had been born into this new life with danger all around. Kassam and more jihadists could show up at any moment. Now the men needed to get out and away.

Blount found his tactical vest, slipped it over his back. Placed the PRC-148 radio into a pouch, slung one of the M16s over his shoulder. Pressed the power button on the GPS; it was a "dagger" model, the Defense Advanced GPS Receiver. To Blount's pleasant surprise, he found the battery still good. After the DAGR initialized, he stored the position of this hell house he'd just taken over. He looked around for his helmet, found it in a corner, put it on. Picked up the KA-BAR, went over to Ivan's body and kneeled beside the dead Russian.

"I know it ain't right to leave you here, bud, but we gotta make tracks," Blount said. "Somebody will come for you later. And I'll make sure everybody knows what you did."

Blount opened Ivan's shirt enough to reveal a necklace that held the Russian's dog tags. He unclasped the necklace and pocketed the metal tags. Next, he unbuckled the belts that had served too late as Ivan's tourniquets. Threaded the black one through the loops of his trousers and the KA-BAR's sheath. Buckled the belt, placed his hand over the pommel of his grandfather's knife. Then he stood up to continue his life's mission.

"Look alive, boys," he called. "Time to move."

"Hey, Gunny," Grayson called from the other room. "I found a bucket of water."

"Good work," Blount said. He picked up the CamelBak and tossed it through the doorway. "Fill this up. It's the only hydration pack I see."

"Aye, Gunny."

"Whatever water doesn't go in the CamelBak, we'll drink now. Don't know how long before we get picked up, and the best place to store water is in your body."

Blount gave the bloodstained gray web belt back to Fender. Then, in the other room, he watched Grayson fill the hydration pack with water and strap it to his back. That task completed, Grayson lifted the water bucket and drank in deep gulps, droplets running down his neck. He handed the wooden bucket to Blount.

Without drinking, Blount passed the bucket to Escarra.

"You next," Blount said.

"*Gracias,*" the Legionnaire replied. He drank from the bucket for a few moments, passed it back to Blount. Blount handed it to Fender. The corporal looked into the bucket, sloshed the remaining water.

"Ain't much left, Gunny," Fender said. "You take it."

"Drink."

With reluctance in his eyes, Fender tipped the bucket to his mouth and slurped. Lowered the bucket, wiped his lips with his sleeve.

"Saved you some, Gunny." Fender handed over the bucket.

Blount drank the final two swallows. He swished the last one around in his mouth for a second, noted the oaken flavor the bucket had lent to the water. For just an instant, it reminded him of drinking well water with a dipper made from a dried gourd.

They finished dividing up the gear. Blount gave the other M16 to Fender. Grayson and Escarra took AK-47s, along with the spare magazines of 7.62 millimeter. They found no food other than half a loaf of black bread. Blount tore it into four pieces and passed them out, keeping one for himself. The men wolfed the bread in seconds.

"Make sure your weapons are loaded," Blount said, wiping crumbs from his mouth. "I wish we had more ammo, but that's all I could find."

"Aye, Gunny," Grayson said.

Blount shifted the M16 off his shoulder. Ejected the magazine, found it nearly full. Smacked it back into the magazine well. Pulled the charging handle. Just in case more bad guys drove up at the last moment, he thumbed the fire selector to three-round burst fire. Checked the windows, saw no enemy.

He opened the door and stepped out into the Sahara.

CHAPTER 30

The guards at Takhamalt airport raised their weapons as Gold drove up to the chain-link gate. The hostile reception didn't surprise her; she was driving a shot-up vehicle with bloodstains along the side.

"Halt!" one of the guards shouted.

Gold had not expected the guards to speak English. She braked to a stop. Tried to lower the cracked power window, but it wouldn't work. Ongondo spoke in the Tuaregs' language, and the two boys held up their hands, fingers spread. Fear showed in their faces. Ongondo spoke what sounded like soothing words. The Tuareg man gripped his arm. Blood had soaked into the blue fabric of the headdress used as a makeshift bandage.

"Who are you?" the English-speaking guard yelled.

The guard wore British-style green camo. Behind him, the boughs of a stunted Algerian oak swayed in the breeze. The winds swept dust across the airport entrance.

Just let us in, Gold thought. Please just let us in. She glanced behind her to see if their attackers had caught up with them. No sign of any pursuers. She took a deep breath, tried to appear as calm and unthreatening as possible.

"I'm with the United Nations," Gold said. "I'm taking these men on an emergency medical flight that will land at any moment. The window will not come down. Let me open the door and show you my identification." She spoke slowly, unsure how much English the man knew.

He nodded, stepped back from the Nissan's door. Lowered his rifle but held his finger near the trigger.

Gold pulled the door lever. The bent door did not open until she kicked it. She reached for her wallet, slowly. Pulled out her ID card, offered it to the man. Beneath the United Nations logo and the UN's New York address, the card read NAME—MS. SOPHIA GOLD. TITLE—UNHCR FIELD SERVICE STAFF MEMBER. EXP. DATE— 4/11/15.

The guard perused the card, passed it back to her. Gestured with the barrel of his weapon.

"Man in there hurt. Your car shot. Why you not go to hospital?"

"We were on our way here when we were attacked by bandits. Our plane will take us to a hospital."

The man lifted a hand mike from where it was clipped on his uniform, talked into a radio in Arabic too rapid and colloquial for Gold to follow. She could not understand the answer that crackled back, either.

Ongondo found his AU identification card. He passed it to Gold, who offered it to the guard through the open door. Ongondo spoke in what Gold assumed was Berber. The guard read the ID, flipped it over, checked the back. Returned the card.

"Go to there," the man said. He pointed to a military hangar separated from the main terminal by an aircraft parking ramp. An aging transport plane—some kind of twin-engine turboprop—sat on the ramp. Whatever it was, it had remained there for a while. Oil stains darkened the pavement under its engines, and bird droppings soiled the windscreen. Gold had seen forlorn, disused airplanes like that taking up space at airports all over North Africa and South Asia.

"We send medic," the guard added.

"Thank you," Gold said. *"Salaam."*

"Salaam."

Gold tried to pull the Nissan's damaged door shut, but it wouldn't close all the way. She didn't care. She tapped the accelerator with her foot and steered to the military hangar. When she parked the vehicle and shut off the engine, she puzzled for a moment about what to do with the keys.

"I was going to leave you this vehicle to take back to the camp when you flew back here," Gold told Ongondo. "But I don't think you'll want to be seen driving around in it now, with all the bullet holes."

"I'll worry about that later," Ongondo said. "Now we just need to get out of here."

Gold handed him the keys. He pocketed them and stepped out of the vehicle. Ongondo opened the Nissan's side door and helped the Tuareg man get out. The man winced with every movement. He held on to his forearm while Gold, Ongondo, and the two boys escorted him into the hangar. Gold pulled on a corroded aluminum door at the back of the hangar, and the door squeaked open.

Inside, pigeons fluttered and cooed in the rafters. The smell of oil and mold hung in the air. An Mi-8 helicopter rested in one corner, its rotors missing. A metal folding chair, its seat rusted through in places, leaned against the wall. Gold unfolded the chair, and the wounded man lowered himself into it. The Tuareg boys brought everyone's bags into the hangar.

Gold hoped fervently that the C-130 would arrive as scheduled. She had no backup plan. She dared not venture out onto the Algerian roads again; if the aircraft diverted for any reason, she and her group would remain stranded at a dust-blown Saharan airport with minimal security.

She kneeled beside the Tuareg man's chair. The man continued to grip his arm, and he bent forward with his eyes closed. Ongondo stood nearby. The hangar's main doors were open, and Gold stared out toward the runway.

"Please tell him I know he's in pain," Gold said. "I'm sorry we can't do better for him right now."

"I did," Ongondo said.

"Thank you. I can't believe we got clear of that ambush."

"You drove brilliantly. Where did you learn such driving?"

"U.S. Army."

"Very impressive."

Ongondo strode over toward the Tuareg boys, spoke in their language. He huddled with them near the derelict helicopter and chatted in tones that sounded almost fatherly. The boys replied with what could have been pleading. When Ongondo walked away from the conversation, he wore a look of dissatisfaction.

"Anything wrong?" Gold asked.

"I tried to get them to tell me about this uncle selling food to Islamists. I think the older boy knows the most, but they all suspected something about his uncle. They don't want to talk until they're away from here. They are very afraid."

"They have reason to be, especially after what they saw today."

"True," Ongondo said. "Do you think those men who attacked us have any connection with Sadiq Kassam?"

"That's certainly a good bet."

A man dressed in the same uniform as the gate guards came into the hangar. He carried a washcloth and a metal box with a red cross on the lid; Gold figured he was the medic. Ongondo spoke in Berber and pointed to the Tuareg man. The medic regarded the man's arm and began to untie the makeshift bandage. As the medic worked, he continued talking with Ongondo.

"He says it would be better to take him to a hospital right away," Ongondo said.

"I know it," Gold said, "but not with bad guys out there looking for us."

The medic lifted the blue bandage to reveal the wound. The Tuareg clenched his teeth. Blood had begun to clot within the fabric, and the cloth stuck to the torn flesh. When the cloth peeled away, the injury began bleeding again. Red droplets spattered onto the dirty cement floor.

The wounded man's son moved closer to watch. At the sight of the blood, he began to cry. Despite obvious pain, the man spoke to the boy with what sounded like words of reassurance.

Given the torn-up wrist, Gold wondered if the injured Tuareg would keep full use of that hand. Lots of small bones there to get shattered. The medic wiped at the wound with the washcloth, and the wounded man let out only the briefest cry of pain. The medic spoke again, and Ongondo translated into Tamahaq. The Tuareg nodded, kept his eyes closed and jaw set.

From the first-aid kit, the medic withdrew a packet of Celox gauze. Gold had seen products like that in the military: the pad contained granules of a hemostatic chemical to aid clotting. For grievous injuries, a medic could pour the granules directly into a wound. But Gold had heard one resourceful pararescueman say that, in a pinch, you could accomplish the same thing with the dry flakes of instant mashed potatoes.

The medic tore open the packet. He wrapped the Celox around the wound, and the fabric adhered as if glued. A crimson stain expanded into the dressing. The medic wrapped conventional gauze over the Celox. Uttered a few words in Berber.

"Our injured friend is very stoic," Ongondo said.

"He would make a good soldier," Gold said.

She checked her watch, walked to the hangar's main entrance. Shaded her eyes with her palm, scanned the sky. Puffy cumulus scudded above, backdropped by pure blue. The sight implied serenity not at all in accord with events around her.

The turboprop grumble of a C-130 told her she wouldn't have to wait much longer. She'd jumped out of C-130s often enough to distinguish their sound from any other plane. The grumble grew to a low growl, and in the distance Gold spotted the airplane churning through the scattered clouds.

"Our aircraft is here," she said.

· Eventually the Herk turned onto final approach, its propellers appearing as translucent discs. As it glided toward the runway, the Tuareg boys joined Gold at the front of the hangar. They watched the airplane in silence, and Gold wondered if they felt frightened about flying for the first time. They showed no fear, only mute curiosity. The attempted ambush had likely reset all their calculations of risk.

The C-130 settled onto the runway, wings rocking slightly. Gold noticed a horizontal green stripe painted on the tail fin below the American flag. Black lettering within the stripe read THE ROCK. An aircraft out of Little Rock Air Force Base, Gold surmised. She had never been there, but Parson had told her about his tactical airlift training in Little Rock: challenging sessions in the simulator, low-level runs through the Ozarks, post-mission debriefs over beers in the club, days off spent hunting deer and ducks. She wondered if Parson knew any of this Herk's crew.

After taxiing onto the ramp, the C-130 shut down. Its propellers slowed to a stop, but its auxiliary power unit kept howling. Gold resisted the temptation to walk toward the aircraft. She operated under different rules now, out of uniform, and she didn't want to make the crew nervous. Eventually a loadmaster emerged from the plane and strode to the hangar. He looked young, in his early twenties. Lanky guy in beige desert flying gear, almost an image of Parson twenty years younger. From the name tag on his flight suit Gold saw he was an airman first class, a very junior enlisted rank.

"Ma'am," he asked, "are you Ms. Gold?"

"I am. Thanks for coming to get us."

"No problem, ma'am. Colonel Parson's orders. Before we left Mitiga, he said, 'If anything happens to her or her people, I'll beat you like you owe me money.'"

Gold smiled. "That sounds like him. I'm sure he was kidding."

"Uh, probably."

At the airplane, the loadmaster helped the wounded Tuareg

aboard, and the boys followed close behind. The loadmaster then gave a passenger briefing, explaining how to buckle the seat belts, where to find the exits.

Ongondo translated for the Tuaregs, who sat in their seats in the cargo compartment and looked around in rapt silence. The crew offered Gold a seat on a bunk at the back of the cockpit. As the fliers prepared for takeoff, Gold watched the navigator, seated at a panel on the right side of the cockpit, aft of the pilots and flight engineer. That had been Parson's station, she knew, before he became a C-5 pilot. Charts covered the nav table, along with a laptop computer running some sort of navigational app. The screen read FALCON VIEW. LIMITED DISTRIBUTION. A little icon in the shape of an airplane rested at a point that represented Takhamalt airport, and a dotted line stretched across the Algeria-Libya border and back to Mitiga.

These charts and maps reflect our need to impose order on the world, Gold mused. They showed borders of our own invention, latitude and longitude, grid coordinates and aircraft identification zones. They implied more order than really existed.

The crew began their checklist for starting engines. They spoke in clipped phrases, flipped switches and pressed buttons with a practiced confidence that Gold found reassuring. In a few minutes all four propellers spun. The flight engineer tweaked knobs and checked needles on the overhead panel, pronounced the checklist complete.

The copilot called for taxi clearance, and the pilot in the left seat released the parking brake. The C-130 lumbered across the tarmac, turned onto a taxiway, rolled along until it reached the hold-short lines.

"Reach Two Four X-ray clear for takeoff," the tower called in accented English.

"Two Four X-ray clear for takeoff," the copilot answered.

"Lineup checklist," the pilot ordered.

The crew ran another quick checklist, and the pilot steered the Herk onto the runway. Without ever stopping, he advanced the throttles. The acceleration pressed Gold's back against the cushion behind her. The noise and vibration doubled, tripled. When the co-pilot called, "Go," the pilot pulled back on the yoke, and the Herk climbed away from Algeria's sands. Gold closed her eyes, allowed herself a moment of relief.

About fifteen minutes later, the aircraft leveled off at altitude. When the chatter on the radios quieted, Gold ventured a question. She pressed her talk button and asked, "Anything new about those missing Marines?"

"Not a word," the pilot said. "But the terrorist sons of bitches released a video of the one they killed."

"I heard about that," Gold said. "Horrible."

She felt a hollowness that went beyond disappointment into something like grief. She had hoped this crew would bring word of progress of some kind.

"I understand you and Colonel Parson know one of those guys," the navigator said.

"We do. Gunnery Sergeant A. E. Blount."

"Very sorry to know your friend's in trouble, ma'am."

Gold nodded, choked back the emotion.

"We worked with him in Afghanistan," she said. "Wish you could meet him."

Gold described the big Marine, so hard-muscled and imposing that he looked like something manufactured and up-armored rather than born. An unholy terror in combat, yet such a gentle giant with his friends that even Afghan children drew to him as a source of protection and security.

"Not somebody I'd want to fool with," the navigator said.

"No," Gold said.

Blount's strength and resourcefulness gave her the only anchor for what little hope she maintained. But no matter how powerful, he was still human. Still vulnerable to bullets, toxins, thirst, hunger, and all the other ways a person could die in a desert combat environment.

For a few minutes no one said anything else. Gold appreciated the crew's concern and courtesy, but she knew what they were thinking: The odds looked bad and only worsened with time. The fliers turned their attention back to their instruments and charts.

"Look at that," the copilot said. Pointed a gloved finger toward something on the ground.

The pilot leaned to his right, peered out the copilot's window.

"Shit, the forecast was right," the pilot said.

Gold unbuckled her seat belt, stood to look. Miles to the south, along a distinct line, the desert turned to khaki-colored vapor. An invisible rope seemed to drag across the desert and lift the fine sands into the air, obscuring the roads and dunes. The scirocco winds again.

"Hope we get into Mitiga ahead of that," the copilot said.

"Me, too," the pilot said.

Gold didn't worry about her own safety; she'd heard Parson talk of making instrument landings through clouds of dust. But the dust storm would make it hard, if not impossible, for aircraft to continue searching for Blount and the others.

She turned away from the cockpit windows, descended the three steps to reach the cargo compartment. In the back of the airplane, Ongondo had gotten out of his seat, as well. He kneeled on the steel floor, speaking with the Tuaregs. The refugees chattered in excited tones, especially the boy who'd been in the fight. She wanted to know why they'd become so talkative, but as a professional interpreter she considered it bad form to interrupt in a moment like that.

But she could surmise a little just from the context: Now that the plane had safely departed Algeria, the Tuaregs had a story to tell.

CHAPTER 31

An ocean of sand stretched before Blount, Fender, Grayson, and Escarra. Guided by his DAGR, Blount led the de facto squad north. The coordinates displayed on the device told him the terrorists had driven him and the other captives farther south than he'd realized. But his position almost didn't matter. He just wanted to get as far away as he could from where they'd been held, and to make contact with friendly forces as quickly as possible.

The hills and hummocks of sand made for slow going; the *SPEED* portion of the DAGR screen read *4 KPH*. Now that the sun had climbed high, it created mirages wherever the terrain lay flat: Silvery water glistened in sheets, only to evaporate when the men approached.

Water wasn't the problem, though. Grayson carried the Camel-Bak, and it still contained drinking water. Blount worried most about getting recaptured. Only a matter of time before Kassam returned to see his prize hostages had escaped. With trucks and four-wheel-drive vehicles, Kassam and whatever henchmen he had left could catch up pretty quickly. Blount doubted he and his sleep-deprived, malnourished team would win the resulting firefight, especially with just the little bit of ammunition they'd scrounged. Best thing would be to get a helicopter ride out of here, so every few minutes Blount made a call on the PRC-148. So far, no answer. He decided to try it again, using the call sign he remembered from the comm card issued to him aboard the *Tarawa*. The ship and the original mission now seemed decades in the past.

"Any station, any station," Blount transmitted. "This is Havoc Two Bravo."

Nothing but hiss.

"Seems like they forgot about us," Fender said.

"I'm sure that ain't the trouble," Blount said. "We just need a plane to fly near enough to hear me on this thing."

"I just can't believe we're out of there," Grayson said. "God Almighty, Gunny, you kicked some ass."

"All you boys did your part," Blount said. "But now you gotta keep doing it. Keep your eyes open, and scan three hundred sixty degrees. If the dirtbags catch up with us, only hope is to see them first and get low."

"Aye, Gunny," Fender said.

A three-hundred-sixty-degree scan showed sun and blue horizon in most sectors but revealed a strange sight to the southeast. In that direction the sky darkened to the color of dried blood.

"What is that?" Grayson asked.

"Dust storm," Blount said.

"God, I hope that doesn't keep a helo from getting to us," Grayson said.

"I was just thinking the same thing."

Escarra glanced back at the red sky, began mumbling in Spanish.

"*Dios te salve, María,*" Escarra said. "*Llena eres de gracia.*" Escarra continued murmuring to himself as he walked.

"What are you saying?" Grayson asked.

Escarra stopped talking in Spanish. Looked at Grayson and said, "Is Hail Mary."

"Ah," Grayson said.

"That's good, bud," Blount said. "We'll take all the help we can get."

To Blount, a Hail Mary meant a long forward pass, but he'd heard of the Catholic prayer. Something about "pray for us now and in the hour of our death." Blount wondered if "now" and "the hour of our death" would turn out one and the same. Those dust clouds sure didn't look like a good sign. The *Tarawa* had steamed through a storm right before this mission, and now weird weather loomed again. Blount thought that if he were a superstitious man, he'd believe he'd passed through storms to the underworld, or maybe to another time.

Sure did seem like they'd come from the land of the dead. Blount had even brought back a two-hundred-year-old pistol in his pocket. He felt the weapon's lock rubbing against his leg. That would more than likely leave a sore spot, but Blount had no intention of ditching the flintlock. He kept it as a symbol of victory. Besides, it was still U.S. government property.

As the men walked, Blount looked them over to assess their condition. Everybody seemed reasonably strong, considering what they'd been through. But he doubted any of them had enough gas in the tank for a long battle if the enemy caught them again. As Blount regarded the men, he noticed a pouch on Grayson's rig: an Individual First-Aid Kit. Blount couldn't be sure, but it looked like his own.

"Hey, Grayson," Blount said, "where'd you get that IFAK?"

"Found it under a chair just as we left. Sorry I didn't see it when you were working on that Russian guy."

"That's all right. I don't think it would have helped him anyway. I think that IFAK's mine, though."

"Sorry, Gunny. Here, let me give it back." Grayson began to take the IFAK off his rig.

"No, keep it," Blount said. "But look in it and see if you find any CAT tourniquets."

Blount always carried his own extra tourniquets. He knew from bitter experience that if you got in a firefight or hit with an IED, you could never have too many.

Grayson unzipped the IFAK and looked inside. Poked through the contents.

"Yeah, Gunny. You got six."

Grayson lifted a handful of the CATs, made of black webbing and Velcro, neatly folded and secured with rubber bands. Each included a plastic rod for use as a windlass to tighten the tourniquet. Each also bore a white tag marked TIME, for recording when the tourniquet was applied.

"Pass 'em out."

Grayson held out a pair toward Blount.

"Nah," Blount said. "Give 'em to everybody else. Six is enough for the three of you to put one on each arm. Y'all put 'em loose over your upper arms. If you get hit, you can tighten it right quick. Saves enough time to maybe save your life. We used to wear 'em like that on patrol in Iraq. If we hadn't been wearing MOPP suits, I'd have made everybody put on CATs when we launched off the ship."

"Aye, Gunny."

Grayson handed tourniquets to Fender and Escarra. The two young Marines slipped the CATs over their arms and showed Escarra how to don his own. The Spanish Legionnaire looked a little puzzled at first.

"Yeah, I know," Fender said. "Seems pretty hard-core. But combat's hard-core, dude."

"Gracias," Escarra said.

"Anybody need more water?" Grayson asked. He held up the tube from his CamelBak.

"Yeah, I'll take a sip," Blount said. He put the tube in his mouth, took one long swallow. Fought the temptation to drink more.

As Blount handed the tube back to Grayson, Fender held up his hand.

"You hear that?" Fender asked.

Blount and the other men stopped walking. Listened. Sure enough, the low, continuous whoosh of a jet sounded in the distance. Blount shaded his eyes with his hand, saw nothing. Reached for his radio. The PRC-148 was a line-of-sight radio, and the line of sight here in the Sahara stretched pretty far. Even farther when talking to airplanes.

"Any station," he called, "Havoc Two Bravo, Mayday. Any station, do you read?"

Blount's idea of paradise took many forms. Maybe it would be something like his wedding day. Or perhaps the days his daughters were born. Or maybe that time during his childhood when he found a good fishing spot under a catalpa tree by a farm pond. The tree's leaves practically dripped with catalpa caterpillars. Young Blount fished all day with unlimited bait right over his head, not a single care on his mind.

But at the moment, heaven came as an answer on the radio. In a French accent.

"Havoc Two Bravo, Dagger One-Seven. Read you Lima Charlie. Please advise."

Blount grinned at the others. Pressed his transmit button.

"Havoc Two Bravo requests emergency extraction for four personnel." Blount read off his coordinates from his DAGR.

"Dagger One-Seven copies all. Very good to hear from you, *mon ami*. Will relay to search-and-rescue."

"Roger that," Blount replied. "Be advised we will keep walking on a northerly heading. Need to get some distance from hostiles." Blount released his talk switch, waited for a response.

"Understood. Maintain a listening watch on this frequency."

"Yes, sir," Blount said. "What type aircraft are you?"

"Dagger is a flight of two Mirages. Ah, stand by for a closer look."

At first Blount wondered what the pilot meant. But as the jet noise grew louder, he realized the French aviator intended a flyover. Not tactically necessary, but one heck of a morale boost for isolated personnel. Blount and his comrades craned their necks, gazed into the azure expanse. At first he saw nothing. But then Grayson pointed to the northeast and said, "There."

Two specks moved in unison across the sky, locked into formation as if connected by an iron bar. When they came nearer, both took on the pointed shape of fighter planes. One began to descend; the other stayed high.

The descending jet grew larger, banked toward Blount's position. The engine noise rent the sky, filled the desert. In a steep bank angle, the Mirage's triangular form become more apparent, gray exhaust and heat waves trailing from the tailpipe.

Blount raised his arm, began to wave. Swung his hand in wide arcs. Grayson, Fender, and Escarra waved, too. The aircraft dropped to what would have been treetop height if there had been any trees. The jet blast rose to deafening levels, and the Mirage streaked low overhead with the finesse of a flying ax blade. Blount noted the weapons mounted on pylons, and the roundel of the French air force. The jet rocked its wings.

"Heavy metal, baby," Fender shouted as the Mirage pulled up into a nearly vertical climb.

"Whoo-hoo!" Grayson yelled. "Find them fuckers and blow 'em up."

The jet burned its way back up to altitude. The men stood silently for a few minutes and watched the Mirage join up with its wingman. The airplanes turned back to the north.

"Okay, boys," Blount said. "This is real good, but don't let your guard down. Look at that dust storm back there." Blount pointed behind him. The rust-colored mass on the horizon grew by the second. "That's gon' be on us pretty soon," he continued. "I don't know if a helicopter can fly in that or not. This day is far from over."

Blount checked his DAGR, tried to lead his team north on as straight a heading as possible. What seemed a simple task turned out to be harder than he expected. Land navigation usually involved setting a course, noting a landmark on that course, then moving toward the landmark. You'd count paces along the way to figure distance. Once you reached the building, tree, ditch, or boulder, you'd take another reading, choose another landmark, and so on. Even in most desert environments you could find a bush or a gulley somewhere along your course.

But here, Blount found only ripples in the sand, each one indistinguishable from another. He'd lead the team a hundred paces and find himself ten degrees off his heading. Not necessarily a problem; he didn't expect to travel far enough on foot to make a difference to a helicopter. But he didn't want to get sloppy and start angling all over Creation. He glanced at the DAGR screen, noted the latest error.

"Let's head a few degrees to the right," Blount said.

"Should we change direction to make it harder for the bad guys to track us down?" Fender asked.

"I don't think it would help," Blount said. "If that dust storm covers our tracks, heading won't matter. And if the storm doesn't cover our tracks, they'll find us easy no matter what we do."

"I wonder if they're coming for us already," Grayson said.

"Wouldn't surprise me," Blount said.

Blount knew even if Kassam could not pick up a trail, the terrorist leader could still find them if he had enough four-wheel-drive vehicles. Just send the trucks out from the hell house in ever-widening circles. Run down tired escapees on foot in no time.

The men trudged through the sand for another half hour. Blount's tactical vest began to chafe. The weight of the flintlock pistol in his pocket started to tug at uncomfortable angles. He shifted his rifle, rested the M16 in the crook of his elbow. Listened closely for the sound of a helo, but heard only breeze, footsteps, and the hiss of his radio. How long could it take to launch a chopper? If it didn't get here pretty soon, that storm might make a rescue impossible.

Now the reddish-brown haze covered half the sky. Blount felt the wind rising. Wisps of fine sand were already lifting from underfoot and ghosting across the ground.

In Iraq and Afghanistan, he'd seen dust storms take different forms. Sometimes gales flung grit like a sandblaster and made walking—let alone flying—impossible. Other times dust hung in the air like fog, lifted by distant winds long played out. You almost didn't notice the dust except for the discolored sky. And when you cleaned your face with a baby wipe, the wipe came away muddy. Blount had heard pilots say landing in that stuff depended on how thick it was and how low it hung.

The storm's approach made Blount impatient. He decided to try a radio call, maybe get an update.

"Dagger One-Seven, Havoc Two Bravo," he transmitted. "You still up?"

No answer.

"Any station, Havoc Two Bravo."

Still nothing.

With only static on the radio, Blount could imagine himself and his men marooned on a waterless planet, pleas for help bouncing through an ionosphere absent of any other human voice. Because he'd made contact with the Mirage, he knew someone would come for them sooner or later. But the vastness of the desert made his team seem utterly, completely alone.

Apparently the others were thinking the same thing.

"Sure would suck to get out of there and then just die of thirst out here," Fender said. "Dry up and leave nothing but bones."

"Why haven't they got to us yet?" Grayson asked.

"Quit talking like that," Blount ordered. "You're on patrol. Act like it." Blount realized he was speaking to himself as much as the others.

Something began to irritate his eyes. It reminded him of cutting onions or peppers, except his eyes didn't tear as much. Blount blinked twice, forced his eyes to water. That brought a little relief. With his index finger, he wiped the notch of his right eye where the tear duct lay. The finger came away smudged with what looked like ground mustard. Almost imperceptibly, the sky had turned darker shades of that color in all directions.

"All right, boys," Blount said. "The dust is about to get thicker. Y'all keep a sharp eye out while you can, 'cause I don't know what we'll have for visibility."

"Aye, aye, Gunny," Fender said.

Blount checked the DAGR again, pointed to correct the team's heading a few degrees. Dust collected in the folds of the men's clothing and gear; the horizon no longer existed. The ground melded with the sky as if the earth and its atmosphere were made of thicker or lighter measures of the same stuff. Swirls in the air seemed to grow solid, then dissipate. The men turned as they walked, checked behind them and on their flanks.

Fender pointed at something to the south.

"Do you see that?" he asked.

Blount pivoted to look. At first the dust in that direction appeared much the same. But after a moment he noticed a thickening along the ground.

He would have dismissed it if not for the way it moved. The wisps and swirls did not dissipate like all the others. A plume traversed the desert at a constant speed, going east to west. No gust of wind ever blew that steady.

"That's a truck," Blount said.

CHAPTER 32

Parson forced himself to concentrate on his job as he fought back a range of emotions. The news of Chartier's contact with Blount elated him, of course. But now he worried whether the rescue choppers he'd just alerted could get there in time; they would launch at any minute. Parson glanced down at the VFR charts on the ops counter, noted their brown depictions of vast expanses of wasteland. The problem would come down to technology versus the weather and the enemy. Could the Pave Hawks pluck four men from the back side of nowhere before the storm or jihadists overtook them?

The next couple hours would tell. The forecast called for winds at ten knots gusting to thirty, starting during this hour. Blowing dust, visibility down to a mile or less.

The ops center door swung open and the four chopper pilots rushed inside. The pilots' flying gear bulged with pouches for radios, flares, and other survival equipment. Their M9 pistols hung in holsters, along with extra magazines. Their enlisted personnel—the flight engineers, gunners, and pararescuemen—were already at the helicopters. He showed the pilots the weather forecast.

"Wish I had better news," Parson said.

"We'll push it hard as we can," one of the pilots replied. "Worst case, we'll just set her down in the desert if we have to."

"Hope it doesn't come to that," Parson said.

"Yeah, me, too," another pilot offered. "Let's get this done."

The pilots stuffed weather sheets into the lower leg pockets of their flight suits and rushed out the door. As they left, Parson heard a familiar sound, the engine start sequence of a C-130. In this case it was an HC-130 Combat King, specially modified to refuel the Pave Hawks in flight. If the helicopters needed extra gas to reach the survivors, they could join up with the Combat King on a predetermined refueling track.

He followed the pilots outside to see them take off. The air had already taken on a strange translucence, softening the edges of distant objects. The effect came as a result of dust lifted high from miles away, now drifting back down to earth. Just a foretaste of what was to come.

Saint-Ex had faced the same kind of weather, Parson knew, with much more primitive aircraft and less reliable forecasts. Parson recalled a description written by his new favorite author: . . . *desert storms that turn the sky into a yellow furnace and wipe out hills, towns, and river-banks, drowning earth and sky in one great conflagration.* Well, Saint-Ex, Parson thought, here we go again.

The crews climbed aboard the two waiting Pave Hawks. Beyond the choppers, the Combat King sat with propellers spinning and red strobes flashing like an all-capable mother ship. The Pave Hawks' rotors began turning, at first languidly, then faster.

Above the noise of rotors and turboprops, Parson heard the whistling sound of jet engines throttled back. He looked up and saw a pair of Mirages on downwind. One entered the break, banked hard to the left, lowered its landing gear. The other extended downwind for several seconds, then turned onto the base leg just as the first jet touched down. A few moments later both fighters rolled along the taxiway, canopies lifted open on their actuators. Parson could see Chartier and Sniper in the lead aircraft, helmets turning side to side as they scanned for ground traffic, oxygen hoses extending from their masks.

Now that the missing men had been located, the mission changed from search to recovery. That meant the Mirages could taxi into parking and let the Pave Hawks and their support aircraft take over.

The helicopters' main rotors came up to speed, spinning in blurred discs. The pulse and thump grew deeper as the blades changed pitch, and the choppers lifted off. The helos flew a few yards above the ground in a slightly nose-low attitude, then began to climb and turn to the south. At the same time, the HC-130 started taxiing toward the runway.

The movement of all these aircraft made it seem invincible forces had gathered themselves, that some inevitable reckoning would soon play out. But Parson knew all too well the frailty of the machines, the fallibility of the people inside them, and the unpredictability of fate.

By the time the HC-130 growled into the sky, visibility dropped further. Buildings on the far side of the airport grew indistinct, as if viewed through translucent glass stained the color of bourbon. Parson waved to Chartier as the Mirages taxied into parking. Then he went back inside to check the weather again and see if the data confirmed his suspicion. Sure enough, a new observation had popped up on his computer:

SPECI HLLM 231700Z 21015KT R29/1500D PO NSC 20/28 Q1020

The first part of the coded observation carried the identifier for Mitiga and a date/time stamp. It was a special observation because it differed significantly from the last one. The rest brought no good news: Winds from the southeast at fifteen knots. The runway visual range along Runway 29 had fallen to fifteen hundred meters and was still going down. No significant clouds, but that wasn't the trouble; PO was the international code for dust or sand whirls. Temperature, 20 degrees Celsius. Dewpoint, 28 degrees. Altimeter setting, 1020 hectopascals.

The captain working the shift with Parson glanced over and said, "How's it looking?"

Parson simplified the codes and data:

"Weather's going to dog shit."

"Great."

Parson worried about visibility, of course, but his concerns extended beyond that. Unlike fog, dust could actually damage aircraft. Dust clogged filters, pitted rotors and propellers, scoured turbine blades. The C-130 flight manual even called for crews not to operate the air-conditioning system on the ground in a desert environment—despite the sweaty misery—to avoid sucking sand into the ducts. The book also said to keep flaps up until ready for takeoff so dust wouldn't foul jackscrews and actuators.

But in flight, crews could do little to minimize damage except minimize time in the air. Normally, you'd just postpone missions until the storm passed. But not this time.

More radio traffic caught Parson's attention. The traffic came on the ops frequency, with the call sign of Gold's C-130 flight from Algeria.

"Kingfish, Reach Two Four X-ray."

The captain at the ops desk lifted the hand mike and answered.

"Reach Two Four X-ray, Kingfish. Go ahead."

"Kingfish, be advised we are fifteen minutes out. We have a patient on board who needs immediate medical attention. Gunshot wounds to the lower arm."

Parson twisted in his seat toward the radio. Had something happened to Sophia? Damn, did she have to get shot on *every* mission?

"Gimme the mike," Parson said. The captain handed it over. Parson pressed the talk switch and said, "Reach Two Four X-ray, who is the patient?"

"Uh, I don't have the name in front of me, sir. He's an Algerian national."

Parson felt a flood of relief, and then he felt guilty for feeling relief. It was bad when anybody got shot. But he couldn't deny he was glad Sophia wasn't hurt. He'd nearly gotten her killed in Afghanistan, and the vision of her bloodied and fighting for her life in a rescue helicopter still haunted him. Parson knew he loved her; he'd admitted that much to himself by now. But none of the in-vogue phrases for these kinds of relationships quite applied. She was not a "work spouse." She meant far more to him than that. Not a "friend with benefits." That implied too-casual sex. "Emotional affair" didn't cut it, either. Their bond—forged under fire and maintained at times by long-distance—defied description.

He keyed the mike again and said, "Kingfish copies all. We'll have E-MEDS standing by. Do you have current weather for Mitiga? Visibility's going to hell."

"Yes, sir, we do. We'll see you soon if we can get in. Reach Two Four X-ray out."

Parson called E-MEDS, the Expeditionary Medical Squadron, to make sure an ambulance stood by. That done, he could only monitor the computers and radios, and wait.

A few minutes later, Parson heard the C-130 call in on the VHF tower frequency.

"Mitiga Tower," the pilot said, "Reach Two Four X-ray is with you on the ILS to Runway Two-Niner."

Parson glanced at the radio, looked out the window at the swirling dust. The sight made him grimace.

"Reach Two Four X-ray, Mitiga Tower," the controller responded. "You are cleared to land."

That made things sound simple, but Parson knew better. Visibility came and went during these storms, and nothing mattered except what the pilots could see when they reached decision height. Depending on the airfield, decision height was usually two hundred feet above ground level for a Category One approach. Very little room for error when you got that low. If the pilots couldn't spot the approach lights or other parts of the runway environment, they had to go around: shove the throttles, arrest the descent, start climbing away on a predetermined missed-approach path. The situation allowed for no fumbling, no hesitation.

Parson remembered an old instructors' saying about flying in weather this bad: Don't consider a missed approach an aborted landing. Consider a landing an aborted missed approach.

He looked out the window toward the runway. The sun had not started to set, but the light—filtered through dust—looked like twilight. He heard the grumble of the C-130's turboprops. Watched the approach end of the runway. Saw nothing. The grumble grew louder. Parson still saw no part of the airplane, not even landing lights. He could imagine the pilots' eyes glued to their instruments, watching the altimeter and the localizer and glide-slope needles. Another call came over the tower frequency.

"Reach Two Four X-ray's on the missed approach."

Parson cursed under his breath.

"Roger, Reach Two Four X-ray," the tower said. "Contact Approach Control on one-one-niner point seven."

"Reach Two Four X-ray over to Approach."

Parson wondered if they'd divert to another airfield or make another attempt at landing here. Under Air Force rules, they couldn't even start an approach unless the weather was reported above minimums. And the visibility changed moment to moment in a dust storm.

For long minutes he heard no engines and no more calls on the tower frequency. He considered checking the plane's flight plan to learn its alternate airport; surely it had headed for Cairo or somewhere. But then another call came on the radio.

"Mitiga Tower, Reach Two Four X-ray's with you on the ILS to Two-Niner."

"Reach Two Four X-ray cleared to land."

Parson stepped outside and again watched the skies above the approach end of the runway. Fine particles stung his eyes. He heard the growl of engines once more. Across the airport, the orange windsock fluttered in a dirty, gusting breeze. Several seconds passed with no sign of the C-130 except its noise signature, and Parson expected to hear it pass overhead in another missed approach.

But one shaft of light penetrated the beige clouds, perhaps a quarter mile from the touchdown zone. Then another appeared. Parson recognized the landing lights of a Herk. The aircraft took shape as if formed from the blowing sand. When the main wheels touched down, puffs of gray tire smoke joined the swirls of dust.

The E-MEDS ambulance began rolling across the tarmac, along with the blue pickup truck of the flight line team. The pickup stopped near an aircraft parking spot. A marshaller got out of the passenger side and stood with two electric wands held above his head. Parson watched the C-130 roll from the runway and lumber along a taxiway, its engines sighing as they shifted into low-speed ground idle. When the Herk reached the apron, the marshaller signaled it to turn left into the parking spot. The aircraft rolled to a halt.

Parson strode across the tarmac to the C-130. After a couple of minutes, the props spun down. The crew door dropped open, a loadmaster stepped out, and Parson climbed aboard. He glanced up at the crew on the flight deck: two pilots, a navigator, and a flight engineer. Clinks and rattles sounded in the cockpit as they unbuckled their harnesses and unplugged their headsets.

"Good job, guys," Parson said. "After that missed approach, I thought you were headed for Egypt."

"Well," the navigator replied, "you said you would kick our asses if anything went wrong."

Parson laughed. "Yeah, I did, didn't I? How's the weather behind you?"

"Varies," the copilot said. "Sometimes you can see a mile, sometimes you can't see anything. I almost hit the go-around button again, but right then I saw the approach lights."

"Yeah," the pilot said. "We were surprised those helicopters took off in this mess. We heard them talking to tower."

"Well, there's a good reason for that," Parson said. "We made contact with the missing Marines."

In the cargo compartment, Gold stood with her back to the crew entrance door. She and a tall African Union officer helped a man get to his feet. The man wore some sort of native headdress. He had a bandage across his wrist. Two men—no, two boys—sat in the nylon troop seats. One of them wore a blue headdress, like the wounded man. Gold turned when she heard Parson's voice.

"That's wonderful news," Gold said. "Did you talk to them?"

"No," Parson said, "but the Mirage crews did. Flew right over them."

"Thank God. I just hope the choppers can get to them."

"Tell me about it."

Parson walked over to Gold, placed his hands on her shoulders. She put one arm around his waist for just a moment, then turned her attention back to the wounded man. The patient stood on his own two feet but looked weak and tired.

"How did he get shot?" Parson asked.

"Long story. I'll tell you inside."

"I guess you guys have had a rough day," Parson said.

"Oh, yeah," Gold said.

The AU officer began talking to the boys in a language Parson had never heard. They unfastened their seat belts and stood up.

"I suppose that's the officer you told me about?" Parson said.

"Yes. He's Major Ongondo. He speaks the Tuaregs' language, and I think those guys have something to tell you."

CHAPTER 33

The murky, dust-laden air reminded Blount of the start of the Iraq War in 2003. At one point during the push north from Kuwait, a dust storm turned the sky to ocher, grounding aircraft and fouling weapons systems. If you blew your nose, it looked like you'd smeared your handkerchief with orange paint.

Back then Blount fought alongside fellow members of a thirty-five-man platoon. Now he'd face whatever was coming with only three other men: Fender, Escarra, and Grayson.

Blount donned a set of dust goggles so he could at least keep his eyes open amid flying grit. The four men lay prone with their weapons, watching the truck at several hundred yards' distance. Its occupants apparently hadn't seen the escapees; the vehicle kept moving toward the west. Its direction of off-road travel supported Blount's suspicion that Kassam had his henchmen driving in wider and wider circles out from the hell house.

"I think it's leaving," Fender said.

"Just keep low," Blount said. "I don't think they saw us, but they could swing back around. Another truck could come along pretty quick, too."

The vehicle disappeared. It did not seem to drive out of sight. Instead it simply dissolved into the dust storm.

Blount shifted his weight a bit to keep pressure off the radio at the front of his tactical vest. He reached into a pocket, found a handkerchief colored in the same digital camo as his uniform. Wrapped it around the PRC-148 to give the radio at least a little dust protection. Fender wrapped an identical handkerchief around his nose and mouth, giving him the appearance of an Old West bandit armed with modern weapons.

The weather made it seem less and less likely that rescue forces could reach Blount and his men anytime soon. Had he cheated death—or postponed it just for a matter of hours? He knew stories of American POWs who made heroic escapes only to get recaptured. During the Vietnam War, Air Force pilot Lance Sijan ejected from his burning F-4 Phantom over hostile territory. Despite a fractured leg and a torn-up right hand, he evaded capture for more than a month. After the enemy caught up with him, Sijan coldcocked a guard and escaped. Blount especially liked that part of the story—a man with multiple injuries who could still kick a bad guy's ass. But the North Vietnamese recaptured Sijan hours later, and he died in prison. In the same war, aviator Bud Day broke his arm when he punched out of his F-100. After his captors found him, they strung him upside down. Day later got away and even made it into South Vietnam. But the enemy found him again, shot him in the hand and leg, and sent him to the Hanoi Hilton.

Those guys had lived up to the Code of Conduct. For Blount, the takeaway from the Code's several articles came down to this: Resist until you got nothing left. If you're in command, lead the fight as long as anybody has the means to fight.

Resisting and evading would get a lot easier if Blount could communicate. He decided to try another radio call. He pulled his handkerchief away from the PRC-148 enough to reveal the transmit button. Pressed the switch and said, "Any station, any station, Havoc Two Bravo."

The only answer came from the wind, lifting powder from the ground so that it looked like the earth smoked. His rifleman's mind, always calibrated for wind and range, estimated the gusts at better than twenty-five miles an hour. Blount did not know the limitations of helicopters and their crews, but he knew these conditions would push the capabilities of both machine and man. He thumbed his transmit switch again.

"Any station," he called, "Havoc Two Bravo."

Static joined the wind in a mixture of blank noise. The absence of any response pulled Blount's fear onto an elemental plane, a primordial dread of the unknown. Nothing existed in the universe except the lifeless ground beneath him, the three men beside him, and the enemy seeking to kill him, lurking somewhere out there beyond the edge of visibility.

"Keep your eyes open, boys," Blount said. "We might be here for a while."

He peered into the beige gloom, searched over the sights of his rifle for any solid objects amid the dust—objects that might signal an enemy's approach. The other men did the same. Nothing out there but a desert trying to lift itself to the sky.

Blount had pretty much given up on the radio when the PRC's hiss broke. A pulsing noise replaced the static, a carrier wave without voice but with the ambient sound of a helicopter in flight. Then someone spoke.

"Havoc Two Bravo," the voice called, "Pedro One-One, do you read?"

The call surprised Blount so much that he nearly let the radio slip from his hand. The other men turned their heads toward him, eyes expectant. Blount gestured toward the open wasteland.

"Keep watch," he said. Then he pressed his talk button and said, "Pedro One-One, Havoc Two Bravo has you five by five."

"Roger, Havoc. On what vehicle did you learn to drive?"

An authentication question, Blount realized, taken from a form he had filled out years ago. The form included statements about him no enemy could know. The document became classified as soon as a service member completed it, and it was sent out to rescue forces if the member went missing. Right now, Pedro needed to confirm Blount was really who he said he was.

"A red Farmall tractor," Blount said.

"That checks, Havoc. Be advised Pedro One-One and One-Two are a flight of two Pave Hawks inbound to you. Do you have an update on your position?"

Blount raised himself on his elbow enough to reach the pouch where he stored his DAGR. Hoped that from a distance he'd appear as but a lump in the sand. Pulled out the device and read off his coordinates to the chopper pilot.

"Pedro copies," the pilot said. "ETA fifteen minutes. Can you say conditions at your position?"

Blount scanned around, stared into the maelstrom.

"Sir, I think the winds are gusting about twenty-five," he said. "Visibility's only several hundred yards. A few minutes ago we spotted a truck, and I'm pretty sure it's hostile. No vehicles or other personnel in sight at this time."

"Roger that. See you in a few, if the visibility holds."

A big *if*. The storm showed no indication of letting up. Blount wasn't a pilot, but common sense told him visibility would get worse near the ground, close to the source of the dust. And that's exactly where visibility became most critical for the aircrew.

"Do you think they can pick us up?" Grayson asked.

"Don't count on it till it happens," Blount said. "If those helos get here and they can't see to land or at least hover over us and drop a basket, they'll just climb up where the air's better and fly home."

Blount strained his eyes, tried to will the blowing sand to part enough for him to see farther. The effort only made him dizzy; for a moment he lost all depth perception and imagined that visibility had dropped to mere feet. Then his eyes focused again and he discerned sand ripples across the ground for several hundred yards.

"Let's spread out a little bit," Blount ordered. "Make sure we're covering a full three hundred sixty degrees."

The men crawled a few feet left or right, shuffled themselves until a rifle aimed toward each cardinal point of the compass. Escarra seemed to understand without translation; he trained his AK-47 due east and peered into the distance. Several minutes went by. All the while, Blount listened to the wind whip the Sahara, and he kept hoping to hear the pounding of helicopter rotors.

Instead he heard a single word in Spanish. Escarra spoke without emotion, without raising his voice. Two syllables from a language Blount didn't speak told him all he needed to know.

"*Mira,*" Escarra said.

Blount looked toward Escarra's assigned sector.

In that direction, a solid point took form at ground level amid the shapeless eddies of flying grit. At first it seemed motionless, but after a few seconds the point began to enlarge and shift to take on the lines and angles of a pickup truck.

"Good eyes," Blount said. "Possible target to the east, boys."

Fender and Grayson rose up slightly on their knees and elbows, turned their eyes and weapons toward the threat. Blount switched his M16 from safe to semiauto, watched the truck approach.

"Keep watch all around us," Blount said.

"Aye, aye, Gunny," Fender said.

This could get complicated, Blount thought, with a firefight breaking out just as the Pave Hawks arrive. Better warn the crews. He lifted his radio again.

"Pedro, Havoc Two Bravo," he said. "Be advised we have a vehicle approaching our position, possibly hostile."

"Roger that, Havoc. Our gunners copy, too."

Blount figured his team had one advantage: four men flat to the ground presented a much lower profile than a truck full of dirtbags. Whoever was in the vehicle probably hadn't seen Blount and his men yet. Now he just needed positive identification of a hostile target.

"I don't have positive ID yet, fellas," Blount said. "But if you see a threat, shoot first and shoot straight, but remember we don't have a whole lot of ammo."

"Aye, Gunny," Fender said.

The truck bounced and wallowed through the sand, and when it came within a couple hundred yards, Blount could see six men kneeling in its bed. Scarves covered their heads and faces, leaving only their eyes exposed. Some wore goggles. All carried weapons—mostly AK-47s, but one had a long tube. A launcher for rocket-propelled grenades, Blount realized, or else a shoulder-fired antiaircraft missile. Either way, bad news for helicopters.

One of the men in the truck bed stood up and placed an AK across the top of the cab. He took aim as the vehicle continued swerving across the desert.

"They see us," Blount shouted. "Fire!"

The men opened up. Blount squeezed off two shots at the jihadist aiming over the cab. The man dropped into the truck bed as his weapon slid forward. The AK clattered across the hood and fell into the sand.

Bullets punctured the windshield. The pickup skidded, began to roll over. Five men and one limp body tumbled out onto the desert floor. The truck came to rest about a hundred yards away, on its right side with its open bed oriented toward Blount and his team. Two men remained in the cab. Blount couldn't tell if those two were hit; they had fallen all over each other.

The terrorists thrown from the vehicle scrambled for their weapons. Blount kept firing on semi-auto, one shot at a time. So did Escarra, Fender, and Grayson. Two of the dirtbags raised themselves and fell immediately as the escapees' rifles popped off rounds and ejected brass.

The sharp edge of rifle smoke salted the air. Two jihadists lay prone, firing. One in front of the vehicle fumbled with his launch tube.

Over the shooting, Blount heard—and felt—the thudding rhythm of helicopters. The crews needed to know what they were flying into. Blount thumbed his transmit switch again.

"Pedro," he called, "Havoc's in contact. Enemy clustered around overturned pickup."

"Copy enemy pickup truck," the pilot answered.

The jihadists' rounds flung little geysers of sand around the men. Escarra cried out when a slug struck his upper left arm. Blount saw the blood begin to redden the Spaniard's sleeve.

Hot, sharp things pricked Blount's face: grit kicked up by bullets striking the ground. The enemy must have heard the choppers, too. The guy with the launcher started looking up at the obscured sky. Blount touched off a shot at him just as he scrabbled around to the other side of the pickup. Missed.

Now the guy could fire at the choppers from behind cover. Not good. The aircraft would come within range at any moment; Blount heard the slap of rotor blades getting louder. Yet, above him, he could still see nothing but a sky filled with dirt.

This whole mess had started when jihadists bagged a helicopter. Not happening again, Blount decided.

"Gimme some covering fire," he yelled. "I'm gon' flank 'em." Blount wanted to move around toward the other side of the truck so he could aim at launcher guy behind it.

Fender, Grayson, and Escarra poured rounds downrange. Blount knew it was a calculated risk to burn through limited ammunition by using it up as covering fire. But he hoped the choppers would open up at any moment with their immense firepower.

One of the terrorists still inside the cab fired out through the windshield. His shots chewed out an opening the size of a basketball in the safety glass. Fender returned fire, ejected an empty mag. While Fender reloaded, Grayson and Escarra kept shooting, and Grayson's weapon emptied. They could keep firing at this rate only for a few more seconds.

Blount leaped to his feet. Sprinted in front of the truck, about forty yards away from it, hoping for a good firing angle. The terrorists' bullets cracked around him. The dirtbags were dividing their fire between Blount and the other three men.

From the corner of his eye Blount saw a helicopter take shape above him. The aircraft appeared gauzy and translucent through the dust, an inanimate object forming spontaneously amid the storm. Close, too. Well within the kill range of an RPG or shoulder-fired missile.

Just before Blount gained a good angle on his quarry, a round struck his tactical vest. The slug failed to penetrate the vest's protective insert, but it knocked him off his feet. Blount tumbled into the sand. He hugged his rifle close as he hit the ground, and he managed to keep dirt from fouling the muzzle of the M16. The flintlock pistol in his pocket dug into his thigh. He coughed, felt a sting in his ribs.

Blount remained on the ground, rolled twice. Ended up in a prone position about twenty yards from the truck's front end, with his rifle pointed at launcher guy. Blount had a clear shot now, and he could see the man's weapon better. Sure enough, an RPG-7 tube.

The Pave Hawks began descending, both finally coming into clear view. Tangible machines now instead of vaporous suggestions of themselves.

Launcher guy situated himself on one knee, raised his weapon. The lead helicopter thudded directly overhead, presented an easy target for an RPG. Blount settled his optical sight on the man's center mass. The dirtbag sighted with his launcher, cheek against its heat shield, fingers curled around its grip and trigger.

Blount fired.

Launcher guy crumpled but held on to his weapon. Blount fired again. The M16's bolt locked open. Empty.

The dirtbag pushed himself up from the ground with one hand. He moved as if a great weight hung across his shoulders. At least one of Blount's rounds had connected, but perhaps not with mortal effect.

Blount pressed his magazine release button, and the spent mag dropped into the sand. He tore open a vest pouch for his one spare mag.

Launcher guy now sat cross-legged, like an exhausted workman taking a break. Lifted the weapon.

Blount clicked the new mag into his magazine well, smacked the bolt release. The weapon slammed closed, deadly once more.

The dirtbag took aim again with his RPG launcher.

Blount opened up, this time on burst fire. Three rounds spat from his weapon just as launcher guy squeezed his own trigger.

The bullets from the M16 tore into the man's shoulders, neck, and head. The grenade sailed wide, disappeared into the sky as if the dust had absorbed it. If the RPG fell back to earth and detonated, Blount never heard it. Too much other noise.

Most of that noise came from the minigun jutting from the side of the Pave Hawk. Its barrels, spun by an electric motor, spewed hot metal at such a rate that the desert floor churned. Empty casings tumbled from a black hose in a hail of glinting brass. When the stream of fire found the truck, the vehicle shuddered and clanked as the gun dismembered it. What remained of the windshield exploded in a splash of white. A body, hardly recognizable as human, slumped through the windshield frame. Another figure lay inside the cab on top of the first corpse. Blood spattered across the punctured hood.

The two men who'd fired from outside the vehicle died last. The minigun's column of fire seemed to drive them into the ground. Their AK-47s fell silent, surrounded by bloody clothing and torn flesh.

Blount watched the wreckage for a moment, checked for any further threats. Kept the first joint of his index finger on his trigger. No sign of movement came from the smoking, riddled vehicle. He pressed his transmit switch and said, "Pedro, Havoc Two Bravo. Hold your fire. Lemme observe your target."

"Pedro copies."

Blount picked himself up, ran forward in a crouch. Up close, he found it difficult to confirm eight separate enemy bodies, but it became clear nothing in that vehicle could ever present a danger again. He pressed his transmit switch again.

"Pedro," he called, "you got a cold LZ."

"Copy that, Havoc. Stand by for pickup."

"Yes, sir. Be advised we have at least one wounded."

Blount slung his rifle and trotted to where Fender, Grayson, and Escarra still lay prone.

"Y'all okay?" he asked.

"Escarra's hit," Fender said.

"I know it."

Fender and Grayson seemed all right. One of them had already tightened Escarra's CAT tourniquet on the wounded arm. Didn't look real messy, so maybe he'd keep the arm. When Blount had last taken refresher first aid, the instructors told him to forget the old-school wisdom that cranking down a tourniquet meant sacrificing a limb. Get a wounded man to the right kind of help in that first golden hour, and miracles could happen.

About eighty yards away, one of the choppers began lowering itself to the ground. The other stayed high for overwatch. Gale from the rotors magnified the blast of the dust storm. Sand flew sideways and drifted over spent cartridges on the ground.

"Let's get out of here, boys," Blount shouted.

The Pave Hawk settled to the sand. The left-side gunner pivoted his weapon, swung the muzzles away from Blount and his men. Two pararescuemen hopped out of the aircraft, wearing specially made helmets that allowed room for headsets underneath. They carried carbines across their chests as they ran to the escapees.

Blount placed his hands on top of his head. Fender and Grayson did the same, while Escarra held out his good arm. Even though Blount had authenticated his identity, the men still needed to look as nonthreatening as possible to a helicopter crew touching down in a combat zone.

"We got one with an arm wound," Blount yelled over the rotor noise.

"We'll take care of him," the first pararescueman said. On his vest hung spare mags, chemlights, pens, and a set of medical shears. A patch of glint tape on the man's arm read PJ.

The two PJs helped Escarra into the chopper. Blount hung back, let Fender and Grayson board next. As the two young Marines buckled into seats made of webbing, Blount climbed aboard. The sight of the aircraft interior, with its dangling cords, winking indicators, fire extinguisher, hand trigger for the hoist control, brought Blount a rush of relief. He felt nine-tenths of the way to his own front porch. The Pave Hawk began climbing as soon as he sat down.

He closed his eyes, savored the motion, let the wind rush over him through the open doors. No, this was more than relief. His fingers tingled with a sense of well-being and gratitude. Dear God, Blount thought, we're all right. We get to live the rest of our lives. Steal away home, like the old song says.

"Oo-rah!" Fender shouted.

Grayson and Escarra began hooting and stamping their feet.

"Fuckin' oo-rah, buddy," Grayson yelled. He clapped Escarra's shoulder on the man's good side. The PJs began to examine Escarra's wound. The crewmen at the two miniguns gave thumbs-up signs.

"Welcome aboard, gentlemen," a gunner called out.

The dust thinned as the helicopter gained altitude. Blount could see the second Pave Hawk flying in formation just off to the side. Since he did not wear a headset he could not hear the crew's interphone chatter, but he supposed they were delivering good news by radio. He watched them smile, nod to one another, pump fists in the air.

As the sun set, the Pave Hawks refueled in the air. The wake turbulence of the HC-130 tanker bounced the helos like a tractor jouncing along a washboard farm path. Made Blount a little queasy, but he didn't mind.

When the Pave Hawks broke away from the big plane, the air suddenly felt smooth. The moon began to rise. Fender called out, "Hey, Gunny. Maybe this is a better time to ask. What do your initials A. E. stand for?"

Blount smiled, considered whether to answer the question the corporal had first asked weeks ago at Sigonella. What the heck?

"Alonzo Erasmus."

"What?"

"You heard me. Alonzo Erasmus."

Fender laughed, punched Grayson's arm. Grayson began laughing, too.

"You gotta be kidding me," Fender said. "We're gonna tell our parents our lives were saved by Gunnery Sergeant *Alonzo Erasmus* Blount?"

"You do that."

CHAPTER 34

Parson couldn't wait to tell Gold the good news that had just come over the radio. As ops center staff cheered and exchanged backslaps, he headed for the locked room normally used to give aircrews their tactics and intel briefings. Gold probably hadn't heard the sounds of celebration; she was in the briefing room.

He knocked on the door, and Gold unlocked it and cracked it open. Inside, Parson saw Major Ongondo and two CIA officers talking with the Tuareg refugees. VFR charts depicting segments of North Africa hung by tacks on the plywood walls. Shelves held stacks of booklets containing instrument approaches and airport data. Ongondo wore an intent expression, and he wrote furiously on a notepad.

"Can you come out?" Parson whispered. "They found 'em. Blount's on the helicopter with three others."

Gold's face brightened. "That's wonderful," she said. She stepped out of the room and closed the door behind her. Someone, probably one of the CIA spooks, locked the door from the inside. Gold gave Parson a tight embrace, then let go of him and returned with him to the ops desk. Whoops and cheers continued to fill the room, and the loudest came from the Marine lieutenant colonel, Bill Loudon. The other Marine officer, Captain Privett, had returned to the *Tarawa* to help get ready for whatever might come next.

"Hot damn," Loudon cried. He picked up a sat phone and punched in a number, presumably to Privett or someone else on the ship. Amid the noise of celebration, he held the phone to one ear and covered the other ear with his hand as he talked.

The door at the front of the ops center swung open and Chartier came in. He still wore his flight suit, but he had shed his G suit, survival vest, and all other flying gear.

"There's our new best friend," Parson said. "Hey, Frenchie. The Pave Hawks picked 'em up." Parson put his arm around Chartier's shoulders, squeezed hard, and said, "Good work, you froggie bastard."

"*Très bien,*" Chartier said with an embarrassed smile. "Nothing could make me happier."

Parson released the Frenchman and said, "Let me introduce you to Sophia. She and I go way back." He turned to Gold and said, "This is Captain Alain Chartier. He flies those shiny Mirages out there. Frenchie, this is my old friend Sergeant Major Sophia Gold."

"Charmed, I'm sure," Chartier said. "You're with the American army?"

"I was," Gold said. "I work with the United Nations now."

As Gold and Chartier chatted, Parson sat down at the ops desk. He gripped the edges of the counter with both hands, closed his eyes, lowered his head. Let satisfaction flow into him like a cool drink of water. He thought of a line Saint-Ex wrote in *Wind, Sand and Stars*:

Every pilot who has flown to the rescue of a comrade in distress knows that all joys are vain in comparison with this one.

Roger that, Saint-Ex, Parson thought. Moments like this didn't come often in a career, and he hoped the Pedro crews and everybody in the ops center could carry this day around with them in their hearts. Maybe it would help sustain them through whatever pains, losses, and setbacks lay in their futures.

Gold pulled over an office chair and sat beside Parson. She placed a hand on his arm but said nothing. Parson felt grateful she was there to share this moment with him, its simultaneous joy and pain. They had gone through so much together, and a lot of it had given no cause for celebration. He suspected she knew what he was thinking, and when she finally spoke, she confirmed his guess.

"It's such good news that Blount and the others are safe," she said, "but I keep thinking about the two who aren't coming back."

Parson leaned back in his chair, pressed his fingers over her hand. The way the light struck her face, with her hair flowing over the folds of her Afghan scarf, she looked like some kind of guardian angel in an epic legend. But in the real world, not even guardian angels like Gold and mighty warriors like Blount could save everybody.

"I do, too," Parson said.

He looked around the room at the tactics officers, schedulers, weather forecasters, and other personnel. For the first time in days he felt he could take a few minutes to catch his breath and clear his mind.

"You know," Gold said, "in a way, Captain Privett was right. Those guys flew into a trap because of bad intel I helped gather."

Parson gave her a quizzical look. "Don't be stupid," he said. "You did your job. You can't help what somebody else did with that information."

Gold fingered her scarf, looked into its fabric as if seeking answers. "That's sort of what I've been thinking about," she said. "I translate and interpret, but I'd like to have more control over what happens next."

"Hmm," Parson said. "You thinking about a career change?"

"Not necessarily. Maybe change the way I go about things, though. Maybe get into some volunteer work."

"Look," Parson said. "I can't think of anybody who's done more good for more people than you. If you want to feed starving children, that's great, and I'm sure you'll do it well. But don't start thinking you have to change the world by yourself. Look around you."

Puzzled, Gold glanced around the room at the ops center personnel.

"Everybody here is a control freak," Parson said. "Everybody's an alpha dog. Wallflowers don't volunteer for this stuff. But we're a team. Nobody has to go it alone."

Gold gave that half smile of hers. Parson thought it was a beautiful expression, and he wished she'd smile more often. He wanted to talk with her more, but that would have to wait. He still had things to do.

"All right, people," he called, "they'll get here before you know it. Let's make sure we got a place for them to sleep and that the medical folks are ready."

"Yes, sir," a lieutenant answered.

By the time the Pave Hawks landed, night had fallen. Sodium-vapor lamps lit the parking apron, and the harsh glow backlit the aircraft. Word of the rescue had spread through the camp, and Chartier and other fliers waited outside with Parson, Gold, and Loudon.

The Pave Hawks taxied from the runway and settled on the ramp with their rotors spinning. After a few minutes the rotors spun down. Figures moved inside the helicopters; Parson craned his neck for a glimpse of the survivors. Finally, a crewman stepped out, followed by two young Marines.

Claps and cheers broke out among the waiting personnel. The Marines helped another man emerge from the chopper, evidently the wounded Legionnaire, who sat down in the back of a waiting ambulance. Then a big black man got out, carrying weapons and gear.

"There he is," Gold said. She put one hand on Parson's arm, pointed with the other. "Thank God," she added.

"They look tired," Loudon said.

"They gotta be," Parson said. He motioned to a Security Police pickup truck several yards away. The truck rolled toward Parson.

"Sir?" the driver said.

"Let's get their weapons and lock them up in the armory," Parson said.

"Yes, sir."

The truck met the Marines as they walked across the ramp. Two SPs got out of the vehicle and began collecting the weapons and gear. Parson, Gold, and Loudon caught up and greeted the men.

"Welcome back, devil dogs," Loudon said. He shook each man's hand, gripping with both of his own. "You done us proud."

"Thank you, sir," Blount said. "Just wish we could have brought back more."

"Said a lot of prayers for you, Gunny," Gold said. She stepped forward and embraced him. Her head came up only to the tape over his chest pocket that read U.S. MARINES.

Blount let Sophia hug him for a few seconds. He placed a wide hand on her back and opened his mouth to speak. But whatever he started to say, he kept it inside. He looked up at the sky for a long moment, and when he turned his gaze back to earth, Parson saw that his eyes glistened.

Though the survivors' exhaustion showed plainly, Blount's face also displayed a look of sublime relief. Parson could relate; he'd been rescued from a similar situation in Afghanistan years ago. But a U.S. and Afghan special ops team had saved Parson. Blount and his men had managed their own escape. Parson looked forward to hearing that story; he almost pitied any idiot foolish enough to trifle with Blount.

"We need to let the docs check you out," Loudon said. "But after that, what do you want first? Food, rest, or a call home?"

"I want to call home, sir," Blount said.

"I do, too, sir," Fender said.

"Same here," Grayson said.

Blount unclasped his tactical vest and twisted out of it. Parson took it from him. The vest felt warm from Blount's body heat. That's right, Parson thought. My buddy's still alive. And the people who fucked with him are probably stone cold by now. Parson swung the vest into the back of the pickup truck. It landed with a thud among the rifles and other equipment.

"I didn't know you and Sergeant Major Gold were here, sir," Blount said. "Real, real good to see you." His voice caught, and the big man struggled for words. "All of you," he added finally. He clapped Fender on the back and said, "Glad you can meet my buddies, here."

Up until then, Parson thought Blount had done an almost superhuman job of maintaining his military bearing. But something finally caused the dam to break—perhaps it was simple exhaustion, perhaps the emotional overload of finding himself suddenly surrounded by people who loved and respected him. Blount's knees seemed to buckle. He caught himself by placing his hands on the edge of the truck's tailgate. He folded his elbows over the tailgate, buried his head in his arms. Blount's shoulders shook but he made no sound.

Fender and Grayson stayed close to him. Neither man spoke, but both of them patted his back and took hold of his arms, just to let him know they were there.

A blue Air Force crew van pulled up. Parson whispered to the driver, "Give 'em a minute."

Blount raised himself. His eyes streamed, but otherwise he regained his composure. "Let's get moving," he said.

Loudon ushered the Marines into the crew van. He held the door for them, and just before closing it, he said, "Guns, I know you like cigars. I got one waiting for you when the docs turn you loose." He slid the door until it slammed shut.

"Thank you, sir." The sound of Blount's bass voice came from within the van as it drove away, flashers on.

Back in the ops center, Parson lost count of how many phone calls he made and received. He talked to AFRICOM, Headquarters Marine Corps, and the Joint Special Operations Command. Chartier called the French Foreign Legion Command in Aubagne, France. Then Parson talked to Marine Corps and Air Force public affairs officers in the Pentagon so they could brief the media. He asked them to hold the news for at least an hour to give the men time to call home.

Finally, Loudon escorted Blount, Fender, and Grayson into ops. Blount let the younger Marines call first. Parson found a bottle of cold water for Blount to drink while he waited, and Gold went back to check on Ongondo's progress with the Tuareg boys. When Blount's turn came to make his call, he went to the phone at Parson's desk. Parson stepped away to give him at least a little privacy, but in the confines of the cramped workplace, he couldn't help but overhear.

"Baby, it's me," Blount said. "I'm safe."

Even through the phone's tinny speaker, bounced through space, the voice of the woman on the other end came in loud enough for Parson to hear. She gave a long shriek of joy and then began speaking hurriedly. Parson could not make out her words.

"I'm fine, baby," Blount said. "Well, I'm a little tired."

Pause.

"I'm so sorry I—"

Pause.

"I'm so sorry I put you through—"

Pause.

"I love you, too."

Though it was none of his business, Parson liked the sound of the conversation. Blount's wife wouldn't let him express any guilt; she was just happy to have him back.

"No, they think I'm all right," Blount said. "They want to do some more tests."

More excited chatter on the other end.

"Yeah, I'm in an ops center right now. Don't know when I'm coming home. Probably soon. I'll let you know."

Slower chatter on the other end. Parson supposed Mrs. Blount was getting her mind around the idea that her husband would be all right.

"Grandpa doing okay?" Blount asked.

Faster chatter.

"That don't surprise me," Blount said. "I wish I was tough as him."

Blount spoke with three other people. From hearing one side of the conversation, Parson surmised they were his kids and his grandfather.

By the time Blount hung up the phone, the news had gotten out. Parson looked up at a TV tuned to CNN and saw the crawl at the bottom of the screen: *Three Marines, one Legionnaire recovered in Sahara . . . Chem attack mastermind still at large . . . UN worker and refugees narrowly escape Algeria assault.*

"Word travels fast," Loudon said.

"Yes, sir, I guess it does," Blount said.

"I got something for you, Guns. Let's go outside."

"Thank you, sir. I got something for you, too."

Loudon and Parson gave each other questioning looks. Blount had just survived capture and slogged through part of the Sahara. What gift could he possibly have?

The three men stepped out of the ops center. Sand barriers and razor wire ringed the tent complex, and a stack of spare sandbags lay in front of the building. Parson, Loudon, and Blount sat on the pile of sandbags. Loudon reached into a chest pocket and withdrew a cigar. From another pocket he pulled a cigar cutter and clipped the end. Handed the cigar and a lighter to Blount.

"It's a Montecristo, Guns," Loudon said. "You've sure earned it."

"Very kind of you, sir."

Blount placed the cigar in his mouth, turned it over a couple of times. Closed his eyes, apparently savoring a luxury he'd thought he'd never experience again. Parson recalled that Blount had grown up on a tobacco farm. Perhaps the taste and smell took the big man home.

"Is that the Cuban Montecristo or the Dominican?" Parson asked.

"Cuban," Loudon said. "Perfectly legal. Bought it in Italy."

"I sure appreciate it," Blount said, teeth clamped around the Montecristo. He flicked the lighter. The flame guttered in the breeze still rolling in from the desert. Blount cupped the fire with his hand, lit the cigar, let a long stream of smoke escape from his lips. The smoke joined the dust still dancing in the air. The rich, sweet scent made Parson think of burning molasses.

Blount stared out across the ramp. He seemed to look past the lamps, past the runway, past the civilian terminal to something deep in the darkness. Parson and Loudon gave him several minutes of quiet. During that time he simply smoked the cigar and said nothing. Each time he took a puff, the lighted end of the Montecristo brightened and crackled. The ash tip had enlarged. Blount tapped the cigar. The section of ash fell away and shattered on the ground.

Finally, Blount said, "Here's what I got for you."

He held the cigar between the index finger and middle finger of his right hand. With his left hand, he reached into a cargo pocket on his trousers. Parson had seen some sort of wooden handle protruding from the pocket but had thought nothing of it. That handle turned out to be the grip of a flintlock pistol—an honest-to-goodness, muzzle-loading, God-knows-how-old antique sidearm.

"Check this out, sirs," Blount said, hefting the pistol. "Kassam left this where he'd held us. I took it with me when we left."

"Wow," Parson said. "That's one hell of a trophy."

Blount handed the weapon to Loudon. The Marine officer held it muzzle up, turned it side to side. Swung open the frizzen, examined the pan. Parson marveled that the parts still worked. To his mind, the old firearm practically glowed with history. Made him think of declarations handwritten on parchment, ships propelled by sail, treaties sealed with candle wax. New and old worlds clashing amid swordplay and musket fire.

"Good common sense, Guns," Loudon said. "You took that bastard's little symbol."

"Yes, sir, but it ain't his. If it's really as old as he says it is, I figure it belongs to the Marine Corps or the Navy."

Even in the dim light, the intricacy of the pistol's checkering and engraving stood out. Parson noticed the lines of grain in the wood, growth rings perhaps from an American tree felled two centuries ago.

"This thing is beautiful," Loudon said. "I wonder if it still fires."

"I don't know if I'd shoot it," Blount said, "but I think it belongs in the museum at Quantico."

"I'll see that it gets there. No, why don't you do it? You should have the honor of presenting it. That is, unless you want to keep it."

"Thanks, sir, but it ain't no more mine than it was Kassam's."

Loudon passed the flintlock to Parson. Parson admired it for a moment, found the pistol heavier than he'd expected.

"That's a great find, Gunny," Parson said. Handed the weapon back to Blount. Blount pocketed it, took another drag from his cigar. Blew out the smoke, which drifted and scattered.

"Thing that bothers me," Blount said, "is I got the pistol from Kassam, but I didn't get Kassam. And I keep thinking about what happened to Farmer and Ivan. This ain't no time to celebrate."

"You did more than your part," Loudon said. "We'll take care of the rest."

Blount said nothing. He just gazed out into the black desert. Glanced down at his cigar. Lifted it to his lips and took another puff. The fire at the cigar's tip lit up enough to cast a glow across his face. Parson noticed that Blount's eyes did not drift unfocused in the aimless stare of the traumatized. Instead he seemed to gauge something, calculate range, estimate wind. Parson knew that feeling: the same one he had when observing an elk through the mil-dot reticle of a scope, preparing to place a shot.

Finally, Blount said, "I just wish we had a target." As he spoke, the ops center's door opened. Gold and Ongondo emerged.

"This is my friend Major Ongondo," Gold said. "I think he can help us with that."

CHAPTER 35

For a second, Blount couldn't remember where he was. He woke up on a narrow bed—a real bed, not a cot or a sleeping bag— with sheets, and a green military blanket over him. Amber light beamed through the walls of the desert tent, though the cold raised goose bumps on his arms. Air-conditioning?

Then he recalled everything. Closed his eyes, stretched, inhaled a great chestful of chilled air. Every cell of his brain expressed gratitude—to his fellow Marines, to the other service members who'd helped recover him, to the men he'd brought back, and to the ones who did not survive.

On the bed to Blount's right, Fender snored. The corporal lay on his back with his left arm off the bed, knuckles against the wooden floor. Once again, Blount noticed the boy's tattoo, just a girl's name: *Anne.* Go home and marry her and treat her right, Blount thought.

Grayson slept in the bed to the left, completely covered by a green blanket that rose and fell with his breathing. No sign of Escarra; the Legionnaire had probably slept in the field hospital, unless they'd already shipped him back to France.

Hunger gnawed at Blount. Fatigue had kept him from eating much last night—just a bowl of cereal at midnight chow before showering and falling into bed. He checked his watch. The analog hands showed nearly noon local time. That was two hours ahead of Greenwich Mean Time, which Blount read in the digital window of his Citizen chronograph. Blount recalled how the terrorists had taken this watch from him—temporarily.

He sat up. Blount wore boxers and a Marine Corps–issued T-shirt. Where were his clothes?

There, at the foot of his bed. Good gracious, somebody had washed his uniform and left it folded by his boots and a set of clean socks. Shirt and trousers, but no hat. He'd worn his helmet off the *Tarawa*. Well, the Corps would have to forgive him for going outside without a cover until he found a new one.

As quietly as he could, Blount dressed and tied his boots. He found a key in a pocket of the trousers. What was that? Oh, yeah; Parson had given him a padlock and key so he could store the flint-lock pistol and other gear in a wall locker. Nice of Lieutenant Colonel Loudon to let him keep the pistol until he could deliver it personally to the National Museum of the Marine Corps. Good excuse for a family trip, but that would come later.

Blount unlocked the locker, swung open the door slowly to try to stay quiet. The pistol remained where he'd left it. Beside it lay his grandfather's KA-BAR in the leather sheath. Blount threaded the sheath onto his belt, closed and locked the locker.

When Blount stepped outside the tent flap, the brightness hit him all at once. He shaded his eyes with his hand, squinted. When his pupils adjusted to the light, he saw four CH-53s on the ramp, Super Stallions from the *Tarawa*. What was going on?

An aerostat, which looked a lot like a World War II barrage balloon, floated above the base. The aerostat carried cameras, Blount knew, to watch for bad guys sneaking up on the perimeter. Didn't take an intel expert to sense the buildup of a new operation in the works.

He made his way toward the chow tent, though he felt a little lost at first. Parson and Loudon had taken him to eat last night, but things looked different in the daylight. Blount followed the smell of food, his boots crunching through the pea gravel. At a table just out-side the tent, he signed a roster on a clipboard. Pumped a squirt of sanitizer into his palm, rubbed it across his fingers. Strong alcohol smell, and the cuts and scrapes on his hands burned.

He stepped inside the chow tent and found it full of Marines and airmen eating lunch.

Someone shouted, "Hey, it's Gunny Blount."

All the service members in the tent put down their plastic forks and knives, rose to their feet, and applauded.

Blount's eyes brimmed. He smiled, waved, felt unsure what to do next. He didn't want the Marines to see him in any raw display of emotion, but he could not escape. The men surged around him. Lieutenant Colonel Loudon embraced him.

"Thank you, sir," Blount said. "Sorry, if anybody saw me outside. I couldn't find my cover."

The Marines laughed. "Don't worry about that, Gunny," Loudon said. "I think you deserve a little bit of a break."

"I appreciate that, sir."

Two Frenchmen in flight suits greeted Blount. One of them shook his hand and said, "You must be Havoc Two Bravo."

"Yes, sir," Blount said, "but now that I'm back, it's Gunnery Sergeant Blount. Your voice sounds familiar. Were you Dagger One-Seven?"

"*Oui*. Alain Chartier. This is my backseater, Sniper."

"I like that call sign," Blount said.

"All right, guys," Loudon said. "Step aside and let the man eat."

"Semper fi," someone called.

Another round of cheers and applause.

Blount found a tray and moved along the serving line. Platters and skillets steamed, attended by TCNs—third-country nationals—in white uniforms. Blount picked up an apple and a banana, made a roast beef sandwich, took a plate of baked chicken and rice and a slice of apple pie. Slid open a cooler box and grabbed a can of iced tea. Found a seat beside Loudon.

"So, what's going on?" Blount asked. "Why'd they fly everybody in here?" Blount tore open a mustard packet, squeezed it onto his roast beef sandwich. Took a bite. Felt his salivary glands activate. Real food for the first time in days.

"Can't talk about it here," Loudon said. "We're briefing officers and NCOs later in the afternoon."

Blount chewed, swallowed, took a gulp of the tea. Not as good as Bernadette's, a little too much lemon, but it would do. He forced himself to slow down, not to wolf his food like an animal, despite his hunger. He wouldn't let an officer—or anyone else, for that matter—see him lose his military bearing.

"What time, sir?"

"Don't worry about it, Gunny. You've done more than your share. We're gonna let you go home on a nice long pass."

"Appreciate it, sir. I'll take you up on that. But as long as I'm here, I might as well stay up on things. The Corps is still paying me."

"All right. Three o'clock. Secure briefing room. You know where that is?"

"No, sir."

"Right off the ops center. You'll see the MPs outside."

"I'll find it."

Loudon excused himself to go prepare for the briefing. Blount finished his sandwich and started in on the chicken and rice. From time to time a Marine would come by and offer congratulations or greetings, but for the most part they left him alone. They seemed to know he needed space to decompress, time to heal. And time to eat: He finished all the food he'd picked up, then went back for another slice of apple pie.

After lunch, he found a tent where the Air Force comms people had set up computers for morale purposes. An Air Force staff sergeant created a password for him, and Blount sat down to e-mail his wife. He wrote:

DEAREST BERNADETTE,

JUST A NOTE TO SAY I LOVE YOU. I DON'T KNOW WHEN THEY'LL SEND
ME HOME, BUT I THINK IT WILL BE SOON. FEELS GOOD TO BE FREE. I'M
OK, NOT HURT. DOCS WANT TO DO MORE TESTS, AND SHRINKS AND
INTEL PEOPLE WANT TO DEBRIEF ME. SO SORRY TO PUT YOU THROUGH
ALL THIS. ARE YOU OK? TELL THE GIRLS AND GRANDPA I SAID HELLO.

A.E.

Blount wanted to tell her more, but he decided that would have to wait. He always took care not to discuss anything that could harm OPSEC—operations security—and he knew the e-mail from here was monitored. He also didn't want some stranger seeing his most personal feelings toward his wife. Bernadette would appreciate just getting an e-mail that said anything; it would reconfirm that he was all right, prove she didn't just dream his phone call last night.

At three o'clock, Blount went to the briefing room near the operations center. Lieutenants, captains, and NCOs sat in rows of folding chairs. A computer and a projector rested on a table at the front of the room, and beyond the table stood a pull-down projector screen. Blount's company commander, Captain Privett, offered a handshake.

"Damn it, Guns," Privett said, "I can't tell you how good it is to see you."

"Same to you, sir."

"But what are you doing here, man? Get some rest."

"I just got about eleven hours of sleep. I'm good. Wanted to see what was going on."

"Well, you probably know more than me."

A sergeant major called the room to attention, and the battalion commander entered. Blount recognized him: Lieutenant Colonel Dixon. Loudon came in behind Dixon. Parson and Gold followed, along with that Kenyan officer, Major Ongondo.

"At ease, people," Dixon said. "Can we get someone to lower the lights?"

A Marine at the back of the room flipped a switch to turn off the front row of lights, darkening the projector screen. Loudon tapped at the computer. A still photo from an aerial video came on the screen. The image showed a grouping of tents and primitive buildings. The surrounding terrain was marked by gullies and dunes. Wording at the lower right-hand corner of the image read SECRET.

"Devil dogs," Dixon said, "Lieutenant Colonel Loudon has worked with air assets to put this mission together, so I'll let him take it from here."

"Thank you," Loudon said. "This briefing is classified secret. Welcome to Operation Iron Maul."

"Oo-rah," someone said.

Blount liked the mission's name. Reminded him of using a maul to split wood back before everybody bought a hydraulic splitter. You'd pound in a steel wedge by swinging an iron hammer as hard as you could. Best workout in the world.

"Based on a combination of human intelligence and aerial surveillance, the terrorist leader Sadiq Kassam is assessed to have encamped at this location just north of the Libyan village of Al-'Uwaynat," Loudon continued. "He has obtained chemical weapons left over from the Gadhafi regime, and he may also have received weapons from Syria."

So that's where he was going when he wasn't cutting off Farmer's head, Blount thought.

"We have with us Colonel Michael Parson from the Air Force, Ms. Sophia Gold from the UN, and Major Ongondo from African Union forces," Loudon said. "They're going to tell you how we know all this."

Parson rose to his feet and pointed to the screen.

"This image came from a video feed from an RQ-4 Global Hawk," Parson said. "In a second I'll ask Lieutenant Colonel Loudon to play the video. If you watch carefully, you'll see this camp doesn't seem to have any women or children in it. Go ahead and play it, Bill."

Loudon tapped his keyboard and the video began moving. Sure enough, Blount saw a bunch of bearded men. Most carried weapons. The video ended and Parson continued.

"This RQ-4 is marvelous technology," Parson said. "I'm an old Air Force guy, and I love me some planes and drones and satellites."

The Marines chuckled, and Parson went on.

"But all those machines are just expensive toys unless we know where to send them," Parson said. "That's when human intelligence comes in—'humint,' as we call it. Making connections, getting people to trust you, understanding life on the ground. I'd like to introduce you to an old friend of mine who specializes in that sort of thing."

Parson explained that Sophia Gold had spent most of her adult life as a linguist in the Army, and that she once talked a senior Taliban commander into ratting out a bad guy.

"That takes talent," Loudon said. More laughter from the Marines. Gold took the floor. She wore khaki tactical trousers with a black nylon belt, and she'd looped a checkered Afghan scarf around her neck.

"A few days ago," she said, "at a UN camp in Algeria, we encountered a group of three Tuareg refugees: two boys and a man. One of the boys said his uncle had delivered grain and vegetables to 'soldiers of God' at an encampment near Al-'Uwaynat. At first they were afraid to talk, and with good reason. But once we got them here to Mitiga, they felt safe enough to open up."

Gold went on to credit Major Ongondo and a Tuareg teenager for the whole thing. They will have performed a great service, she explained, if this stops another chemical attack. She asked Ongondo if he wanted to say a few words.

The major stood, faced the seated Marines, and said, "Ms. Gold gives me far too much praise. I will say only that I thank you for helping stop these men from using terrible weapons against civilians. Our brothers in Nigeria have a proverb: 'Ashes fly back into the face of him who throws them.'"

"Damn straight," Parson said. Gold, Parson, and Ongondo took their seats, turning the briefing back over to the Marine officers.

"Analysts now believe Kassam keeps at least part of his weapons cache at the location you saw on the screen," Loudon said. "All personnel at this target are considered hostile. The Air Force plans to hit it tomorrow with what they call 'agent defeat' weapons."

Loudon changed the slide to show a B-2 stealth bomber. He explained that the B-2 would hit Kassam's lair with CBU-107 Passive Attack Weapons. PAWs destroyed targets through kinetic energy rather than explosions, which made them ideal for wiping out a chemical weapons cache. Less chance of spreading a toxic cloud.

"The bomb opens up and releases a bunch of penetrator rods," Loudon said. "Think of it like hitting a target with a whole lot of big bullets. I know you guys can relate to that."

Laughter rippled through the room. Now the mission's name made even more sense to Blount. Strike the enemy with solid metal.

"Our job is simple," Loudon said. "At a safe distance from the target, we will set up a blocking force. Any bad guys manage to get out of the objective area, we take 'em down. We'll also lase the target for the B-2. As you might imagine, we will do all this in MOPP Four." He added that once the bomber exited the battle space, the French would provide air support with their Mirages.

Loudon changed the slide again. The new image was all text. At the top, it read *BPT*. That meant, be prepared to do the following. The bullet statements read:

- Establish blocking force
- Kill/capture enemy personnel who escape target area
- Conduct bomb damage assessment

Maybe a little tricky in execution, but simple in concept. Take away the bad man's toys. Blount loved it. Ivan and Farmer would have loved it, too, Blount thought.

He remembered his grandfather's words about not letting revenge burn you up. But this wasn't fury-blinded vengeance; this was a Marine Corps mission. Blount wanted in. He waited to speak to Loudon after the briefing ended.

"Sir," Blount said, "I'd like to go."

Loudon stared at him.

"Are you serious?" Loudon said. "Your mission now is to get debriefed and to rest up. You know that."

"Yes, sir, and I'll do all that. But I want to go with you tomorrow."

"Gunny, I think that shit they slimed you with is messing with your mind."

Blount didn't appreciate that remark. He didn't expect to get treated like a hero for wanting to go. But he did expect to get taken seriously.

"Sir, due respect. Don't patronize me."

Loudon turned his gaze down to the floor like he knew he'd said something wrong, then looked up at Blount again.

"I'm sorry, Guns. I didn't mean it that way. Let's talk outside."

The two men stepped out of the briefing room and sat on a wooden bench outside the ops center. Starlings twittered on a nearby satellite dish. In the distance, a KC-135 glided toward a landing.

"I had to listen to what they did to Farmer," Blount said. "I didn't see it but I heard it. I had to leave behind a good man in the Legion because he got killed helping us escape, and we couldn't carry him through the desert. And I saw what that poison did in Sigonella to my old platoon commander."

Loudon watched Blount speak, then looked out across the air base. Dug the toe of his boot into the gravel at their feet.

"I understand you want payback," Loudon said. "I would, too, in your boots. And I admire what you want to do. But the Marines are a big brotherhood. You don't have to do everything yourself."

"I know, sir. But I want to be part of this one."

"What if something happens to you, after all you've been through? How would we ever tell your wife?"

That made Blount pause. He worried about that, too. Before he could respond, he noticed something moving in the gravel. A camel spider nearly as wide as his palm crawled through the rocks toward the bench.

"I been thinking about that," Blount said. "But I figured something could happen when I get back to the ship. Something could happen on the flight home. I could have a wreck turning into my driveway. If I wanted to be safe all the time, I'd work in an ice-cream store. And then somebody'd rob the place and shoot me. Ain't no such thing as safe. But taking out Kassam will make the world a little less dangerous."

Part of Blount's mind knew his words rang a little hollow. Let me go on a mission because it's dangerous everywhere? A thin rationalization, maybe. But he couldn't come right out and say he needed vengeance.

"Gunny, this is a highly unusual request," Loudon said. "It's not even up to me."

The camel spider reached the bench and began climbing.

"Sir," Blount said, "can you at least ask?"

"I don't know. I think if—"

On the seat of the bench now, the camel spider began crawling toward Blount. Blount unsnapped the sheath holding his World War II KA-BAR. He withdrew the knife. Made a quick downward stab.

The blade stuck upright in the wood. Impaled the spider.

CHAPTER 36

In the early-morning darkness, four Super Stallion helicopters lifted off from Mitiga. Stars strewn across the North African sky shimmered like a luminescent mist. Blount rode in the lead aircraft, Loudon beside him. The Corps had granted permission for Blount to take part in this op, but only if he remained with Loudon and the command element. Loudon and his staff would observe the attack from a rise several hundred meters from the target, and they'd issue orders and call in air support as needed.

Blount would have preferred to get closer, to join one of the fire teams encircling Kassam's hideout. But higher-ups had decided Blount's direct knowledge of Kassam and his henchmen could provide good input to Loudon and Loudon's ops officer. Perhaps he could identify Kassam—dead or alive—after the air strike. The thought of the terrorist leader in cuffs or a body bag filled him with expectation.

Blount appreciated the chance to see this thing through to the end, even if *seeing* was all he'd get to do. And he had to admit this made a lot more sense than sending him into the middle of what Marines called "the point of friction." His family had gone through enough already. The Corps had public relations to consider, too. Blount's name would soon appear all over the news—the Marine who escaped his chains to free his buddies and kill the bad guys. Couldn't let him take crazy chances now.

"Thanks for this, sir," Blount shouted over the noise of rotors and engines. "I reckon you went out on a limb for me."

"Yeah, I did, Gunny," Loudon said. "If you get hurt, I'll kill you."

Blount nodded. He shifted in his seat, checked his gear again. He still carried the M16 he'd brought with him on the first mission, but he wore a brand new MOPP suit. The gas mask rested in a carrier on his side. Night vision goggles, now in the stowed position, added weight to his helmet. The other men wore the same equipment, and they gripped an assortment of weapons—including many for hitting bad guys at a distance: An AT4 rocket. An M40 sniper rifle. An M107—a semiautomatic .50 caliber monster. The M107 gunner had loaded his weapon with Raufoss rounds, incendiary projectiles with a tungsten core, capable of setting cars on fire. And one Marine assigned to Loudon's command element had a laser designator to provide pinpoint guidance for the bombs from the B-2 aircraft.

All that weaponry made him want to use some of it. He felt like a bullet with a hang fire—the cartridge primer popped and sizzling but delayed in igniting the powder. The round had to go off, but when and how?

Blount looked over his equipment one more time, and he saw something he'd not noticed earlier. Some kind of stain marred the receiver of his M16. He looked closer and realized it was a bloody thumbprint. His own, judging from the size. Whose blood? Maybe Ivan's. Maybe Rat Face's. Maybe even Farmer's. In an instinctive reflex to keep his weapon clean, he wiped away the stain. Now he wanted even more to see destruction visited on his tormentors.

By the green glare of a penlight, Loudon studied his objective area diagram. The chart trembled with the vibration of the aircraft as Blount looked on. From the contour markings, he could tell the terrain did not lie as flat as the area where he'd been held captive. This land featured hills and outcroppings, some fairly steep but not high.

Loudon wore a headset, and he pressed a talk switch to speak with the chopper crew. Blount, without a headset on this flight, could not monitor the conversation, but an announcement from Loudon told him the subject matter.

"Five minutes to refuel," the lieutenant colonel shouted. "Gonna get a little bumpy."

Blount looked forward toward the cockpit. With the unaided eye, he could see only the soft glow of NVG-compatible lighting on the instrument panels. Nothing visible out the windscreen. But when the helo began to turn a few minutes later, Blount pressed a release lever and clicked his NVGs into place. The black night turned to a glimmering green, with the bulk of an Air Force HC-130 directly in front of the Super Stallion.

Just as Loudon had warned, the helicopter began to bounce in the HC-130's wake turbulence. A pair of hoses extended from the airplane's wings, a funnel-like drogue at the end of each hose. Blount's stomach began to churn just a little, the effect of the irregular motion. Other than that, he felt pretty good. He'd slept well until alert time, and whatever the exposure to toxins had done to his body, the effects seemed to have worn off, at least for now.

Even without a headset, Blount noted the cross talk on the radios and interphone. Some of the fliers had their headphone volumes turned up loud enough for Blount to catch tatters of conversation. He could not make out the words, but he could just barely hear the short syllables, the static-scraped phrasings of technical procedure. Voices devoid of all emotion, conveying nothing except command and response. The sound of long study and training.

A drogue loomed large in the windscreen, and the helicopter's refueling probe eased into it. The gurgle of fuel flowing through lines joined all the other noises of wind, engines, and electronics.

Blount and Loudon both checked their watches. The refuel had come right on time, and this mission depended on precision timing. The blocking force needed to get into position only minutes before the bomber strike, so as not to alert the enemy. The B-2 could not release its weapons without a call that the choppers had cleared the airspace. And the Mirages could offer no support to the men on the ground until the B-2 was gone.

350 | TOM YOUNG

After several minutes on the hose, the Super Stallion broke contact with the tanker. As soon as the helo banked out of the wake turbulence, the ride became smoother. Blount turned off his NVGs to save the batteries. He might need them one more time, at landing, and after landing he'd switch them off for good. The air strike would take place in morning nautical twilight. That first hint of sunrise would wash out night vision goggles.

The other choppers refueled, and the formation made a final turn on course to the objective. The men spoke little as the aircraft neared the target. The gunners manned their weapons, belts of ammunition curving from the breeches like metallic serpents.

For the remainder of the route, Blount tried to let his mind enter a neutral place. He had a lot of strong feelings to keep at bay right now if he wanted to think like a professional, especially after seeing the blood on his rifle. He sought not to go blank or tune out, but rather to leave all his channels open so his training could kick in quickly for any given problem. As a student of the martial arts, he was reminded of drills when he had to close his eyes and wait for a classmate's mock attack. No point in anticipating what was coming; that could lead you to do the wrong thing and get your butt kicked. He forced himself into a kind of silence, but it was the silence of a shark gliding the depths: a lot of potential power that might get set off unpredictably. Just stay loose and alert, he told himself. Breathe deep. Battle Zen.

The sound of wind and rotors shifted into a different key, and the Super Stallion began to descend.

"Three minutes," Loudon shouted.

The Marines straightened in their seats, prepared to exit the helicopter in the order assigned. Blount turned his NVGs back on.

The three minutes passed quickly. When the aircraft touched down, the crew chief yelled, "Go, go, go!" Blount unbuckled his seat belt. Loudon jumped out of the helicopter, followed by a radio operator, the forward observer with the laser designator, and a fire team of four Marines. Blount got out last, and the helicopter lifted off to place other fire teams who had remained in the aircraft.

As expected, Blount found himself on top of a rocky rise that overlooked a vale of sand. Through his goggles he saw the helicopters depositing men into positions surrounding the vale. At the center of the sand bowl, four tents—about the size of American twenty-five-man tents—stood pegged beside five mud-brick structures. The buildings looked like they might have served as some sort of base camp for nomads at one time.

A higher ridgeline rose to the east. Beyond it, as viewed through NVGs, skyglow beamed as if an electrified city of crystal lay just out of view: the first hint of sunrise, and the end of usefulness for night vision goggles.

"Time to go MOPP Four, gentlemen," Loudon said.

Blount switched off his NVGs, removed his helmet. Pulled his gas mask out of its carrier and donned the mask, checked its seals. Placed his helmet back on over the mask and pulled on his butyl gloves. The other men suited up the same way.

He inhaled long and slow through the gas mask filter.

Now he wanted to kill.

The scent of the mask's rubber sparked anger within Blount quick as steel and flint might ignite a load in that old pistol. He knew smells could trigger memories with a power denied all the other senses, and this particular odor wiped away his battle Zen. The last time he'd suited up like this, he'd lost friends, found himself delivered into the hands of people who wanted to saw his head off. Kassam was still out there, probably in that compound below. The rational part of Blount's mind registered surprise that rage had flared in him so hotly. His grandfather had warned about vengeance burning you up, but he hadn't expected it to feel like actual flames.

With all the fire teams in place, the four helicopters clattered away to the north. Blount wanted to check his watch again to note the B-2's time over target, but now the watch lay buried under his glove and MOPP suit sleeve, and he could not expose any skin. As far as he was concerned, the bomber couldn't get here soon enough. Every second gave those terrorists another moment of life they did not deserve.

He did not have to wait long. As the terrain below filled with the milky light of dawn, Blount thought he heard the whisper of jet engines way up high. He could not be sure; it might have been only the breeze or perhaps the sound of men breathing through gas masks. Behind the cover of a boulder, Loudon kept his eyes on the target. The forward observer manned the laser designator, which looked vaguely like a spotting scope on a tripod. The observer aimed his infrared beam, invisible to the naked eye, at the target.

Loudon conferred with the observer and one of the radio operators. Spoke into the handset of a PRC-119, holding it close to the voicemitter of his gas mask.

"Spirit Five-Four, this is Thor Six," he said. "You are cleared hot."

"Thor Six," came the answer, "Spirit Five-Four copies we are cleared hot."

A light came on in one of the tents down below. Faint voices shouted in Arabic. Perhaps the enemy had heard something. For a moment, nothing else happened. Seconds ticked into minutes. Blount wondered if the bomber had aborted. He looked up. If the B-2 was there, it flew so high Blount could not see it.

Then a staccato fluttering filled the air. The noise reminded Blount of the wing beats of a field lark startled from a pasture, amplified by a factor of hundreds. At first the sound made no sense. But then he realized what he heard: heavy metal ripping through the atmosphere at terminal velocity.

Blount had seen plenty of ordnance blasts, but nothing like this hail of anvils. When the weapons struck, the ground leaped and rolled. The tents flattened. A geyser of debris and dust lifted into the air as the buildings began to disintegrate. Even at a distance of hundreds of meters, Blount felt the impacts resonate inside his chest cavity. Solid projectiles jackhammered the desert floor. The noise made Blount think of standing under a trestle while a train crossed it just as clouds thundered. He had never witnessed an earthquake, but he imagined the rending of tectonic plates might sound something like this.

Despite the absence of high explosives, sparks and fire leaped amid the raging of a miniature sandstorm. Blount figured the source of ignition could have come from anything—perhaps the fuses of chemical weapons or even flame spewed from an oil lamp as the lamp got crushed. No telling what weird effects might result from that much steel hitting with that much force. He wanted it to go on forever.

"Beautiful," Loudon said.

Blount simply nodded and kept his eyes on the target area.

The desert grew still again, save for a drifting cloud of dust and smoke. Blount wondered what poisons that smoke might contain. The sun crested a notch in the eastern ridgeline, and light spilled into the sand bowl as if a levee had broken. Blount felt almost . . . disappointed. Was it over so soon? Loudon spoke into his radio, this time on a ground channel.

"Hold your positions," he said.

As the smoke cleared and the sun rose, the effect of the CBU-107 Passive Attack Weapons became more apparent. The tents had disappeared altogether. Whatever they had covered lay in sand-covered ruin, lumps of rubble no more than three feet high. The PAWs had also flattened most of the mud-brick structures, though part of one of them remained standing. That structure appeared to have been made up of three rooms. Two of the rooms remained nearly whole, shattered walls leaning inward.

"Nothing passive about that, was there?" Loudon said.

Blount shook his head.

Though Blount found the air strike impressive, it left him feeling hollow. He'd wanted to kill Kassam with his own hands, see the dirt-bag's eyes fill with fear, hear the rasp of his last breath.

More jet noise came from above, this time low, and loud enough to be unmistakable. Blount tilted his head—he had to crane his neck farther than usual because of the gas mask—and he saw two Mirage fighters streak by in close formation. The aircraft grew smaller with distance, banked into a turn.

Nothing moved in the target area, though Blount spotted two vehicles he'd not seen earlier: an SUV and a pickup truck like the one that had carried him to the hell house. They had been parked on the other side of the compound, screened by structures that no longer stood. The vehicles looked dirty but otherwise untouched. The CBU-107s had struck with such accuracy that they'd hammered the target and nothing else—not even trucks only yards away.

Loudon went over to the radio operator, lifted the handset of the PRC-119.

"All stations, Thor Six," he called. "BDA team move into place. Exercise extreme caution."

Loudon, Blount, and about twenty other Marines from various positions around the target area began to head downhill. The bomb damage assessment team would take photographs and try to deter-mine exactly what the bombs had destroyed.

Blount glanced over his shoulder, back up the hill. The sniper with the .50-cal watched and waited, his spotter beside him with an observation scope. The BDA team continued moving toward the devastated compound. Blount wished fervently that he'd find Kas-sam's body, to provide proof positive of the dirtbag's death. But at this distance he saw no bodies at all—only shattered bricks, crum-bling walls, and two intact vehicles.

Loudon continued leading the descent down the outcropping into the sand bowl. The lieutenant colonel nearly lost his footing in a slip-pery chute of loose stones, and he stumbled ahead of his radio operator. To maintain balance he took a long stride downhill and let the momentum carry him. Nearly at a run, he reached the edge of the sand bowl. Pebbles bounced and rolled across the ground behind him, and he came to a stop about fifty yards in front of the other men.

At that instant, movement caught Blount's eye, something within the few walls still standing. Could anyone have survived that air strike?

Before Blount could call out a warning, three men ran from within the bombed-out structure. One wore a dark tracksuit. The other two wore green field jackets, and all were bearded. They moved too quickly for Blount to determine if Kassam was among them. One dived into the pickup, and the other two jumped into the SUV.

"Fire," Loudon shouted.

From behind and above him, Blount heard the deep slam of the .50 cal M107. A Raufoss round tore a flaming hole in the pickup's engine compartment just as the vehicle started to move. The pickup ground to a halt, smoke seeping from under the hood. The driver jumped out. The M107 boomed again. This time the Raufoss slammed through the driver's torso. The body collapsed in a smoking heap.

Marines opened up on the escaping SUV, but the bullets seemed to have no effect. Maybe the vehicle was armed, or maybe the range had become too great for the M16s.

The M107 fired once more. An orange flash and a wisp of smoke showed the Raufoss had found its mark, but the vehicle kept accelerating. The sniper sent another round, and the SUV only moved faster.

"Don't let that thing go," Loudon shouted. "Call the Daggers."

Blount stood closer to the radio operator than Loudon, and every second counted. The radio operator swung the PRC-119 from his shoulder and made a quick adjustment to the channel selector. As Blount reached him, the man held out the handset and said, "You're on Dagger's frequency, Gunny."

Blount grabbed the handset, lifted it to his gas mask's voicemitter.

"Dagger flight, Thor Six Bravo with a fire mission," he called. As he spoke, he watched the SUV growing smaller. A trail of dust rose behind it. Maybe Kassam himself was in that vehicle. If so, he was getting away. Please answer me, Blount thought. Please, please, please come up on freq.

"Thor Six Bravo, Dagger One-One, say your fire mission," a voice responded. Very familiar. Yeah, that French pilot, Chartier. With the backseater they called Sniper.

Perfect, Blount thought. Time to talk a round onto a target.

"Sir," Blount transmitted, "my position is objective area as briefed. Target is a vehicle heading south, away from objective area. Will not be marked."

Blount released his talk switch, waited for a response.

"Dagger One-One copies target is a moving vehicle south of objective."

Vengeance is mine, Blount thought. Maybe that went against the Good Book, but he couldn't help it. He had to summon all his self-discipline just to use proper radio procedure.

"Yes, sir," Blount said. "Thor Six Bravo requests bombing or strafing attack. Run-in heading roughly one-niner-zero, pull out at your discretion. I can observe and will not control. Over."

"One-niner-zero, pull out our discretion," Chartier said.

Go get 'em, Blount thought. Hope your boy Sniper's as good as you say. Reckon this makes me Sniper's spotter.

Jet noise rose from a distant whisper to pealing thunder. Blount gazed at the sky above him. At first he saw no aircraft. He'd lost track of their position, but he knew they'd attack from the north. He followed the sound as best he could.

There.

Blount spotted two dark specks moving in unison above the northwest horizon. When they turned, their wing flash clearly identified them as a pair of fighters. The Mirages rolled onto a southerly heading. One of them began to descend.

"Thor Six Bravo," Chartier called, "Dagger One-One has target in sight."

"Dagger One-One cleared hot," Blount answered.

On the ground, the vehicle appeared only as a distant feather of dust. Out of range now for infantry weapons. But not for infantry talking to air.

The descending Mirage began to level off several hundred feet above the desert floor. Its roar seemed to fill the entire Sahara. When the jet streaked overhead, Blount noticed the clusters of fins and oblong shapes underneath the wings: an aircraft laden with death, but to Blount, laden with justice.

After the Mirage rocketed past the compound, one of the weapons fell from the jet. The bomb made a slight change in direction as it dropped, perhaps riding a laser beam from the Mirage. As if drawn by a magnet, the weapon steered directly to the moving SUV.

Flame erupted, blotted out the vehicle. An instant later the sound reached Blount's ears. More crack than boom, sharp and hard. Black smoke belched from the point of impact. Burning masses hurled themselves skyward—chunks of the SUV, accompanied by dozens of smaller embers. From the central swirl of flames, blackened debris flew in arcs, streamed smoke and fire, and bounced onto the desert floor.

The Mirage pulled up, banked into a climbing turn.

Blount raised both arms. In his right hand he brandished his rifle; his left hand he clenched into a fist. From within the gas mask, he let out a long monosyllabic growl, a victory cry. Sweat poured into his eyes and he didn't care.

"Precision-guided whoop-ass," Loudon shouted.

Several Marines began to yell.

"Oo-raaah!"

"Gotcha, baby."

Blount keyed his mike again.

"Good hit, Dagger," he called. "Nice shot."

The radio hissed for a moment before Chartier called back.

"Copy that, Thor. *Merci*. Do you require another pass?"

Blount scanned the target area. No movement. No gunfire.

"Negative, sir."

"Roger. We'll remain on station until we reach bingo fuel."

The sun now appeared as a bronze ball, fully risen above the horizon. The last whorls of red marbled into a sky growing bluer by the minute. Clear visibility stretched for miles; Blount noted with satisfaction that the helicopters would have no trouble coming back for him and his fellow Marines. The weather itself seemed to acknowledge Blount's right to get home.

But before he went anywhere, he wanted to make sure Sadiq Kassam had made a permanent change of station—to hell. Blount couldn't wait to find Kassam's body in the rubble and wreckage. He wanted—needed—to look into Kassam's dead eyes.

He joined the bomb damage assessment team searching the target area. Blount, Loudon, and ten other Marines began picking their way through the crumbled bricks and collapsed walls of the compound. The men snapped photographs, jotted notes, paced off distances.

One Marine stopped, and with a gloved finger pointed at something on the ground. He took a photo as other men came to look. Blount trotted over as fast as he could in heavy chem gear, hoping to see Kassam's corpse.

But it was only a foot, still inside a Russian-style black leather boot. Elsewhere in the rubble the Marines found a hand, several fingers, even a jawbone with bloody teeth. Nothing identifiable except through dental records or DNA analysis. Blount stepped over to Loudon's side.

"Sir," he said, "do you think the CIA or somebody has a DNA sample from Kassam or one of his relatives?"

"I seriously doubt it," Loudon said.

The only identifiable body was that of the man who'd tried to drive away in the pickup. The Raufoss round had all but blown him in half, but the face was still intact. A face Blount had never seen before. Younger than Kassam, with a much sparser beard.

So, where was Kassam? He's gotta be here, Blount thought.

What Blount really wanted was to find the terrorist leader alive, to make sure Kassam knew who took him out. And then to choke the life out of him slowly, to make him suffer like he'd made that boy Farmer suffer. He kept imagining his hands around that dirtbag's throat. Blount still remembered what his grandfather had said about vengeance. But by God, vengeance had its place.

Blount, Loudon, and a few of the other Marines hiked south to the SUV destroyed by the Mirage. The explosion had left a shallow crater in the desert floor. The wreckage seemed . . . incomplete, not enough to have been a vehicle. Twisted, burned metal lay surrounded by blackened sand. With anticipation tingling down to his fingertips, Blount walked over to the largest chunk of seared steel. Kassam's body had to be here.

Inside the twisted beams and sheet metal, Blount found human remains—but what remained came closer to fossil than corpse. His excitement over the Mirage strike corroded into simmering wrath. A skeletal black husk stared back at him, the flesh seared away to leave little but an openmouthed skull. A crisp film covered the ribcage; Blount couldn't tell if it was shriveled skin or melted clothing. The arm bones ended in a general scattering of ash and debris, with no hands visible. Perhaps the intense heat had burned them away, bones and all.

The very face of death, the skull seemed to mock Blount. He looked into the eye sockets, and he wished he could grant this dirtbag three more seconds of life, just to ask, "Who were you?" But the burned bones looked like they could have been dead a thousand years. For the moment, at least, they were impossible to identify.

The last time Blount had felt so powerless came rushing back to him. In his mind he saw Sadiq Kassam spattered with Farmer's blood, holding a dripping machete.

"Guess you got the last laugh on these bastards, Guns," Loudon said.

Blount turned away from the wreckage, slung his rifle over his shoulder, peered out across the Sahara. He felt the flames inside him building, spreading like fire in a tobacco barn raging through dry, cured leaves. "I don't know, sir," he said. "Kassam could still be out there."

Loudon placed his boot on the singed engine block. "We'll find out soon enough," he said.

Or not, Blount thought. And even if we do get Kassam, how long before a new chief dirtbag takes his place? And how long before another terrorist cell gets its hands on weapons of mass destruction? Blount saw his grandfather on Iwo Jima facing an enemy that could appear from nowhere and melt away just as quickly. You could throw fire and steel, kill in sickening numbers, and still never know when the enemy would pop up behind you.

He wanted to assail his enemy right now, to open fire, to thrust with a blade, to smash with a boot, fist, or elbow. He wanted to cut loose with a flamethrower like Grandpa, get payback in grand style. But he had no place to throw the flame. Nothing burned but his own spirit. He balled his hands into fists, walked in a circle, dragged deep breaths through the filter of his gas mask.

"Guns," Loudon said. "Are you all right?"

Loudon stood over a piece of an axle. The blast had burned away the tires completely. However, one rim remained bolted onto the axle, giving it the appearance of a giant steel mallet. Blount looked down at the incinerated metal.

"Give me that," Blount said. Forgot about the "sir."

Blount charged toward Loudon. Loudon stepped back, eyes widened in fear. But Blount didn't want to hurt the lieutenant colonel. He wanted that axle.

He leaned over and grabbed it with both hands. Yanked it up from the ground the way a weaker man might lift a baseball bat. Blount hefted it by the broken end. At the other end, sand streamed from the edges and grooves of the bare rim. Blount ran at the chunk of wreckage that contained the scorched remains.

He swung the axle over his head like a battle-ax. Brought it down hard on the twisted metal frame of the destroyed vehicle. The impact made a loud clang. Dust and ash bounced from the burned steel.

"Guns," Loudon said. "What are you—"

Blount wasn't listening. He swung the axle again, sweating inside his gas mask. The rim at the end of the axle whanged once more into the wreckage.

"I'm gon' get you," Blount growled. He drew back the axle for another blow, wielded it like a maul. This time the impact tore away some of the wreckage that encased the burned body.

The blackened skull heightened Blount's rage. As he raised the axle again, the effort twisted his gas mask so that the facepiece dug into his nose. He ripped the gas mask off and flung it to the sand.

"Gunnery Sergeant Blount," Loudon shouted. "You will place that mask back on your head!"

Blount heaved the axle again. Ignored Loudon's order. He smashed the rim into the grinning skull inside the wreckage. The skull exploded into flying shards of bone and soot.

Blount took in a long breath of unfiltered air. It went down clean; he felt no sign of chemical poisoning. But then he realized the insane chance he'd taken.

"Marine," Loudon shouted. "You *will* pick that mask up off the deck and replace it on your face."

Horror replaced Blount's wrath. He'd let emotion break down his military bearing, his common sense, even his devotion to family. He'd let rage overcome judgment. After all he'd survived, he'd risked losing his life, widowing Bernadette, leaving his kids fatherless, in a fit of fury. He dropped the axle. Grabbed the mask, pulled it over his head. Sweat slickened its seals and straps.

Heart throbbing in his chest, Blount remembered the nausea and weakness he'd experienced from his earlier exposure to chemical weapons. He thought of Kelley writhing on the ground in Sigonella. What if Bernadette had had to learn he'd died the same way, and so unnecessarily? What if he never got another whiff of her lavender shampoo, never got to see his girls riding the new pony? He'd nearly thrown it all away.

"I'm sorry, sir," Blount said. "I'm sorry." He leaned against the burned and battered wreckage of the SUV. Loudon walked over to him and put his hands on Blount's shoulders.

"That's not the Gunny Blount I know," Loudon said. He no longer used his command voice, but he poked a finger into Blount's chest when he spoke his next sentence: "You better get yourself squared away."

"I know it, sir. It's just—I had to hear what they did to Farmer."

Loudon took a step back.

"We all saw the video, Guns," Loudon said. "We all loved Farmer."

Blount didn't reply. He just stared at the horizon and listened to the silence of a desert returning to the proper stillness of morning. Breathed in, breathed out. Let the flames inside him flicker down to embers.

"Payback is too big to carry in one man's seabag," Loudon said. "Let us finish this, whatever's left to finish. You need to go back to your family for a while."

Blount knew he'd probably never get the revenge he'd craved just moments ago. But he considered what he did have: He remained alive and healthy, despite his recklessness. He still had his family.

Blount thought of Grandpa in his room at the senior center, coping with his own flames of anger.

"You know, sir," Blount said, "my grandfather warned me about not getting eat up with vengeance. He said if you gotta fight, fight to protect and not to punish."

"How's that?" Loudon asked.

"Grandpa fought in the Pacific. He said revenge will burn you up like a flamethrower and turn you into something you don't like."

Loudon turned his eyes down to the charred ground, seemed to consider what Blount had said.

"Your grandfather's right, Guns," Loudon said. "You can't let a mission turn into a vendetta. You let that happen, and part of you never goes home."

Had that happened to Grandpa? Blount wondered. Did part of him still fight across the black sands of Iwo Jima? Blount wondered if he, too, might leave a portion of himself always at war, fighting across the sands of North Africa, the mountains of Afghanistan, and the alleyways of Iraq.

The radio interrupted his thoughts. Chartier called again. "Thor Six," the Frenchman said, "be advised Dagger flight is bingo fuel. Do you require further air cover?"

This time Loudon answered. He stepped over to the radio operator, lifted the handset and said, "Negative, Dagger. I think we're done here. We'll see you back at base."

Blount looked up toward the reverberation of jet engines. Two flecks of metal traversed the sun's glow as the Mirages joined up in close formation and turned to the north. The pair of fighter planes rose higher, grew smaller and fainter, until they became but a memory. They left Blount standing on the desert floor, a long way from home.

THE STORY BEHIND *SAND AND FIRE*

In the first days of the Iraq War, my Air National Guard crewmates and I flew a C-130 Hercules to an airfield in Numaniyah, southeast of Baghdad. We carried tons of Meals Ready to Eat to Marines who had pushed north from their line of departure at the Kuwait border. We didn't stay long; the devil dogs helped offload the MREs quickly, and we took off to return to our base in Oman.

But during our short time on the ground, I could see the fatigue in the men's faces, and I wondered what they'd experienced and what challenges lay ahead of them. I heard not one word of complaint, and I saw in those faces not just exhaustion but an unshakable commitment to the mission and to their fellow Marines. They lived in pretty rough field conditions, and I felt guilty about flying back to my air-conditioned tent and hot meals. These guys seemed willing to endure any hardship to carry out the core mission of a USMC rifle squad: "to locate, close with, and destroy the enemy."

This is my fifth novel in the Parson and Gold series, but the first with a focus on the Marine Corps, and the furthest from my personal experience in the Air Force. I wanted to make the novel as authentic as I could, so I reached out to the Marines for help with questions about tactics, weaponry, and Marine Corps culture.

The Corps allowed me to observe an exercise at Fort A.P. Hill, Virginia, and to chat with instructors at the Weapons Training Battalion at Quantico. Much of what I learned in those visits, especially with regard to Marine Corps Scout Sniper training, made its way into this novel.

When I put in requests to visit USMC units, I appreciated the way Marines did business; they gave prompt replies with a refreshing absence of red tape and foot-dragging. Ask a Marine a question and you'll get a straight answer.

As a former reporter in civilian life, I noticed something else that impressed me. Marine Corps leaders trust their people. Many times when I visited a corporation or other institution as a journalist, a public relations official would sit in on every interview, listening for any word that strayed from approved corporate spin. On Marine bases, however, senior leaders allowed me to speak with junior officers and enlisted personnel without a PR officer standing over them every minute.

Make no mistake: Marines are very conscious of their public image. But they don't seem to live in fear that a private will say something stupid. I suppose they have two reasons for that: One—they have more important things to worry about. Two—Marines are professionals, not usually given to stupid comments.

Formidable as they are, however, Marines don't win wars by themselves—not even those as tough as Gunnery Sergeant Blount. So I tried in this novel to demonstrate how different services, and even different services of other nations, work together toward a common goal. If you spend much time around the modern military, one of the watchwords you hear often is "jointness." That means teamwork between various branches of the military. In both exercises and real-world missions, my Air Guard career gave me opportunities to work with the Marines, the Navy, and the Army, as well as the armed forces of several countries, including Britain, France, Germany, Chile, and Bangladesh. I don't think the general public realizes how much international cooperation goes on, and I hope this novel brings that picture into sharper focus.

Readers of my previous novels may remember Blount's introduction in *The Renegades*. He began as a minor character, but I got so much positive feedback about him that I decided to give him a star turn in *Sand and Fire*. I certainly enjoyed writing him, and I hope readers enjoy getting to know him better.

Though this book required me to research Blount's branch of service, I needed only to call on my past to write Blount's recollections of farm life. Blount's memories of Southern tobacco fields are my own. I grew up on a Carolina farm, where my parents, Bobby and Harriett Young, taught me the value of hard work. Incidentally, my parents continue to live on that farm. "Blount's" catalpa tree is dead now, but the ponds still contain fish, the fields still produce crops, and the woods still harbor game.

I can't say I know anyone exactly like Blount; he's a composite of people I've known. So is his grandfather, for that matter. I used to hunt quail and pheasant with a retired Marine lieutenant colonel who had survived some of the most hellish fighting imaginable in the Pacific campaign during World War II. Though he told lots of stories, most of them had to do with garrison life. I heard him talk about combat against the Japanese just once. Even on that occasion he said very little: "We had to dig those bastards out." And in reference to severe losses among officers and senior NCOs in one particular battle: "We lost a lot of high-priced help." On most days he preferred to talk about dogs, birds, and wildlife management.

This novel describes chemical weapons attacks against civilians in Sicily and Gibraltar. Those incidents are, thank God, fictional. But they reflect events that did take place in Iraq in 1988 and in Syria in 2013. The threat of chemical weapons in the hands of terrorists and rogue nations represents a nightmare scenario, and chemical weapons are easily produced. Each day that goes by without their use comes as a result of hard work by intelligence agencies, military personnel, and international groups such as the Organisation for the Prohibition of Chemical Weapons.

On a personal note, as I wrote this novel I retired from the Air

National Guard after twenty years of military service. I can scarcely find the words to express my gratitude to my brothers and sisters in arms for their friendship and professionalism.

While you read this, many of my friends in uniform remain in harm's way. As the guardians of an elected democracy, they serve in your name no matter how you voted. Never send them into battle lightly. Always keep them in your thoughts and prayers.

TOM YOUNG
Alexandria, Virginia
July 2014

ACKNOWLEDGMENTS

A few months before I finished this novel, I made my last flight as a member of the Air National Guard. After landing, I descended the crew ladder of the C-5 Galaxy and saw dozens of my squadron mates and dearest friends waiting for me. A fire truck had pulled up near the aircraft's parking spot for the traditional spray-down of a retiring aviator. My buddies gave the hose to my wife, Kristen.

Payback time.

Kristen didn't just throw a few drops in my general direction; she opened the valve and let me have it. Full force—in a good-natured celebration of a closing chapter. To the cheers and laughter of the squadron, I learned something interesting: A fire hose can blast you so hard you have to turn your head to breathe. Then I gave Kristen a soggy embrace in my dripping flight suit.

She had earned a little fun with that hose. For two decades she had put up with the war deployments, the long absences, and all the inconveniences and uncertainties of life as a military wife. Not only that—she had also served as my adviser and writing coach, critiquing each manuscript line by line, draft after draft.

I owe a word of thanks to several of my comrades-in-arms. Instructor pilot Joe Myers served in a number of leadership positions in the 167th Airlift Wing, and I logged many pleasant hours of flying with him. Now in retirement, Joe reads all my manuscripts and helps keep me straight on technical details.

Retired brigadier general Wayne "Speedy" Lloyd, former commander of the West Virginia Air National Guard, provided valuable input on how my character Michael Parson would go about leading an air expeditionary group. General Lloyd spent a tour running a forward air base in Kyrgyzstan, and the aircraft operating out of that base included French Mirage jets. He provided a great account of his time there in my nonfiction book, *The Speed of Heat: An Airlift Wing at War in Iraq and Afghanistan*, and his stories informed my description of Mirage crews in this novel. (Yes, they really had a masseuse.)

Dennis Philapavage, a former helicopter pilot turned C-5 driver, gave me helpful details about choppers, especially emergency egress procedures. Fellow flight engineer Al Rigdon, a former KC-135 boom operator, told me about boomer checklist items for aerial refueling.

My brother, Ron Young, and his colleague Bill Oestereich—both black-belt martial artists—helped me conceptualize Gunnery Sergeant Blount's fight scenes. They came up with a good idea as soon as I described the scenario: If he's chained, they said, he'll use those chains as weapons.

Longtime friend Jodie Tighe helped refresh my dim memories of French as I penned the character of Mirage pilot Alain Chartier. *Merci beaucoup*, Jodie.

Air Force veteran Drew Pallo very kindly provided memories of serving at the old Wheelus Air Base, before it became Libya's Mitiga International Airport.

I'd like to thank Tony Scotti's Vehicle Dynamics Institute for a great course on Protective/Evasive Driving. That course helped me evade errors as I described Sophia Gold's escape from a vehicle ambush.

The Marine Corps contributed a wealth of information for this project. The views expressed by the characters herein do not necessarily reflect the official views or policies of the United States Marine Corps. Any mistakes are purely my own. I'd like to express my appreciation to the Marines of the Weapons Training Battalion at Quantico for their input on sniper training, and to one of the Fleet Antiterrorism Security Teams—Alpha Company— for allowing me to observe a mission rehearsal exercise.

Several retired Marines also provided very helpful details about the Corps. (Note that I didn't say ex-Marines. Once a Marine . . .) They include Lieutenant General Jack Klimp, Major General Paul Lefebvre, and former aviator Jim Porto. A tip of the hat goes to my cousin Elizabeth Watts for introducing me to General Klimp.

As always, my thanks to the team at Putnam and Berkley for the privi-lege of working with them. They include Putnam president Ivan Held, Putnam publisher and editor in chief Neil Nyren, and Berkley executive editor Thomas Colgan. Thanks also to Alexis Welby, Michael Barson, Ashley Hewlett, Sara Minnich, Kate Stark, and everyone at Penguin Random House.

My agent, Michael Carlisle, makes it all possible, along with his colleague Lyndsey Blessing. Author and professor John Casey helped me get this adventure started. I also owe thanks to old friend and mentor Richard Elam and to author and editor Barbara Esstman for their help in fine-tuning the manuscript. Thanks also to Bobby Siegfried for proofreading. In various ways, each of these folks helped me bring this story to you.